LITTLE,
BROWN

LARGE
PRINT

For a complete list of books by James Patterson, as well as previews of upcoming books and more information about the author, visit JamesPatterson.com or find him on Facebook.

THE NOISE

JAMES PATTERSON
and J. D. BARKER

LITTLE, BROWN AND COMPANY
NEW YORK BOSTON LONDON

Little, Brown and Company
Hachette Book Group
1290 Avenue of the Americas, New York, NY 10104

First edition: August 2021

ISBN 978-0-316-49987-3 (hc) / 978-0-316-27905-5 (large print)

Library of Congress Control Number: 2021939757

Printing 1, 2021

LSC-C

Printed in the United States of America

THE NOISE

CHAPTER ONE

TENNANT

THE FOREST HAD A particular scent to it, a dewy moistness off the Columbia River mixed with Douglas fir, ponderosa pine, red cedar, hemlock, and maple. Overnight, a fog had rolled down from the peak of Mount Hood, the sun crackling over the ghostly landscape, glistening shadows marred by flecks of white, now warming with dawn.

Sixteen-year-old Tennant Riggin took each step over the earth with practiced care, her footfalls silent as she avoided the twigs, fallen branches, leaves, and pine needles, her leather boots leaving no trail. Just as Poppa had taught her.

Three feet to her left, her eight-year-old sister, Sophie, took no such precaution. She crashed through the underbrush, thrashing her crooked walking stick as if intent on waking all of Mother Nature's creatures who dare to still be sleeping when she had to be awake.

"Will you be quiet?" Tennant urged.

"I will not," Sophie fired back. "If you wanted quiet, you shoulda let me sleep."

"Momma wants you to learn. You need to hunt, too."

"Coulda learned an hour from now just as good. What makes you think you caught anything at all, anyway?"

Sophie was annoying, but she was right. While Tennant's traps had improved substantially over the years, they weren't as good as Poppa's. Half the time, her bait was gone or her post snapped, or the noose was missing. Yesterday she'd seen a plump hare jump right into one of her twine nooses, but successfully break free, running off with her bait and half her trap in tow. She'd caught it, but only after nearly an hour. She hadn't told Momma or Poppa that part. Sophie knew, though. She'd perched on a rock and laughed as her big sister chased that damn rabbit.

Tennant set six snares yesterday, made with wire this time rather than twine.

The Riggin sisters were fourth-generation survivalists, both born within three hundred yards from where they now stood, and neither had ever left the woods of Oregon. They'd heard stories, they knew there was another world out there, but they had no desire to see it. More than once, Grammy Riggin had sat them down and told them the horrors of the outside world, with its pollution and greed and waste, and on her deathbed last fall she made them promise never to take part in that debauchery. Tennant told her she never would. She swore to it. She loved their little village of 187—correction—188 with the birth of Lily last week—and that outside world didn't concern her. Saying that Sophie felt the same might have been a bit of a white lie. Sophie had started asking questions when Kaitlyn and Jeremiah's boy Kruger went to Portland for nearly three months. He came back different, and Tennant had caught Sophie watching him, following him around, listening to the things he said. She was nosy for an eight-year-old, and most folks around here hushed up when she came round. Not Kruger, though. He seemed to like having her ear.

They both heard the scream, and froze. A baby's wail, a keening from up ahead. A desperate rattling in the brush.

"Oh, stars, you got one!"

Rabbits made the most horrible of sounds when frightened or injured.

But there shouldn't be any sound. When set properly, a snare ought to choke the rabbit to sleep, death a moment later. Quick. Humane. Efficient. This wasn't the sound of a dying rabbit. This was one fighting for escape. Something had gone wrong.

Another scream, about twenty feet away, louder than the first.

A third, this one more faint, beyond the first two. Tennant had set six traps in total, all with the new wire.

The excitement melted from Sophie's face. Her eyes got wider as the screams grew louder. The blood left her cheeks, and she went pale, near tears. "Make it stop, Tennant."

Tennant carried a small jar of beeswax in her pack for tick and bug bites. She fished it out, scooped some on her fingertip, and pressed globs of wax deep into each of her ears, reducing the screams to dull, muted cries. She held the jar out to her sister, who waved it off—too messy for little Miss Prissy.

Sophie covered her ears instead.

Tennant dropped the wax back in her pack, retrieved her knife, and extended the blade. "Come on."

Sophie didn't move. Instead, she planted her feet firmly and shook her head. She said something, but Tennant couldn't make out her words through the wax.

Tennant heard something else then, not from the forest but from deep in her mind. A ringing. First faint, barely audible, but steadily growing. A single tone gaining strength, joined by others, shrill, louder.

Hungry. Ugly. There was a pressure, too. As if her head were filling with water and didn't have enough room. Cold sweat trickled down the back of her neck. The world swooned, her vision clouded, and Tennant felt like she might pass out.

She thought it was all in her mind until she glanced over at Sophie, whose eyes welled with panic—her sister's mouth hung open as she looked up into the trees, toward the dull gray of the morning sky, her hands cupped tightly over her ears.

The sound grew louder.

Deafening.

A crescendo of screams.

As if every human, animal, and creature of Mother Earth all cried together in fevered pain.

Tennant was on her knees, her sister curled up beside her, as Poppa burst from the bushes with a rifle slapping against his back, Momma behind him. She didn't feel Poppa scoop her into his arms, didn't remember it. She blinked and they were running through the trees, toward Bill McAuliffe's barn at the far edge of the village. She blinked again, and Poppa was lowering her through the trapdoor into the cellar. Momma handed Sophie down to her and Tennant tried to catch her, but instead they both tumbled down the steps to the dirt floor, landing in a heap.

Tennant caught a glimpse of Poppa's eyes as he slammed the door down from up above, Momma behind him, their faces white as paper and skin stretched tight with pain. She'd never seen eyes so bloodshot.

This sound.

This loudest of sounds.

Somehow, grew louder.

Oh, God, why didn't Poppa and Momma come down, too?

CHAPTER TWO

TENNANT

SOPHIE'S SCREAM CUT THROUGH Tennant like a dull, rusty blade.

Her sister's voice blended with the horrible wail coming from both everywhere and nowhere all at once. Her bones wanted out of her skin. The dirt floor of the cellar pulsed with the penetrating hum. Dust and dirt jumped, stirred angrily through the stale, musty air.

Tennant rolled from her back to her side, dug her fingers deep into her ears against the sound, yet the deafening cry managed to dig further—past her fingers, through the wax, a knitting needle clawing at her brain, scraping the inside of her skull, cracking against the bone.

What had started as a single high-pitched tone had grown to all sounds—high and low, both deep and shrill—screeching, shrieking, all at once.

The cellar wasn't large. Ten by ten, at the most.

The dirt walls were lined with wood and cinder-block shelves filled with canned goods, beef jerky, powdered milk, gallons of water, wheat.

All of this came to life, vibrating from the sound.

Cans and packages tumbled from the shelves and crashed to the ground. A bag of flour burst.

The walls groaned as the weight of the earth pushed in from all sides.

The boards of the ceiling rattled as if stomped on from above.

Still, the sound grew louder.

Tennant had no idea she was screaming, too, until she ran out of breath and choked on the air—dirt, dust, flour—all filling her lungs at once. She coughed it back out, forced herself to stand, clawed at the cellar door.

Why had Poppa locked them in?

They'd die down here.

And Momma and Poppa out there?

On the ground at her feet, Sophie's hands and arms wrapped around her head, her knees pulled tight against her chest. Blood dripped from the corners of her eyes, from her button nose, seeped out from between her fingers over her ears. Thick, congealed blood, dark red, nearly black. One of her hands shot out and wrapped around Tennant's ankles and squeezed so tight the pain brought her back down to the floor.

The sound grew louder.

Tennant wanted to hold her sister, but her arms and legs no longer obeyed her. Her heart drummed against her ribs, threatened to burst. She couldn't get air, each gasp no better than breathing water. Her eyes rolled back into her head, her vision first went white, then dark, as the walls closed in. The cellar no better than a grave.

CHAPTER THREE

TENNANT

WHEN TENNANT WOKE, HER eyes fluttered open on muted darkness. Light crept down from above, leaking from between the cracks in the ceiling boards, flickering over the dust hovering in the air, finding her on the floor, on her back, her right leg twisted awkwardly beneath her.

Utter silence.

The silence so complete, Tennant thought she could no longer hear at all. Then she remembered the wax in her ears and clawed it out, sat up, gathered her senses.

"Sophie?"

Tennant had experienced earthquakes before. Two she recalled vividly, and neither had left the cellar in such disarray. Most of the shelves had collapsed. Those still in place were bare, the ground littered with their contents. Canned berries and jams had exploded, their sweet scent mixing with the dust, shards of glass everywhere. The once-familiar room looked foreign to her.

She spotted Sophie tucked into the corner, crouched, rocking side to side on her feet. Matted hair and blood covered her face. Her eyes were wide but unfocused. Her lips moved in some silent conversation.

Tennant shuffled through the debris and went to her. Every muscle in her body ached, as if she'd spent the day in the cornfield or baling hay.

When she reached out to Sophie her sister didn't respond to her touch, only continued to mumble, although Tennant couldn't make out the words.

Her eyes were bloodshot, like Momma and Poppa's. She was horribly pale, too. Cold to the touch. "Sophie, can you hear me?"

Her sister didn't respond.

Tennant wrapped her arms around her, tried to stop her from rocking, but her sister continued to move side to side.

Tennant leaned in closer, brought her ear to her sister's lips.

Sophie's incoherent mumbling was barely a whisper. Tennant didn't know what her sister was saying, but there was urgency to the words. Her head nodded as she spoke, her eyes flickering about the room without really looking at anything at all.

Tennant snapped her fingers.

Nothing.

She slapped her.

She didn't want to, but it *did* work.

The rocking stopped. Sophie sucked in a breath and went rigid. Her gaze fixed on her sister.

Tennant pressed her palms to Sophie's cheeks. "You okay?"

Sophie stared at her for a moment, confused. Then her hands went to her ears, her fingertips digging inside. Tentatively at first, then more fevered, aggressive. Tennant grabbed her wrists and tried to make her stop, but she was so strong.

Both their hands came away bloody—Sophie screamed, and that only made things worse. She slammed her hands against the sides of her head. "Can't hear! Can't hear!"

Tennant tried to pull her arms away, but Sophie just slapped at her, banged the sides of her head again, each blow more harsh than the last. "No! No! No!"

"Sophie! Stop!"

Smack.

Smack.

Smack.

She started rocking again, faster than before—left to right, right to left, back again.

Smack.

Smack.

Smack.

Sophie pushed her back, sending Tennant tumbling across the floor into a barrel of cornmeal.

She had to get them out of there. She knew Bill McAuliffe kept an ax down here. Normally, it hung on the wall in the far right corner, but now she found it on the ground under a pile of powdered milk cartons.

Tennant hefted the heavy ax and scrambled up the steps to the trapdoor. With the blade facing up, she gripped the handle with both hands and swung up at the door. She aimed for the hinge but struck the wood about four inches off-center. She repositioned and swung again. On the third hit, the first hinge snapped. The second hinge took five blows. The door fell in, and sunlight streamed down through the opening.

Dropping the ax, Tennant went back down into the cellar and grabbed Sophie's hand. "Come on!"

At first, she thought her sister would fight her, but instead she was on her feet. She pushed past Tennant and raced out into the open air.

"Wait!" Tennant hollered after her, bounding up the steps.

There shouldn't be daylight.

CHAPTER FOUR

TENNANT

THE MCAULIFFE BARN WAS GONE.

Tennant found Sophie standing where the barn door had been, her back to her. The roof of the old building was missing, the walls nothing but a crumbled ruin. Cracked and splintered boards littered the ground, hay tossed about wildly. Only a single post remained, sticking awkwardly out from the earth, no longer straight, but like a finger pointing east on a bent knuckle.

The air was still, filled with unsettling calm.

Tennant crossed over to her sister, each step heavier than the last, as she realized what Sophie was looking at.

Their village was gone, too.

Leveled.

Not a single structure still standing. Even the stone well, near the village center, had been reduced to nothing but a hole in the ground with the heavy stones as far as twenty feet away embedded in the dirt.

There were no people. No bodies. No wildlife.

Tennant's stomach twisted into a heavy knot.

Poppa had told them about tornados, but he also told them they were rare in Oregon. She had never seen one, but nothing else could explain this.

Her hand was on Sophie's shoulder, and she must have squeezed too hard; her sister shook her off, slowly started rocking again—left to right, right to left.

A dog barked across the emptiness, and Tennant's head swiveled toward the sound.

Zeke.

She found herself walking toward him in a half daze, towing Sophie by the hand.

They found the yellow Labrador cowering in the remains of their home, nothing more than a shivering puddle of fur pressed against the flattened hearth of their fireplace, the chimney a pile of rubble beside him.

Tennant fell to the ground and buried her face in his body. "Hey, boy. It's okay. It's okay."

At first, he didn't seem to notice her. Then he tentatively lifted his head and licked her cheek.

Sophie remained standing, her feet moving in place, her gaze lost in the direction where their room should have been, beyond that to the empty space of their parents' room. She choked back a sob. "Where are Momma and Poppa?"

Zeke whimpered and buried his face in the crook of Tennant's arm.

"How did you escape this, brave boy?" she asked him.

He only buried his face deeper.

Sophie's eyes narrowed and she raised a hand, her finger pointing at something in the distance, toward the center of the village.

"What?"

She didn't answer. Tennant couldn't be sure she even heard her. Her stiff finger quivered, and she started toward whatever it was she found.

Tennant chased after her, Zeke reluctantly following—his snout first on the ground, then sniffing at the air, a steady whine from his throat as he chuffed with concern. A bumblebee crawled out of the flattened grass and took flight—the only other sign of life she'd seen since leaving the cellar.

Sophie had stopped beyond the well, near a large reddened heap surrounded by matted grass.

Tennant froze, unsure if she wanted to get any closer. A voice in the back of her mind told her not to, told her to turn and run in the opposite direction, put as much distance between her and this place as she could.

Zeke lowered himself to the ground. His tail thumped once, then went still.

Sophie rocked again—left to right, right to left. Her small hands closed into fists and opened again in a steady rhythm like the ticking of a clock.

A metronome.

"What is it, Sophie? What'd you find?"

No answer came, but Tennant hadn't really expected one. The blood seeping from Sophie's ears had slowed but hadn't stopped. She feared her sister would never hear again.

Tennant sucked in a breath, forced herself to move. She made her way to Sophie's side.

She'd known the scent of death since her earliest memories. Momma had once told her she'd grow used to it, and she told Poppa that she had. That had been a lie. The familiar sickly-sweet odor crawled through the grass like a venomous snake, silent and fierce.

Death came from the pile at Sophie's feet. But what really frightened her was that the scent of death was everywhere.

The bloody mass at Sophie's feet was a horse. Beaten, pulverized, a horrid mound of flesh lay in opened waste, intestines and innards strewn about from a ragged tear in the animal's dark, glistening fur, as if it had burst under the pressure. She'd never seen anything like it.

About twenty feet to their left, a horde of dark flies

filled the air, dipping down to the ground and back up again in a fevered dance. Tennant couldn't see what they were feasting on. She didn't want to.

Beside her, Sophie rocked. Right to left, left to right, *tick, tock.*

She reached over and squeezed her sister's shoulder. "We should go."

As she took a step back, her foot rolled and she nearly fell.

Half-buried, a single leather work boot protruded from the ground.

A boot she recognized.

Poppa.

CHAPTER FIVE

TENNANT

WHEN SOPHIE ALSO SPOTTED the boot, her bloody hands went to her mouth. She shuffled to the side and let out a guttural wail.

Zeke jumped to his feet and began to bark, but rather than go to the girls, he fell back. His bark fell to a low growl as he watched them both warily.

Tennant's legs went weak and she dropped to the ground. There was no mistaking the boot—the intricate pattern, the stitching, the deep scratch across the back of the heel from last summer when he caught it on a sharp rock in the river attempting to net trout.

Poppa's boot.

Her gaze went to the growing hordes of flies in a dozen or more places just around the village. She'd been doing her damnedest to ignore them, not wanting to know what was there.

Now Tennant forced herself to stand and go to the nearest flies. She had to. She had no choice. When she came close enough to see it was a goat, the air left her lungs and didn't want to go back in.

"It's not Poppa, Sophie, it's only his—"

Sophie took off—darting across the center of the village toward the trees on the opposite side. With a single huff, Zeke went after her, a blur of yellow.

Tennant ran after them both, and although Sophie's legs were only a fraction of the length of hers, her little sister somehow managed to pull ahead. She crashed through the bushes and underbrush with complete abandonment without any regard for the sharp branches and thorns biting at her skin, smacking her in the chest, arms, and face. Sophie pressed on at a pace so quick, Tennant lost sight of her altogether. If not for Zeke, she would have lost her sister for sure.

Nearly ten minutes later, as Tennant's chest burned and her legs ached, she forced herself to push ever harder. Because Sophie was racing straight for the forty-foot drop of Dalton's Crevasse—the Devil's Doorway—without any sign of slowing down.

CHAPTER SIX

MARTHA

THE HEADSET WAS FAR too large for Dr. Martha Chan. Even with the band adjusted to the smallest setting, they kept slipping down her forehead—she found herself holding them in place, alternating from her right hand to her left and back again whenever her arm got tired. They did the job, though. The heavy thwack of the helicopter rotors were reduced to a rhythmic thump with the metallic breathing of her pilot amplified over the speakers.

"I'm sorry about that," he said again. "They're the smallest I have."

He'd apologized twice now.

At only five foot one, Martha was no stranger to things not fitting, particularly when it came to military aircraft. After getting picked up at just after two in the morning from her apartment in San Francisco, she'd been shuttled to a C-1 transport plane at Yerba Buena Island, rushed from the Army sedan up the steps and into one of the jump seats on the port side of the aircraft. She'd felt like a child as one of the pilots helped secure her with a double-banded belt, tugging it tight over her shoulders. She'd noted his fatigues bore no name badge or insignia of any kind; same with the other pilot. Aside from the two of them, she was alone in the large aircraft as it lumbered down the tarmac and took flight.

Two hours later, they'd touched down. The moment the plane stopped moving, the pilot was back, unfastening the safety harness and ushering her down the steps to the awaiting EC135 chopper less than fifty feet away.

"Where are we?" Martha had asked, attempting to take in the airfield as they ran, ducking as they approached the spinning blades, her leather overnight bag slapping against her leg. She could see nothing beyond the lights of the airstrip and a group of hangars off in the distance. The night sky was black and gray, filled with dark, churning clouds. Even the moon had abandoned her.

"I'm not at liberty to say, ma'am."

The too-large headphones had been sitting on the backseat of the helicopter. She'd put them on and adjusted the microphone as her escort closed and locked the door, then ran back toward the plane.

Her new pilot had looked back at her and nodded toward a large manila envelope on the seat beside her. "Ma'am? Please place your cell phone in that envelope. I was told to collect all communication devices before I'm permitted to go airborne." He glanced at her Apple Watch. "That, too, please."

Martha frowned. "The watch isn't cellular. I just use it to track my fitness information."

"Please, ma'am. I have orders."

She sighed. She knew better than to argue with military personnel. He'd sit here for the next two weeks and wait on her before he'd violate orders. None of these guys seemed to think for themselves. She supposed that was appealing for some, but not for her. Mark, her ex-husband, would be the first to tell anyone willing to listen that Martha was a control freak of the highest degree. In the final months of their marriage, they'd had blowout arguments over things as ridiculous as who got to control the television remote. Understandable, considering his choice in programming was shit, but the arguments didn't stop there—they'd managed to find a way to fight about damn near everything. Fighting might have been the only thing they were good at. Two strong-willed type-A personalities under the same roof was bound to end bad, always did. The twins held them together that last year. Without those two, they would have called it quits a long time ago.

Christ, the twins.

This coming weekend was her turn to take them.

Nobody had told her how long she'd be gone this time. They never did.

A two-hour flight in the transport plane from the airbase in San Francisco could put her anywhere in the western United States—Idaho, Utah, Arizona. Maybe Wyoming, Colorado, or New Mexico. Even Baja, although she hadn't seen any sign of the ocean. She had no way of knowing what direction they'd flown. She didn't like not knowing where she was. She liked communication blackouts even less.

Martha powered down her phone and smartwatch, dropped them into the envelope, and handed it up to the pilot. The chopper was airborne a few minutes later, soaring through the night.

From the window, she studied the distant skyline. "What city is that?"

The pilot glanced out the window, then at her in the mirror. "I'm not at liberty—"

She waved a hand and cut him off. "—not at liberty to say, I understand."

They flew in silence for thirty minutes. The pilot was the first to speak. "You're not military," he asked. "Are you some kind of doctor?"

"What makes you think I'm not military?"

"Your clothes, that leather bag. The way you're gripping your armrest. My military passengers tend to sit back and enjoy the ride, happy for the downtime. You look like you're ready to jump. Civilian."

Martha released the armrest and nudged her headphones back up on her head. “Doctor, yeah.”

“Where’d you go to school?”

“I did my undergrad in biology at UC San Francisco, then four years at Hopkins studying trauma surgery. After that, I got my psychology PhD from Berkeley.” She was looking out the window again. “Are those mountains down there?”

He ignored her. “That’s a lot of school.”

“I like school.”

“Kids?”

Martha nodded. “Boy and a girl, twins. Emily and Michael.”

“How old?”

“Eight.”

“Good for you.”

Light started to creep up over the horizon. They were heading east.

“I’ve got a little boy, name’s Tim, after his grandpa. He’s going on thirteen now.” The pilot showed her a photograph of a boy with a mop of white hair holding up a fish.

“Tighten up your belt. We’re about to land.”

Through the window, she spotted a familiar landmark. Mount Hood. She and Mark had gone camping up here once, back when things were good. So this was Oregon.

CHAPTER SEVEN

MARTHA

THE EC135 TOUCHED DOWN in the grass about thirty feet from two other helicopters, and a fiftyish man in a tan uniform with dark-olive pants ran out from the porch of the cabin, one hand holding his hat, the other shielding his eyes as the blades kicked up dust and dirt.

Martha took off her headphones and fumbled with the latch on her belt.

The man opened her door and shouted over the engine noise. "I'm Hoyt Rayburn with Forest Rangers. Welcome to Zigzag Station. Can I help you with that?" He snatched Martha's bag from the seat before she had a chance to answer and helped her out of the chopper.

They were halfway to the cabin when the helicopter shot back up into the sky.

Martha turned and frowned. "He still has my phone and watch."

The blades of one of the other choppers started turning as a transport helicopter lowered a concrete barrier to the ground on thick cables, setting it down next to several others already in place. There were people crowded around, directing the work. The noise was deafening.

"What?" Rayburn shouted back.

"Never mind."

One hand still on his hat, he yelled, "Let's get you inside. They're waiting on you."

Another truck pulled up. Some type of military transport. A few men jumped out the back and began unloading rolls of chain-link fencing.

Martha followed Rayburn up the steps and into the building.

He closed the door behind her, took off his hat, and brushed the dust off. "They've got a crane on the way to finish up the barrier, but the powers that be didn't want to wait so they brought that thing in from Kingsley. Probably scaring the wildlife half to death."

"Why are they building a barrier?"

"Dr. Chan?"

A man in jeans, black boots, and a white button-down shirt stood in a doorway toward the back of the room. He was about Martha's age, with thinning dark hair cropped close to his head. "In here, please."

Martha didn't move. "You are?"

He didn't answer. Instead, he turned and walked back into the room.

"DIA," Rayburn said softly. "At least I think so. He got here first. I heard him on the phone."

"Defense Intelligence Agency?"

"Now, Dr. Chan," the man called out from the other room.

Rayburn handed Martha her leather bag. "Best to keep that close."

Zigzag Station was larger than it appeared from the outside. The walls of the main room were lined with educational displays—photographs of local wildlife with detailed descriptions and histories stenciled beneath protective plastic. Martha imagined this was the kind of place schoolchildren visited on field trips. There was a counter off to the far right covered in pamphlets and brochures for local tours and outings. There were several vending machines, too, stocked with water and soda, candy and energy bars. Although the exterior of the cabin was covered in siding, the interior was made up of exposed beams and white oak, most likely sourced locally. There was a fireplace, but it didn't look like anyone had used it in some time, more for show now.

As she stepped through the doorway at the back, three more people looked up at her from around a large oak table. Two men and a woman. One man wore a suit, the second was in a sweatshirt and jeans, the woman wore a tank top and yoga pants, her hair pulled back in a ponytail. Martha pictured a crew similar to the one that collected her picking this woman up from the middle of a morning jog somewhere. Without a word, they all looked back down at the large stack of papers in front of each of them.

The man from DIA pointed toward a vacant spot. Another pile of pages there, a black ballpoint on top. "Please take a seat, Dr. Chan."

"I'd like to know what we're doing here."

"No speaking until you've read and signed the NDA. You'll need to initial each page in the bottom right corner as well."

Martha frowned. "NDA? I have Top Secret clearance."

The man in the suit fought back a grin and flipped to the next page of his papers.

Martha glared at him. She wasn't in the mood for this. Not at this hour. "This funny?"

Without looking up, he said, "*We all* have Top Secret clearance, Doctor. *We all* argued with this upstanding civil servant, and *we all* found ourselves no better for it. Best to read the document and sign so we *all* can get on with it."

He spoke with a slight accent. British, but faint. Like he came to the States as a child.

The woman in the yoga pants glanced up at Martha, offered her a soft nod, then went back to reading.

Martha placed her bag in the corner of the room, sighed, and dropped down into the vacant chair. "Can I at least get some coffee?"

CHAPTER EIGHT

MARTHA

THE TOPMOST PAGE OF the thick document simply read, OFFICE OF THE JOINT CHIEFS.

As Martha read, two others joined the group and were handed NDAs of their own. A man and a woman, both in their mid to late forties. Although dressed casually, Martha caught a glimpse of a lab coat stuffed into the man's bag, which was simply a canvas shopping bag. From their soft grumblings, she got the feeling they had been picked from a lab somewhere, and not allowed time to pack.

Thirty-seven minutes passed before the last person slid their NDA across the table to the man from DIA. He placed each of them carefully in an oversize leather briefcase, snapped the locks, and set it behind him on the floor against the wall.

Martha leaned forward in her chair. "Now can you tell us what this is all about?"

He studied each of their faces in turn, then looked down at his watch. "Shortly. We're waiting on one more."

"Introductions, then?" the man with the British accent said. "I'm Sanford Harbin with NOAA."

"A climatologist?" Martha asked.

Harbin nodded.

"Interesting. I'm Martha Chan, a civilian liaison with the military for medical crises, and a PhD in psychology at Berkeley."

"Dr. Chan. Pleasure. I read a paper you wrote about a decade ago on the negative psychological effects of overpopulation in first-, second-, and third-world populations," Harbin said.

"I read that paper, too," the man in the white sweatshirt and jeans said. "My name is Russel Fravel. Astrophysicist. I'm with Garner out in Boulder." Fravel, an African American, his hair graying at his temples, studied her from behind round, silver-framed glasses. "You estimated the planet could sustain nine to ten billion people at maximum. A bold statement, considering many others post numbers nearly double that. Some accused you of attempting to start a panic, considering we're close to hitting your number."

Martha shifted uncomfortably in her chair.

"I'm Dr. Brenna Hauff, planetary biology," one of the latecomers said. She pointed a thumb at the man to her right. "This is Dr. Brian Tomes, geology. We're both with NASA in Houston."

"NASA?"

This came from the young woman across the table in the tank top and yoga pants.

She pursed her lips, mulled this over. "A climatologist, an astrophysicist, geologist, biologist, and a shrink. All brought together by the Department of Defense? My money is on alien invasion."

Martha tilted her head at her. "And you are?"

"Dr. Joy Reiber. Department of Agriculture. I was set to give a speech today in DC and couldn't sleep, so I figured I'd get a little exercise." She jerked a thumb back at the man from DIA. "Mr. Holt kidnapped me near Washington Mall."

"I hardly—"

She glared at him. "You showed me some bogus badge and rushed me into a van with two of your cohorts. I damn near maced you."

Harbin looked up at him. "Mr. Holt, is it?"

Holt cleared his throat. "Keenen Holt. State Department."

"Are we being invaded by little green men, Mr. Holt?" Harbin's accent made the statement sound even more absurd than it was, yet nobody laughed.

An alarm went off—Holt's watch. He silenced the beeping, checked the time, and glanced over at the door with a frustrated sigh. "Best to just get started."

From a shelf behind him, Holt retrieved a laptop, which he set on the table. The screen came to life when he opened it. He sorted through some emails, located one. "I'm going to play a statement for you. I need you to pay close attention."

He clicked on an attachment, and an image of an older man, bald, wearing a gray suit and red tie, filled the screen. He had a mole on the corner of his right cheek and deep bags under his eyes.

"That's Frederick Hoover," Harbin said. "He's looked better. I worked with him on a project for the US Navy about six years ago. I believe he's with DARPA now. Or at least he was the last time I spoke to him."

DARPA, the notoriously cutting-edge research arm of the DOD—this was getting odder and odder, Martha thought.

Holt pressed the Play button.

"I apologize for the short notice, the ways and means necessary to bring each of you to your current location," Hoover's video began. "As you may have already surmised, the nature of the anomaly requires the utmost secrecy, and your cooperation is greatly appreciated. I would be remiss if I failed to point out that the NDAs you've signed clearly state that a violation of the Secrets Protection Act of 2008 carries a minimum of five years in military prison and a maximum penalty of death under the Treason Act as defined in Article III, Section Three of the United States Constitution. Should you speak to any unauthorized personnel, those individuals will be subject to the same. At this point, all your communication devices should have been turned in to an appropriate handler. If you've retained any form of communication device, you are hereby ordered to relinquish it immediately. Failure to do so will result in immediate charges, imprisonment, and replacement on this team. I ask that your handler pause the video at this point in order to give you the opportunity to turn in any remaining forms of communication."

Holt pressed pause.

"Christ," Harbin muttered.

Tomes, the NASA geologist, dug through his canvas bag, pulled out an old BlackBerry, and tossed it on the table, his face red.

Holt took the phone and slipped it into his pocket. "Anyone else?"

No one moved.

He started the video again.

"I imagine you to be curious as to why you are here. Understandably so. And while I would like to offer an explanation, I'm hesitant to do so. I fear sharing our current theories and analysis of the anomaly may prejudice your own opinions and theories, and we'd prefer you approach this situation without such handicaps, at least for your initial exposure. We will reevaluate upon debrief. In a moment, you will be transported to the anomaly. We ask that you do not consult one another until after your individual debrief and return to base. We'd prefer to hear your individual thoughts before you compare notes."

At that point, the video ended.

"*The anomaly,*" Reiber repeated portentously.

Martha didn't like this one bit. "Why a taped message instead of a live conference? Seems like just a way of avoiding questions."

Brenna Hauff, the other NASA scientist, leaned over the table and pointed at the screen where the email was still open. "Look at the cc list here—Joint Chiefs, White House, about a dozen addresses with NSA..."

Holt reached over and closed the laptop before she could read the rest. "Your point of contact will be me. If necessary, I'll initiate a conference with members of the distant team."

"Our *handler,*" Harbin said with an edge to his voice.

"Correct."

"Since when does the Defense Intelligence Agency run scientific ops?" Martha asked.

"Oh, this is clearly a military concern, not scientific," Fravel pointed out.

“I never said I was DIA.” Holt locked the laptop in the leather briefcase with the NDAs. “We’re wasting time. I need everyone in the choppers. You can leave your personal belongings in this room. We’ve got a two-hour window.”

Martha watched him leave and head out the front door of the ranger station.

Nobody moved.

After about a minute, Tomes tapped his pen several times on the table. “I don’t know about the rest of you, but I’m curious.” He got up and followed Holt.

“Me, too.” Reiber stood as well, tugging her tank top down with her left hand. Martha noted some kind of tattoo on the small of her back but couldn’t make out what.

Martha got up. The rest did as well.

Outside, she eyed the concrete and chain-link barrier going up around the perimeter, nearly half done now. More trucks had arrived while they were inside.

Harbin was studying it, too. He leaned close to Martha, whispered in her ear, “If they’re taking us to this *anomaly* in helicopters, clearly a distance from where we stand, aren’t you the least bit curious as to what they’re trying to keep *out* of this little slice of heaven?”

CHAPTER NINE

TENNANT

DALTON'S CREVASSE BROKE THE forest in half. Stretching nearly half a mile north and south, and nearly twenty feet wide at the center, it was a ragged, angry crack in the earth nicknamed "the Devil's Doorway." Poppa had said it was formed by a long, dry, ancient river or maybe an earthquake. Momma told her God had gotten angry and tried to tear the mountain in half. Both had claimed it had no bottom, and anyone who slipped off the edge would fall forever. Tennant and Sophie had spent hours throwing rocks over the side, listening for them to hit bottom but they never did.

Two footbridges crossed the expanse, one about a quarter mile south, the other to the north.

Sophie didn't stop; she didn't even slow. The sight of that edge seemed to invigorate her.

While Tennant found herself gasping for breath,

Sophie only seemed to gain energy and speed. Her tiny legs moved with ungodly energy and purpose.

As they approached the crevasse, Zeke's barking grew insistent, panicked, filled with whines and cries. He tore through the tangle of branches, slipped on some leaves, regained his footing, and bounded after Sophie. He reached her about fifteen feet from the edge, getting under her feet, trying to trip her up.

This slowed her, if only a little. Tennant ignored the burning in her legs and chest, and forced herself forward. She cut through the last of the trees, closed the distance, pushed off a rock, and leaped at Sophie.

Her fingers brushed the back of her sister's jacket, rolled over the fur at the bottom, and slipped off the top of her jeans. Tennant's shoulder cracked against the rocky earth and a sharp, white pain cut through her vision. Her outstretched hand closed around Sophie's ankle, and she yanked her leg out from under her. Sophie fell forward, dropped hard on the rocks, and went still.

"Sophie!" Tennant cried out, scrambling to her hands and knees, less than a foot away from the edge. Gravel and earth crumbled away, fell down into the black.

Sophie was awake but stunned. She stared up at Tennant with those terrible bloodshot eyes.

Zeke shuffled back several steps watching them, a low growl in his throat.

There was blood on her sister's face, the sides of her head, on her neck. Not from the fall, but from her mouth, ears, and nose. Tennant ran her hands over the back of Sophie's head, through her hair, and didn't find other injuries. But she felt hot to the touch, feverish.

"Hey, can you hear me?"

There was another growl. Tennant realized it hadn't come from Zeke, but from Sophie. Her eyes narrowed and her tiny hands reached up, scratched at Tennant's face, punched her chest. She managed to get a hold of Tennant's braid and yanked her head sideways with incredible strength.

How was she so strong? Adrenaline?

Tennant grabbed her wrists, pinned them to her sides. The girl struggled like a wild thing caught in one of her traps.

"Stop, Sophie, stop!" Tennant wrapped her arms around her in a tight hug and pulled her close, like Poppa.

Sophie went limp, buried her face in Tennant's shoulder, and began to sob.

Yet when Tennant loosened her grip, Sophie tried to slip away toward the crevasse again. She brought her knee up and caught Tennant in the gut, knocking the wind out of her. She tried to dive for the edge.

Only by sitting on Sophie's chest, using her weight, did Tennant manage to hold her down.

"Let me go, you fucking bitch!"

The voice came from Sophie but wasn't hers—too deep, guttural, this inhuman thing.

Zeke dropped down to his belly and whimpered, shuffled back.

Sophie snarled, twisted, her feet and hands lashing out. "Get off me, you fucking cunt!"

Pink tears tinged with blood dripped down her face.

Her nails slashed the air, just missed Tennant's eye.

Tennant slapped her.

It had worked once before, but this time it seemed to anger her. Her sister screamed out a torrent of awful, filthy words, some Tennant had never even heard. Then she realized she wasn't speaking English but some foreign tongue. Momma had taught them some Spanish, but this was something else.

Sophie's head thrashed side to side as she yelled, screamed, shouted these terrible things in a fit of rage.

This was all too much. Tears welled up in Tennant's eyes, too. She found herself crying with her sister, trying to hug Sophie even if she didn't want to, as she tried to fight her off.

Glancing back in the direction of their village, Tennant hoped someone would come out of the woods—Momma, Poppa. Someone, anyone. But nobody did.

She'd never felt so alone.

CHAPTER TEN

TENNANT

TENNANT USED THE SPARE wire in her pack to secure Sophie's hands behind her back. She also wrapped her belt tight around her sister's legs just above her knees, forcing her to move at a slow shuffle. Even so, the moment Sophie was back on her feet, she dove for the edge of the crevasse again. Had Tennant not been there to grab the hood of her coat, she would have surely gone over.

Most of the words leaving her sister's mouth were incoherent gibberish and angry curses but for one brief instant—when Tennant had pulled her back and slammed her down into the rock again—Sophie had looked to the west and pointed, a single name rolling off her tongue: *Anna Shim*.

Tennant hadn't seen anyone and didn't know anyone by that name. When she called out nobody answered, but Sophie had continued to gaze off in that direction, her disturbed eyes fixed. From the maps Poppa had shown her, Tennant knew there was nothing that way but wilderness for a hundred miles. She supposed there could be campers, maybe even hunters or poachers, but most of those folks tended to stay on the west side of Mount Hood. Rarely did they cross the peak and venture down this side. Too much work, too remote. Poppa once said these part-time survivalists would be the first to go when the end came. He said they would flee their homes in the cities with their unfamiliar gear and prepackaged foods and find themselves lost in the woods. Bears and mountain lions would make quick work of them. But then the villagers would find their gear and put it to good use.

"Annnnnna," Sophie murmured again, her red eyes still on the west, staring beyond the crevasse off into the trees.

"There's nobody out there." Still holding her sister's hood, Tennant gave it a tug. "Come on. We gotta go back."

She wasn't sure if Sophie could hear her or even understand her. She'd snapped her fingers near her sister's ears several times and gotten no response. When she spoke to her, the words seemed lost on her, meaningless. Zeke was more responsive.

Sophie started rocking again—left to right, right to left, swaying back and forth.

Tennant gave her a push back in the direction of the cellar. Poppa and Momma had put them there for a reason. That's where they needed to wait.

She tried not to think about the boot, or the look on their faces. She told herself Poppa and Momma would be standing there over the cellar door, angry that they'd left, and she was fine with that. They could be as angry as they wanted, as long as they were there.

Sophie didn't move at first, only rocked in place, then she looked up into the sky and started forward in an awkward shuffle because of the belt around her legs. Tennant held tight to the hood of her coat so she couldn't run off. For nearly ten minutes, Zeke trailed behind them, darting in and out of the bushes. When he realized where they were going, he ran off ahead. He didn't seem to want to get too close. He eyed Sophie suspiciously and grumbled softly when she looked his way.

As they approached the village, Tennant looked for the roof of Bill McAuliffe's barn poking through the trees. She hoped all this had been a bad dream and the barn would be there and the village beyond that, their little house. Her stomach sank as they entered the clearing where the barn had stood, stepping over the fallen boards and beams to make their way to the cellar door.

The air buzzed with flies, stank of death.

No sign of Poppa or Momma.

When Tennant opened the trapdoor, Sophie took a step back.

With her hands and legs bound, she wasn't sure she could get her sister down the steps if she fought her. She couldn't untie her, though, no way.

About a dozen feet away, Zeke took a seat where the barn door had stood.

Tennant snapped her fingers at him and pointed down into the hole—maybe Sophie would follow him down.

Zeke only looked back at her. He lowered himself to the ground and rested his snout on his paws with a soft whimper.

Tennant cursed at him and knelt on the ground in front of Sophie. "Poppa and Momma will be back for us, so we need to wait here. Do you understand? Poppa will know what to do." She reached up and stroked her sister's tangled hair. It was damp with sweat, sticky with blood. "You need to rest. You're getting sick."

A gurgle rose from Sophie's throat, but she said nothing. She didn't so much look at Tennant as *through* her. She was facing west again.

"There's food down there, water. Aren't you hungry?" Tennant tried to edge her toward the cellar, toward the steps.

Instead, Sophie's arms jerked, her shoulders

wrenched. She yanked at the wires binding her hands.

"Don't do that."

The gurgle turned to a deep growl. Sophie jerked again. Her entire body spasmed.

"You're going to hurt yourself!"

When Tennant looked at her sister's hands, she realized Sophie must have been tugging at the wire the entire time they walked. Her wrists were covered in bloody welts.

Sophie yanked again. The metal dug in even deeper.

"Don't!"

"Untie... now," she breathed in that ugly voice, pumping her wrists. Blood trickled down over the wire, a drop landing in the dirt at her feet.

Tennant reached for her sister's arms, not to untie her but to hold her still long enough to get a better look. At first, Sophie let her, but when she realized she wasn't removing the wire, she pulled away. Tennant saw enough, though. She'd have to replace the wire with something else, maybe rope or cloth, something softer. She'd need bandages, ointment.

"Untie!" Sophie charged her. Shoulders hunched, she leaped forward in a blur.

At last check, the eight-year-old only weighed fifty-five pounds, but when she slammed into Tennant, it was with the force of a small truck. The air burst from Tennant's lungs, her feet went out from under her, and she fell backward with Sophie on top of her. She huffed angrily, glared at Tennant with those red, puffy eyes, then reached for her own head, grabbed a handful of hair, and yanked it out. The bloody clump fell from her fingers, fluttered through the door in stringy strands of blond.

The two of them dropped through the open cellar door and rolled down the steps, landing hard in a heap on the earth floor, gritty dust pluming up around them.

CHAPTER ELEVEN

MARTHA

WITH TWO PAIRS OF bucket seats positioned opposite each other, the passenger compartment of the EC135 held four people. Martha Chan and Sanford Harbin sat next to each other, facing Russel Fravel and Joy Reiber. Keenen Holt, Brian Tomes, and Brenna Hauff were in a second chopper following behind them. They were airborne within a few minutes of boarding, and although Martha could see the pilot's lips moving, she could no longer hear him through the headphones—apparently, he was speaking on another channel. She had hoped to gather additional information—locations, size of deployment, general chatter. You could learn a lot listening in on an open radio channel, all those voices speaking to one another sometimes forgot you were there. Any child could tell you the best information was always gleaned from adults speaking in hushed voices one room over, thinking you were asleep.

"Who do you suppose was late to the party?" Harbin said, his voice thin over the headphones. It seemed the passengers were all on the same channel, at least.

Martha turned to see a pensive look on his face. "What?"

"Our lovely handler, Mr. Holt, said we were expecting one other person. Someone he wanted at that little dog and pony show but not someone he felt important enough to wait on."

Joy Reiber pulled the elastic band from her hair, gathered her blond locks together again, then replaced it. "That shit was hiding something."

Beside her, Russel Fravel chuckled. "DIA hides *everything*. That's their job. If you caught him with his pants down and his pecker in his hand and asked him what he was doing, he'd tell you he was brewing coffee and make you believe it. We've got to assume everything he's telling us is utter bullshit and piece together whatever is happening on our own. He's just as likely to feed us disinformation as the truth."

Reiber frowned. "Why bring us all this way and lie? How can they expect us to determine anything without all the relevant facts?"

Harbin nodded in agreement with Fravel, then told Reiber, "We're here to find all the jigsaw pieces scattered about, someone else has been tasked with putting the puzzle together. Most likely Frederick Hoover, the man in that video message. That's the only way to explain the involvement of DARPA."

"You said you knew him?" Martha pointed out.

Harbin nodded again. "And I know how he works. In that video, he looked tired, run-down. When he's on a project, particularly something time-sensitive, he goes all in, to the point of self-neglect. I've seen him go days without sleep or a shower. He doesn't eat unless someone reminds him. Doesn't shave. Whatever is going on here, he's been working on it for several days at this point, maybe longer."

"An alien invasion," Reiber said flatly, looking at Fravel. "That's why you're here."

Fravel waved a dismissive hand at her. "I've spent my entire adult life staring up into the cosmos, and I can tell you with relative certainty if there was someone else out there close enough to stop by and visit, we would have found them by now. This is something else."

"Then why bring in an astrophysicist?"

He shrugged. "No idea. My work focuses on the study of a star's life cycle. I can't imagine how my particular skill set is useful here. Besides, if something as far-fetched as an alien spacecraft approached this planet, I would have heard about it through a colleague. We have a worldwide network and tend to share data. Even the Chinese and Russians are cooperative. We try not to let politics dictate our work."

Harbin leaned forward. "There must be a reason each of us is here. What are you working on at this moment? Of all the astrophysicists in the world, why you?"

Fravel thought about it for a moment. "Lately I've been following QV89, an asteroid about the size of a football field. Catalina Sky Survey first found it back in '06. Its current path will bring it close to earth this September, but it doesn't pose a risk."

"Are you sure?" Harbin pressed.

Fravel chuckled again. "If you're concerned that it's really going to hit the planet, and the government's lying about it in order to avoid a panic, I can safely tell you it is not. I'm the guy tracking its trajectory. If we were all going to die, you'd see me on the internet, on television . . . I'd tell everyone. They'd have to lock me up to keep me quiet. This is something else."

Martha turned to Reiber. "You're with the Department of Agriculture, right? What are you currently working on?"

Reiber glanced out the window, then back to Martha. "I study pollination. Specifically how it's impacted by the decline in the world's bee population. That's what my speech today was supposed to be about." She let out a sigh. "God, I hope I don't lose my grant over this. In a few hours, several hundred academics are going to gather at the Babson in DC, and I'm clearly not going to be there. The timing of this couldn't be worse." She looked out the window again. "If we're in Oregon, I don't think this is about bees. The closest large-scale decline in honeybee population is north of here, in Washington—a good three hundred miles away. I must've been dragged here for another reason."

Harbin's eyes were back on Martha. "And you? The focus of the paper I read was overpopulation. That's hardly a problem out here. What's their interest in you?"

Much of what Martha did was classified. She weighed what she could tell him. "I'm typically brought in to help deal with the psychological effects of large-scale medical emergencies—bird flu, SARS, Ebola, coronavirus. Lately I've been focusing on isolated measles outbreaks. Like Dr. Reiber said, Washington State would be the closest. I'm not aware of anything in Oregon. What about you?"

Harbin sighed. "For the past three years, I've been studying the impact of fluctuating tides on coastal urban centers. We're heading in the opposite direction of the ocean right now. I can't think of a single reason for the powers that be to rush me out to this place."

Martha looked back out the window at the

landscape below. There was no denying the beauty—deep green forests, icy blue lakes. Wild, still relatively untouched by the barbarism of humans. The land below them looked so peaceful, serene. As they flew by the peak of Mount Hood, she couldn't imagine what could possibly be happening—

She saw it then and gasped. "Oh, God."

CHAPTER TWELVE

MARTHA

SANFORD HARBIN LEANED OVER Martha and looked out her window. "Well, I find that very odd indeed."

Across from Martha, Russel Fravel adjusted his glasses and peered out his own window. He spoke slowly, processing his thoughts as he said them aloud. "Difficult to say from this height, but I'd estimate the width to be around twenty yards. Looks like it starts at that crevasse and peters out somewhere in the woods." He glanced over at Harbin. "You're right. Very odd. Why would they bring us in to investigate tornado damage? There's not a single meteorologist on the team."

"We didn't bring in a meteorologist, because what you're looking at wasn't caused by a tornado," a voice said over the radio.

Holt.

You could learn a lot listening to an open radio channel. All those voices speaking to one another sometimes forgot you were there.

Damnit.

Joy Reiber blew out a frustrated breath. "If you brought me here for a tornado, I'll be—"

"It's *not* a tornado," Holt insisted. "The average width of a tornado's path is three to five hundred yards. Obviously, this is nowhere near that wide. I've been told the width of this path isn't on par with the destruction left behind. If this had been a tornado, the estimated wind speed necessary to create this damage would be around two-hundred-fifty miles per hour. That would make it an F4 on the Fujita–Pearson scale. The minimum width of an F4 is point-three miles. That's a little more than five hundred yards. Our path is no more than twenty or thirty yards wide. A tornado of that size would be considered an F1, with wind speeds of no more than one-hundred-twelve miles per hour—not strong enough to leave this kind of damage. Like I said, this wasn't a tornado."

Harbin was shaking his head. "I don't think you could make that determination from this swatch of land. An average is just that, an average. I've read about F4s and even F5s with maximum wind speeds that didn't conform to the norm. I recall one in Kansas about fifteen years ago that clocked in at two-hundred-seventy miles per hour and only left a path thirty yards across—what we're looking at is on par with something like that, an anomaly as you called it earlier."

Reiber had unfastened her safety harness and was bent over Fravel with a hand on his shoulder. The physical contact clearly made him uncomfortable, but he didn't say anything. His eyes were on her black sports bra under her loose tank top. When he noticed Martha watching him, he turned back to the window.

Fravel said, "The damage, though. The ground cover has been flattened. Some of those trees are snapped in half. Others appear to be ripped from the ground and tossed aside. That looks like tornado damage."

Martha had to agree. The chopper hovered above the crevasse, angled so they could get a better look. As Fravel had said, the path was about twenty yards wide, nearly a straight line, virtually everything within that path either flattened or gone altogether, as if someone had run a wide bulldozer through the tall redwoods in preparation for a road.

In the cockpit, the pilot spoke silently into his radio, then pulled right on the stick and slowly began following the path through the woods, hovering no more than twenty feet over the ancient trees.

"It's damn near a straight line," Harbin said to nobody in particular. "No variation in the width."

Reiber pulled a pair of field glasses from a black mesh storage bin beside her seat and peered down. "This happened recently. I'd say within the past several hours."

"How can you tell?" Martha asked.

"There's no discoloration in the fallen trees or flattened shrubs. Everything's still bright green."

Harbin glanced at her. "How long, exactly?"

She shrugged. "Hard to tell from this height, but to me, the fallen trees appear no different than the live ones. Discoloration begins immediately on branches separated from the trunk, the moment they lose their water supply. I'd guess more than two hours but less than six."

Harbin said nothing to this, only frowned.

Martha understood what he was getting at. "They started pulling our team together *before* this happened."

He nodded. "That means they either anticipated this event—"

"—or caused it," Fravel finished his thought.

The helicopter followed the path for nearly a mile before coming upon a large clearing. From the far end, another helicopter took off and buzzed past them, most likely heading back toward base camp at Zigzag. The ground was teeming with people, some in yellow hazmat suits. Various types of equipment stood—some of it still in cases. A large, white tent occupied the far corner of the clearing.

Harbin said, "We've got the leveled remains of several buildings down there. Houses, maybe? Some kind of colony?"

"Probably preppers. I've hiked Mount Hood, came out here with a boyfriend about five years ago," Reiber said. "These woods are full of doomsday preppers, survivalists, naturalists... thousands of people living off the grid. They break from society and make a life out here. Some even raise families."

Martha thought of her twins back home. "I can't imagine raising children out here."

"Look there." Fravel was pointing toward the east. "We've got another path. Not as wide as the first one we saw."

"I've got three more on this side," Reiber said. "They converge below, in the clearing."

Harbin glanced at each of them, then pushed the microphone on his headset closer to his lips. "Holt, are you still with us?"

"Yes, Doctor."

"Multiple paths through the woods, all converging here. Like streams feeding a river. Equal damage on all. Is this what you meant? Why you're certain it wasn't a tornado?"

"Yes."

Harbin went on. "They come together here, consolidate, then continue to that crevasse, end there, correct?"

"Correct."

"What's at the bottom of the crevasse?"

Holt fell silent for a moment, then: "We'll discuss that back at Zigzag. In a moment, we'll set down. I'd like to remind you of your instructions—you're welcome to study anything you find, but we'd like you to keep your opinions to yourself until we debrief. You'll have one hour and forty-seven minutes on the ground."

CHAPTER THIRTEEN

MARTHA

MARTHA SHIELDED HER EYES from the rising sun. "Where are Tomes and Hauff?"

"The two from NASA?" Harbin asked.

Martha nodded. "Weren't they right behind us?"

Their helicopter had set down on the far end of the clearing, about ten yards from another one. A half dozen more tents were going up. There were more people here than Martha had first thought.

Holt was on a sat phone, pacing about ten feet away. He covered the mouthpiece. "You'll see them back at Zigzag." He pointed at one of the newly erected tents. "That's you. You'll find all the gear you need already inside. One hour, forty-five minutes, then back in the chopper."

Martha still had no idea what specifically she was supposed to do here. She opened her mouth to ask him, but he had paced off in the other direction, back on his call. "I really don't like that guy."

Harbin didn't answer. His face had gone white. He was staring at the ground.

"What is—" Martha followed his gaze and felt something drop in the pit of her stomach. "Oh, my God."

Harbin glanced at her, then knelt. He took a pencil out of his pocket and tenderly picked at what he had found. "I think this is a chicken. *Was* a chicken."

Martha lowered herself beside him and fought back the urge to vomit. "It's been pulverized. Flattened."

"By what?" With the tip of the pencil, he pried a couple of the feathers up. The ground was saturated with fresh blood. "Look at that, that was its beak. Bones are mush, like roadkill that's been on the highway for a week, ground down to damn near nothing."

Martha looked around. "This isn't a road. I don't think you could even get a vehicle out here. Nothing substantial."

"We're in the middle of that path we saw from the helicopter." He raised a hand and pointed west. "Look at the ground—branches, twigs, grass—decimated. Like something carved a trench through the wilderness."

Reiber walked over and pointed at a small group about thirty feet away, all dressed in yellow hazmat suits. "That team, they're using Geiger counters. If they're worried about radiation, why weren't we given suits?"

"Holt's not wearing one, either," Harbin pointed out. "I'd think if there were truly a concern, he'd be the first to put one on."

Reiber turned and looked toward the east, followed the path as far as she could see. "This couldn't be some kind of asteroid or meteor crash, right?"

Harbin shook his head. "Anything like that would cause immense friction. This entire area would be scorched. Nothing's burned, just flat."

"Airplane crash?" Reiber offered.

Martha had ruled that out from the air. "Not wide enough. No debris. And Harbin's right about the scorch marks. We'd see that with an aircraft, too."

Then there was the smell.

Martha had been to crash sites before. The scent of death drifted through the air here, but it wasn't right for an aircraft. Not the sickly sweet odor she remembered. This was more like meat that had turned. She wandered over to the edge of the anomaly, amazed at how obvious that line was. The flattened earth, the damage to the trees and brush, all of it ended in a perfectly straight line, like a wall—small branches to thick trees, snapped off. She felt that was important—they weren't sheared or cut, they'd been broken.

Some of the branches had blood on them. Sticky,

nearly dry. Flies buzzed about, hungrily collecting what they could.

"Dr. Chan!"

Martha turned.

Harbin was standing near the tent Holt had said was theirs. He gestured her over and disappeared inside.

She found him with Russel Fravel, both staring up at a topography map taped to a whiteboard, a satellite photo next to it. Notes were written along the right side in blue ink. Black plastic cases lined all the walls, the covers open—an electron microscope, four laptops slotted into foam in another, collection containers and labels in the third, audio and video recording equipment, measuring tools, a Geiger counter similar to the one the other team was using . . . a relative crapshoot of scientific instruments, nothing specific to the task at hand.

Reiber had crouched next to one of the cases. She was studying the outer shell. "This one is Navy, that one over there is from NTSB." She frowned and looked back out the mouth of the tent. "If this isn't a crash, why would NTSB be here?"

Martha and Harbin both shook their heads.

Reiber considered this for another moment, then removed a small video camera from the case, snapped off the lens cover, and switched it on. She panned the room, studying the image on the display. "Night vision and FLIR built in. Nice."

"FLIR?" Harbin asked blankly.

"Forward-looking infrared radar," Reiber said without looking up. "Thermal imaging. Great for mapping hot and cold spots."

Fravel motioned Martha over and tapped on the satellite image. "This was taken three weeks ago. I count seventeen different structures. Clearly some kind of settlement. These larger buildings look like bunkhouses or maybe some type of central meeting space. This looks like a barn. Then we've got a number of smaller buildings, probably single-family dwellings—most have chimneys." He pointed at a cluster of shadows next to one of the larger buildings. "Those look like ATVs to me—probably how the locals got in and out of this place. The terrain is too rough for anything larger."

Martha stepped closer to the photograph and frowned. "I didn't see any of those things when we flew in, did you?"

Fravel shook his head. "That's because they're not there anymore."

"Did the people leave? On the ATVs?"

"I don't think so. I only count four vehicles in this image. It's possible they had others parked somewhere else, but by all accounts, this was a fairly large settlement, at least a hundred people. No way they all got out at once."

"Then where did they go?"

Fravel shrugged. "Maybe they left on foot?" He drew an imaginary circle around their current location on the topography map. "Plenty of places to hide out here. Maybe they're watching us right now. No way they survived if they didn't hide."

He went back to the satellite image. "Look at this." With his fingertip, he indicated something round near the center. "That's a well."

Stepping to the mouth of the tent, he said, "*That* well."

Martha followed his finger to a hole near the center of the clearing. There were stones scattered around the edges, but otherwise, it was gone. She turned back to the photograph, then back to the clearing. There were several buildings near the well in the photograph, but she didn't see them anymore. "Where did these go?"

"They've been completely leveled," Fravel said. He indicated one of the buildings. "I found this one. The boards are still there, but they've been crushed, embedded down into the dirt, as if someone plowed through this place with a heavy steamroller. From the chopper, I saw additional debris in the woods, along the length of the anomaly. At first glance, it appears something rolled into this village, carried everything away, and crushed the disintegrating pieces. To me, this looks like flood damage without the water. Pressure and force. Something with substantial momentum."

"Think of our chicken," Harbin muttered. "It might have been a balloon stomped under the foot of a giant. Organic matter nearly gone, only the hard bits left."

Fravel turned back to the photograph and indicated the well again. "The amount of force necessary to dismantle concrete and stone is thousands of pounds of crushing power, possibly millions. A human body is composed of sixty percent water. No way a person could ever survive a force like that."

Martha shivered. "Are you saying that's why we can't find anyone? The force that did this was strong enough to obliterate them?"

"It's a theory."

"You were told not to share your theories until after your debrief back at Zigzag."

This came from Holt. He was standing at the mouth of the tent.

Martha turned to him. She'd had enough. "We're civilian contractors. We don't fall under your hierarchy." She gestured at Fravel, Harbin, and Reiber, then back to herself. "If you want answers, we need to talk these ideas out. If we try to work this problem in a vacuum or if you or whoever it is you answer to attempts to filter our data or control the flow of information, you'll slow us down. We may not solve this at all."

"One theory spoken aloud infects all others," Holt

replied. “It’s now impossible for you to consider anything without your subconscious weighing your thought against what Dr. Fravel said.” He shifted his weight to his left foot. “I need each of you at the top of your game. If you get stuck on one idea and narrow-mindedly chase it down the rabbit hole, we’ll lose valuable time.”

Martha took a step closer. “Are we in danger? At least tell us that much. Is there residual radiation?”

“We haven’t found any radiation.”

“But you’re obviously concerned, or you wouldn’t be checking.”

“We’re checking *everything,*” Holt countered. He eyed everyone for a moment, then stepped back out into the clearing. “There’s something I want you to see.”

CHAPTER FOURTEEN

MARTHA

THE EXTENSIVE TESTING GOING on, the diversity of it, told Martha one simple fact—they had no idea what they were looking for. Whoever was running this operation was casting a wide net to see what they caught.

As they walked past what was once the village well, Martha watched someone in a hazmat suit lower a collection tube to retrieve a water sample. The team with the Geiger counters had moved on to the far end of the clearing. At least a dozen people, including Reiber, were documenting the scene with both still cameras and videos. Another pair were standing about twenty feet away, holding what Martha recognized as PCG meters—these measured air quality. Everything from relative humidity to barometric pressure to air content was being measured. The Earth's breathable atmosphere is typically comprised of 78 percent nitrogen, 21 percent oxygen, a little less than 1 percent argon, with trace amounts of carbon dioxide, neon, helium, methane, krypton, and hydrogen. Martha knew these particular meters were designed to look for anything outside the normal scope down to the microbial level. She'd seen them used at crash sites in the past. They had also been used extensively in Kuwait and Iraq when it was thought chemical weapons were at play.

The stink of death in the air came in ebbs and flows, and as they followed Holt across what was once the village center, it grew worse. She couldn't help but think about what Fravel had said. Was it physically possible for a human body to disintegrate from pressure?

Harbin tapped Martha on the shoulder and pointed off to their left—a mound in the dirt. It took a moment before Martha realized this was once a horse. Flattened and crushed, several gray ribs reached up toward the sky, others were snapped in half. A blanket of flies writhed over the exposed muscle, tendons, and tissue.

Her stomach lurched again, and when she saw Harbin's pale face, she knew she wasn't alone. She covered her mouth and nose with her hand, took several steps closer, then knelt near the corpse, careful not to get too close. The stomach was exposed; it had burst, the contents pooled out around it. She leaned over, tried not to breathe, and waved her hand to scare away the flies.

"What do you see?"

"Eggs, from the flies. Several hours old. By this time tomorrow, they'll hatch into maggots."

Harbin understood. "That confirms your theory. They put our team together before this happened."

"This way, Dr. Chan. Dr. Harbin," Holt called out from up ahead.

A few paces behind Holt, Reiber was recording everything. She lowered the video camera, glanced back at them worriedly, then continued on.

Holt led them beyond the edge of the village to a secondary clearing. Several chimneys still stood; others had toppled over. Another leaned precariously to one side, ready to fall at any moment. Debris covered the ground—logs, boards, the remains of furniture and clothing. At least two dozen people clambered around the scene. They wore white jumpsuits with no distinguishable markings indicating who they worked for.

Holt stopped and turned back to them, gesturing around. "You saw this from the air, and I've confirmed with sat photos—several hours ago, these were crudely constructed single-family dwellings."

"You mean homes," Harbin replied. "This is where the people of this place lived, laughed, and cried.

Until very recently, someone was very happy here. Do we know how many 'someones'?"

Holt shrugged. "At best guess, just shy of two hundred."

"Have you searched the surrounding woods?"

"They're not in the woods."

"Is what Fravel said correct? Were these people somehow vaporized? A group of this size can't simply vanish."

Holt pursed his lips but didn't answer.

"Was there some sort of crash here, or do you suspect some kind of weapon?" Harbin pushed.

"I have orders. I'll be able to disclose more when we return to Zigzag."

Martha was ready to punch this guy. If she wasn't half his size, she'd lift him off his feet and shake him.

"Listen," Reiber said. She was standing several feet off to the left, her eyes closed. The camera was dangling from her hand but still recording.

The group fell silent for a moment, then Holt said, "I don't hear anything."

"Exactly. No birds, no wildlife at all. Only insects."

"They got spooked, ran off. Understandable, under the circumstances."

"Yes," Reiber agreed. "But they haven't come back. Animals are quick to return to their homes once the danger has passed."

"I need all of you to focus," Holt interrupted. "We

have forty-three minutes left before we need to head back." He pointed off toward a smaller path coming out of the woods on the far side of the clearing. The ground was flat, the small trees and branches were cracked. "We saw that from the air. We're calling them 'feeders.' There are several—smaller anomalies coming in from the woods and converging at this point. Upon convergence, the anomaly appears to grow exponentially in size and continue on from here, destroying these dwell—*homes,* and moving on to the village where the destruction intensifies. From there, it appears to continue back into the woods, growing in size, until it reaches the crevasse where it ends."

Martha took several steps toward the "feeder," various pieces of timber and glass crunching under her feet. The cracked branches were green, fresh.

Harbin asked, "Could this be some type of seismic activity?"

"We ruled that out early on," Holt replied. "We've got small fault lines all around this area, but they don't coincide with the feeders or the main line of the anomaly."

Reiber panned the camera from where they stood, to the feeder, then traced the path as far back as she could, expertly working the digital zoom button. "I think all of us keep going back to natural events, understandable, but there's nothing natural about any of this. This is either man-made—some kind of weapon—or something else."

Harbin stifled a chuckle. "Your little green men?"

Reiber ignored him and continued to record.

"This is what I wanted you to see," Holt said.

Martha glanced over at him. He was standing next to the remains of a wall; splintered siding, lying flat on the ground, cracked down the center. At one point, it had been white, but the paint was faded and chipped, half peeled away. Written across, spanning nearly the entire piece, were two words in large, blocky letters—

DEAF! DEAF!

Harbin cleared his throat. "Is that blood? Someone wrote it with blood."

Holt took a pen from his back pocket, knelt down, and used the tip to point at the first word. "See how the dirt has been brushed away?"

"Someone brushed the dirt away, then wrote the words," Harbin finished his thought. "This was written *after* the anomaly struck. After the wall was on the ground."

"Exactly."

"So we have at least one survivor, somewhere."

Reiber gasped, nearly dropped the camera, and pointed.

There was a human nail embedded in the wood on the bottom of the second exclamation mark.

Martha stepped closer. Her right foot caught on something, and when she looked down, she realized it was a hand sticking up from beneath several layers of clapboard.

CHAPTER FIFTEEN

MARTHA

MARTHA FELL TO HER knees and began pulling away the boards. "Help me!"

Holt didn't move.

Harbin grabbed at the splintered wood, took a large piece about six feet long, and tossed it aside, then tugged at another. "Watch for nails."

Reiber stood frozen, a hand clasped over her mouth.

Martha hoped for a survivor, but as they uncovered the body, that hope quickly faded. They found not one but two people. When she spotted the gray clumps of hair and what was left of their heads embedded in the ground, Martha rose to her feet and had to step away. She watched as Harbin reluctantly uncovered the rest. Her eyes welled up.

This elderly couple had been holding hands, Martha could determine that much, but otherwise she found it impossible to determine where one body ended and the other began. Their ruined clothing, sopped with dark, pulpy blood, twisted with the crushed remains of their flesh. She'd seen bodies at crash sights, she'd witnessed the life leave someone while working in the ER back at Hopkins, but this was an image Martha didn't want in her head.

"My God, they're still warm," Harbin said softly, tentatively touching what might have been a forearm.

Reiber, who hadn't moved, slowly raised the camera and pointed it at the bodies, spoke in a timid voice, "Switching to thermal." She studied the screen for a moment, then turned to Martha. "89.8 Fahrenheit. Surrounding air temp is 58."

Martha chewed the inside of her cheek, did the math. "The human body drops about one and a half degrees every hour after death until it reaches air temperature. Accounting for the low air temp, I'd put time of death around four hours."

Harbin stood back up and looked out over all the fallen homes. "Reiber, what is the distance on that camera?"

"For thermal?"

He nodded.

"I'm not sure," Reiber said. "I'd guess about fifty feet."

He waved a hand toward the clearing. "Can you..."

She was already raising the camera. Moving slowly, she panned from left to right, then back again.

She went rigid. Her eyes grew wide as she repeated the motion again, staring at the small screen. “I’ve got heat sources…everywhere. At least two dozen, maybe more.” She looked up. “Under the debris. Nothing over ninety degrees.”

Dead. Everyone.

Holt put two fingers in his mouth and whistled. Two men in white jumpsuits stepped out from the remains of a house about forty feet away and looked at him. When he pointed down toward the bodies at their feet, they both nodded. The one on the left reached down, pulled a black bag from a nearby pallet, and unfolded it.

A body bag.

An entire pallet of body bags.

He didn’t approach them, though. Instead, he laid the bag out flat near his feet while the other man produced a small shovel and began to scoop—

Martha’s stomach lurched.

She turned swiftly, away from the others, took several steps, and tripped over a pipe. She fell hard to the ground, landing awkwardly on her left arm, her head smacking against the damp earth. Her vision went white for a moment, and as it cleared, she spotted the remains of a cradle lying on its side a few feet away. A swaddled blue blanket had fallen out. From within the folds, two icy-blue eyes stared back at her.

A baby, lifeless.

Martha shuffled backward, scrambled to her feet.

Holt's eyes went from her to the swaddled blanket, lingered there a moment. "I'll have someone..."

Martha didn't hear the rest. She turned her back on him, staggered to about twenty feet away, and sucked in several deep breaths. "Get your shit together, Martha," she told herself.

She didn't, though. At the thought of a baby out here, she lost it. She buried her face in her hands and tried to hold back the tears, but there was no stopping them. She sobbed. Martha wanted nothing more than to get back on a plane, get to her twins, and hug Emily and Michael for the next week, not let them out of her sight.

She felt a hand on her shoulder and realized it was Joy Reiber.

"I'm... sorry. I don't usually..." Martha stammered.

Reiber shushed her. "It's okay. I get it. I've got a little girl back home."

It wasn't okay, though. As a trauma surgeon, she'd seen much worse. Emotions had no place in an operating room, no place in a disaster, certainly no place here.

Several more minutes passed before she was able to pull herself together.

When Reiber led her back to Harbin and Holt, the blue swaddled blanket was gone.

Harbin gave her a soft nod before turning back to the words written in blood on the cracked wall.

DEAF! DEAF!

"I'm at a loss," he said more to himself than the others. Looking to Holt, he asked, "Anything else like this?"

Holt shook his head. "Nothing yet."

Kneeling down, Harbin's finger hovering above the words, he slowly traced each letter. "The desperation... fright... certainty they would die... these are the last two words this person or persons chose to communicate. The fact that they had time to write the message, and to write it in blood, tells us something, that's possibly more meaningful than the words themselves."

Holt frowned. "I don't follow."

Martha understood. She wiped her nose with the back of her hand. "If you're standing in the middle of a tornado, you don't have time to stop and write a message. By the time you realize you're in danger, it's too late to react."

"We know this wasn't a tornado."

Martha rolled her eyes. "Tornado, flood, missile attack... whatever the anomaly was, it's obvious it struck hard and fast." She gestured out over the flattened houses, then turned back to Harbin. "To your point, the person who wrote this, stood in the middle of it, while it was happening, and left this message."

Harbin's eyes lit up. "A sonic weapon of some sort?"

The doctors all looked at Holt.

Holt shook his head. "We ruled that out. Sonic weapons don't produce the power necessary to create physical damage on this level. At their strongest, they burst eardrums, cause pain, disorientation, bring on nausea or discomfort. They might shatter glass, but they're not capable of punching a hole through a piece of plywood, let alone down a tree or a building."

Harbin said, "You're speaking to US technology. What about the Chinese or the Russians? Some foreign actor? Is that why Frederick Hoover is mixed up in this with his cohorts at DARPA? Is this something experimental? Maybe satellite-based?"

"I've been assured by people much smarter than me that sonic weapons, both current and future, are not, and will never be, capable of delivering the damage we're witnessing here. Frankly, if they were, we'd see a military push to replace conventional weapons. Chemical weapons, nuclear, even most conventional, they leave a residual aftermath. This is..."

"This is what?" Martha asked.

Harbin huffed. "Clean. He was going to say clean. Isn't that right, Mr. Holt?"

Holt didn't answer.

Harbin faced Martha and Reiber. "We've got no radiation, and a swift, targeted destruction. The military considers that to be a clean weapon. Highly desirable." He stood and wiped his hands on his slacks. "If this was a weapon, I guarantee someone is trying to figure out who possesses it. If it wasn't a weapon, Hoover and those at DARPA are interested because they want to know if it could be turned into one."

"Lovely," Reiber muttered.

She'd filmed the entire exchange.

A group of Army Rangers, three men and a woman, approached them, stepping carefully over the debris. To Holt, the woman said, "Sir, we've got something."

CHAPTER SIXTEEN

MARTHA

WALKING ALONG THE CENTER of the anomaly, Martha and the others followed the four Rangers toward the large crevasse they saw from the air. She found it amazing how cleanly the damage cut through the forest.

She was quickly reminded of the violent devastation when they came upon the remains of a barn. One support beam stuck up out of the ground like an old, crooked finger scratching at the sky. Hay was scattered about. If there had been animals inside, there was no sign of them now.

Martha found the silence unnerving. Not a single bird chirped.

Two other Army Rangers watched them approach from the center of the debris. Tense, weapons at the ready.

Holt kept glancing at his watch.

"If there's no radiation," Martha said, "why are you so concerned with the amount of time we spend here?"

Harbin said, "I believe Mr. Holt thinks the bogeyman might come back."

"Could it?"

Holt appeared frustrated. "We don't know what *it* is. Best to remain cautious. I've been ordered to limit exposure to two hours until we know more."

With the camera up, Reiber slowly walked the perimeter of the barn. The soldiers carefully avoided the lens, turning with her so she only got shots of their backs. Martha noticed none of them wore name tags on their uniforms.

The female Ranger led them to the center of the barn. There was a trapdoor in the ground, open. She produced a bulky cassette recorder with RADIOSHACK stamped into the old, chipped plastic. "We found this inside, on the top step, sir."

Holt took the recorder from her, turned it over in his hand, then pressed Play.

Static.

A young girl's voice: *"Momma? Poppa? We're okay. Where are you? We're going to number two. We'll wait for you there."*

More static.

Holt rewound the tape, increased the volume, and played it again. When the message finished, he looked up at the others. "Teenager, maybe? Hard to tell."

"She said 'we,'" Martha pointed out. "We've got at least two survivors."

Harbin said, "Play it one more time?"

Holt did.

"She doesn't sound deaf to me."

"You can't always tell," Reiber said. "I knew a girl in college who'd only been deaf for two years, and her inflection and tone were perfect."

Harbin shrugged. "If she didn't write that message on the wall, that means we have more survivors; that's my point."

The Ranger pointed the barrel of her weapon at the open trapdoor. "We've cleared the space. It's tight, but you'll want to go down there, sir. There are signs of a struggle."

"A struggle?"

"On the ground, to the right of the steps. Possibly more. Hard to tell, sir."

Holt nodded, took out a flashlight, and started down the steps.

Harbin leaned in close to Martha. "I'm not a fan of confined spaces. I think I'll sit this one out."

She patted his shoulder and followed down behind Holt.

A storm cellar.

Holt stepped down onto the dirt floor: Martha, too. Reiber remained on the steps, panning the camera.

Shelves lined most of the walls, many of them

toppled. The various canned goods and boxes they once held littered the floor, made it difficult to maneuver the tight space. A bag of flour lay in the far corner, burst, covering everything in a thin layer of white dust.

Holt knelt beside the steps, where the Ranger had mentioned.

When Martha looked down, he was picking at something with the tip of his pen.

She frowned. “Is that hair?”

Holt nodded. “There are bits of scalp, too. Blond. Any chance you grabbed a sample bag from the tent?”

Martha shook her head.

“Here.” Harbin tossed one down to him from the opening above.

Holt carefully bagged the hair, slipped it into his pocket, and stood, looking around. “Tough to say if all this damage was from some type of fight or the anomaly itself.”

“Why would someone fight?”

Holt walked over to one of the toppled shelves and studied what looked like blood on the edge of the board. “Tense situations tend to bring out the worst in people. Maybe they saw this as a safe space and there wasn’t enough room for everyone who tried to get down here.” He found more blood on a can of corn on the floor. He picked it up with the tips of his fingers and held it in the flashlight beam. “Blood happens in an accident. People get hurt. Hair doesn’t come out in clumps unless someone or something pulls it.”

His watch began to beep. Holt glanced down at the display and tapped a button to silence the alarm. “Time to go.”

Martha didn’t move. “We can’t leave—we’ve got a survivor out there. A young girl!”

Holt gestured for Reiber to go back up, then started up the steps behind her. “Two hours, max. That’s my orders.”

“I’m not going to leave a frightened little girl out in the woods!”

From above, Holt called back, “Not your problem, Doctor. You’re here to determine the cause of the anomaly, not search and rescue. The Rangers will find her.” Turning to the soldier at the top of the steps, he said, “Is he here yet?”

“Less than a minute out, sir.”

Holt scribbled something on a piece of paper and handed it to the woman along with the old cassette recorder. Turning to his right, he said something Martha couldn’t make out, then pointed down at her.

Two other soldiers appeared up above, looking down from the trapdoor. The two who had been guarding the barn.

"Less than a minute out," Holt repeated. "It's covered, Dr. Chan. Get your ass on the chopper, or I'll have these fine gentlemen carry you."

"You wouldn't."

"Try me."

Martha hesitated another moment, then cursed under her breath and huffed up the steps.

CHAPTER SEVENTEEN

FRASER

LIEUTENANT COLONEL ALEXANDER FRASER peeled off his Velcro name tag and slipped it into the manila envelope on the seat beside him. His wallet and cell phone went in behind it. He handed the envelope up to the chopper pilot, who stuffed it into a leather bag.

"Approaching forty-five, one-twenty-one now, sir. Stand by to disembark."

"Understood."

He glanced back down at the debrief documents in his hand.

45.3736 degrees north, 121.6960 degrees west. Western corner of Mount Hood, Oregon. Several hours ago, he'd been asleep in his barracks at Lewis–McChord, just south of Seattle. The president asked for him, a munitions expert, specifically. He'd been given fifteen minutes to wake, shower, and prep for departure. Because he always kept a go-bag at the ready, he finished with six minutes to spare.

The video conference with the joint chiefs on his way to the airfield had been brief. He was told to treat this event as an attack on American soil. Employ the utmost secrecy.

He didn't ask any questions, never did.

He had only one concern—the debrief stated civilians had been employed as part of the investigative team.

He sighed.

Civilians.

Fraser's father had been career Army, his grandfather before him. Neither had achieved a rank higher than captain. Neither had lived long enough to see him achieve that rank or surpass it. He lost his grandfather to cancer. His father to Afghanistan. He hadn't seen his mother in nearly four years. She lived in El Paso, and he had little time or inclination to take leave.

Having graduated high school early, at the age of seventeen, and with letters of recommendation from his father and several high-ranking officials close to his father, he was accepted into West Point two months later. He majored in defense and strategic studies, took extra classes over the summer rather than return home, and graduated at the top of his class exactly four years later. From there, he shipped to Fort Benning in Georgia for Basic and began a series of deployments where he quickly moved up the ranks, becoming one of the youngest lieutenant colonels in the Army at the age of thirty-five.

Civilians got in the way, slowed things down.

Cogs.

Fraser liked a smooth-turning wheel.

The debrief folder contained several photographs—he took them out and held them next to the chopper window one at a time. Whatever caused the damage down below worked in a straight line, a damn near perfectly straight line, from what he could see from the air.

In Iraq, he'd seen entire villages flattened by drone attacks, Patriot missile batteries, even MOAB, Mother of All Bombs bunker-busters. They all left a similar scar behind—a crater with burnt, disheveled earth and debris radiating out from the center. He'd been briefed on foreign advanced weaponry just last week, assured by the joint chiefs that no foreign actor had assets in their sky, no new satellite-based weapon or laser fired from space. The latest threat out of Russia was called 3K22 or "zircon"—a hypersonic missile capable of traveling at speeds up to two miles per second. Current missile defense systems were useless at that speed. Didn't really matter; intel suggested 3K22 was at least several more years from use.

His money was on the Chinese.

Nearly all electronic devices contain one or more components manufactured in China. Recently it was discovered that many of those connected devices—everything from cell phones to wi-fi toasters—

contained firmware that could be used for surveillance purposes. Even worse, much of the internet backbone contained hardware developed by the Chinese. In private circles, Fraser had heard talk of something called the Black Dragon Switch—a program linked to all these devices, capable of taking them over with the flip of a switch. Theoretically, they could shut off the lights and attack us while we fumbled around in the dark.

Sneaky bastards, the lot of them.

"Ten seconds to ground, sir. Stand by."

Reaching for his watch, Fraser set a timer for two hours.

He slipped the photographs and documents back into the debrief folder, sealed it, and handed it up to the pilot. He was out the door before the skids of the chopper touched down. Ducking low, shielding his eyes from airborne dust, he ran across the small field to a waiting Ranger.

Fraser shouted to be heard over the helicopter. "I was told to report to someone named Keenen Holt."

One hand on her hat, she nodded toward the west. "Gone, sir. Back to base camp. Time window expired. He gave me this for you— " She handed him a beat-up cassette player and a scribbled note.

The note read:

Contain them!

CHAPTER EIGHTEEN

MARTHA

DR. MARTHA CHAN STARED out the small window near the front door of Zigzag Station, a cold cup of coffee in her hand. Holt had finished with her twenty minutes ago, and now she was free to observe all that had happened while they were gone. Army personnel had managed to complete the barrier around the perimeter of the ranger station: concrete blockades at the bottom with ten feet of chain-link fencing bolted to the top, capped off with glimmering razor wire. Every few feet were red signs reading, DANGER—HIGH VOLTAGE. Soldiers were walking the length of the barrier in pairs, at least a dozen. Four more manned the only access gate. Two helicopter pads had been established within the perimeter, four more outside the gate. Numerous helicopters—EC135s, several smaller ones, and a large troop carrier, were in constant motion, ferrying people between Zigzag and the anomaly.

Tents had gone up, too. She counted fifteen of them, all within the confines of this newly formed compound.

Martha stared at the fortified fence between her and the outside world.

Harbin's words echoed back, *Aren't you the least bit curious as to what they're trying to keep* out *of this little slice of heaven?*

During the flight back, their microphones had been disabled, making it impossible for them to speak with one another. Upon landing at Zigzag, soldiers escorted them to individual tents. She'd been alone for nearly an hour before Holt retrieved her, brought her to a tent he claimed as his own, and sat her in a chair facing a video camera on a tripod.

"Summarize your thoughts on what you just saw for me."

Martha first looked at him, then directly into the camera. "I don't have a fucking clue what I just saw. I need to call my children."

"When we're finished."

During thirty minutes of useless back-and-forth, a medical tech checked her blood pressure, hearing, eyesight, and drew three vials of blood that she placed in a small silver case and carried out of the room.

He'd finally dismissed her, told her to wait here

while he talked to Harbin, Fravel, and Reiber. She hadn't seen Brian Tomes or Brenna Hauff, the two from NASA, since they left.

He'd given her a sat phone, at least there was that, but when she dialed her ex-husband, she only got voicemail. She really needed to hear her children's voices right now. Something about a kid's voice made everything all right.

Finishing the coffee, she retrieved the phone and hit redial. Unlike a cell phone, this one took about twenty seconds to connect. The line rang twice and again went to voicemail. "Goddamn you, Mark." She waited for his recording to finish, then left another message. "Hey, it's me. Sorry for the strange number. Please pick up or call me back. I want to talk to the little ones. All right. I'll try again in a little bit."

She disconnected.

Martha could picture the cocksucker staring down at his phone and just not answering, the kids probably within arm's reach. Emily had a play tonight at school. Michael had a lacrosse match. She should be there. No doubt Mark would play up the fact that she wasn't. He'd scribble something down in his little notebook for their next custody hearing. "Sorry, kids, Mom must be busy."

The door opened and Harbin came through, Fravel a few paces behind him.

"Where's Holt?" Martha asked.

“Still grilling Reiber.” Harbin stepped up beside her at the window. “I don’t like this one bit.”

Fravel collapsed into a chair, eyeing the sat phone in her hand. “Does that work? Can I see it?”

Martha tossed the phone to him, watched him peck in a number. After about half a minute, he left a message, disconnected, and set the phone down on the table. “Did he ask either of you about crop circles?”

Harbin’s eyebrows went up. “Crop circles?”

Fravel nodded. “You know, patterns cut into fields of wheat and corn.”

Martha and Harbin both shook their heads.

Fravel went on. “He showed me pictures of several different ones around the world, but he focused on one in particular near Steens Mountain, about three-hundred-fifty miles from here. It was this giant Hindu symbol called a Shri Yantra mandala. Two Air National Guard pilots spotted it from nine thousand feet on a routine patrol on August 10, 1990. They flew this route daily and swore it wasn’t there the day before. This thing was huge—13.3 miles of lines carved into a dry lake bed. Each line measured exactly ten inches wide and three inches deep—large, perfectly shaped squares, circles, and triangles, all coming together to create this ancient symbol. The Army went out to investigate, and when they got up close, they didn’t find any sign of tool marks.

No tire tracks in or out, nothing but the ones they created."

"Haven't they proven those things to be hoaxes?" Martha asked. "Kids using boards to stomp down the crops, that kind of thing?"

Fravel leaned back in the chair and spread his hands. "Some, sure, but the file he showed me was marked Top Secret. He has closeup photos of the lines—ten inches wide, three inches deep, 13.3 miles in total. *No visible tool marks*. Holt asked me, 'when a group of astrophysicists are locked in a room together at a conference and the alcohol is flowing, what theories come out?' "

"And what did you tell him?" Harbin asked.

Fravel shrugged. "There's a small group of people who think they could be messages—labels, tags, branding—whatever you want to call it."

"Made by who?"

"Are you really going to make me say it? There are no aliens. It's a statistical improbability."

Harbin clucked his tongue. "You have to admit, there are similarities between crop circles and this anomaly. Think about what happens when you press your hand down into the sand at the beach. You may be able to compact it some, but most will displace. A depth of three inches is significant. The anomaly shares signs of immense pressure, the perfectly straight lines of a geometric shape, even the smaller feeder lines we saw converging with the main line. These are all similar to crop circles."

"But much larger," Fravel said softly.

Harbin nodded. "Much, much larger."

Fravel's eyes went wide as he considered this.

Outside, a large helicopter came in low and fast. It set down on one of the newly constructed pads near the far corner of the compound.

Holt appeared at the mouth of a tent nearby, shielding his face from flying dust.

Brian Tomes jumped out of the helicopter, followed closely by Brenna Hauff. She spotted Holt, quickly stormed over to him, and punched him square in the jaw.

CHAPTER NINETEEN

MARTHA

MARTHA SHOT OUT THE door and ran toward Holt and the two NASA employees, Harbin and Fravel behind her. When they reached them, Hauff was beating on his chest with her fists. Holt had one hand on his nose and was attempting to block her blows with the other. Tomes had his arms wrapped around her waist and was trying to hold her back.

Martha grabbed Hauff by the wrist, but she was surprisingly strong. Her clothing and protective gear were stained with blood; Tomes', too.

"This bastard lied to all of us!" she spat out, her face red. "He told us he didn't know what happened to the rest of the people from that village!"

Holt took his hand away from his nose and looked at his fingers. There was a little blood, but not much. She hadn't broken it. "I never said that."

Back at the landing pad, a ramp opened on the

rear of the helicopter. Two soldiers in green fatigues walked out carrying a black body bag. They crossed the small field and disappeared into the mouth of one of the tents. A small sign near the door read MEDICAL. A moment later, two other soldiers appeared, went to the helicopter, and retrieved another. From where Martha stood, she counted at least a dozen more similar bags inside the chopper's cargo hold, stacked floor to ceiling.

All eyes went back to Holt.

Hauff fumed, her face bright red. "There must be a thousand people down there!"

"Down where?"

"In that crevasse!" she replied. "Me and Brian, we rock climb. He just had us rappel down the side into..." Tears welled up in her eyes. "What the fuck was that?" She lunged at him again, nearly broke free from everyone.

Holt stood his ground and wiped his hand on his pants. "I'm just following orders, same as everyone else here. You have a problem, take it up with Washington."

"That's a bullshit excuse, and you know it. You could have warned us!"

Martha held up her palms. "Let's all calm down."

Brenna Hauff gave Holt one more icy glare, then shrugged off the others and stomped off to the side, wiping her nose and eyes. "We couldn't get to the bottom, it's too deep, but there are bodies everywhere. Impaled on the rocks, caught up in cracks and outcroppings. Pieces and chunks of flesh on the walls..." She looked down at her bloodstained gloves, peeled them off, and tossed them on the ground.

The soldiers walked past them carrying another bag. They vanished in the tent.

Harbin eyed Holt. "You said there were about a hundred people in the village. How can there be a thousand down there?"

"She's exaggerating."

"Fuck you," Hauff shot back.

Holt lowered his voice and spoke slowly. "There's no way to know how many are down there. Like she said, the crevasse is too deep. We've tried thermal, but the crevasse was caused by a fissure. The escaping heat screws with the sensors. We've pulled out twenty-seven so far, brought back half. The others are in a chopper behind us. We'll retrieve as many as possible. In the meantime, I need to file a progress report in twenty minutes, and someone is bound to ask me for a cause of death. I intend to have an answer."

He started for the tent. "Dr. Chan, you're a medical doctor, you're welcome to join me. I want the rest of you back in the ranger station. You've been debriefed; you're free to discuss your findings. I've been authorized to share additional details with you—I'll be there shortly to fill in blanks."

“Where’s Reiber?” Harbin asked.

“Studying vegetation and ground samples taken from the anomaly site,” he called back over his shoulder before disappearing inside.

Martha looked back at the others.

Harbin offered her a soft nod and silently mouthed the word *go.*

She turned and went after Holt.

CHAPTER TWENTY

MARTHA

INSIDE THE TENT, MARTHA found Holt in a small antechamber changing into scrubs and a mask. He tossed a set to her, sealed in a plastic bag. "Put these on."

She tugged the scrubs on over her clothing and followed him through a narrow hallway lined with a series of heavy plastic curtains—each weighted and sealing automatically behind. The temperature dropped between each, and when they stepped through the last one, she estimated the air to be in the fifties.

The tent was much larger than it appeared from the outside, at least sixty feet in diameter with halogen lights hung from cables strung across the ceiling, bathing every inch in bright white. Several operating areas had been set up in the center of the room. Lined on the floor to the left of several large support poles were black body bags, far more than the ones that came in on the helicopter with Tomes and Hauff. Each bore a number written in blocky letters on white tape. The highest number she spotted was 106, but they didn't appear to be in any kind of order.

Martha followed Holt to a man huddled over one of the tables. Three blinking video cameras were positioned on tripods, angled down toward the center.

She expected introductions, but none were made.

Even in the chilled air, the man's forehead glistened with sweat. He'd been working awhile. He glanced up at them for a moment, his eyes fixating angrily on Holt, then turned back to the table. "This is the sixth one I've examined so far, a male, thirties or forties, subjected to extreme trauma. Nearly every bone is broken. His rib cage is damn near pulverized. Scapula is dust." He shuffled down the table and pointed at the remains of his leg. "The femur is the hardest bone in the human body, look at it—it's a splintered mess. This man was crushed. All of them were."

"Was he pulled from under one of the houses?" Martha asked.

The man looked up at Holt again. "Has she been cleared?"

Holt nodded. "Dr. Chan came in this morning from San Francisco under special request of Frederick Hoover. She's toured the site and been vetted. You're clear to speak freely."

He sighed and looked at Martha. "I'm Dr. Fitch from Grace in Seattle. Got here a few hours ago." He moved back to the head of the table. "Look at the skull," he said. "See these breaks? Most impacts have a central point of collision, and the breaks branch out respectively—worst at the center, less so as distance increases. What you're looking at was caused by thousands of pounds of force applied equally over every portion of his body and sustained for at least a minute, maybe longer. Like he was placed in a large vise or one of those machines used to crush cars."

The first two soldiers pushed through the plastic curtain, carrying another black body bag. When they started toward the others along the wall, Holt stopped them. "Place that one on the table here." He gestured toward a wide aluminum gurney beside them.

Fitch glared at Holt with frustration. "I need to finish all the others first. You promised me more help. Where is it?"

Holt ignored the question. He stepped over to the body bag and tugged the zipper open.

Martha swallowed and covered her nose as the smell lofted up.

The body inside was of a woman, maybe in her sixties. It was difficult to tell. Her clothing was shredded. Her right arm and most of her face were covered in abrasions. She was missing a shoe. Her ankle on the other foot was bent at an unnatural angle. No obvious signs of bruising there, so the break had occurred postmortem.

Fitch's gray eyebrows were bushy, unkempt. He stepped closer. "What's that odor? That's not decomp. Where did this woman come from?"

Holt told him.

"Interesting." He reached down with a gloved hand and raised her right arm, his fingers inching tenderly from her wrist to her elbow. "There's a break here, in the ulna. This feels like a standard fracture, not from extreme pressure like the others."

Reaching to his left, he picked up a device that looked like a large camera with a dome over the lens. A MaxRay portable X-Ray machine. Martha had used one before in Honduras and more recently at the crash of an Airbus A310 outside Houston. This unit was a little smaller, appeared new.

Fitch raised the device, pointed it down at the woman's body, starting at her head and working his way down. He stared at the digital display for several seconds, scrolling through the images. "We've got numerous fractures, but these appear to be related to her fall."

Her eyes were open slightly, both lined with red. He reached down and pulled back her left eyelid. "This is peculiar."

Holt stepped closer. "What?"

Martha saw it, too. "The blood came from her lacrimal."

"Her what?"

"Her tear duct," Fitch said. "This woman was crying blood in the moments before she died." Turning her head, he studied her ear. "There's blood in the ear canal, too. She was hemorrhaging."

Martha ducked down and looked at her mouth. "Here, too."

Fitch pressed a finger into her cheek and frowned, did it again. From there, he moved down to her neck, his fingers walking down the line from her chin to her clavicle. He peeled off one of his gloves and did it again. He looked up at Holt. "When did this woman die?"

"We'd estimate within the last four to six hours."

This seemed to confuse Fitch. He located an infrared thermometer on the table at his side, pointed it at the woman's forehead, and pulled the trigger. A red dot appeared on her forehead. He frowned at the display, scanned her again on her neck, then her arm and also an exposed portion of her thigh. "I'm getting a consistent temperature of 102.8. If she's been dead that long, her temperature should be much lower, not feverish." He cocked his head at Martha. "What does that odor smell like to you? Be honest."

Martha didn't want to say it out loud, but she did anyway. "Barbecue. Cooked meat. I've smelled it at crash sites. It's familiar, but I don't see any burn marks on her body."

She found a box of gloves, pulled on a pair, took up a pair of scissors, and began cutting away the woman's clothing. They found signs of hemorrhaging at all orifices.

Leaning in close, she smelled the woman's skin. "I think the odor is coming from her sweat glands. It's consistent across the woman's body."

Holt, who had remained silent through most of this, finally said, "What does that mean?"

Martha looked at Fitch, who simply shrugged his shoulders. She told Holt, "This woman's body temperature rose significantly prior to death. She was cooking from the inside out."

CHAPTER TWENTY-ONE

TENNANT

THE SMELL OF BAKED beans drifted up out of the small pot on the propane stove and seemed to inch up the walls of Fallout Shelter Number Two, to the heavy crossbeams holding the ceiling up, and back down to the dirt floor like a sentient investigation of their new surroundings. Tennant fully understood baked beans and cooking odors were not alive, but it helped her to think of them that way. If Poppa were there, he'd tell her to use the creative portions of her brain, turning this into a little game, an adventure, even.

Curled up under her feet, Zeke's tail thumped against her ankle. He'd remained close since they got here, insisting on physical contact. If she moved a foot or two in either direction, he shuffled over and pressed against her, his soft whimpers saying all that needed to be said.

"Sophie, you can have the bacon if you want it," Tennant said over her shoulder, slowly stirring the beans. "I know that's your favorite part."

Momma had told Sophie manufacturers used the least desirable bits of swine in these cheap cans, parts better left unknown. That didn't seem to sway her in the least.

"Do you want the bacon, Sophie?"

Behind her, Sophie let out a soft grunt. This was followed by a guttural sound, deep and angry.

Zeke whimpered again and pressed his snout down into the dirt.

Tennant's everything hurt, her nose most of all. When they got here, she found the first aid kit and took six ibuprofen tablets, then she located a small hand mirror and set the break herself. Poppa had taught her how, but he'd shown her on Tabby Mexler after Tabby fell out of a tree and busted hers good. Waiting a day or more could mean you'd have to not only reset the break, but also crack newly formed cartilage and bone—break the bone again—just to put it right. She'd done it fast, pressing her palm on the left side, then giving herself a hard slap from the right. She felt the damaged bone grind and lock into place. She'd heard it, too, a deep crunch in her head. The pain came a moment later, and she fell into the corner and screamed for nearly five minutes, until the pain returned to a dull throb.

Of course, all of this took place *after* she secured Sophie.

Inside Number Two, Tennant found some more rope and tied her sister to the wooden bench in the back corner. Her grandpa had made the bench out of an old oak tree that had been struck by lightning. She knew it weighed a ton, she remembered hauling it here with Momma, and there was no way Sophie would break the arms or legs, even if her fever was making her stronger.

She was burning up.

Tennant didn't have a thermometer, but there was no question about a fever—a hundred something for sure—and it was getting worse.

A thick sheen of grimy sweat glistened on her skin, but when Tennant tried to give her medicine to bring her temperature down, her sister refused to open her mouth. She clenched her teeth and jerked her head from side to side until Tennant finally gave up. When Momma and Poppa got here, they might have to take her down to the stream. Tennant remembered two springs ago when Abigail Cruther's flu turned feverish and she didn't respond to the meds, she had to be carried, thrashing and fighting, down to the spring near Borden Hill. She was only nine, but the adults had to work in shifts of three to hold her down in the water. That took nearly three hours, but her fever eventually broke.

There was no way Tennant could manage Sophie on her own.

She had to wait.

Someone would come.

On the stove, the beans began to burn, and Tennant slid the pot off the flame before switching off the propane.

"Do you want a hot dog?" she asked her sister. "I'll make you one if you'll eat it. I'll make you two, even."

Tennant didn't much like the freeze-dried hot dogs. Even when boiled in water, they never seemed to taste quite right, not like the refrigerated ones. She'd had those once, and they were *so* good. Sophie had never seemed to care. She'd eat those horrible protein bars Poppa liked so much, too, even though they tasted like sawdust. She scooped a serving of the beans onto a plate and turned back to Sophie.

Her sister had gone silent. Her head was cocked oddly to the left, her eyes rolled up to the side, staring at the ceiling.

As Tennant took a step closer, she noticed Zeke was looking up, too. His ear twitched.

Her heart jumped. "Is someone here, boy?"

He gave her a quick glance, then looked back up, a soft growl in his throat. His tail thumped once against the floor, then went stiff.

Like before, the ringing started deep in her head,

as if someone tapped a fork against the side of a glass bottle off in the distance, barely audible. Instead of fading away, though, the ringing grew louder.

She dropped the plate of beans and frantically glanced around the room, her eyes landing on the first aid kit still open on the table. She shuffled around the contents, found a wad of cotton balls, and pressed two into her ears. Her sister remained still as a statue as she pressed cotton into her ears, too. Even Zeke didn't fight her, but she had to work fast—he was trying to scurry under the table.

The sound grew louder.

Even through the cotton, that single tone increased. Tennant couldn't tell if it was getting closer, amplifying, or both, but within moments the sound was everywhere, louder than her own screams.

CHAPTER TWENTY-TWO

TENNANT

TENNANT DUG HER FINGERS into her ears, jammed the cotton in as deep as it would go, but it didn't seem to help. The sound was as loud within her mind as it was everywhere else. The table began to vibrate. As she watched, the first aid kit shuffled across the table and fell to the floor.

Sophie tried to stand.

She got up in one quick, spastic motion as if every muscle in her body tensed at the same time. The rope around her hands, arms, legs, and feet all went taut, and somehow she managed to lift grandpa's heavy bench off the ground for nearly a second before the weight of the thing won out and pulled her back down. Her lips were moving, not in a scream but words, a flurry of words, but Tennant couldn't hear her above everything else. She pressed her palms tight over her ears as the sound grew louder—cacophonous and frantic—the screams of a million people in the worst possible pain—the shouts of those who would rather be dead—as if she were hearing those trapped in the fires of hell.

Tennant pressed her eyes shut, and when she opened them again she was on her knees with no memory of falling to the ground. The room pressed in on her from all sides, as if the underground space were filling with water and didn't have enough room to contain it all.

Her heart pounded. Each beat a hammer blow.

Sophie jerked up again, and this time she managed to raise the bench up for nearly ten seconds before both she and the wood crashed back down to the ground.

Zeke backed away from both of them, scurried from under the table on his haunches and into the far corner even as canned goods began to jump off the shelves and land around him.

Tennant pressed her eyes shut, pushed her palms against her skull, tried to keep it all out, but the noise just grew louder.

A shelf toppled beside her.

Dirt rained down from above. Dust and chunks of earth breaking out from under the support beams and shattering on the ground, the pieces dancing away as vibration grew with the noise. Scrambling into a half crawl, she managed to get under the table with Zeke; more of the ceiling came down.

"Sophie!" she shouted, unable to hear even herself.

Her sister was standing again, this time somehow managing to hold the bench up by her bindings. Her mouth was open in a scream, blood trickled from the corners of her eyes, from her ears.

Tennant felt wetness on her own face. She managed to pull her palms away from her ears only long enough to realize there was blood on her hands.

CHAPTER TWENTY-THREE

MARTHA

MARTHA FOUND THE OTHERS in the room at the back of the ranger station, Harbin standing up at the whiteboard and the others sitting around the oak table. A pot of coffee sat between them, along with several half-eaten sandwiches. The board was covered in loosely organized text in shaky handwriting—

Natural Event:

Tornado
Flash flood
Pressure vortex
Heat fissure
Unknown storm type

Man-made:

Biological weapon
Sonic weapon
Space-based?
Extraterrestrial?

Misc:

Virus
Mass hysteria
Suicide pact?

In the top left corner, he'd written *DEAF! DEAF!*

As Martha entered the room, Harbin was busy drawing a line through *flash flood*. "The ground was dry, there was no evidence of residual water, and today's weather wasn't ideal to dry the area out as quick as it would need to for this to be plausible." He looked up at Martha and pointed at a shelf near the door with the tip of his blue marker. "They brought us a wide assortment of sandwiches—bologna on white and bologna on wheat. They taste like someone made them a week ago and just remembered they left them in their car. Better than nothing, I suppose."

"I don't think I can eat right now," Martha replied, falling into a chair. She'd spent the last several hours helping Dr. Fitch conduct autopsies, and her stomach was in knots. By the time she emerged, the sun was gone.

She told them what they'd found.

Reiber was first to speak. "Same thing with all of them?"

Martha nodded. "The ones found in the village died of wounds created by immense pressure. The ones found in the crevasse were... cooked, apparently suffering from an extreme fever."

"At what kind of temperature?" Harbin asked.

She didn't really have an answer, not a viable one, anyway. "The highest human temperature on record was an Atlanta man named Willie Jones who in 1980 somehow survived heatstroke with a temperature of 115.7 degrees. At anything greater than 111.2 Fahrenheit, brain damage, convulsions, shock, cardio-respiratory collapse, organs liquefy... Death is almost a certainty."

Harbin put the cap back on the marker and set it in the tray under the board. "I don't mean to press, but you didn't answer my question. What temperature would be necessary to facilitate the damage you found in the autopsies?"

Martha looked at the faces around the table, not sure she wanted to say it aloud. "One-twenty, maybe one-twenty-five. Not just a spike, but for a sustained period of time."

Brenna Hauff sat slumped in her chair, her skin

horribly pale, still visibly shaken. More to herself than to the group, she said, "I touched one, and he was hot. Hotter than a living person. His eyes were filled with blood, gorged with it, ready to pop." The word *pop* seemed to amuse her. She repeated it again, barely a whisper. A grin edged the corner of her lips, vanishing when she realized Martha was watching her.

Fravel took off his glasses and cleaned the lenses with a napkin. "Suppose for a moment the human body could generate a fever that high, what would be the cause?"

Martha turned nervously from Hauff. She had discussed this at length with Dr. Fitch. "It would have to be something viral. We took blood samples from bodies found in the village and in the crevasse, though, and found nothing abnormal."

Tomes reached for his coffee and slowly turned the Styrofoam cup in his hands. "Microwave."

Harbin's eyes narrowed. "Microwave?"

Tomes nodded at the cheap white microwave next to the coffee maker. "Microwaves heat from the inside out. Maybe we're looking at some kind of microwave-based weapon."

Harbin considered this, picked up the marker, and took the cap off. He started to write *microwave* under *Man-made* and paused. "Microwaves occur naturally, too, don't they?"

Tomes nodded, but when Harbin looked over at Fravel, he waved him off before he could ask the question. "Solar flares contain microwave radiation, but it's minimal, barely detectable by the time they reach Earth. If it were possible for one to get here with the necessary targeted strength, you'd see half this mountain missing, the electrical grid would be down, major chaos."

"Even if microwaves were responsible for the heat, they wouldn't explain the injuries derived from pressure," Reiber pointed out.

"She's right," Tomes said. "What we witnessed was twofold, heat *and* pressure." He held out each of his palms in turn, then brought them together. "Someone or something paired these two forces together... intentionally."

Harbin nodded in agreement, returned to the board, and finished writing *microwave* under *Man-made*. He added the word *weapon,* then took a step back. "By *something,* I suppose we're back to extraterrestrial again, aren't we?" He circled the items under *Man-made* and drew an arrow pointing back at *Extraterrestrial.*

"When Aliens Attack," Hauff said in a low voice. "Told you."

"Where is Holt?" Martha asked. "He said he'd share additional information after he filed his report. Did he come by here?"

"Bastard turned tail and got on a chopper before we could corner him," Reiber said. "We think he went back to the anomaly."

"How long ago?"

"A while. Probably right after he left you in the medical tent. Apparently, the two-hour window doesn't apply to spooks."

"Shit."

Harbin looked around the room. "Where's his sat phone?"

Reiber plucked it from a counter behind her and tossed it to him. "Gonna phone a friend?"

"Hoover, if I can remember the number. It's been awhile." He half-looked down at the display, while tapping the side of his head, coaxing it out. When it came to him, he dialed. After a few seconds, he put the call on speaker. The line rang for nearly a minute before timing out. No voicemail, just three quick beeps in succession and dead air. He hit several buttons and frowned.

"What is it?" Martha asked.

"The call log self-erases. No record of whoever Holt has been talking to."

Martha looked over at the corner where Holt had set down his briefcase earlier, but it was gone.

"He took it with him," Harbin said, following her gaze.

"Figures."

"What about that forest ranger, Rayburn? I haven't seen him since we got back."

Tomes gestured toward the newly built wall outside. "My guess? There's no place here for a civilian without clearance. They probably sent him packing after he showed them how to turn on the lights."

Martha let out a sigh. She'd liked Rayburn.

Harbin returned to the board and studied all they had written down. "We've listed known items when our answer is clearly an unknown."

Fravel rubbed his temples. "Known is all I've got. I left my crystal ball back in Boulder."

"I need sleep," Hauff said, her eyes on the dark window. "Nobody told us where we should sleep."

"What time is it?"

Tomes glanced at his watch. Analog. Apparently, he'd been allowed to keep it. "Nearly eleven."

Zigzag had gotten oddly quiet, Martha noted. The constant thump of helicopter rotors was gone. Even the buzz of people around the tents seemed to have slowed. Only the patrolling soldiers along the perimeter appeared to be out.

"I need a shower," Reiber said, still wearing her jogging clothes from morning. "I saw a tent earlier tagged as *Latrine,* showers and sleeping quarters can't be far." She stood and stretched. "I don't know about the rest of you, but tomorrow I'm done. Fuck Holt, fuck all of them."

Hauff got up, too. "Hear, hear."

The others began to stand. Fravel said, "There's a shower in the back of this building. Down the hall and to the right."

Still looking up at the board, Harbin cleared his throat. "Let me leave you with one last thought, something Dr. Chan pointed out to me earlier. Whatever we saw today, Holt's *anomaly,* took place after they rounded all us up. That means they either caused it or had reason to believe it would happen."

"Because it happened before?" Fravel speculated.

Harbin nodded. "And could happen again."

CHAPTER TWENTY-FOUR

FRASER

WITHOUT MAKING A SOUND, Fraser held up his closed left fist. The five Army Rangers behind him immediately froze.

Back at 45-121, he'd listened to the recording. He'd then been shown the storm cellar carved into the ground at the center of what had once been a barn. He'd studied the footprints in the cellar's dirt floor and had casts made. The voice on the tape had been female, young, probably a teenager. The larger of the two sets of prints most likely belonged to her. The smaller ones were clearly a child between four and eight. The two had fought; there were clear signs of a struggle. That struggle had continued up the steps, through the remains of the barn, and out into the forest. The younger of the two was either being dragged along or shuffling her feet—her steps were too close together to be considered a normal walking gait.

He'd gathered the small team and followed the tracks into the woods.

The note from Holt was in his uniform's breast pocket.

Contain them!

Like him, the Rangers deployed to 45-121 were hardened, the elite. Past experience of war and death hadn't prepared any of them for what was found here. These people weren't killed by the known weapons of war. And while he wasn't frightened by the unknown, he had a deep respect for it.

He'd been told more than a hundred people from this village were missing and believed dead, the cause still unknown. Information indicated there were only two survivors, the two girls he now tracked.

If not a contagion, what kind of threat could two young girls possess?

He was under no illusion children couldn't be as dangerous as adults. In Iraq, he'd witnessed a twelve-year-old girl walk up to a Humvee with an explosive vest hidden beneath her clothing and detonate. But what happened here wasn't caused by a bomb, not one he recognized, anyway. He'd seen enough of this so-called anomaly to know that.

Unknown.

Children.

Fraser stared down at a bloody rag in the path. Looked like it had once been part of a shirt.

The two girls had followed the anomaly west for several miles, then veered north. The girls weren't simply wandering through the forest; they had a destination in mind, though their path was nothing more than footfalls. Aside from the girls' prints, he found a handful of tracks from adults taking care not to leave evidence. He had yet to find any kind of booby trap, but he was fairly certain they were out here.

According to his GPS, the bloody rag at his feet was nearly three miles from the center of 45-121, the village, but their route had taken them nearly perpendicular with one of the feeder trails. Even though he couldn't see it through the thick woods, he estimated they were no more than a quarter mile from that particular trail, slowly converging with it.

When he touched the cloth with the tip of his finger, he found the blood to still be tacky—no more than a few hours old.

He turned to the Ranger behind him. "Any heat signatures?"

Holding the small scanner at arm's length, she slowly panned the surrounding trees. "Too dense, sir."

"What about from the air? Can we get one of the choppers to scan?"

The communications officer stood next in their single-file line. He shook his head. "The tree canopy is preventing sat-comm—no line of sight. I can try again if we find a clearing or higher ground."

Fraser nodded and turned back to the bloody rag. From his pocket, he retrieved a plastic Ziploc bag. He placed the rag inside and put it back in his pocket.

The girls' tracks continued north.

Standing, he raised his M4 carbine rifle again and continued after them.

CHAPTER TWENTY-FIVE

MARTHA

MARTHA ROLLED ONTO HER back, and her cot let out a soft squeak. Although the temperature couldn't be more than sixty degrees, her clothing was soaked with sweat, and while she didn't remember falling asleep, she must have. Through the tent window, the moon had crossed nearly half the sky. Thin beams of light cascaded down, bluish-white, the heavens dotted with stars never visible in San Francisco. She tried to forget all the horrors she had seen today, the unnerving knowledge that Holt had not yet returned. Focus on the beauty of nature instead.

It wasn't working.

Reiber snored softly from the cot beside her. Hauff one over, her body jerking slightly as she outran some monster in dreamland.

Fravel, Harbin, and Tomes were in the next tent.

Their names, all six, were written on white tape on

the doors—women in one, men in the other, both tents side by side. They'd searched a number of the other tents, too, and found them empty.

Before disappearing into the mouth of the men's tent, Harbin had leaned over to Martha and said, "I counted six different helicopters earlier. There's only one here now. Where are the others?"

Martha rolled back onto her side.

Zigzag was accessible by road. It was meant as a way station for tourists, after all, but she hadn't seen a single nonmilitary vehicle since she arrived here. She wondered what they were telling the carloads of adults and children as they approached the roadblock, what excuse they offered before ruining their weekend plans of camping and hiking.

Martha forced her eyes to close. When she did, icy-blue eyes stared back at her from beneath a matching blue swaddled blanket. Icy-blue eyes surrounded by the pale, cold skin of a dead child. The baby's mouth opened, let out a horrified cry.

Eyes open. *Christ.*

She was exhausted, her body needed rest, but her mind wouldn't let her. If it wasn't images of death, her thoughts filled with the girl who had made that tape, wandering in the woods. She thought of her own kids, Emily and Michael, alone and scared out there. From the sound of her voice, this girl couldn't be much older. Martha remembered a Stephen King book she'd read years back, *The Girl Who Loved Tom Gordon,* little Trisha McFarland lost in a New England forest, a wendigo on her heels. From somewhere in the corner of her half-conscious brain, her mind reminded her that Trisha's wendigos thrived out east, not here.

We have our own monsters here. Sometimes they have baby blues or matted gray hair. Oh, my, how they screamed before—

Her heavy eyes snapped open yet again, and this time she sat up with a frustrated sigh. Hauff and Reiber both continued to sleep.

Oh, how she envied them.

Pulling on her hiking boots, she crossed over to the mouth of the tent, peered out, and saw no one. With one more glance back at the two sleeping women, Martha slipped out into the night air.

CHAPTER TWENTY-SIX

MARTHA

MARTHA FOUND HARBIN SITTING on a crate outside his tent smoking a cigarette. There were three more crushed butts on the ground near his feet; he'd been there for a little while. He watched her walk over with a tired eye, slid to the side, and patted the space next to him. "I suppose we should worry about those who are able to sleep after what we've seen today. I think I'll dodge those demons just a little bit longer."

He dropped the cigarette to the ground, stomped it out, and removed another. He offered one to Martha, but she declined. "I gave them up in college."

"Wise girl." Lighting the tip, he held the smoke for a moment, then let it slowly drift out from the corner of his mouth. With his free hand, he gestured off to their left. "I found Holt's tent. He's three over in that direction, but aside from a muddy pair of socks balled up in the corner, there was no sign he even set foot in there. Sheets and blanket are still folded on his cot. He hasn't slept in it."

"You went inside?"

Harbin offered a sly smile. "I'm not above riffling through that sly piece of shit's possessions, if given the opportunity. There was nothing in there, though. No bags, no computer, no notes, no nothing."

"He can't still be at the anomaly?"

"He's somewhere other than here, and he's most certainly not alone. How many people do you think we have in this little camp of ours?"

Martha thought about this. "Maybe a couple hundred. Between the troop carriers, all the soldiers erecting the tents, construction of the surrounding barriers, civilians. There may have even been more, it's hard to tell. Why?"

He gestured in the opposite direction. "Those long tents over there are troop barracks, meant to hold fifty each. I took a peek in those, too, and I only counted twelve soldiers. We've got a handful of others on patrol around the perimeter and guarding the equipment, two working the mess hall, four more near the medical tent where you conducted those autopsies earlier. I counted twenty to thirty total, plus our little ragtag team of six. Even if I'm conservative and assume there are others hidden away in some of these tents, a large number of people appear to be missing."

"They might be back at the anomaly, or maybe they returned to their base for the night. There are several military installations around here, probably more comfortable and better equipped. There's no reason for them to spend the night here. Maybe that's where Holt is, too."

"Maybe."

As they spoke, Harbin raised an infrared thermometer in his left hand, pointed it off at something in the distance, and pulled the trigger. When the temperature appeared on the display, he frowned. He'd done this three times since she sat down.

"What is it?"

"These are accurate from a distance, right? I've never used one before."

Martha held out her palm. "May I?"

He handed the device to her. It was heavier than the one she had at home. "This is military grade. I imagine pretty accurate as long as there is line of sight and you're reading a flat surface. Why?"

He nodded forward and to the left. "Point it at that tent over there, near the ground."

Martha followed his gaze, pointed the thermometer, and pulled the trigger. The display read fifty-two degrees.

"Now the tent directly to the right of that one, also near the ground," Harbin instructed.

This time, the display read 102.

For reference, she then pointed the thermometer at the ground a few feet in front of them. That read sixty-three degrees.

Harbin retrieved the thermometer from her and shielded it with his hand as two guards on patrol walked silently by. He didn't speak again until they rounded the corner and disappeared from view. When he did speak, he lowered his voice. "While you were conducting autopsies, I took some time to acquaint myself with our camp. I found a nice, quiet spot and watched the helicopters come and go, unloading their cargo. I counted two hundred and fifty-seven body bags before I was collected by Holt's people and told to wait in the ranger station."

"Two hundred fifty-seven?"

Harbin nodded.

That didn't add up. "Holt said there were only about two hundred people in the village. Could he have been wrong?"

"He doesn't strike me as the kind of man to get his facts wrong."

"Then where did the others come from?"

Harbin didn't have an answer for that. He looked back at the tents. "As they unloaded the bodies, a handful were brought into your medical tent for autopsy. The rest were divided among those two tents—some went into the one on the right, the others went to the left."

Martha frowned. "That doesn't make sense. Why would they store some of the bodies at a higher temperature?" Even as she said this, she understood what he was alluding to. "You don't believe..."

Harbin went on before she could continue. "I took a walk around those two tents. Both have large portable air-conditioning units attached and wired into the generator system. The first time I looked, both only had one, but over the past few hours, two more have been added to the tent on the left."

"The hotter one?"

He nodded. "And yet, the temperature appears to be rising. Two degrees in the past thirty minutes alone."

"That can't be the bodies. Body heat can't do that. A dead body doesn't produce heat at all. It's physically impossible."

"How confident are you that we aren't dealing with some form of radiation?"

"Fitch and I didn't find anything with the dosimeters. We'll need to see the results from the samples, but I'm fairly confident. Holt said they tested for it back at the anomaly and found nothing. I've seen radiation poisoning before—there are far more differences here than similarities."

"And you *only* found the elevated temperatures in the bodies pulled from the crevasse, correct?"

She nodded. "The ones found in the village were

crushed, but body temp was consistent with estimated time of death."

"Where is Dr. Fitch now?"

"I'm not sure."

Harbin sighed, raised the thermometer again, and pointed it at the tent. He tilted the display toward her—103.

Still climbing.

Martha stood and started toward the two tents.

"What are you doing?"

"I want another look at those bodies."

CHAPTER TWENTY-SEVEN

TENNANT

WHEN TENNANT WOKE, SHE sucked in a breath so hard she choked on it. She rolled to her side and clutched her knees to her chest as each gasp tried to claw back out from the inside with savagely sharp nails. When it finally stopped, she found herself on her back, slowly rocking back and forth, dust continuing to rain down on her from the boards of the ceiling above.

At first, she thought she was deaf, but then she remembered the cotton she'd shoved in her ears when that sound returned.

When was that?

Minutes ago?

Hours?

She had no idea. She didn't know how long she'd been out.

With the tips of her fingers, she pulled the clumps

of cotton from her ears and dropped them on the floor. Both were soaked with blood.

The silence became a dull ring.

The camping lantern had fallen from the storage shelf and was half buried under a bag of rice in the corner of the shelter. Dust seemed to hover in the now still air, hanging silently in the gloom of the light.

Tentatively, she touched each of her ears, then her nose. Although her fingers came away moist with blood, the actual bleeding appeared to have stopped. Her nose still ached something awful from the hit Sophie had given her earlier, but even that felt a little better.

Under the table, Zeke faced away from her. At some point, the cotton had fallen from his ears to the dirt. He burrowed his belly into the ground and thumped his tail with a nervous tempo—a heavy thwack, followed by seconds of silence, then another. His worried eyes were fixed on Sophie.

She sat on the bench, blood dripping from the wounds on her wrists and ankles where her bindings had bitten deeper during her struggles. The gag Tennant had fashioned from one of Poppa's old shirts was on the ground, bits of it still caught in Sophie's teeth.

When Tennant first looked at her, her sister's gaze was lost somewhere in the dirt at her feet, her chin pressed against her chest as she glared down, but she somehow felt Tennant watching, and her head came up with one quick jerk, a twist of her neck fast and hard filled with the protests of grinding, clicking bones. Her head then slowly tilted to the left, until her ear nearly touched her shoulder. A single drop of blood fell, this stringy thing of red, and dripped down the side of her arm.

"Tennnnnnant," Sophie said, her voice low and filled with gravel. "Untie... Tennnnnaaant."

The words dangled from her lips.

When Sophie jerked both her wrists up with a loud crack, her bindings slapped against the bench and Tennant jumped back.

Zeke's tail thumped, and he let out a soft whimper.

"Siiister, love you, Tennnnnnant. Untie siisster."

The cotton Tennant had shoved into Sophie's left ear oozed out on a thick gob of dark blood and fell onto the corner of the bench. Blood ran from her sister's nose and eyes, too, thin lines against her horribly pale skin.

She took a step toward her sister and tentatively reached for the cotton still in her other ear.

A grin edged the corner of Sophie's mouth. Her tongue darted out, snakelike, and lapped up a bit of the blood trailing down from her cheek. "I won't huuurt you, siiisster, not my Tennnnnnant."

Zeke's tail thumped again, and he shuffled back on his haunches.

Tennant shrunk back, then asked, "Do you still have a fever?" As the words left her mouth, Tennant realized how high and wobbly her own voice sounded. She was stronger than that. Momma and Poppa had taught her to be much stronger.

Unwilling to give in to fear, Tennant took a step closer to Sophie and held her hand out. She didn't have to touch her sister's forehead to feel the heat.

Tennant had killed a deer the week prior with a shot from her bow, the arrow piercing both lungs, just as Poppa had taught her. She had gone to the animal in its final moments and cradled its soft head. She had found herself looking into the deer's eyes as she stroked its neck, her other hand on its heart. She felt the wild beats slow and fade away to nothingness. Momma had once said if you paid close attention, you'd see the spirit rise to the heavens in the moment the eyes shift from the living to the dead, and Tennant believed she had.

As she looked into her sister's eyes, they seemed to be caught in the instant right before that moment, as if her spirit wished to escape but found itself tethered to her body much like Sophie was tethered to the bench.

"You have preettty hair, Tennnant," Sophie said softly in that thick voice. "Braid my hair like yoourrs?"

Spittle rolled off the side of Sophie's lip and hung

from her chin, thick with mucus and tainted with flecks of blood.

Her sister smelled.

She smelled not only of the sweat and dirt of the day but something else, a scent Tennant recognized. A smell that had no place on the living.

Tennant found herself unable to move, her hands and feet frozen in place.

"Untie me, and I'll brush your preettty hair," Sophie went on. "One hundred strokes on the left, one hunnndred more on the right, will leave yoouur hair sooo soft and liiight."

Momma used to say this when she was younger, as she drew a brush through her hair, counting aloud with each stroke. Hearing the words from her now felt wrong, tainted.

Sophie grinned at her, that horrid grin as she watched her with those dead eyes.

Tennant managed to shake her head.

"Untie me, you fucking bitch whore!"

Her sister screamed this out with the ferocity of a trapped beast loud enough to rattle the few cans still perched on the shelves. She jutted forward, taking the heavy bench with her nearly a foot before the weight of it won out.

Zeke let out a yelp, and Tennant shuffled back several steps before turning, climbing the steps, and pushing out through the door into the cold night air.

CHAPTER TWENTY-EIGHT

TENNANT

THE SKY WAS BLACK, punctured with the light of a million stars, the constellations Poppa had taught her all looking down from the heavens upon her mountain, her home. Tennant drew in several deep breaths and slowly let each out, washing away the grime and filth that had filled her lungs as the shelter collapsed around her. She wanted to force away the stench of death she'd smelled seeping from her sister's pores, that now clung to her clothes, her skin, her hair.

Down in the shelter, Sophie let out another scream, and Zeke came bounding up the steps. When he spotted Tennant, he ran to her and nuzzled her legs.

She reached down and scratched behind his ear. "She's sick, boy."

Momma and Poppa will find the recording, and they'll be here soon. Help Sophie get better.

Oh, how she wanted to believe that.

The idea of slipping a pill between her sister's lips, her teeth, sent a shiver down her spine. She'd sooner reach into the mouth of a black bear and stroke its tongue.

The air felt oddly still. No wind, not even a breeze.

Glancing around, Tennant realized there were no animals, either.

Rabbits, skunks, opossums, raccoons—none of the creatures normally out at night were active. She hadn't been bitten by a single mosquito, and while they weren't so common this high up the mountain, it was rare to go this long without a single bite.

Bending down, she scooped up a rock and tossed it into the brush about ten feet away.

Nothing.

She threw several more, and not even a squirrel or chipmunk scurried out. In the trees, she didn't see a single bird or owl. More times than not when she visited this particular shelter, she had found bats—Poppa had said they like the cool dampness found underground. There had been no bats when she and Sophie first arrived.

About five years ago, a wildfire scorched the south side of the mountain, threatened to spread near their village, and sensing the danger, the animals had left. She and Sophie had perched out on Logan's Bluff and watched scores of deer, bear, and other creatures run not only from the flames below but the smoke and the potential path. The fire had been out for nearly two weeks before they returned.

Much like a fire, that sound, whatever that was, had frightened everything off. Nothing else could explain it.

Sophie let out this gut-wrenching scream, and Tennant jumped. She went on for nearly a minute before her voice finally trailed off and she went back to muttering. Her shrill cries echoed down the side of the mountain like the waters of a geyser erupting from the shelter and rolling down through the woods.

Aside from Tennant and Zeke, not a single creature stirred.

Not a single *wild* creature.

At first, Tennant didn't see the light down below, at least a half mile away; the tree cover was too thick. But as Sophie's screams died away, the light shifted, pointed up toward them, and Tennant knew it was a flashlight. The single light became four or five, all sweeping back and forth through the trees.

Momma or Poppa?

But even as she thought this, the lights seemed too bright to be one of the old flashlights they had back at the village.

She heard voices then, anxious voices.

Unknown voices.

Pulling Zeke behind her, Tennant scrambled back to the shelter and pulled the door closed.

From the pale light in the corner, Sophie let out a soft hiss. “Anna Shim,” she whispered anxiously. “Annnna shiiimmm.”

CHAPTER TWENTY-NINE

MARTHA

MARTHA AND HARBIN FOUND two guards positioned outside the medical tent. Both stepped into their path, blocking the entrance. Before either had a chance to speak, Martha said, "I'm looking for Dr. Fitch."

The first one shifted his weight from his left foot to his right. His right cheek was dotted with acne, and while the Army had tried to bulk him up, his uniform hung loose on his rail-like frame. "I don't know a Dr. Fitch, ma'am."

Like the other soldiers, neither guard wore a name tag.

"Dr. Fitch and I are in the middle of conducting autopsies, and I need to take another look at the bodies."

The second guard raised a small tablet and took a photo of her, then tapped the screen. After a moment, he showed the screen to the first soldier, then looked back at her. "Dr. Chan, correct?"

Martha nodded.

"I'm afraid your authorization window for Medical has expired." He paused for a second and frowned. "Frankly, you should be resting. You're scheduled to return to the anomaly in three and a quarter hours."

"I am?"

The soldier stared at her, blank-faced.

"Nobody told me."

"Do you need help locating your bunk?"

Martha took a step closer. "Like I said, I conducted several autopsies earlier with Dr. Fitch. I need to confirm something." She gestured toward the tent. "In there."

The soldier raised the tablet again, this time pointing the camera at Harbin. After scrolling down the screen, he said, "Dr. Harbin isn't green-lit for Medical at all. I suggest you speak to your handler or commanding officer."

"Where can I find Keenen Holt?" Martha asked, her heart thumping at the sight of the younger soldier tightening his grip on his weapon.

"I don't know who that is, ma'am."

Nodding at the tablet, Harbin spoke. "Does that contain a record of everyone at Zigzag?"

Again, the soldier's face went blank. He didn't answer.

Harbin offered a disarming smile and nodded at the tablet. "We hate to be a burden, but Holt is our…our handler. We need you to direct us to his current whereabouts."

Rather than run a search on the tablet, the soldier lowered the device back to his side. "I'm sorry, ma'am, I'm afraid I can't do that."

Martha took another step closer, rolled back her shoulders, and did her best to make all five-foot-one of her tiny frame look intimidating. "If you prefer, I can contact your commanding officer. The powers that be went to a lot of trouble to get both Dr. Harbin and me here, and you're preventing us from following through on our orders."

The soldier took a step closer, his chest nearly touching hers. "Intimidation tactics only work in the movies, ma'am. I won't let you into this tent without authorization, period. If you continue to harass me, I will have you brought to the brig until this can be sorted out. I strongly suggest you return to your quarters."

"Just tell us where Holt is," Martha pushed. "Please. We'll get out of your hair."

He gave Martha a frustrated glance, sighed, and went back to the tablet. After several clicks, he said, "Mr. Holt returned to the anomaly at 16:32 and hasn't returned."

The younger soldier shuffled slightly at the statement but said nothing.

Martha opened her mouth to ask another question when automatic weapons fire cracked somewhere near the east side of the camp.

CHAPTER THIRTY

MARTHA

"THAT CAME FROM NEAR the helicopters," Harbin said, turning to the east.

From the radios attached to both soldiers' belts, a voice said, *"Unauthorized movement, Sector Five. Two, maybe three bogies."*

Harbin grabbed Martha's arm. "Come on."

Together, they ran between the tents through the camp. Dr. Fravel was standing outside his tent, shirtless in a pair of sweatpants, his eyes swollen with sleep. He stared at them as they ran by.

The soldiers reached the helicopter pads, weapons at the ready. Three more were on a platform looking out over the wall toward the forest beyond the grass surrounding Zigzag.

One of the soldiers on the platform leaned out over the razor wire, the barrel of his weapon trained on something off in the woods, a faint red laser barely visible on the fog settling over the mountain. Like the soldiers guarding the medical tent, he was just a kid. Looking around, Martha realized how young they all looked. She stepped up to a female soldier with cropped red hair. "Who's in charge here?"

The woman gave her an irritated glance, then shouted up at the other soldiers. "Morrison? What's going on?"

"I saw at least three out there just past the tree line!"

"I don't see anything," the soldier beside him said. He was working a large floodlight, sweeping it back and forth across the trees.

"Three what?" Harbin asked, peering out through the chain-link under the platform.

"There!" Morrison shouted before pulling the trigger and releasing another three shots in rapid fire.

"You're firing on US soil!" Martha shouted out.

He ignored her. His weapon swept to the right, and he fired again.

"Morrison! Stand down!"

This came from the soldier with the red hair standing next to Martha.

He glanced down at her, eyes wild and face white, then turned back to the woods and raised the gun again.

"Morrison!"

The soldier next to him on the platform placed a tentative hand on his shoulder and said something Martha couldn't make out.

Morrison didn't move at first. His frantic gaze remained fixed on the trees, then his finger slowly lifted from the trigger and he lowered the weapon.

The redheaded soldier looked up at the man operating the light. "Ebbs, you see anything?"

"Negative, ma'am."

To another soldier about twenty feet down the platform: "Griffin?"

Without looking away from the woods, he shook his head. "I think it was deer, Sergeant. I saw three of 'em run off."

"Sergeant?" Martha repeated the word softly.

She gave Martha a quick glance, then scowled back at the soldier who fired the shots. "Damnit, Morrison, take thirty. I don't want you back on the wall until you've got your head straight." Raising her voice. "The rest of you spread out and stay sharp. We're not here to bag the local wildlife! Nobody touches another trigger, unless there is a confirmed threat!"

Weapon slung across his back, he climbed down off the wall and approached her sheepishly. "It wasn't deer, Sarge. We haven't seen any animals out there."

"We're all running on fumes. I should have pulled

you an hour ago. Take a break, get some food in you, and come back in thirty. Relieve Ebbs next. Understood?"

He nodded and walked in the direction of one of the longer tents. Barracks, Martha presumed.

When he was gone, the woman's hands slipped over the various items attached to her belt in some kind of self-inventory: handgun, several clips of ammunition, canteen. Then she made a brisk start toward the only remaining helicopter. A troop carrier, larger than the one that brought Martha in. The rotors were turning slowly but picking up speed. Several soldiers climbed into the back.

"Wait!" Martha shouted, chasing after her, Harbin a few paces behind.

When the woman got to the helicopter, she barked out orders, then started to climb inside.

Martha caught up to her as she was about to close the door. "Wait, damnit!"

One foot in the door, the other still on the skid, she turned back to Martha. "You should be in your tent, Doctor." Shooting a disconcerting look at Harbin, she added, "Him, too."

"So you know who we are?"

"It's my job to know who everyone on my base is."

"Is it also your job to know *where* everyone from your base is?"

The woman looked her over but didn't respond.

Martha noticed a small scar on her left cheek, a thin white line puckered at the top.

"Are you heading to the anomaly?"

Inside the helicopter, three soldiers were strapping into bench seats along the walls. Unlike the helicopter Martha came in on, this one was utilitarian. All harsh lines, exposed metal, and worn, chipped paint. Once buckled in, they tossed an oily rag back and forth, checking their weapons and wiping down various parts in some practiced ritual Martha didn't follow.

The redheaded sergeant looked in on them. "I want all of you fully loaded and ready to move the second we've got boots on the ground. No less than three spare clips and plenty of water. I don't know how long we'll be gone."

She then turned back to Martha. She seemed to be weighing several options as her eyes bounced from Martha to Harbin and back again.

"We're trying to find Keenen Holt," Martha said. "He's been MIA since this afternoon."

"I can't help you."

"We were brought in to investigate the anomaly, and now it feels like we've been left up here to fend for ourselves. Zero resources or useful information." Martha shot her finger out and pointed back toward Medical. "I've got a tent full of dead bodies that seem to be getting hotter with each passing second. That's not possible, but it's happening, and it's happening fast. The only person who seems to have any idea what's going on is at the anomaly. I need to talk to Holt, and I need to talk to him now."

"You're not authorized to go— "

Martha cut her off. "I'm scheduled to go back in a few hours. Check if you don't believe me. You either take us there, or I'm done. I'll head back to San Francisco and bust this wide open—see how the Army reacts when carloads of reporters show up outside this little prison you built live-streaming video around the world."

The sergeant's gaze didn't falter. When she glanced over at Harbin, he simply shrugged and said, "I'm with her. I can't speak for the other scientists brought in, but I imagine they feel the same."

She glared at both of them for nearly a minute before blowing out a frustrated breath. "Get in. We should already be in the air."

CHAPTER THIRTY-ONE

FRASER

LIEUTENANT COLONEL ALEX FRASER tightened his grip on his M4 carbine rifle as he hovered over the two sets of tracks they'd found in the mud. Clearly children, one older, one young. The younger one might be injured, maybe from the struggle back in the shelter at the old barn.

If not for the shuffling trail left by the younger girl, the older child would have proven a worthy adversary, maybe even a challenge. As they followed the trail, her tracks vanished repeatedly. She'd had training, was purposely placing her footfalls on leaves, branches, and rocks in an attempt to conceal her path.

Then they heard the scream. In the mountains of Afghanistan, he'd learned from the best. The Taliban had used sound, perfecting the ability to project off the harsh surfaces, generating noises in one place and bouncing it to others in order to set up elaborate ambushes that had taken the lives of more than one of his friends.

And when the girl's scream shot at them from the mountain up above, he followed the sound back up through the trees, off the cliffs, until he was certain he'd pinpointed the source. All of this happened in less than a second, and a moment later, he and his team were hoofing it up the side of the mountain, unwilling to let these two children pull ahead of them.

Then they found the tracks.

The tracks led them farther up the mountain.

They followed the tracks slowly, with caution, until they came upon a small clearing where they abruptly vanished.

Fraser signaled for his team to stop and dropped to one knee.

The tracks didn't stop. They'd been brushed away and covered with leaves, branches, and pine needles. Carefully concealed, reminiscent of the Taliban.

Fraser lowered his night-vision goggles, flicked them on, and studied the surrounding area.

No movement.

He switched to infrared and looked for heat signatures.

He expected to see rabbits, deer, birds—tiny blips of red from the wildlife no doubt watching him, but there was nothing. Earlier, one of his men had pointed out the eerie quiet of the forest, as if all the wildlife had vanished, and at first he'd written that off. Now he was beginning to wonder if those animals knew something he didn't.

At the center of the clearing, surrounded by greens, yellows, and blues in his goggles' display, was a square outlined in a faint line of red.

Heat.

The square was about three feet in diameter, and when he switched back to standard night vision, he found it virtually invisible—nothing but dirt and dry leaves about six feet to the right of a large ash tree.

He switched back to IR, the square visible again.

This was either a trap set in the clearing or a trapdoor with another underground bunker or cellar much like the one they'd found under the barn.

Number Two.

There was no sign of the girls anywhere in the clearing.

Contain them!

With a series of hand gestures, Fraser instructed his team to position themselves around the outer edge of the clearing, weapons trained on the center. When the others were in position, he slowly edged forward, his M4 also trained on the opening. His boots barely leaving the ground, he rolled his foot from toe to heel with practiced care as he inched forward. If this shelter was as large or larger than the other one, he could very well have been standing over them right then. His Kevlar armor protected his head and torso, but if the girls were armed, a single shot fired from below would rip right through him.

One little sound to give away his presence.

One panicked pull of the trigger.

When he reached the edge of the structure, he found the hinges of a door on one side, then located a rusty handle.

He signaled his team into position, all weapons trained on the door. Fraser let his own M4 hang down his back, gripped the handle with his right hand, and raised his left fist into the air, using his fingers to silently count down from five.

CHAPTER THIRTY-TWO

FRASER

AT ZERO, FRASER MOVED fast. He yanked up on the door, threw it back. As he crashed down to the earth and tumbled away, he expected the harsh crack of one or more shots, braced for the pain of one of those shots hitting him. Gravity took over and he was at the edge of the clearing in an instant and back on his feet a moment later.

"Don't move!" someone shouted.

"Drop it!" another yelled out.

There was a clatter from down below, a muffled gasp.

Several of his team scrambled closer, the red beams of their laser sights slicing the dark and disappearing down into that hole.

Nobody fired.

"Clear!"

"Clear!"

"Clear!"

One by one, the team sounded off.

Silence.

Fraser stepped up to the opening and peered down inside.

A girl of about fourteen or fifteen stared back up at him. A hunting knife was on the ground at her feet. Her face was covered in dirt and crusted blood, black and blue beneath. Looked like her nose might be broken. Her dark braided hair hung matted and filthy. Her once white shirt was torn in several places, caked with dirt and stains. She wore baggy jeans, at least a size or two too large, cinched at the top with a rope in place of a belt.

She stared up at him with a fire in her eyes, burning with a mix of fear and distrust.

Contain them!

"We're not here to hurt you."

Her eyes darted from the red laser dots slipping over her chest to the soldiers up above, then to Fraser before she took several steps backward, attempting to fade into the dark recesses of that pit.

"Wait...no...don't move. It's okay." Fraser held out his left palm to her. His right hand reached around his back and wrapped around a stun grenade. He looped his index finger through the pull ring and teased it about halfway out.

"Can you step back out into the light, honey?"

She was trembling, but he didn't think it was from

fear, more likely adrenaline. As he watched, her left leg moved slowly back. Not much, just enough to provide additional support. As she did this, she flexed the fingers on her right hand. Her eyes glanced off into the gloom at her left for an instant, then were back on Fraser.

He moved a little closer. "I don't want to see anyone get hurt. Not my team, not you. From what I've heard, you've had a very traumatic day. We're here to help you. We have food, water, shelter, medicine..."

"We have all those things," she replied, her voice barely a whisper.

We.

"Who's down there with you? Is she hurt? We found blood."

"Leave us alone. We don't need your help." She took another step back, half her body now lost to the dark.

"You need to stay in the light, where we can see you."

"Okay," she said softly. With a swift jump, she vanished into the dark.

Fraser yanked the stun grenade from his belt, ripped out the pin, and threw it down into the hole. His team had been ready for it—moving fluidly to the side and away from the blast as he rolled to his left a moment before the grenade went off with a loud thud and a flash of bright white light.

Down into the hole, then. Quick, practiced, three

of them disappeared down the steps with their weapons at the ready as the bang echoed out over the mountain.

Fraser followed behind them.

They found the girl on the floor in the back corner curled up in a ball, her hands pressed against her ears, her eyes closed. He scooped up the knife she'd held earlier and tucked it into the back of his belt. If she'd been going for a weapon, he didn't see one. There was nothing on the ground around her but canned goods and busted bags of flour and grain. "Secure her, bring her up."

"Lieutenant?"

He turned, followed the soldier's flashlight beam to the opposite corner of the shelter, and felt the hair on the back of his neck stand.

Another girl.

She was tied to a bench, blood dripping from wounds on her wrists and ankles where she had tried to break free. Her hair and clothing were caked with muck and more blood. It trailed out from her ears, nose, even the corners of her eyes.

That wasn't what threw Fraser, though. It was the expression on her face. The stun grenade was on the ground near this girl's feet. It had gone off right next to her. By all accounts, she should be incapacitated, like the other girl. She wasn't, though. Instead, a slight grin played at the corners of her lips. There was a shimmer in her bloodshot eyes, and he didn't like that at all. As she stared at him, her head tilted slightly to the left, her tongue darted out and lapped up a bit of blood on one corner of her mouth, and she spoke in a voice that had no business coming from the body of a young child. Deep, guttural, filled with gravel.

"Anna Shiiimmmm," she said, with a slight nod of her head, her grin growing.

CHAPTER THIRTY-THREE

FRASER

"GET THEM OUT OF here," Fraser ordered, breaking eye contact with the girl.

He didn't see the dog.

None of them did.

The yellow lab leaped up from behind a fallen shelf and crashed into Fraser's chest, sending him tumbling to the ground. In an instant, the animal was standing on his chest, fangs around Fraser's neck.

One of the soldiers raised his M4 and leveled the barrel inches from the dog's head.

Fraser held out his hand, gestured for him to wait.

"Easy, boy," he said in the calmest voice he could muster.

The dog's teeth pressed into his flesh but didn't break the skin. When Fraser tried to sit up, the dog bit down a little harder. Warm breath and saliva dripped from his mouth.

"He could be rabid, Lieutenant," the soldier said.

"He's only protecting the girls," Fraser replied, doing his best to keep his voice calm. "You won't hurt me, will you, boy?"

The dog let out a soft growl mixed with a whimper.

"Labs are very protective of children. We've invaded his space. He sees us as a threat, that's all. Give him some food."

"Lieutenant?"

"A ration bar or something. Offer him some food."

Reaching into a Velcro pocket on his vest, the soldier took out an energy bar, tore the wrapper open with his teeth, and held it out to the dog.

The dog glanced at it, growled, and tightened his grip on Fraser's neck.

So much for that.

"Zeke, *nieder,*" the older girl said from the other side of the room. She was on her feet, still visibly shaken from the stun grenade, but recovering quickly. Two soldiers held her arms. *"Nieder. Komm."*

The dog's eyes glanced over at her. He whimpered again, then released his grip. He stepped off Fraser's chest, went to the girl, and sat at her side, his body pressed against her leg.

Fraser stood, wiped the dirt from his uniform, and looked at the girl. "German?"

She didn't respond, only eyed him warily.

He didn't have time for this. "Take her up top. We'll sort this out back at 45-121."

In the corner of the room, one of the soldiers stood in front of the girl tied to the bench. "What about her?"

Fraser glanced over but when his eyes met hers, he found himself looking away. "Get those ropes off her, treat the wounds, and prep her for the walk back."

"Yes, sir."

"No!" The older girl yanked free of the two soldiers leading her toward the stairs and jumped in front of the younger girl, blocking the man reaching for the ropes on her hands. "You can't untie her! She's sick!"

Fraser rolled his eyes at her. "If she's sick, why is she tied up?"

The soldier leaned in closer. "She's sweating pretty bad, Lieutenant. Could be a fever."

"Last I checked, you treat that with meds, not rope."

The older girl said, "She's hysterical, dangerous. She tried to hurt herself. You gotta keep her tied up."

"She the one who broke your nose?"

The girl nodded.

"What's your name?"

She pursed her lips, didn't answer.

"She your sister?"

No response.

The younger girl sat quietly on the bench, watching all of this, that sinister grin still on her face. To the extent her bindings permitted, her right foot slowly dragged back and forth in the dirt, digging a small trench with the tip of her toe. Her hands, secured to the arms of the bench, gripped the wood tight enough to turn her fingers white. She didn't look right, though. Those eyes. Those damn eyes. Could be jaundice, that yellow color. That was never good. Sweat trickled down from under her matted hair, through the caked blood and grime. The collar of her shirt was stained pink with it. She couldn't be more than seven or eight.

"What does she have? Sick with what?"

Again, the older girl didn't answer.

"Is it contagious? Do you have it?"

This time, she shook her head.

Would she even know? Would she tell him?

Contain them!

Turning back to the soldier, "Clean up the wounds as best you can. Get her ready to move in five minutes." He brushed past the older girl and stomped up the steps. "We've got eight klicks back to 45-121! Everyone prep to move out!"

CHAPTER THIRTY-FOUR

MARTHA

A LARGE FLOODLIGHT LIT up the ground below them as their helicopter climbed up and over Mount Hood and dropped back down the other side. As they swept over the trees, rocks, and foliage, Martha found the sight strangely surreal, as if she were watching on television rather than through the narrow window at her side. Harbin sat next to her on the bench seat. They hadn't spoken since taking off.

The sergeant—Martha had learned her name was Riley—and the other soldiers sat on the opposite bench. Weapons now resting in their laps, barrels pointed down.

"Approaching 45-121," the pilot's voice announced over their headphones.

45-121? Apparently, the anomaly had a new name.

Sergeant Riley's lips began to move, and Martha

realized she and the other soldiers were speaking on a different frequency.

As if reading her mind, Riley reached to the dial next to her head, gave it a fast turn, and faced Martha and Harbin. "When we land, I want both of you to stay in the chopper until I give the all-clear, understand?"

Martha looked around at the uneasy faces of the soldiers sitting across from her, but she was tired of the secrecy. "Why? What's wrong?"

Riley's eyes narrowed, and she leaned forward. "Do... you..." she said slowly, deliberately, "... understand?"

Beside her, Harbin nodded.

Martha sighed, nodded, too, then turned back to the window.

They passed over the crevasse, and the path of the anomaly came into view. It seemed more pronounced than before, this wound carved into the earth. The foliage within it and along the sides had discolored from a healthy green into a darker shade. *Dead or dying,* she thought.

The moment they touched down next to four other helicopters, the soldiers were on their feet and out the door, Sergeant Riley in front.

Martha waited for the last one to go, then she removed her headphones and unbuckled her safety harness.

Harbin grabbed her arm. "Wait."

"Why? I don't answer to her. I'm gonna find Holt and—"

Harbin cut her off. "Didn't you see it?"

"See what?"

"Something's very wrong."

"See what?" Martha repeated.

Harbin unfastened his harness, removed his headphones, but stayed in his seat. "When we approached, I didn't see a single person down below. Not one. Where are they?"

"It's dark." She tried to shrug him off, but he only tightened his grip.

"I...I can read lips."

"Huh?"

"My sister was born deaf, and when I was a child, I learned sign language and lip reading along with her. It was always this little game of ours; a language the two of us could speak together...this secret thing. Sergeant Riley didn't realize I knew what she was saying...when she spoke to the others."

Martha looked for Riley and her team; she could no longer see them. Over their heads, the blades of the helicopter slowed and came to a stop. Their world got very quiet. Up front, the pilot was busy scribbling on a clipboard. He still had his headphones on, couldn't hear them.

She didn't move from the bench. "What did she say?"

He glanced over the ruins of the empty village, toward the trees. On his lap, he twisted his fingers nervously together.

"Harbin? What did she say?"

"They lost contact with the teams at the anomaly... here... several hours ago." He nodded out the open door. "As you saw, they'd been ferrying people between here and Zigzag at a fairly rapid pace. At some point, that becomes a one-way trip. I think they realized it after Holt departed. When they understood something was wrong, they sent another team and lost contact with them shortly after that. Riley was ordered to conduct recon. She told her team it was probably just a radio problem, some kind of interference with the mountain or a residual effect from the anomaly itself, but it was clear from their expressions nobody believed that nonsense. I'm not sure she believed it, either."

"There must be a satellite pointing down here—military, NSA—probably a dozen satellites."

Harbin just shrugged his shoulders.

"How many people are missing?"

Again, he shrugged.

"Eighty-four."

This came from the pilot.

Both Martha and Harbin looked up at him. Neither had seen him take his headphones off.

Martha's mouth fell open. "Eighty-four?"

He nodded. "Sixty-eight personnel already on the ground, four in the EC135 your friend Holt hitched a ride on, twelve more in the other recon chopper. Radio contact has been a problem since we got here, something to do with all the iron in this mountain. They've had us all moving at such a fast clip, unable to really talk to one another. Nobody realized there was a problem until the choppers stopped making the return trip."

He had a gun in his hand. Martha hadn't noticed it at first. Some kind of semiautomatic. As he spoke to them, his finger moved cautiously over the trigger guard. The pilot's gaze remained on the trees and village outside the windshield, his head slowly swiveling back and forth.

Martha stood and went to the open door. She could now see Riley and her team. They were about a hundred feet away, the beams of flashlights mounted to their guns slowly moving through the remains of the village. She realized most of the tents were no longer standing. Cases of equipment were strewn about. It must have rained here, too. Everything looked wet.

"We should wait here," Harbin said again from behind her.

Martha knew she couldn't do that. She stepped down out of the helicopter, her shoes sinking into the muddy ground.

CHAPTER THIRTY-FIVE

MARTHA

THE AIR WAS ODDLY still and smelled sweet. Not necessarily from wildflowers or even the rain, more like someone had coated everything in a mist of antifreeze. Some man-made scent that had no place here.

Of the original four helicopters, three were large troop carriers, the other an EC135, like the one she'd first arrived on. She crossed the makeshift landing pad to the empty EC135.

Riley's team had moved farther on. They were picking through the remains of the tents about a hundred yards away. Although their voices carried, she couldn't make out what they said.

Harbin must have changed his mind. He came up behind her with a flashlight. He held a dosimeter, too. "I found this on the ground over there."

"Does it work? Any radiation?"

He shook his head. "Readings are all low."

"Can I see the flashlight?"

Harbin handed it to her, and she ran the beam over the back of the helicopter. The doors were all open. The exterior was streaked with blood.

"That's a handprint," Harbin said, pointing. He held his palm about an inch over the surface and followed the blood forward.

"There's more on the seat," Martha said, the light playing over the interior. "Some on the glass over there, too."

"Is that Holt's briefcase?"

It was. Partially tucked under the seat in the footwell.

Martha pulled the leather briefcase out and tried the latch.

Locked.

"We'll take this back with us." She handed it back to Harbin.

Harbin dropped the briefcase between them with an audible gasp.

"What is it?"

His face had gone white. He pointed down at the bag. "There's...a fingernail embedded in the handle."

Martha pointed the flashlight and saw that he was right. Her stomach crawled, and she had to look away.

"We should go back to the helicopter and wait for Sergeant Riley."

"I can't do that."

"Whatever is happening here is well beyond whatever we were brought in to investigate. You have a family, for God's sake. You shouldn't be here."

Images of Emily and Michael popped into Martha's head, and she realized they were the reason she *needed* to be here. Whatever this was, they had to stop it. *She* needed to stop it. That's how she kept her children safe.

Martha left the briefcase on the ground next to the EC135 and proceeded to check the other helicopters, Harbin following behind her at a deliberately slow pace. She found more streaks of blood. The windshield on one of the troop carriers was spiderwebbed with large cracks. She couldn't imagine what kind of force was necessary to break the glass on a military aircraft.

She'd finished with the last helicopter when Harbin said, "Have you noticed the ground?"

Martha pointed the flashlight beam down. Other than depositing Holt's briefcase, she hadn't seen it.

Aside from their own tracks, the ground was filled with muddy footprints.

As she played the light over the prints, she realized exactly what Harbin meant, why this was peculiar—nearly all the footprints were heading in the same direction—west—through the village, toward the wide mouth of the anomaly path into the woods.

She raised the beam and pointed it toward the trees.

It was too dark to see much, but that didn't matter. She knew where that path ended.

Harbin was first to say it aloud. "We'll have to check the crevasse when the sun comes up."

"But... why?"

"I told you both to wait in the helicopter!" The beam of Riley's flashlight jerked across the ground as she stomped over to them.

"There's nobody here," Martha said softly, still staring off into the trees.

"You don't know that."

"They're all dead," Martha said. "Did you find any bodies?"

Riley shook her head. "That doesn't mean they're dead."

Martha exchanged a look with Harbin but let it go. She started back toward the EC135.

"Hey!" Riley shouted. "What did I just tell you?"

"Shoot me," Martha replied without bothering to turn around. She ducked around one of the troop carriers and crouched next to the briefcase.

Riley came up behind her, followed by Harbin. "What is that?"

Martha picked up a twig and used it to knock the fingernail out from the leather handle. Then she set the case down on its side and tried the locks again. "Holt's briefcase. He understood what was going on. There might be something useful in here." She picked up a rock and cracked it against the lock. The blow didn't even scratch the metal. She hit it again.

Riley said, "Holt is DIA. I can't let you open that. I seriously doubt your clearance level covers whatever is inside there."

Martha ignored her, hit the briefcase again. "Why the two-hour window? Do you know anything about that?"

"Stop hitting the case."

Martha dropped the rock and picked up a larger one, then brought it down hard on the lock. Still nothing. "He felt it was important nobody stayed here for more than two hours. Do you know if that was to limit exposure, or was it because he knew whatever caused the anomaly would repeat on some kind of cycle?"

This time when she hit the lock, there was a spark, the metal gave, and it popped open. She then went to work on the second one, bringing the rock down hard with a satisfying crunch.

"You'll be brought up on treason charges, you understand that, right?"

Martha ignored her. "If this event is occurring on some kind of schedule, where are we in that cycle? Is it going to happen a minute from now? Or did it just happen and we have nearly two hours?"

"The blood we found on the helicopters wasn't fresh," Harbin pointed out. "If the event cycles, it occurred some time ago. We're either in the middle or possibly the tail end of Holt's window."

"All the more reason for you both to get back in the helicopter," Riley countered.

"Did your superiors explain the two-hour window to you?" Martha brought the rock down again. "Because this impacts you and your team just as much as it impacts us. Whatever happened here took everyone in the camp, not once, but twice—"

"—that we know of," Harbin interrupted.

"That we know of," Martha repeated. "It doesn't seem to care if you're a soldier or civilian, man or woman. Whatever this is has no prejudices, no preferences. And it's clearly coming back. The only real question is when."

She brought the rock down again, hard, and the second lock snapped off.

Martha tossed the rock aside and opened the briefcase.

CHAPTER THIRTY-SIX

MARTHA

INSIDE HOLT'S BRIEFCASE, MARTHA found his laptop and power cord, a blank notepad, several loose pens, and the NDAs each of them had signed.

She opened the laptop and pressed the power button. Nothing happened.

Harbin knelt down next to her. "Battery?"

The laptop had a fingerprint reader, but as far as she knew, that wouldn't keep it from starting. She pressed the power button again, harder. Still nothing. "Shit! Shit! Shit!"

Riley stiffened. "Shhh!"

"Don't tell me— " Before she could get the rest of the words out, Harbin clamped his hand over her mouth and pointed toward the woods.

The beam of a flashlight momentarily cut through the black from deep in the trees, then vanished again. A second later, it reappeared, brighter, closer. The first beam was joined by a second, then a third.

Riley gestured for them both to get behind the helicopter before turning back toward the members of her team. All three of them were on the opposite side of the village, out of earshot, barely within visual. She tapped a button on the small induction radio resting under her jawbone and said softly, "Bogies, multiple, approaching from the west." Without waiting for a response, she knelt in the mud and sighted her weapon on the mouth of the path as the lights grew closer.

Harbin removed his hand from Martha's mouth and slowly edged around the side of the helicopter, moving with a surprising amount of stealth for a larger man. Martha followed behind him, pushing the briefcase through the mud with the toe of her shoe until it was out of sight, too.

Safely concealed, Martha cupped her hands on the helicopter's side window and peered through. Although the glass was filthy, smeared with blood, she could still see the path.

Two soldiers came into view. Only visible for a moment before they turned off their flashlights, Martha didn't recognize either of them. In the moment before those lights flicked off, both raised their weapons and pointed them in her general direction. She thought she caught the outline of several others behind them, but she couldn't be sure.

On the ground, about half a dozen feet from where Martha hid, Sergeant Riley lowered the night-vision goggles attached to her helmet and switched them on. She tapped the button on her radio again. "Do you have visual?"

Martha couldn't hear the other side of the conversation, and she found that frustrating. If someone answered, she had no idea what they said. As her eyes adjusted to the dark, she saw at least four soldiers near the mouth of the path now. Two had crouched down low, the first two remained standing, their weapons sweeping slowly over the devastated expanse of the village.

Riley unsnapped a small box from her belt and heaved it into the bushes—it landed about a dozen feet from the others, and all weapons quickly turned in that direction. She pressed another button on her radio. "This is Sergeant Kristine Riley with the United States Army. Identify yourself."

Her voice didn't come from where she crouched in the mud, but instead from whatever she'd thrown—some kind of amplified speaker.

One of the soldiers who had been crouching in the path rose and turned his flashlight back on. He flicked the beam on and off twice, and shouted, "I'm Lieutenant Colonel Alexander Fraser! Lower your weapons! We're coming in!"

"Understood!" Riley got to her feet and let her gun fall to her side. She pressed the button on her radio again. "Stand down."

From the opposite end of the village, flashlight beams began to blink back on as Riley's team came into view again—they'd spread out and assumed a defensive stance.

Martha and Harbin stepped out from behind the helicopter.

Riley crossed the open field and spoke to the one who'd identified himself as Lieutenant Colonel Fraser. He was tall, at least six-four, wide shoulders; he towered over her.

Again, Martha couldn't hear. "Can you read their lips? Like you did in the helicopter?"

Harbin shook his head. "Too far away. My eyes aren't what they used to be."

Riley had her arm out, gesturing toward the remains of the village as she spoke rapidly. No doubt telling him about the missing people. Who knew what else.

No more secrets.

"Screw this," Martha said, before stomping out across the field toward the two of them.

At first, she didn't see the stretcher held by two other soldiers about twenty feet back. Nor did she see the teenage girl held still by two more soldiers. It wasn't until she got close that she realized both were secured with zip-ties and gagged.

Martha turned, ready to run back to the helicopters, but Riley and Fraser stood, blocking her path.

CHAPTER THIRTY-SEVEN

MARTHA

MARTHA PLANTED HER FEET firmly and pointed back behind her. "Why the hell are those two children tied up?"

Sergeant Riley held her palm up. "Calm down, Doctor."

Her eyes narrowed. "I want both of them released immediately!"

"It's not that simple," Riley said.

Lieutenant Colonel Fraser stared out at the empty village, his eyes darting from the structural debris to the ruined tents and destroyed military hardware. He looked over at the helicopters and then at the abandoned vehicles—several ATVs and a Humvee. He turned back to Riley. "You're telling me every single person who was in this camp... *is missing*?"

Riley reluctantly nodded. "We lost radio contact yesterday. Several teams were dispatched, and we lost contact with them, too. Frankly, I was told you and your team were missing as well."

He waved a hand absently behind him, toward the girls. "We were in the woods, searching for those two. Found them about eight klicks out hunkered down in a shelter. We...we lost contact, too, and assumed it was due to the terrain."

Fraser didn't seem like the kind of person who got rattled easily, but he clearly was. He took off his helmet and ran his hand over his short hair. "What the hell happened here?" He said this last bit more to himself than to anyone else. Martha watched as he knelt and got a closer look at all the tracks, then turned and stared back in the direction they'd come.

Martha shook her head and said, "I want those girls untied." She started toward them, and a tall soldier with arms like tree trunks blocked her path. His broad chest might have been a wall. When Martha tried to go around him, he side-stepped. "Get the hell out of my way!"

Without looking up from the footprints, Fraser said, "Those two may be the only survivors of this thing, and the younger one appears to be running a fever. She may be infected with a related condition. The older one drew a knife when we attempted to rescue them. She's dangerous. I'm under orders to get them both back to quarantine."

"They're children."

"Irrelevant."

Harbin had taken all this in without saying a word. He stepped closer to Riley and Lieutenant Colonel Fraser, the dosimeter still in his hand. "If you're worried about a contagion, why aren't any of your men wearing protective gear? They've made direct contact. A drop of blood, a sneeze, a brush against the sweat covering that feverish child...any one of those things can easily transmit a virus, yet you've taken no steps to protect yourself or your team. Why is that?"

Fraser ignored him, continued to study the footprints.

"You've already been told it's not contagious, haven't you, Lieutenant?"

"We found no sign of a virus, or any contagion, for that matter, during our autopsies back at Zigzag," Martha pointed out.

Harbin held up the dosimeter. "And it's not radiation."

With the barrel of his gun, Fraser traced the outline of a boot print in the mud.

Martha couldn't see his face. "I'm a medical doctor," she pointed out. "At the very least, I can stabilize the sick one. If they're the only two still alive from all this, you'll want to keep them that way."

This seemed to give him pause. He stood, his back still to her. After about a minute, he turned to the soldier blocking Martha's path. "Let me see the sat phone."

The soldier detached the phone from his belt and held it out to him, unwilling to move from Martha's path.

Fraser took the phone, extended the antenna, and walked off toward the helicopters as he dialed.

Harbin gestured for Martha and Riley to step closer. "There's a second elephant in the room," he said quietly. "We've been here for nearly an hour. Unless someone understands Holt's reasoning for two-hour windows, I suggest we board one of the helicopters and figure out our next step back at Zigzag, maybe examine the children there. I seriously doubt we're the least bit safe here."

Riley eyed him for a moment, then looked down at her watch. She blew out a frustrated breath. "Give me a minute."

Martha watched as she walked over to Fraser, barely visible in the dark, the phone pressed to his ear.

Harbin shoved the dosimeter into his pocket and looked nervously toward the woods, then seemed to study the debris around his feet.

Around the side of the large soldier, Martha gave the older girl a reassuring nod. The girl stared at her, still as a statue. On the stretcher, the younger girl had twisted her head in their direction, watching Martha, Harbin, and all the others. Her face was covered in filth, lined with dried tears and trails of blood. Her lips moved in some silent conversation. When she noticed Martha watching her, her eyes narrowed. She seemed to speak faster, more deliberately, and a little voice deep in Martha's mind told her she may not want to know what the girl was saying.

CHAPTER THIRTY-EIGHT

MARTHA

"WHY WON'T HE LET me examine them?" Martha said over the helicopter's communication system.

"He will, back at base," Sergeant Riley replied from the bench opposite her. "He agreed to that much."

After disconnecting his call, Fraser spoke briefly with Riley, then rushed everyone into the choppers. Many checked their watches, trying to determine where they fell in Holt's window—though none of them had a clue when that particular clock started ticking. Martha had Holt's briefcase braced between her legs as she shifted her weight on the uncomfortable metal seat. She expected Fraser or Riley to try and take it from her. Neither had.

They'd taken two helicopters—Riley and her team in this one with Martha and Harbin, Fraser's team and the girls in the other. Martha had argued the girls should fly back with them, but Fraser wouldn't budge.

Harbin nodded at Riley. "Do you know him?"

She shook her head. "Only by reputation. He's one of the youngest lieutenant colonels in the Army. He comes from a career military family; that's one way to move up the ranks fast. Many think he's destined to be our next defense secretary, maybe the joint chiefs' office. I know the president trusts him."

Riley seemed off, Martha thought. Shaken. "Who did he call back there?"

At this, one of the soldiers glanced up, then looked back down at his weapon.

Riley simply said, "Superior officer," then closed her eyes and leaned her head back against the helicopter's shell. A not-so-subtle end to the conversation.

Harbin slipped a note into Martha's hand:

Give me Holt's briefcase when we touch down. I'll take it to Fravel and the others. Can't let Army get it first. You see to the girls.

Martha gave him a swift nod and crumpled the note in her palm.

As they circled Zigzag and came in for a landing moments behind Fraser's helicopter, the sun began to creep over the mountain peaks to their east. Martha couldn't decide if it was the most beautiful thing she'd ever seen, or a mask, a funeral shroud inching over the dead beneath its folds.

CHAPTER THIRTY-NINE

MARTHA

TRUE TO HIS WORD, Harbin took the case and disappeared off into the tent city that was Zigzag before anyone could give him a second glance.

Riley ushered her team to one of the command tents to debrief.

Martha went straight to Fraser's helicopter—the girls were already gone.

She spotted Fraser talking to the pilot and stomped over. "Where are they?"

Fraser gave her an irritated glance, then turned back to the pilot. "Understood?"

"Yes, sir."

Martha punched Fraser in the shoulder. "Goddamnit, where are they?!?"

"Whoa, calm down, Doctor. I told you that you could see them, and you can. We just need to lay down a few ground rules first."

"Ground rules?"

Fraser dismissed the pilot and started walking away from the helicopters at a brisk pace.

Martha did her best to keep up, but her legs were much shorter than his. She practically had to run. She'd be damned if she was going to ask him to slow down. "What ground rules?"

"I don't know you, Dr. Chan. You're a thin file I read on a plane. Your actions will define who you are to me, whether I consider you to be valuable. This entire situation is obviously sensitive. Anything you learn needs to be run by me before you share it with anyone, including those people Holt brought in with you. I want my own people to vet them first."

Martha had no intention of doing that. "Sure," she told him.

"Second," Fraser said, "that other guy—"

"Harbin," she interrupted.

"Harbin. He was right. Those two girls are the only known survivors of whatever is happening out here. I need to understand the whys and hows of that. Are they just lucky, or somehow immune?"

"Immunity implies that this is viral, and I already told you—"

"Yeah, yeah, yeah. Not viral, not a contagion. I don't want to hear *what this is not*. Don't waste my time with theories. I only want to know what *is*. Facts. Nothing else. I let you in there to see those girls, and you have one sole purpose—determine why they are not dead. Once you know that, you tell me. I'll pass the information on to people much smarter than you, who will decide how we keep others from being dead."

Martha stopped walking and glared at him.

He went on several more feet before turning back toward her. "I'm sorry, did I offend you?" He paused for a second, then added, "Let me be perfectly clear. You see two girls, I see rats in a lab necessary to solve a problem. Do we understand each other?"

There were a million things she wanted to say to him, but instead she only nodded.

"Good."

He started moving again, crossed the barrack tents and led her to Medical. Three guards were posted out front now, and Martha noticed two others on the side of the tent installing another air-conditioning unit. When she started for the door, he held out a restraining arm. "This tent is off-limits." He pointed to a smaller tent across from them, another guard posted at that one. "You'll find them in there. Everything you need should be inside. If not, ask the guard, and he'll see that you get it."

With that, Fraser stepped into Medical, leaving Martha alone, her head spinning.

CHAPTER FORTY

MARTHA

UNLIKE THE TENT ACROSS the path, with its prefab plastic sign labeled MEDICAL, someone had hastily written EXAM 1 on a strip of white tape and placed it above this tent's opening. The guard standing beneath the sign offered Martha a soft "Ma'am," and stepped aside, holding the flap open for her.

Another guard was stationed inside, his gun loosely trained on the tent's two occupants. Although it was cool under the thick canopy, his shirt was damp with sweat. He pointed the barrel at the ground as she came in, then raised the weapon after she passed.

"Is that necessary?"

"Orders, ma'am."

"Orders," Martha muttered.

The tent's interior was only a fraction the size of Medical, maybe half the space of her sleeping quarters. Several black plastic crates lined the leftmost wall, their open lids revealing a wide assortment of medical equipment and supplies. In the center of the room was one of the aluminum examination tables she'd used earlier, freestanding halogen lights erected on each end bathing the shiny metal in harsh light.

The younger girl, still secured to the stretcher, had been left on top.

She twisted as Martha entered, a bob of matted blond hair moving with her and slapping against the table. Her fingers, arms, and legs all appeared tense—stretched as if caught in a jolt of electricity—the cords of muscles and veins testing her thin body and skin.

From one of the plastic black bins, Martha retrieved a laser thermometer identical to the one Harbin had used earlier, pointed the device at the girl's exposed forearm, and pulled the trigger.

The display read 103.6.

Not good.

She was just a child, maybe seven or eight. Because she was positioned with her head nearest her, Martha couldn't see her face, but she could hear her, mumbling softly, some incoherent babble. She appeared to be crossing back and forth between a delusional state and alert, each turn lasting only moments, oblivious to the pain brought on by her injuries. Not uncommon with a fever this high.

The soldiers had wrapped the young girl's

extremities with cloth before tightening the plastic ties, and while those strips were soaked with blood, it became painfully clear she'd be much worse if the girl had been secured without them—tugging, pulling, twisting—this relentless movement making matters worse. She'd have to get the temperature under control.

The older girl sat in a folding chair in the back corner, her bound hands in her lap. She had looked up as Martha entered the room but hadn't said anything.

Both girls were covered in bruises and scratches. They smelled as if they hadn't bathed in days. Their clothing was frayed and worn, threadbare, the colors muted to nothing but dull beige and grays. Martha couldn't imagine living out here, removed from civilization. The simplest of conveniences and medical care far enough out of reach, they might not even know such things existed. She wondered if these girls had ever set foot in a well-stocked grocery store, or a movie theater, or a school. Had they been out here their entire lives?

As subtly as she could, Martha pointed the thermometer at her and pulled the trigger again. A little red dot appeared at the base of her neck.

98.4.

"The older one tried to jump from the helicopter right after takeoff," the guard said. "Lieutenant

Colonel Fraser caught her by the belt, one foot hanging out like she thought she could fly."

Martha set down the thermometer and went over to her. She crouched down to get to her eye level. "Have you ever flown before?"

The girl shook her head.

"It can be frightening the first time, but I assure you, you're in good hands."

"We need to go back. They won't find us here." She spoke with a strange accent; not quite Canadian nor the familiar sound of a typical northwest American. Her vowels were slightly more pronounced, drawn out. Other words sounded clipped. The word *here* came out more like *her*.

"Is that your sister?"

She glanced nervously over at the table, then down at her hands without a word. Her left knee began to bounce nervously. She had severe bruising around her nose and a noticeable break at the ridge line. Fractured within the past twenty-four hours. "Who set your nose? Was it her? Is she your sister?"

She didn't look up, didn't answer.

"If it was her, she did a fantastic job. I'll clean it up for you and apply a bandage, but I don't think I could have done better myself." Martha gave her a reassuring smile. "I'd bet money the two of you are sisters— the way you've looked out for each other. After an experience like that, she must be grateful to have you. You've done an incredible job keeping the both of you safe, but you can relax now. I'm here to help. We all are. My name is Martha. What's yours?"

"Will you take us back?"

Martha didn't want to lie. She'd learned early on with her own kids that children saw through even the slightest half-truth, and she needed this girl to trust her. "When it's safe," she told her. "First, let's get you and your sister cleaned up, treat your injuries, and get some food into you. I bet you're tired, too. Maybe when we finish, we'll get you some cots so you both can rest. She is your sister, isn't she?"

The girl hesitated for a moment, then looked up at her with tired eyes and nodded. "Can you help her?"

It was Martha's turn to nod.

"Her name is Sophie."

Martha smiled at this. "That's a beautiful name. What's yours?"

Again, she hesitated. She held her bouncing knee down with both hands, and finally said, "Tennant."

"And she is your sister?"

Tennant nodded.

"Pleasure to meet you, Tennant." Martha placed her hand over the girl's and tapped at the zip-tie. "If I remove this, do you think you can help me with your sister?"

Tennant's knee stopped bouncing. She nodded.

Martha reached for a pair of scissors. Behind her, the soldier cleared his throat but didn't make a move to stop her.

She clipped off both ties and examined the girl's wrists and ankles. They were pink, but the plastic hadn't been tight enough to break the skin.

"Thank you," Tennant said softly, rubbing her wrists.

"Can you tell me how long Sophie has had a fever?"

Tennant stood and walked over to the table. When she tried to take Sophie's hand, she jerked away.

Martha came up behind her, and for the first time got a good look at the younger girl's face. Her skin was sickly, horribly pale beneath a sheen of grimy sweat. Her eyes were yellow with jaundice and lined with burst vessels. Like the bodies they'd autopsied, her tear ducts and ears appeared to be hemorrhaging. Not as bad as the others, but still evident. Most likely worsening. There was blood in the corners of her mouth, too. Between her teeth. She was breathing in short, shallow gasps, sucking the air in and letting it out quickly with a wheeze.

When she realized Martha and Tennant were standing over her, she gave her bindings another frustrated pull, then went still. Her eyes narrowed, and she looked at the two of them. "Anna... anna... anna shim... anna shim."

"Who's Anna Shim?"

"I don't know. She just keeps saying it. Can you help her?"

Martha took her temperature again.

104.1.

Climbing.

To the guard, she said, "I'll need some ice and a vessel I can submerge her in. Like a bathtub."

"A bathtub?"

"Just tell Fraser."

He nodded and spoke into his radio.

Sophie's back arched. Her arms and legs shot out, testing the limits of her bindings. Fresh blood appeared where they met her skin through the damp cloth. She held there for an impossibly long time, then collapsed back onto the stretcher, wasted and defeated, only to jerk back up a moment later.

"Can you help her?" Tennant asked again in a voice that sounded much younger than her years.

Martha nodded and quickly began riffling through the medications, bandages, and other supplies.

She tried not to think about the bodies in the other tent.

The ones growing hotter.

CHAPTER FORTY-ONE

MARTHA

AN HOUR LATER, MARTHA sat at the table in the small room at the back of the Zigzag ranger station with Harbin, Russel Fravel, and Joy Reiber. Holt's laptop sat between them. They'd powered it up and tried so many different passwords the system now required them to wait one minute between each attempt. They had no idea what it could be. Harbin had even gone back and searched Holt's tent in hopes of finding something that might provide a clue, but even the muddy socks he had found the last time were gone.

Brenna Hauff was out in the main room watching the door—when they came to take her back to the crevasse, she'd refused. Brian Tomes had reluctantly gone. Martha pretended not to hear when Harbin pointed out the laptop's fingerprint reader, told him to keep it in mind if he found Holt's body. Tomes had simply nodded as if this request were no more obscene than "pick up a gallon of milk at the store." Then he walked off toward the awaiting helicopter. Sergeant Riley had boarded that one, too. They'd last seen Fraser on the opposite side of the camp, where they appeared to be reinforcing the newly constructed wall.

When the timer on the laptop ticked to zero and the password box reappeared, they consulted the list of possible passwords they'd made on the whiteboard.

"Try *Patriot* again, but replace the letters with numbers and symbols, like *P@tr10t,*" Reiber suggested.

Fravel shrugged, keyed in the word, and hit enter. The box flashed red, and the timer reappeared. Fifty-nine seconds...

"How many doctoral degrees do we have in this room and not a single hacker?" Harbin balked. "We're not going to get in with blind guesses."

"Ironically, Holt is probably the only one who would know how to bypass computer security. I imagine that's a skill they teach when they hand out their magic decoder spy rings," Reiber said.

Fravel pushed the laptop back several inches and scratched at a stain on the table with his fingernail. "If I had a USB drive and access to the internet, I could get in."

"Well, we have neither of those things," Harbin muttered.

The clock ticked back down to zero. Fravel keyed in another word, hit enter, and the timer reappeared.

"What did you try?"

"*Spook,* but with zeros."

Martha went to take another sip of her coffee and realized her mug was empty.

Before she could get up, Harbin took hers along with his and walked over to the coffee maker for refills. Nobody else was drinking coffee. When he sat back down, he said, "Tell us about the girls."

Martha hadn't stopped thinking about them. "I had to sedate the younger one, Sophie. Then I got an IV in her with a mix of saline, high-dose NSAIDs, and antibiotics. The ice helped. I managed to get her fever down to 102, but without knowing the root cause, I feel like I'm stalling the inevitable. I found nothing abnormal in her blood work. Her current state aside, she's actually remarkably healthy. So is her sister. I cleaned up their wounds, redressed their bandages. There's not much more I can do."

"And she couldn't tell you anything? The older one?"

Martha shook her head. "Nothing useful. Their father rushed them down into a storm cellar, and they rode it out underground. That's how they survived. She thought it was a tornado, so loud it shook the ground. She took her sister to a second shelter in hopes of reuniting with their parents. They were there when another one hit indirectly. She only recalls two instances."

"Does that mean Holt was wrong about the two-hour window?"

Martha shrugged. "Who knows."

Fravel typed in another incorrect password.

Nobody bothered to ask him what he entered.

"Where are they now?" Reiber asked.

"Resting. I don't think either of them has slept much. The older one managed to stay upright long enough for a shower and some food, then she passed out the moment her head hit a pillow. Maybe when she wakes up, she'll remember something else."

Harbin considered all this. "Tennant and Sophie, right?"

She nodded. "Can I see the sat phone again?"

Reiber had used it last—but hadn't gotten through. She slid the phone across the table to her, and Martha dialed her ex-husband for the third time in the past hour. For the third time, she got only voicemail. There was no point in leaving another message. She hung up. The clock on the wall read quarter after ten—he should be at work by now. The kids in school.

Fravel keyed in another password. "Oh, fuck."

"What?" Martha asked.

He turned the laptop toward her so she could see the display. Rather than resetting to one minute, the countdown timer was now ticking down from an hour.

"That was a longshot anyway," Harbin said, slouching in his chair.

Reiber brushed a loose strand of hair from her eye. "Any idea why the younger girl has been affected and not the older one?"

Again, Martha shrugged. "If this were viral, I'd look for immunities in Tennant. Possible inoculations she may have received earlier in life that her sister had not, like chickenpox, or measles, but that's not the case. I sequenced Sophie's blood and compared it to Tennant's and a sample from both sets of victims in the tent—I didn't find anything out of the ordinary. No common thread, either. Tennant said her sister was with her all yesterday morning, right at her side, and yet somehow she was affected, and Tennant was not."

"Unless the symptoms are late to present in Tennant," Harbin pointed out. "Maybe age is a factor."

"During the autopsies yesterday, Dr. Fitch pointed out the bodies we found in the village leaned more toward the extremes—either infants or the elderly. The ones in the crevasse, the ones with the fever-like symptoms, seemed to be the healthiest, most virile of the group."

"Wouldn't Tennant fit that definition more so than her sister, Sophie?"

Martha took another sip of coffee and nodded. "If we go by age alone, yes. That made me wonder if there was some other inherent difference. Something that hasn't presented or isn't apparent."

"Like a genetic marker? Do you have the testing equipment?" Harbin asked.

"Gotta love the Army," Martha said. "I asked for something, and ten minutes later they wheeled in a brand-new NovaSeq 6000. That's a million-dollar piece of hardware. It can run a full sequence in a few hours. I'm running both girls, several samples from bodies found in the village, and some from the bodies found in the crevasse. The hot ones."

Harbin perked up at this. "So he let you in that tent?"

Martha shook her head. "He had the samples brought to me, said Fitch collected them yesterday. They're not letting anyone in that tent."

From the other room, Hauff shouted, "Soldier coming toward us! Coming in fast!" She ran back in and fell into one of the empty chairs.

Fravel scrambled to his feet, unplugged the laptop, and shoved everything into the cabinet above the coffee maker.

CHAPTER FORTY-TWO

MARTHA

"WHY JUST US? WHY not the others?" Martha asked as she and Harbin followed the soldier through the camp, leaving the others in the Zigzag ranger station.

"You'll have to ask Lieutenant Colonel Fraser, ma'am."

He led them to Fraser's tent and held the flap open for them.

Fraser was on a sat phone, standing behind a folding table set up as a desk with a laptop and several stacks of folders and notepads. When they entered, he hung up the call, set the phone aside, and gestured toward two chairs. "Sit."

"Everyone should be here," Martha said.

"Sit," Fraser said again, the irritation clear on his face.

Harbin gave her a glance that seemed to say, let's

hear him out, then lowered himself into one of the folding chairs.

Martha sighed and fell into the seat beside him.

Fraser eyed them both for a moment, then slid a sheet of paper across the desk.

Martha leaned forward. “Is that an executive order?”

Fraser nodded. “The president instituted a no-fly zone over 45-121. He’s quarantined a swath approximately sixty miles across the mountain and surrounding area.”

“Infected area,” Harbin read aloud.

“*Affected* is probably a more apt description, but it’s not my place to correct the president’s grammar. Roadblocks went up yesterday, and all air travel has been rerouted.”

“Why air travel?” Martha asked. “Is that to keep the press out?”

He pulled out a folder from the stack next to his laptop and dropped it between Martha and Harbin. “Whatever’s happening isn’t isolated to the ground. A private jet went down yesterday, a Hawker 800XP, ten souls on board. All dead. Came down in a valley on the east side of the mountain. Very remote. The White House is using the crash as an excuse to keep everyone away.”

“This means the anomaly isn’t just a ground-level event.” Harbin looked up at Fraser. “Do we know their altitude?”

"Twenty-three thousand feet," Fraser stated flatly. "We recovered their data recorder. They engaged autopilot shortly after takeoff from Portland, switched to manual directly above 45-121, then immediately went into a dive. Voice communication with the tower was limited to takeoff. They were en route to Vegas and somehow got caught in the path of the anomaly. From what little we know, there doesn't appear to be mechanical failure—the pilot switched off autopilot and put the plane in a steep dive. He downed the craft intentionally."

Harbin had the folder open and was flipping through a series of photographs. The plane shot nearly straight down and hit the ground nose-first. There was hardly anything left. "How did the data recorder survive this?"

"No idea. They found a fully intact suitcase as well."

Martha had seen that sort of thing before at other crash sites. Even in near total destruction, the strangest items sometimes survived with very little damage. She'd once investigated a downed 737 in Malaysia, and someone found an undamaged bottle of Moët buried under the remains of a wing.

Harbin asked, "If a plane got caught in the anomaly, does that mean we are, in fact, dealing with a satellite-based weapon?"

Fraser smirked at this. "Satellite-based? Who told you that?"

"We were speculating yesterday."

Fraser shook his head dismissively. "According to some report out of USGS, the anomaly originated from below, not above. They traced seismic readings down nearly 2,900 kilometers."

"Twenty-nine-hundred kilometers? That would put it nearly to the Earth's core. That can't be right."

"Yet it is, according to them anyway."

"Who is USGS?" Martha asked.

"United States Geological Survey," Fraser said flatly. "Another team Holt brought in."

Harbin said, "We need to speak to Frederick Hoover."

"Not possible. Not right now."

Before Harbin could respond, Fraser turned back to Martha. "What can you tell me about the girls?"

She repeated everything she'd told the others earlier.

Fraser listened, stone-faced. When she finished, he said, "So you've learned nothing."

"This takes time."

"We don't have time."

Martha closed her eyes and pinched the bridge of her nose. She was getting a headache. "Do you have any kind of record of the people who live on the mountain? Tennant said her sister keeps asking for someone named Anna Shim, but she has no idea who that is. She said there was nobody in their village by that name. Sophie said the name several times while I was treating her. Seemed insistent about finding her, almost desperate."

"Anna Shim?" Harbin repeated.

Martha nodded. "Tennant said there's nobody in the surrounding villages by that name, either, but it could be one of the outliers. She said they tend to keep to themselves."

Fraser frowned. "What's an outlier?"

"That's what they call the people who choose to live alone on the mountain rather than with one of the groups. Outliers. Extreme loners."

"Jesus. Even society's outcasts have outcasts." Fraser shuffled through the folders on his desk, located one, and opened it. "These people don't exactly fill out census data or pay taxes. They raise families out here, live, die, all of it completely off the grid. That makes tracking them problematic." He found a list of names and ran his finger down the page. When he reached the bottom, he flipped to the next page. "They do like to read their books, though. They read a lot of books. This is a list of people who have memberships at the three nearest libraries—Parkdale, Hoodland, and Stevenson. Blue dots mean they have no reported income. Red means they're collecting some sort of government assistance—some of them have no problem taking from the system, they just don't like to pay in." He flipped to the third page. "Names highlighted in yellow have a criminal record."

Martha glanced over at Harbin. He'd closed the folder on the crash and was staring at the cover, his mind elsewhere. His index finger tapped against his temple, as if trying to coax out a thought.

Fraser finished the last page and sighed. "Several Annas, but nobody named Shim. Doesn't mean much. She could be out there somewhere. Or it could be some make-believe imaginary friend."

Harbin broke from his reverie and looked up at Fraser. "What's going on with the bodies in the medical tent? Why are they getting hotter?"

"Who says they're getting hotter?"

Martha leaned forward, frustrated. "You need to stop holding back."

Someone knocked on the frame of the tent.

Fraser looked up. "Yes?"

A soldier stepped inside and quickly saluted. "Sir, we've had another attack."

"Where?"

"Barton. A small town about fifty miles east of here. It's . . . it's bad."

Fraser nodded. "Get the rest of the team and meet me at the helicopters. We're in the air in ten minutes." He closed the lid on his laptop and looked at both Martha and Harbin. "You're both with me. I don't want word of this getting out just yet."

CHAPTER FORTY-THREE

MARTHA

"WHAT DO WE KNOW about Barton?" Martha said in the helicopter. They'd taken one of the troop carriers, six soldiers in addition to Fraser. Harbin was in the seat next to her. She'd had just enough time to grab some medical supplies and throw them in a bag and check on the girls. Tennant was still sleeping. Sophie was awake but unresponsive, her eyes fixed on the ceiling. With the medications, her temperature seemed to be holding around 102.

Fraser looked up from the documents in his hand. "Small town. A little more than four thousand residents on the edge of the Columbia River. Not much to speak of—couple stores on the main street, bank, car dealership. Several housing developments. Most near the water. Former mining town trying to reinvent itself."

As he read, Martha noticed his arms for the first time. They were both covered in scars. There was an old burn covering most of his right forearm. On his left arm, he had a long surgical scar that started at his elbow and extended to his wrist. Most likely from a surgery to repair a break in the humerus. He'd seen his share of combat, there was no doubt about that. He had another scar on his neck. This one began just below his jawline and disappeared under the collar of his shirt. Unlike the surgical scar on his arm, this one was ragged, more of a tear. Most likely from shrapnel or an accident. In many ways, his body told a story, and not a pleasant one.

Fraser set the stack of pages on his knee and focused on Harbin. "I've spent a good portion of my career interrogating people. Taliban, ISIS, Afghans, South America. Gitmo...you know what they all have in common, Doctor?"

Harbin met his gaze.

Fraser went on. "The eyes. There's always something in the eyes. When questioning someone, I can always tell when they've told me everything or if they're holding back. The best of liars can't hide it. All they can do is try and mask it. You're one of the better ones when it comes to concealing your thoughts. That's not a skill you picked up in NOAA, is it, Doctor?"

A thin smile edged Harbin's lips. "Did you come to that conclusion on your own or read something in my file?"

"A little bit of both."

"What's he talking about?" Martha turned to Harbin, her eyes narrowing.

Harbin's gaze remained on Fraser. "I did a small stint in British intelligence before joining NOAA. That's not exactly a secret. You can't hide that sort of thing when applying for high clearance in the States. I'm sure the Lieutenant Colonel read the highlights. My past service may very well be why I was brought in here."

"The good doctor was in training to be a spy," Fraser said.

Harbin waved him off. "Hardly. I was barely an analyst. Even in my twenties, I didn't have the fortitude for fieldwork. One of my professors at Cambridge felt I had a brain for the analytical and made several phone calls on my behalf. Before I knew it, I found myself working for Her Majesty. Long hours behind a desk writing reports nobody would ever read was hardly rewarding. I quit less than two years in, furthered my studies, and applied with NOAA."

None of this was a surprise to Fraser. "But you also went through MI-5's basic training program, which includes crash courses on interrogation techniques and deception."

"Same as you, I suppose. Same as anyone who does a stint in a military branch."

"That takes us back to my original point," Fraser said bluntly. "You're keeping something from me."

Harbin gave Martha a quick glance, then turned back to Fraser. "I'm not sure it's worth mentioning, so I haven't. That's all."

Now Martha was curious. "What is it?"

"Anna Shim."

"You know who she is?"

How could he, though? He'd seen the same information she had. Less, really.

"Not a *who,* a *what.*" Harbin paused a beat, then said, "I think she may be trying to say anahshim, not Anna Shim. I don't think it's a name at all."

"What is *anahshim*?" Fraser asked.

"I only know the word because I studied the Tanakh years back, the Hebrew Bible. I studied the Torah as well, but I always found the Tanakh particularly fascinating because it was the foundation for so many of our modern religions. And, again, this is probably nothing, which is why I didn't— "

Martha cut him off. "—Harbin."

Harbin looked down at his hands. "Anahshim in ancient Aramaic means *people.*"

"People," Fraser repeated flatly. "If that little girl is receiving any type of education at all out here in the middle of nowhere, I seriously doubt it includes some long-dead language."

Harbin held his hands up. "Like I said, it's probably nothing."

Over the communication system, the pilot said, "Sir,

we're approaching Barton. Two miles out. Taking us down to one thousand feet."

Fraser unbuckled his harness, braced himself on the frame of the helicopter, and crossed over to the door. He yanked up the release handle and pulled it open.

Martha instinctively shrunk back in her seat as air blasted in from outside and rolled through the interior of the large cabin. She'd thrown on a jacket, but that did little to fight back the chill. There was an acrid scent in the air, too—burnt hair.

They spotted the smoke around the same time. A large section of Barton was burning.

As Fraser had said, the small town of Barton was positioned along the edge of the Columbia River and flanked by a thick forest leading back up into the mountains. Much like the anomaly, Martha quickly spotted several narrow paths within those trees—nearly straight lines through the brush and foliage, spread as far apart as nearly a mile. She counted seven in total, and all of them converged into one wide swath about a quarter mile west of Barton. That singular swath—a bare, smoking brown mass of utter devastation—led straight into town.

CHAPTER FORTY-FOUR

MARTHA

"FIND SOMEPLACE TO SET down," Fraser instructed the pilot. "Try to keep us clear of the fire."

They'd made several passes over the small town and found no movement, no signs of life. Flames had consumed several buildings on the west side of town—some warehouses along the water, something that looked like an old mill. All the houses appeared to be intact, although Martha had noticed several mailboxes lying on the ground, trees, even a swing set, all toppled and crushed. On their second pass, they'd circled a school with no playground—Martha assumed a high school—all the windows blown out. The cars in the parking lot looked steamrollered from some unknown pressure coming from above. The tires on most of the cars had burst, the rims buried in the cracked asphalt.

Other than two fire trucks still in their bays at the

station, they hadn't spotted a single emergency vehicle. No ambulances, no police cars, nothing, neither stationary nor on their way to the town.

The pilot took them back around and settled as far from the fire as he could, in a Wendy's parking lot at the east end of Barton. When they touched down, he said, "We've got fairly high wind—twenty- to thirty-mile-per-hour gusts. Without anyone fighting it, the fire will spread fast."

"Understood," Fraser replied, jumping out. "Keep the engines hot. Be prepared to move out."

The soldiers filed out behind him, Martha and Harbin after them.

Everyone clustered around Fraser. "Spread out in pairs. Stay on comms at all times. Stay east of the flames. Use masks if the smoke gets heavy. No heroics. We're here for recon only—no weapons unless in self-defense. You find anything of note, you radio me. You find any survivors, you radio me. Watch for security cameras—if you can safely collect the footage, do it. Be prepared to move out in one hour, maybe sooner if that fire gets too close."

They were off then, three teams of two.

Martha found herself looking at an old Volkswagen Bug, yellow, covered in rust, at the drive-thru pickup window. Like the cars at the school, the vehicle had been flattened. She spotted what looked like an arm in a flannel shirt sticking out the driver-side window.

When she started toward it, Harbin grabbed her by the shoulder. "Don't. You can't help him."

She shrugged him off. "It's okay."

She needed a closer look.

The driver was dead. That wasn't what drew her in, though; it was his arm, his hand. Still pinched in his fingers, he was holding out a credit card toward the open window, something she'd done herself countless times. The name on the card was David something; his thumb covered the rest.

"He didn't even get a chance to react," Martha pointed out. "Christ, he didn't even drop his card as something crushed him inside his car."

The drive-thru window itself was intact, but the glass doors at the front of the fast-food restaurant had been shattered. The glass sparkled on the concrete sidewalk. Martha crossed the parking lot and knelt down to get a better look, a puzzled expression on her face.

"What is it?" Harbin asked.

She stood and turned toward the pharmacy next door. "Look at all the buildings. All this shattered glass, it's on the outside. As if there was an explosion from the inside."

Before he could respond, she stepped through the ruined doorway into the restaurant. Inside, she found upended tables and chairs, food, packaging, condiments, purses, a flipped children's stroller. Thankfully, the stroller was empty. There was only a single body—an elderly man on the floor next to a booth in the far corner, his head and face nearly flattened into bloody pulp. His mangled walker was just out of his reach. The power was still on, and an old Paul McCartney song came from the speakers in the ceiling. The unmistakable scent of burnt food drifted out from the kitchen.

"Two of the windows are blown out, too," Harbin pointed out. "But I don't see any outward signs of an explosion. No burn marks, no central detonation point."

A chill passed through her, and Martha wrapped her arms around her chest. She felt like she was standing in a tomb.

Outside, they found Fraser staring off into the distance through a pair of digital binoculars. "This is far worse than it looked from the air. Possibly countywide. Same as 45-121, but the devastation is more widespread."

"Maybe there's a direct correlation to the number of people," Harbin suggested. "Larger population may mean more damage."

Fraser considered this. Although he tried to hide it, as he had done back at the village, Martha could tell he was shaken. There was a man under that tough veneer.

She wandered across the intersection; there were three more bodies on the sidewalk. Two women and a man, all older. Martha took out the laser thermometer and pointed the device at each of them. "Body temperatures are all in the low nineties, normal for people who died in the past few hours."

"Elderly again," Harbin pointed out. "That's consistent with what Dr. Fitch told you they found in the village. Whatever this is seems to take the healthy and leave the weak behind."

Martha pointed the thermometer back at the body in the Volkswagen and got 92.6. There was no way to tell how old he was.

"All the cameras here are damaged." Fraser lowered the binoculars. "There's a strip mall about a quarter mile that way with a grocery store and a bank. There's bound to be more. Maybe tougher quality."

Without waiting for a reply, he started off down the road.

CHAPTER FORTY-FIVE

MARTHA

THE WIND GUSTED UP, carrying with it the smell of smoke. When she looked back in the opposite direction, Martha couldn't see flames, but the sky was thick and black, an angry churning cloud hanging over the small town growing larger with each passing second.

Where were the first responders?

She cupped her hands around her mouth and shouted, "Hello! Is there anyone here?"

Martha sometimes had trouble sleeping, and before her divorce, she'd climb out of bed, careful not to wake her husband, and wander the house—check on the twins, walk through each room. The house always felt different at those late hours—smaller, like a bubble. Every noise carried. When she shouted down the streets of Barton, the town felt very much like that sleeping house.

“We should stick together,” Harbin said beside her.

Martha nodded, and the two of them followed after Fraser.

Like all the other businesses, the glass doors and most of the grocery store’s windows had shattered outward; same with the bank next door, the dry cleaner, the comic book shop, and the beauty supply store at the far end. With the exception of a twenty-something woman in a wheelchair, all the bodies found were either older people or children.

Fraser was kneeling on the sidewalk in front of the bank, running his fingers through a wide gouge in the concrete. The remains of a camera were on the ground next to him, nothing but a ruined pile of plastic and glass. He looked up, toward the corner above the door.

Martha followed his gaze. The mounting bracket was still up there, but the metal was twisted with gleaming silver around the edges. Frayed wiring dangled from a hole in the brick behind the bracket. Someone, or something, had torn the camera out.

“That’s at least eight or nine feet, right?” he said to her, his attention back on the gouge.

“At least,” Martha agreed. “What do you think that is?”

He slowly shook his head.

“Even if someone destroyed the camera, it was

recording up until the moment they pulled it down," Harbin said.

Fraser got to his feet and stepped over the broken glass into the bank. There were four other cameras in various positions around the interior, but on closer inspection, they realized the lenses were shattered. The anomaly had destroyed everything inside made of glass.

They found the security system and recording equipment in an office near the back. The desk was upended. An ergonomic chair was lying on its side up against the wall, a hole punched through the backrest. The armrest had been torn off and was in the hallway. Half a bagel slathered in cream cheese sat on a credenza.

Although the security monitor was spiderwebbed with cracks, it still worked. Fraser replaced the chair and sat in front of the equipment, studied the controls for a moment, then clicked through several screens on the attached computer. "Looks like they had eight cameras in total. The system is still recording, but there's no signal coming in."

He brought up a menu, found a series of time-stamped files, and began clicking through them, working back from the most recent. He'd gone back more than two hours before the black boxes on the screen came alive.

"There!" Harbin blurted out.

"Two hours and twenty-three minutes ago," Fraser said.

The time stamp in the corner of the monitor read twelve minutes after eight in the morning. Most of the shots were of the bank's interior, and other than a security guard crossing the frames, the bank was empty. Most likely, they didn't open until nine. Using the mouse, Fraser clicked on the exterior camera above the door. The image zoomed in, filled the entire monitor, and sound came through the speakers. Several people walked by on the sidewalk. The far edge of the camera's vision caught traffic on the road.

Fraser clicked fast-forward, and the image sped up. At 8:24, the image blinked out and the screen went blank.

"Too far," Harbin said.

"I can do without the play-by-play, Doctor."

Fraser slowly rewound the recording, stopped one minute before the picture cut out, and hit Play.

A man and a woman approached the door.

Fraser turned up the volume. They were talking about the football game that had aired the night before.

The woman produced her keys, unlocked the door, and the pair slipped inside.

A man jogged past the camera.

An SUV drove by.

Fraser turned up the volume a little more.

A brunette in a white blouse and tan skirt appeared, tried the door, found it locked, checked her watch, then cupped her hands over the glass and knocked. She glanced back over her shoulder impatiently, then turned back to the door. She must have seen someone inside—she smiled and waved. Her face twisted, then the smile vanished, her mouth fell open, and she slowly turned, looking out toward the parking lot.

"Do you hear that?" Martha asked.

Fraser and Harbin both nodded.

A hum, slowly getting louder.

"What's she looking at?"

"We can't see because of the angle of this camera," Fraser replied.

The hum grew louder.

The woman on the screen took several steps away from the door, more of an unconscious shuffle.

Someone screamed.

The squeal of tires.

A man's voice shouted something incoherent.

The hum grew louder.

The security system's speakers reverberated with it—this deep bass.

More screams. More shouts.

The woman covered her ears, her head swiveling back and forth, eyes wide with panic.

Louder.

"What the hell is that?" Martha said, her own voice rising to be heard.

The bass mixed with a high-pitched shrill, a horrible keening—nails on a chalkboard multiplied by a thousand, the wail of an animal caught under car tires, the screech of a living thing caught in fire—none of these things compared to the sound, the abhorrent bedlam pouring from the speakers.

Fraser reached over and lowered the volume. It did little good, though. The sound continued to grow louder.

Martha found herself covering her ears, but the sound oozed through her fingers, crawled into her head, scratched at the interior of her skull like an icepick scraping at the soft tissue of her brain.

On the screen, the woman dug her palms into her ears and fell to her knees.

The image went black.

"The lenses shattered!" Fraser shouted, his face registering shock at just how loud he had to speak to be heard.

The sound grew louder.

He turned the volume down even further, but it did little good. The sound mixed with the screams of people, desperate shouts and cries. All of it together.

Louder.

"Turn it off!" Martha screamed. "Just turn it off!"

Harbin reached over Fraser, grabbed the speakers,

and yanked them hard enough to sever the wires. He threw them across the room. They cracked against the far wall and fell.

All went abruptly quiet.

Fraser's face was stone-white, frozen, locked on the blank screen. He had the computer's mouse in his hand. Somehow he'd managed to crush the plastic, cutting his palm.

Martha found herself trembling, unable to stop.

She needed to move.

Get out.

CHAPTER FORTY-SIX

MARTHA

"IT'S THE SOUND," MARTHA said. She had an oxygen mask over her mouth, but that did little to keep her from coughing. The mask was too large and kept slipping down her face, obscuring her vision. Her eyes burned with the smoke. The attached tank was clipped to her belt.

They were back inside the helicopter with four of the soldiers. Two more were still out there somewhere.

"Sound can't crush cars," Fraser stated flatly. He was staring out the open door down the main road into the thick smoke, one finger on the button for his microphone. He tried to raise the other two soldiers again, but they didn't respond. Fifth time now.

The blades of the helicopter churned above, stirring the dark, soupy air with a heavy *whoosh*. Two-thirds of the town was burning now. They hadn't realized the flames had reached the bank until they were back outside. Fraser had managed to dump the security system recordings to a micro SD card.

"Sir, we need to go," the pilot said over the communication system. "If the smoke gets much thicker, it could choke the engine."

"We'll give them another minute. If they don't make it back, we'll reposition a little farther down the road."

"Deaf, deaf," Harbin muttered.

Martha found herself looking at him. "What?"

"Back at the village, remember? Someone wrote the words 'deaf, deaf' on that wall in blood, *after* the anomaly hit."

Martha didn't follow. "So the sound made them deaf?"

Harbin shook his head. "I think they were able to write it, I think they survived the anomaly, because they were deaf. They lost their hearing before it hit. They lived because they couldn't hear the sound."

Fraser tried to radio the soldiers again but got nothing. He continued to stare into the fire, half-watching Harbin. "If someone was deaf, how would they know there was a sound at all?"

"You saw the video, the way that woman covered her ears and reacted. They would have seen something similar, read the signs. Maybe they could read lips. They probably would have felt it—if not the vibration of the sound itself, then the chaos it was causing all around them. Who knows. Someone without the use of their ears is keenly aware of sound, but in a very different way than the rest of us."

Fraser got to his feet and scrambled to the door. "There!"

At first, Martha didn't see them. The smoke was like a living wall, a mix of black, white, and grays rolling over the cracked blacktop and around the sides of buildings, a tide rolling in over a desolate harbor. A sea of death.

Three shadows, staggering along at a slow shuffle.

"They found someone," Harbin said.

"Stay here." Fraser jumped from the helicopter and ran toward them, one hand on his mask, the other holding the small oxygen tank clipped to his side. When he reached them, he handed his mask to one of the soldiers, who held it to his face for about twenty seconds, then handed it to the other soldier. They then pressed the mask to the face of the person between them.

"It's a woman," Martha said. "She's not moving. I think she's unconscious."

Her arms were draped over the soldiers' shoulders, her toes barely touching the ground, dragging.

"They need to hurry," the pilot said. "I'm getting stall warnings. We've got a minute, maybe two at the most."

On the opposite end of town, something exploded.

The heavy boom threw all of them to the ground; black smoke belched up along with a rain of debris. A gas station, maybe? Too big to be a car.

Fraser was the first to scramble back to his feet. He picked up the woman's limp body and draped her over his shoulders, continued toward the helicopter with heavy steps, the other two close behind him. When he reached the door, Harbin and Martha helped get the woman inside, pulled her to the center as Fraser and the others climbed in and collapsed on the floor. "Go!" Fraser called out over the comm, before launching into a coughing fit.

Martha pulled the two remaining oxygen masks down off the wall, handed one to Fraser and the other to the soldiers beside him.

Fraser gave her a grateful nod and pressed the mask to his face.

"Hold on," the pilot said.

Martha tightened the straps on her harness and wrapped her fingers around the thick nylon, gripped them as tight as she could.

The moan of the engine grew deep as the blades above increased speed. Another alarm sounded, this one filling the cabin with red and white flashing lights. The helicopter began to rise, lurched, and dropped back down to the ground.

"Smoke's too thick." The pilot groaned. "The engine's not getting enough air!"

Outside the door, the street was aglow in orange and reds, the sun lost behind black smoke and floating soot. The fire was less than fifty feet away, the flames crawling toward them, inching up the walls of a pharmacy and the side of Wendy's, engulfing the bookstore across the street.

Up front, the pilot frantically flicked several switches, adjusted something to his left, then tugged at what must have been the throttle. The engine noise went deep again, they rocked and lifted slowly off the pavement. When the motor sputtered, they dropped several feet. He increased speed. The engine screamed in protest, but they continued to rise. They were at least a hundred feet in the air when the engine sputtered again, and they dropped at least ten or more. Martha felt her stomach slam against her heart.

"Hot air pockets!" the pilot shouted. "Hold on!"

They continued to climb, nearly straight up, dropping as they ran into more hot air. They were nearly a thousand feet up before finally leveling off.

The moment it was safe to do so, Martha unsnapped her harness and crouched down over the woman on the floor. "She's not breathing!"

CHAPTER FORTY-SEVEN

MARTHA

"SHOULD SHE BE IN restraints?" Joy Reiber asked, looking down at the woman on the cot.

Martha reached to the table beside her, picked up one of the laser thermometers, and pointed it at the woman's forehead. She showed Reiber the screen. "She's 98.4, normal. Nothing to indicate she's been affected. I see no reason to restrain her."

After CPR, Martha managed to stabilize the woman in the helicopter, and while she remained unconscious, her breathing and heart patterns had leveled off. When they arrived back at Zigzag, Fraser had her transported to Martha's tent. Medical was still off-limits, and Martha didn't think it was a good idea to put her in with the girls.

The soldiers said they found her on the steps of a recording studio located in the basement of a house two blocks off the main street. Like most of Barton, the house was engulfed in flames. She'd been semi-conscious, unresponsive, most likely in shock and suffering from deep smoke inhalation. There was a nasty bump on the back of her head, probably from a fall. Martha had placed her on oxygen, an IV to get her fluids up, and a steady drip of trazodone—a serotonin reuptake inhibitor—in case she had a concussion. She was maybe in her early to mid-twenties. Her shoulder-length blond hair was tipped in pink, her left ear had six piercings, while her right had only one. She was wearing tight black leather pants and a thin white tank top.

"I think we should restrain her," Reiber pushed. "At least until she's awake and we know what we're dealing with. What if she's traumatized? Or hysterical? She could hurt herself."

Martha didn't see the point in arguing. She shuffled through the medical supplies they'd brought her, found four padded Velcro straps, and secured them around the woman's wrists and ankles. "Better?"

Reiber nodded. "There…there were no others?"

"Survivors?"

"Yeah."

Martha shook her head. "Just her. It was like the village—nearly everyone was missing, and those left behind were dead." She dropped into a chair, closed her eyes, and rolled her head on her neck. She ached all over and had several bruises from the helicopter ride back. "Where is everyone?"

"Fravel is in his tent working on Holt's laptop. Still no progress there. Tomes and Hauff are analyzing samples from Barton—soil, water, that sort of thing."

Martha had already run preliminary tests on tissue samples collected from some of the bodies in Barton and found nothing unusual. She didn't expect organic samples to turn up anything, either.

"Martha!"

Martha and Reiber looked up—Harbin came through the open doorway of her tent, his face red and dripping with sweat. "It's the girls—Fraser played a copy of the recording!"

Before she could respond, he was gone again, racing back the way he'd come.

"Stay with her!" Martha shouted to Reiber as she pushed out of the chair and chased after him.

The two soldiers outside the girls' tent stepped aside as she ran up, uneasy looks on their faces.

She found Harbin inside, Fraser and three other soldiers, too. Tennant was sitting on the floor, her back against the wall and her knees pulled tight against her chest. She was rocking back and forth, her eyes pinched shut and her hands over her ears as she cried.

Sophie stood against the back wall, cornered by

Fraser and the other three. As Martha came in, her head jerked up and she glared at her like a caged animal. By the looks of it, she'd broken her bindings, torn them right off. The straps were on the ground near her upturned cot. The bandages Martha had wrapped around her wrists and ankles were red with fresh blood. Spit dripped from her mouth, down her chin. There was crusted snot around her nose. Her eyes had gone from the jaundiced yellow of earlier to red, lined with burst vessels, filled with a mix of burning hatred and fear.

One of the soldiers took a step closer and reached for her shoulder, but before he could get a grip on her, she lurched to the side and swiped at his arm. Her sharp nails dug into his skin and left four glistening tracks behind. The soldier jumped back, cursing.

Fraser's head swiveled toward Martha. "Sedate her!"

Sophie's eyes went wide, and she backed deeper into the corner. "Let meeee gooo!" she hissed. The voice sounded nothing like the little girl before them. It was too deep, too coarse, this gravelly thing resigned to crawl out only in the deepest dark, some creature of nightmares clawing up from the underside of a mattress, the thing that huddles in the back of the closet and waits for the witching hour to feed.

"Goddamnit, Doctor, sedate her!" Fraser said again.

Calmly, Martha said, "Dr. Harbin? In the supply case back at my tent, you'll find propofol. Please fill a syringe with one hundred milligrams and bring it back here."

Harbin disappeared out the tent.

Martha took a step closer to Sophie.

Sophie huffed, her eyes filled with suspicion.

"The rest of you, back up," Martha said.

"No," Fraser countered. "Reynolds, flank her from the left. Lopez on the right. Tighten up a circle around her and—"

With lightning speed, Sophie reached out and grabbed the soldier closest to her—Lopez, Martha thought, but she wasn't sure—Sophie yanked the man toward her, twisted his arm at the wrist, and wrenched up and sideways. With a sickening crack, his forearm snapped, the bone splintered and tore through the material of his uniform. He let out a shriek and crumbled to the floor at her feet.

The rest of them stared at her in utter shock. She couldn't weigh more than forty-five or fifty pounds. How could she—

Sophie's hand shot out again, managed to snatch Fraser's sleeve, but he pulled back and to the side, ripped away from her.

Martha took a step closer, held both her palms out. "Sophie, it's okay. We're not going to hurt you. We just want to help."

Sophie shuffled backward until her shoulders pressed against the wall of the tent. Sweat dripped down from her hair, over the sides of her face. Her clothing was soaked in it, and she stunk of ammonia. Martha knew that smell—it meant her kidneys weren't able to process the urea in her body fast enough, and she was excreting nitrogen in her sweat. It meant her body was losing the fight against the fever and her organs were beginning to fail. Even from several feet away, Martha could feel the heat emanating from the girl. She'd torn her IV out, and without the medications, whatever was happening to her had come back with a vengeance.

"Sophie, let me help you. I'm on your side."

Maybe the only one who's on your side.

The girl's face jerked toward her, tilted to the left until her ear was nearly touching her shoulder. "Take care of meeee like lil Emiiily and Michael? That how you take care of meeee? You abandon them in some loveless hoouse, leave them to wilt and rot in the smog and filth of San Cisssco. Leave theem wit all the Anna Shimmm. Tooo manny Anna Shimmm. Bodies pressed close, until can't nooo longer breathe. Stifled. Choking."

Martha's heart thumped. *How did she know her children's names?*

Sophie's tongue leaped out, licked at the salty sweat on her upper lip. "Emiiily and Michael will run with Anna Shimmm. You all will. *We* all will." Sophie began to rock back and forth, her weight shifting from her left foot to her right and back again, slowly picking up speed.

Harbin came back into the tent, a needle in one hand, the glass vial of propofol in the other. He came up behind Martha and slipped the loaded syringe into her hand, his eyes locked on Sophie. “Will a hundred milligrams be enough?”

Martha had no idea.

“I’ve got something else,” Harbin said before backing out of the tent. A moment later, he returned with a yellow lab on a leash. He smiled at the little girl. “Someone wants to say hi to you, Sophie.”

Sophie’s dark eyes locked on the dog, a glint of recognition. Her head straightened back up. “Zeeeeeke.”

The dog whimpered.

Martha jumped forward and buried the syringe in the little girl’s neck.

CHAPTER FORTY-EIGHT

MARTHA

ONE HUNDRED MILLIGRAMS OF propofol wasn't enough, not to knock her out, anyway, but the dose slowed her down long enough for Martha to inject her two more times, 350 milligrams in total. Enough to drop a grown man of four times this little girl's weight.

"Help me get her back on the table," Martha said.

Sophie's pulse was strong. There was no way to know how long she'd be out.

Martha quickly went to the soldier with the broken arm, conducted a cursory exam, and injected him with a measured field hypodermic of morphine. The lines on his face slackened.

"Sit tight, give that a minute to work through your system," she told him reassuringly. "Try not to move."

Martha didn't know where he got it, but when

Fraser produced a straitjacket, she was grateful. Sophie had split her original bindings as if they were made of paper, and after what she did to that soldier's arm, they couldn't risk her getting free again. Martha quickly cleaned and redressed Sophie's wounds. Then, with Harbin's help, the three of them got her in the straitjacket, back up on the table, and tied her down with thick leather belts.

When finished, Martha turned on Fraser. "What the hell were you thinking playing that recording?"

His eyes narrowed. "I'm not your subordinate, Doctor. Check your tone."

"Fuck you."

Martha moved the IV pole next to Sophie's head and expertly slipped a fresh cannula into the jugular vein at her neck. She then made several adjustments to the medication dispenser's touchscreen. I'm increasing her antibiotics and anti-inflammatory meds, the propofol, too."

"How long can you keep her out?"

"Indefinitely, I suppose. But considering her body's rate of absorption, the speed at which she's processing the meds, I'll have to monitor her closely and continue to make adjustments. This...this illness is progressing, speeding up. She doesn't have much..."

Martha cut herself off. She'd forgotten about the girl's sister.

Tennant was still on the floor. She hadn't moved.

Her face was buried against her knees with her hands over the back of her neck.

"I'll take care of your sister, Tennant. I promise."

Tennant looked up at her but said nothing. She stretched a hand out toward the dog, and he shuffled over to her, buried his snout against her neck.

In the opposite corner of the tent, the soldier with the broken arm groaned softly. The medication had kicked in, but he still had to be in a tremendous amount of pain.

Martha went over to him and crouched at his side. She took a closer look at the wound. "This break is far worse than I thought." She glared up at Fraser, who was standing over her shoulder. "I can't fix this here. We need to get him into Medical."

"Medical is off-limits."

"Then your soldier will lose his arm."

"I'll bring you what you need."

"We don't have time for that."

Harbin said, "I can assist. I've had field training."

For a moment, Fraser looked like he might argue. Instead, he instructed one soldier to stay and keep an eye on the girls and told the other to help him carry the injured man. "Follow me," he told Martha and Harbin.

The soldiers outside Medical gave them a wary glance as they carried the other man past them and into the tent.

Inside the antechamber, Martha and Harbin quickly changed into scrubs, latex gloves, and a mask before pushing through the curtains into the chilled air of the main theater. Fraser and the other had placed the injured man up on one of the open tables. There was no sign of Fitch inside, nobody else, either. The scent of bleach and ammonia filled the air. The various tables and instruments had all been scrubbed clean, the space shined as if it had never been used—if not for the body bags lining both walls. There were more now, many more. The highest visible number written on a bag was 257. As she stepped closer, she realized the ones on the right all bore higher numbers, marked with red stickers, than the left. She tried not to think about it. She had to treat the injured man.

"I need you and your people out of here. This will require surgery, and just by being here, you're a potential infection risk."

"I'll change into scrubs," Fraser said.

"I want you out. You'll just get in the way." To Harbin, she said, "Find the portable X-ray machine. Do you have any experience with anesthesia?"

Harbin nodded.

"We'll need some O negative, too. I think he nicked the cephalic." Martha turned back to Fraser and glared angrily. "Out!"

To her surprise, he nodded and left, motioning for the other man to follow.

When they were gone, Harbin said softly, "I hope you don't really need me to administer anesthesia. I may be a doctor in title, but there's not much call for that with NOAA."

She shook her head. "The break looks bad, but it's a fairly straightforward fracture."

"I figured as much."

She gave the soldier another injection of morphine along with a local in his arm, whispered to him, "Just lie back and relax."

His eyes rolled back into his head as he fell into a semiconscious state.

"We have maybe five minutes before I can start on him," Martha said, turning back to the two stacks of body bags. She frowned. "Is that . . . ?"

She already knew the answer.

Steam was rising from the body bags stacked on the right.

CHAPTER FORTY-NINE

MARTHA

AT FIRST, MARTHA THOUGHT it was some trick of the lights, but as she neared, she realized a dull haze hung over the black bags on the right side of the tent, a thin shimmer. The thick plastic bags glistened with condensation, and the ground around them was damp.

The room was cold enough for her to see her breath, but as she neared those bags, the temperature climbed, became downright balmy. From the instruments near one of the exam tables, she retrieved an infrared thermometer, pointed it at one of the bags on the top, and squeezed the trigger. A little red dot appeared on the moist plastic.

The display read 105.

Martha frowned and pointed the thermometer at another bag, this one two rows down from the top, in the middle row of five. The temperature read 103.

She tried several others, and the lowest temperature she found was 101.

"Try the ones on the left," Harbin suggested.

She took several readings. The other body bags ranged in temperature anywhere from 61 to 79.

Pointing the thermometer at the ceiling, she got a reading of 57. The ground measured at 52. She checked several more body bags on the right; all read over 100. "Holt said there was no radiation."

"Holt said a lot of things," Harbin replied.

Martha returned the thermometer to the table, riffled through one of the black supply cases stacked beneath it, and found a short-range dosimeter among the other emergency medical equipment.

Martha switched on the device and watched the LCD screen come to life. She expected an alarm or warning beep, but none came. While some radiation was detected, it was well within normal parameters.

She took several steps toward the body bags on the right, her eyes fixed on the small screen. Nothing changed, though, even when right next to them.

"No radiation," Harbin said.

"None...outside the bags," she replied. "When I worked trauma at Johns Hopkins, the hospital maintained a stock of body bags specifically designed to shield radiation. I don't see the nuclear warning label here, and I remember those as being a little thicker, but otherwise they looked the same. These might be some variation."

Martha reached for the zipper on the closest bag and hesitated—the plastic felt warm and wet.

The dosimeter still read nothing out of the ordinary.

Martha tugged down the zipper.

Steam rose up from the opening in a dense cloud, crawled over her mask, and slipped over her exposed skin on the sides of her face, her forehead. Even through the mask, she smelled it, this putrid odor, a mix of seared flesh and sulfur. Rot and sour earth. All at once, she was reminded of red tide, walking along the beach as a child only to find thousands of dead fish along the shoreline baking in the sun.

Inside the body bag, the light fought to find a face, inched around the splayed plastic down into the shadows over long, greasy hair.

"My God," Harbin breathed.

A woman.

Age unknown.

Indeterminable.

Her eyes were open, but there were no pupils, no irises, nothing resembling an eye at all—the sockets were filled with a thick yellow pus. This mucus had dripped down the sides of her face and dried to a crust. Mixed with blood, similar discharge came from her nose, mouth, and ears—all her orifices. It had begun pooling in the bottom of the bag. Her skin had taken on a translucent appearance, milky, with thick, visible veins. Numerous fractures were apparent, more than Martha could count. The same pus drained from scrapes and cuts in her skin.

Heat radiated from her body. Martha checked the dosimeter again but found no signs of radiation. This was something else.

During the autopsies, Fitch had pointed out the bodies found inside the crevasse had somehow been cooking from the inside out. If Martha didn't know any better, she'd suspect this woman was melting, liquefying from the heat. And somehow, it hadn't stopped with death. In fact, it appeared to be accelerating.

From the vents in the wall, cold air bellowed out in white, wispy clouds.

Harbin opened three other bags and found more of the same. "If this isn't radiation and it's not viral, what can cause this?"

"What the hell are you doing?" Fraser was standing near the tent's entrance, glaring at her, one hand on the gun at his hip.

Martha froze over the body bag, trying to think of an excuse to offer up, when a scream tore through the camp.

CHAPTER FIFTY

MARTHA

MARTHA ROSE AND STOMPED toward him. She wasn't about to be intimidated. "Was that one of the girls?"

Fraser's grip tightened on the butt of the gun. His eyes jumped from Martha, to Harbin, to the soldier lying on the exam table, and back again. His face grew red. "Do I really need to babysit you?"

"You're withholding information," Martha pushed. "Where's Dr. Fitch? Where's Holt? Why are you keeping us from these bodies?"

Fraser stepped up to the exam table and looked down at the semiconscious soldier. "You're allowing one of my men to suffer so you can snoop around. I thought doctors were supposed to have ethics?"

"I'm waiting for the medications to take hold," Martha fumed. "Don't try and twist this into something it's not."

"So snooping is what? Busywork? Sorry, maybe I should have left you with a magazine."

"I was specifically brought in to determine the medical ramifications of the anomaly. How can you expect me to provide answers when I'm not privy to all the facts?"

"I'm following orders."

"So am I," Martha countered.

Harbin zipped up the open body bags and crossed the tent. "Lieutenant, Dr. Chan and I will set your man's broken arm. That is not a question. But when we're done, you need to sideline the bureaucracy and tell us what you've been told, what you know."

Fraser was growing impatient. "I'm a soldier in the United States Army, Doctor. I'm part of a rigid chain of command. That chain of command exists for a reason. Information is disseminated as needed, and I fully understand that I don't need to know all the details, I only need to know what is necessary for me to complete my existing orders, my mission. Those below me, including this man lying on the table, understand that as well. This is not a question, this is not an option, this is fact. Anything less is chaos."

"We're already in chaos, Lieutenant. You saw that firsthand this morning in Barton."

Fraser didn't answer.

Harbin fell silent, too.

"Who screamed?" Martha asked again. "Was it Tennant?"

Fraser turned to her, then said, "Most likely, that was our witness. I came to get you when she started to stir. I thought it was important you were there when she woke. Now I'm not so sure."

"We should talk to her together," Harbin said. "Come up with a plan *together*."

"I should lock you both up."

"Then this situation grows worse. I think you know that," Harbin told him.

Fraser eyed both him and Martha with uncertainty. Finally, he patted the side of the exam table. "Set his arm, then meet me out front."

CHAPTER FIFTY-ONE

MARTHA

MARTHA SET THE BROKEN arm with the help of Harbin and a soldier named Klara Fields, who had training in combat triage. The break in the man's skin required twelve stitches. Once done, they left Fields to apply a cast and administer an IV.

Forty-two minutes had passed.

They found Fraser standing outside Medical. As they stepped out, he only started walking back toward Martha's tent at a brisk pace.

Martha and Harbin exchanged a quick look and followed.

Inside, they found their witness sitting up in her cot, a blanket draped over her shoulders, but still visibly trembling. Reiber was holding her hand. The two of them looked up as they stepped inside.

She appeared to be in her twenties, but her eyes

belonged to a frightened child. Wide and moist with tears, bloodshot and lined with broken vessels.

"My name is Dr. Martha Chan," Martha said softly. "I imagine you've been through quite an ordeal. How do you feel, physically?" She reached for a thermometer and took her temperature—98.8, normal. "Any injuries? Do you feel sick at all?"

One of her eyebrows was singed. There was a slight burn on her left cheek, not serious.

She heard the question, but it took her a moment to process the words. When she spoke, her voice was timid, with a slight rasp. "My throat hurts. It hurts when I breathe, in my chest. My lungs."

"No doubt from the smoke." Martha took out a penlight and told her to open her mouth. "They pulled you out of a fire. You're lucky to be alive."

"Is the studio gone?"

"The studio?"

She looked down at her hand, still in Reiber's. "I was recording an album at Crawlspace Records. I guess the recordings are gone. Oh, man, I'm a shit for even thinking that, aren't I? Worrying about some recordings after..." Her face shot up. "Oh, Christ, did you find Eddie? He went out for smokes, and he didn't...oh, man, please tell me you found Eddie!"

"What's your name, dear?" Harbin asked.

"Raina Caddy."

Reiber gave the woman's hand a reassuring squeeze.

"I've got some of your songs from iTunes. You're pretty good."

Fraser stepped closer. Although he didn't say anything, his large frame was intimidating.

Raina shrunk away, inched deeper onto the cot, her eyes on the gun at his hip. "Why are there soldiers here? Where am I?"

Martha knelt down in front of her. "Can you tell us what happened, Raina?"

Her eyes jumped from Fraser and the gun to the other people in the room. The trembling had stopped, but now she looked nervous. "I... I don't know that I can."

"Sometimes, with a traumatic experience, your brain will block certain memories. If you try to recall the last thing you do remember and work forward, step by step, the rest will come back."

"That's... that's not why."

"Then what is it?"

Her gaze dropped to the floor. "I may have taken some pills."

"What kind of pills?"

She pursed her lips. "I don't know. Blue ones. Eddie had them. Said they'd help loosen me up."

"Blue ones," Martha repeated flatly.

Raina nodded. "A yellow one, too. But I only took half of the yellow one. Eddie took the other half. I think they made me see stuff."

"They were hallucinogens?"

"I think the yellow one was. I took a whole pill last night, and we didn't get anything done. The room kept moving, like the walls were breathing. It freaked me out. My fingers wouldn't work right, I could barely hold my guitar. That was too much, so Eddie told me to only take half."

Fraser loomed in silence.

Raina looked up at him. "Can he arrest me?"

"No," Harbin replied. "He can't do anything to you."

"I don't have any left, anyway. Eddie had them."

"What's the last thing you do remember?" Martha pushed.

Raina lowered her gaze again and bit the inside of her cheek as she thought it over. "It wasn't real. It couldn't be."

"What wasn't?"

"Maybe I should have only taken a quarter."

Reiber squeezed the girl's hand again. "It's okay, just tell us."

The memory must have replayed in Raina's mind, because her face went white and she started to tremble again. Her back stiffened. "We took the pills, then Eddie realized he was almost out of smokes. He said he wanted to run to the store before they kicked in. I was down in the basement, listening to the track we recorded the day before yesterday. I wasn't happy with the bridge and wanted to come up with something else. I started to get really thirsty. I mean *really* thirsty. So I went upstairs to the kitchen to get a glass of water. I don't think the pills hit me yet, because other than the thirst, I felt okay. No moving walls or nothing. So I went upstairs, and I was standing at the sink and I saw it through the window." She paused for a second, then shook her head. "That had to be when the pills kicked in."

"What exactly did you see?"

She looked up at Martha. "A stampede."

"What, like cattle?"

Raina shook her head. "Not animals...people."

CHAPTER FIFTY-TWO

MARTHA

RAINA SHIVERED AGAIN AND seemed to shrink. Her eyes darted around the room but looked at nothing in particular as her brain tried to process the thoughts flooding back. When she spoke again, her voice sounded so small. "It . . . it was like a river, a giant mass, all moving together. Thousands of people, just . . . just running. Practically on top of one another, they were packed so tight. And fast, oh, man, were they fast." She paused for a moment. Her eyes grew wide and her head slowly shook back and forth. "They had this haunted look on their faces, like they didn't know where they were . . . blank . . . numb . . . like sleepwalking, mechanical, emotionless. Some of them looked really tired, but they just kept going, oblivious to the pain, exhaustion. They had to be tired, nobody can . . . they . . . oh, God . . ."

"What?" Reiber said softly.

Raina's eyes filled with tears. "One of them tripped, an older woman. She collapsed and went down right there in front of Eddie's window, right in front of me. The others didn't even slow down. They ran over her. She disappeared under them, there were so many. They didn't slow down for anything—cars, yards, fences, other people moving too slow—if something or someone was in front of them, they went right over the top."

Her voice fell off again. Martha could see her growing agitated, her pulse quickening, the early signs of PTSD settling in. When she started speaking again, Raina was no longer talking to them but more to herself, thinking aloud. "I remember looking out the window at them, watching this...unfold. They were completely silent. The window was open, I could hear the sounds of them running, all those feet, and holy shit was that loud, but the people themselves? They didn't make a sound. Not a single gasp, grunt, or cry, and that was the weirdest part—how quiet they all were. It didn't seem real."

Raina looked up at Martha. "That had to be a hallucination, right? From the pills?"

Images of the trampled bodies back at the village flooded Martha's mind. The elderly couple, still holding hands. The baby in a carriage. Not just the bodies but devastated buildings, shacks, and other structures. The stones around the well. The paths through the trees, the brush...could all of that really have been caused by people?

"Doctor?" Raina interrupted her thoughts. "It wasn't real, right?"

Martha looked over at Harbin. She expected him to be watching Raina, but instead his eyes were fixed on Fraser. Fraser caught her glance and subtly shook his head *no.*

"Doctor?" Raina said again.

Martha's gaze hung on Fraser for another moment, then returned to the girl. "Most likely it was the pills. Do you mind if I take a blood sample? It may help us identify what you took."

Raina nodded.

Martha found a needle in the medical kit and wiped Raina's forearm with an alcohol swab. Raina turned away and cringed when the needle went in. "If...if it was real, where were they going? What were they running to?"

A murky silence settled over the room. Nobody had an answer for that.

"It probably wasn't real," Reiber told her, offering a reassuring smile.

"Probably not," Fraser finally said before turning to Martha and Harbin. "Doctors? A word with you outside?"

Martha pressed a cotton ball to Raina's arm and

wrapped it tightly with gauze. "When was the last time you ate?"

She had to think about this for a minute. "Lunch yesterday, I suppose."

"Maybe you can help her find something?"

Reiber nodded and helped her up from the cot. "Come on. I saw about two thousand boxes of macaroni and cheese in the mess tent."

They were halfway out the door when Harbin spoke up. "Raina, one more question?"

She turned to him. "Sure."

"The studio down in the basement, is it soundproof?"

"Oh, yeah. Eddie's got one of the best places around. I came in from LA to use it. You can't hear anything down there." At the thought of her missing friend, Raina's face went slack again. She turned and shuffled out the door.

When she and Reiber were gone, Harbin looked to Fraser. "We'll need access to satellite imagery. Contact with all the local authorities in the surrounding communities. Blockades. Blockades everywhere. You said the president closed off the mountain and surrounding area? The airspace? We need to expand that. The CDC should be here. I have no idea why they're not. And— "

Fraser held up a hand. "Slow down, Doctor. This can't be people."

"It most certainly can."

"I'm not going to start issuing directives on the word of some junkie."

Martha frowned. "I don't think she's a junkie. She's a musician who—"

"Who took a hallucinogenic to spark a little creativity, I get it. That's not enough. Start by analyzing that blood sample, figure out what she was on. Then look for similarities between her blood and the samples from the village. Compare those to the samples we took from Barton."

"You need to contain this," Harbin insisted.

"That's precisely what we're doing."

"Then how did it get from the mountain to Barton?"

A phone rang then, startling all three of them. Martha realized she hadn't heard a single phone ring since arriving here.

Fraser pulled a sat phone from his belt, looked at the display, and frowned before answering and walking to the opposite side of the tent. Aside from multiple *yes, sir*s, they couldn't make out any of the conversation. He spoke for several minutes, then disconnected. When he returned to them, he looked slightly flustered. "How quickly can you get those two girls ready for travel?" he said to Martha.

"Tennant and her sister?"

He nodded.

This took Martha aback. "Well, Tennant isn't a

problem, but Sophie shouldn't be moved at all, not in her current state. I don't think—"

He just started shaking his head. "You wanted answers? This is your chance. We're leaving in ten minutes."

CHAPTER FIFTY-THREE

MARTHA

FRASER DIDN'T TELL THEM where they were going. Immediately after takeoff, the helicopter banked north, crossed over the Yakama Indian Reservation, and leveled off at about four thousand feet following the mountain range. She knew they'd crossed over into Washington, but beyond that, she wasn't sure. That had been nearly two hours ago.

Tennant sat beside her, strapped into the bench seat. Her hands gripping her safety harness, knuckles white. Her eyes were fixed on her sister, strapped to a gurney secured to the floor and still unconscious. Martha had increased Sophie's sedatives and checked her vitals about every ten minutes. She'd managed to keep the girl's temperature in check, hovering around one hundred, but her blood pressure was through the roof and she was breathing in long, hard gasps.

Harbin sat across from them, next to Fraser.

Soldiers sat on either side of her, weapons nearby. Both were ordered to ensure Sophie remained secure. Martha was worried someone might overreact and forget they were dealing with a sick little girl.

Over her headphones, the pilot said, "On approach to McChord. Prepare for landing. East field."

"Lewis–McChord Air Force Base?" Harbin said, turning toward one of the windows.

Martha glanced out too and watched as the pilot maneuvered over one of the runways and began following it toward the opposite end of the airfield and a group of hangars.

When Tennant let out a soft whimper, Martha took her hand. "It's okay. We'll be on the ground soon."

The skin of Tennant's fingers and palm felt rough, callused. She had the hands of a manual laborer beyond her years.

With expert precision, the pilot set the chopper down about fifty feet from the largest of the hangars, and Martha heard the blades above slow to a deep thump.

Fraser was first out of his harness and to his feet. He told the two soldiers, "Take both girls to 185. They're expecting you. Doctors, you're both with me."

"What's 185? I need to stay with Sophie and monitor—"

"It's okay, Doctor. I'll take good care of her."

Martha turned toward the voice.

Dr. Fitch was standing at the helicopter door with two orderlies. He looked tired. Wind from the blades above twisted and tossed his hair. He was holding it out of his face with one hand. There were heavy bags under his eyes. "I've been kept apprised of her current situation. I'll get her situated, and you can join us when you're through." Before she could respond, he nodded at the orderlies—they jumped up into the helicopter and went to work on the straps holding Sophie's gurney to the floor.

Tennant's hand tightened in Martha's. "I'm staying with Sophie."

Martha gave Fitch a quick look, and he nodded.

She pressed a hand to the side of Tennant's face. "I'll be there soon, okay?"

They all climbed down out of the chopper, and Martha watched as they wheeled the gurney away, Tennant at her sister's side, the soldiers close behind.

"They're waiting on us," Fraser said impatiently. "This way."

He led them toward a side door on the hangar. The large overhead was closed. A marine officer was stationed there, which Martha thought was odd. "Isn't this an Army facility?"

"Not today," Fraser replied.

The marine officer produced a retina scanner, raised the device to Fraser's face, and pressed a button. He studied a small display on the other side, then motioned him through. He then scanned Harbin and Martha. Martha was curious where they'd gotten their retina data. Nobody else had scanned her. She hadn't agreed to anything like that.

When finished, the marine pointed at a door near the end of the hallway behind him. "Through there, sir."

Martha and Harbin followed Fraser down the hall, through the heavy steel fire door, into the main bay of the hangar.

Martha gasped.

The light-blue and white hull of the giant aircraft glistened under the halogen floodlights mounted in the girders of the ceiling. On the tail of the Boeing 747 was the number 28000 printed in large block letters directly below the American flag. The door was open. Wide, retractable steps protruded to the concrete floor. Additional marines and about half a dozen people in dark suits stood surrounding the aircraft.

"I'll be damned," Harbin said softly.

"I'll be damned," Martha repeated as her heart thumped in her chest.

She'd only seen Air Force One on television and in pictures.

The plane was much larger in real life.

CHAPTER FIFTY-FOUR

MARTHA

THE PLANE WAS ALSO FILTHY.

As Martha and Harbin followed Fraser up the steps toward the door, she noticed the hull of the plane was covered in dust and dirt, caked on in some places. She imagined this was nothing unusual for a jet. She supposed most images of the iconic plane were Photoshopped and edited much like those of the world's most famous models, slightly larger than life, unattainable. Air Force One was a symbol of this great nation. Not only did it represent the office of the president, but also the thoughts and beliefs that built this country. Martha imagined a team of people traveled with the plane to ensure it always looked camera-ready.

So why was it dirty?

They were met at the top of the stairs by another marine with a secondary iris scanner. From there, they stepped onto the plane into a very narrow corridor paneled in dark wood with the presidential seal embedded in the wall. Martha noted the spotlight in the ceiling above it was either off or dead.

"Follow the corridor to the end and make a right, sir," the marine instructed Fraser with a salute.

The corridor opened upon a large room that spanned the width of the 747. Martha recognized the space from numerous photographs over the years, presidential photo ops with dignitaries and members of the press corps. The walls were paneled in a rich mahogany. The tan carpet was so plush Martha wanted to sink into it barefoot. Oh, Christ, she was wearing hiking boots. Muddy hiking boots, at that. Jeans and a tan button-down shirt no doubt covered in sweat stains. When was the last time she'd showered? She could only imagine what she smelled like. She caught a glimpse of her wild hair in a mirror and had to turn away. Was this really how she was going to spend her first (and probably only) moment aboard the most famous plane in history?

"Had I known where we were going, I might have shaved and dabbed on a little cologne," Harbin said in a low voice, reading her mind. Somehow, Fraser managed to appear impeccable in standard-issue fatigues. She noticed his name tag had been affixed to the Velcro at his shirt pocket. She wasn't sure when he'd done that.

As they stepped into the room, at least a dozen faces looked at them. The president's press secretary was there, along with General Norman Westin, whom she recognized from a recent appearance on *Meet the Press,* and Samantha Troy, acting director of the NSA, seated on a couch. General Westin gave Fraser a slight nod, then went back to his conversation with Deputy Press Secretary Jeanna Brazzell.

She also knew, from press conferences, the faces of the director of Homeland Security, the president's chief of staff, and two others. Six others were seated in plush leather chairs surrounding a maple table. Martha recognized the secretary of defense and members of the Homeland Security Council, as well as people from the National Security Council. They all looked tired. The lines of their faces and dark circles under their eyes told Martha a good many people hadn't slept recently.

When a man in khaki pants and a navy-blue shirt stepped out of a door at the back of the room, the first thought that went through Martha's head was *He's much shorter than I expected.* The second thought was *Why was that man with him?* The president's gray hair was slightly ruffled, and he hadn't shaved in at least two days. She noticed a stain on his shirt. It looked like coffee, small, but there, under the breast pocket. Reaching for a cloth napkin on the credenza just inside the door, he dipped it in a glass of water and scrubbed at the stain before giving up and tossing the napkin aside. He leaned into the shoulder of the man who had entered with him, said something at his ear, then shook his hand.

The president turned from him and faced the three of them for the first time. He, too, looked tired, run-down. "Lieutenant Colonel, thank you for joining us on such short notice."

"Sir." Fraser saluted.

The president eyed Martha and Harbin. "These were Holt's people?"

The use of *were* was not lost on Martha.

Fraser nodded. "There are four others, but I only had time to personally vet these two. This is Dr. Martha Chan and Dr. Sanford Harbin. I apologize for our appearance. We came directly from the field."

"Pleasure to meet you, sir."

"Sir," Harbin said. He reached across the table to shake the president's hand.

The president turned back to Fraser. "The survivors from Mount Hood?"

"They're with Dr. Fitch right now, in 185."

The president considered this, then nodded. "Good, good. Find someplace to sit. We need to get started."

As they took seats and moved closer to the table, Martha tried to get another look at the man who had entered with the president. Dressed in a deep-scarlet cassock and white rochet was Cardinal Manual Kitzmiller, the highest-ranking member of the Catholic Church in the United States.

CHAPTER FIFTY-FIVE

FRAVEL

DR. RUSSEL FRAVEL YAWNED, sat back in his chair, and admired his handiwork. After nearly twenty-four hours of bad password attempts, he'd given up on that approach. He knew the fingerprint scanner was a waste of time, too. On a whim, he tried placing a piece of cellophane tape over the scanner and pressed down with his own finger, but that didn't work. So much for the crap he'd seen in the movies. Knowing Holt most likely used his fingerprint to unlock the laptop brought on another problem. The fingerprint scanner eliminated the need for a memorable password. The laptop was as secure as the front door to Fort Knox.

When that thought had popped into Fravel's head, he'd had a revelation.

What if he didn't use the front door?

Like most buildings, computer systems were

designed to keep people out but did little to restrict the movements of those already inside.

This thought paired with another.

Unlike the movies, government employees were subject to budgeting constraints and the slow movement of bureaucracy. Computers and operating systems were sometimes five to ten years old. Laughable when compared to the average teenager's gaming PC. Even agencies like the NSA, who wrote much of their own operating code, were forced to run it on outdated equipment.

When Fravel realized this, he'd rebooted Holt's laptop and paid close attention to the opening sequence. When the password box came up almost immediately—before the operating system itself loaded up—he had his answer. This meant both the fingerprint reader and password were handled by the laptop's BIOS, or the hardware itself, not the operating system.

From a design standpoint, this would seem extremely secure. And it was, unless you had a screwdriver and a few spare parts.

In one of the Army's black plastic supply cases, he found a set of screwdrivers. From the lab where Tomes and Hauff were working, he commandeered another laptop and an external hard drive with a USB connection.

Back at his own tent, he went to work.

He removed the screws from the back of Holt's laptop and laid each of them out on the table in the order removed in case he'd have to put things back together. He lifted off the cover, set it aside, and located the small solid-state hard drive. Only four screws held the drive down. He took those out, too. He then dismantled the external hard drive he'd taken from the lab, removed the SSD from the enclosure, and replaced it with the drive from Holt's laptop before putting the enclosure back together again.

Fravel then booted up the spare laptop, logged in to Windows, and plugged the external hard drive containing Holt's drive into the USB port. An Explorer window appeared, neatly listing the contents in folders organized in alphabetical order.

All of this took him less than thirty minutes.

Fravel leaned forward in his chair and studied the various folders.

There was a large one called *LinuxRD27* with the operating system, then hundreds of small folders. Some had names that made sense, others appeared to be random sequences of letters and numbers, most likely encrypted. He clicked through several of the folders and found nothing but gibberish. He'd been afraid of that—even though his little hack had granted him access to the data on the drive, Holt's operating system had encrypted the information, leaving it unreadable. He searched about a dozen other folders and found more of the same.

Fravel caught himself cursing as he clicked through folder after folder, file after file, and got nothing but error messages. Then he opened up a new window and typed **.mp4* into the search box. The asterisk was considered a wildcard character, and *mp4* was the standard file extension for video files. He clicked on *advanced search* and checked off a box to search the entire drive.

Nearly two hundred videos came up in the search.

He sorted the results by date and double-clicked on the first one.

The video of Frederick Hoover with DARPA, the one Holt had played for them when they first arrived, began.

Fravel minimized the window and took a closer look at the search results. The video wasn't stored in one of the encrypted folders but instead appeared in a *temp* folder. Suddenly, it made sense—when Holt played a video, the encryption software wrote a local copy into the *temp* folder without encryption so the operating system's video player could play the file. Data in temp folders was as the name suggests—*temporary*—routinely overwritten as space was needed. This file, and a few hundred more, had not been overwritten yet.

Fravel copied all of the files to his laptop, then began to play them, one at a time.

What he was seeing…

His heart began to thud against his ribs. He felt the blood rush to his face. His skin prickled with it, and he had to remind himself to breathe.

This couldn't be true.

This was physically impossible.

Yet, Frederick Hoover laid it out in this matter-of-fact tone as if he were communicating a recipe or driving directions. The man's face was utterly emotionless.

He watched three more videos before he had to stop.

He couldn't keep this information to himself. He needed to tell the others. Tomes and Hauff were in the biology tent. Reiber was with that girl they'd brought back from Barton. He wasn't sure where Doctors Chan and Harbin were, but he'd find them—this couldn't wait. Not another second.

Fravel scooped up the laptop and external drive and ran out of the tent.

That was when he heard a strange sound.

A low hum, quickly increasing in volume.

CHAPTER FIFTY-SIX

MARTHA

"WE DON'T HAVE A name for it," General Westin began. "Frankly, I'm not sure I want to name it. I want to locate and eradicate the cause before we get to the point of requiring a name."

The interior lights of Air Force One dimmed, and a large video screen came to life on the wall at the fore of the cabin with the presidential seal emblazoned at the center.

"For the record, what you are about to see has been classified *Echelon,* meaning discussion must be contained to people within this room. Your understanding and acceptance of that was detailed in the paperwork each of you signed for the Joint Chiefs' office."

The general raised a remote and pointed it at the screen.

The presidential seal was replaced by grainy footage

of a parking lot with a ramp leading up into a garage in the far corner.

"This is a shopping mall in Herdon, Oregon, about thirty miles outside of Barton. You've all read the lieutenant colonel's report."

Several murmurs rolled through the group.

The time stamp in the corner of the screen read six minutes after eleven in the morning. About half the lot was full, and several cars moved through the frame. A woman approached a parked minivan with several shopping bags and two children following closely behind. She keyed the button on her remote, and the back door opened. The kids climbed inside, she placed the bags on the floor in front of them, then closed the door and walked around to the driver's side and got in. Two slots down, a pickup truck pulled into an empty space and a man got out and started walking off to the right—presumably toward the mall—the same direction the woman and children had come from.

Someone ran by him, practically a blur, they were moving so fast. Not heading to or from the mall but perpendicular to it, heading in the direction of the parking garage.

Two more people quickly rushed through the frame, following the first.

Six more.

Then at least a dozen.

An elbow caught the man from the pickup truck in the shoulder and sent him spinning. Another runner clipped him in the leg. Martha watched in horror as he tripped and dropped to the blacktop a moment before more runners appeared—so many now—they ran right over the top of him. He twitched and jerked as feet cracked down on his legs, his back, his head, like heavy pistons. Martha let out a gasp as the man stopped moving, then vanished under a sea of people.

More runners came into the frame.

They filled every inch of blacktop. Others raced up bumpers and ran across the cars themselves—trunks, roofs, hoods—metal and plastic giving way under their feet as tires exploded and vehicles fell under the weight.

The woman in the minivan had started to back out and slammed on her brakes as the first runner crossed behind her. As the crowd grew, she had no place to go. Within moments they were surrounded, then buried under the masses as people raced all around and over them. Martha thought of the children in the back, thought of her own children. There were so many runners she only caught glimpses of the van, and each time the roof was a little lower. She didn't see the windows explode out—one second they were there, then they weren't, then she lost sight of the van altogether as more runners converged on the scene.

There were so many.

Hundreds? Thousands? As the seconds ticked by, Martha lost track. The group just got bigger. An endless stream of runners, these people.

The video had no sound, and Martha took no comfort in that. Her mind filled in the missing screams. She heard the children in that minivan, she heard the crunch of bone. She heard each destructive footfall as the horde of people continued to grow in size. Their faces were expressionless, and while their legs moved with unimaginable speed and power, their arms hung loosely at their sides like dead appendages.

In the upper-left portion of the screen, a light pole toppled over. Another fell about twenty seconds later. Immediately after that, the pole holding their camera collapsed, and the screen went dark.

The general paused for a moment, then said, "We have one more shot, and I find this one particularly disturbing."

Martha couldn't imagine anything more disturbing than what she'd just seen, but then the camera switched to another angle, this one focused on the side of the parking garage. The entrance ramp of the garage was completely engulfed—the runners moved in and around the building in much the same way they had overtaken the cars—like a swarm of ants—the blacktop, the concrete, all lost around them. She watched them disappear inside. Some smashed into the exterior walls, and without a moment's hesitation, they rerouted and continued forward. Faces and limbs were covered in blood, scrapes, and scratches—even broken limbs didn't slow them down. They pressed against the wall in their path in a desperate fevered fury. Some slammed into it repeatedly until they found a way around or through, but they didn't slow or stop.

The rush of people hadn't tapered in the slightest when the first of the runners appeared at the top level of the garage. From this distance, Martha couldn't tell if it was a man or a woman. More poured out behind them, and she imagined the interior ramps crammed with this unrelenting group as the top level began to fill, too. They didn't stop as they raced out into the sunlight. Instead, they tore out across toward the edge.

"Don't tell me they're going to—" the cardinal's words cut off as the first body tumbled over the side, then a dozen more, two dozen after that. A hundred. No hesitation. Not the slightest pause. Martha thought of the crevasse, and she could tell from the expression on Harbin's face he was thinking the same.

The first few hit the blacktop below, bounced, and went still. Necks bent at ungodly angles and snapped. Arms and legs twisted and popped. The pavement quickly grew dark and red.

More fell. They just kept coming. This continual flood of bodies rolling over the side and tumbling down into the growing heap below. Five hundred or more now. The bodies were at least three thick when Deputy Press Secretary Jeanna Brazzell let out an audible gasp. "One just moved. Oh, no, that one, too!"

Martha watched as those falling now, cushioned by the previous bodies, began to crawl away from the pile. Others rolled off on broken limbs, dislocated arms dangling loosely at their sides. Some tried to stand on destroyed legs and toppled back over. Others still managed to get to their feet and begin running again. As the bodies continued to fall, as the mountain of these people grew, more got up and continued on, oblivious to any injuries they may have sustained.

Thousands.

"How many stories is that?" the president asked in a low voice.

"Not enough," the general said before switching off the video.

CHAPTER FIFTY-SEVEN

MARTHA

GENERAL WESTIN STARED AT the blank screen for a moment before speaking again. "From what we've gathered, the horde doesn't stop for anything. They just keep moving forward, up, over, and around, anything caught in their path—just like you saw here. They don't eat. They don't speak. They don't scream. They only run. Even injuries don't slow them down. We don't know if they feel pain, but if they do, they demonstrate no outward signs of it. Their only desire is to keep moving."

"Toward what?" the president asked.

"Anna Shim," Harbin said softly.

"Excuse me?"

Harbin gave Martha an uneasy glance, then continued. "The little girl we have in our care, Sophie, the one who appears to be…infected…by whatever this is, has continually said *Anna Shim*. At first, it was believed this was a name, and maybe it is, but in ancient Aramaic it means—"

"People," the cardinal said, cutting him off. He looked up at Harbin. "You're speaking of anahshim?"

Harbin nodded. "I think this group, this horde, is drawn toward other large groups of people, population centers, anahshim. When they encounter others, they're adding to their numbers."

The president looked him dead in the eye. "You used the word *infected,* yet I've been repeatedly reassured this is not a communicable contagion."

Samantha Troy, acting director of the NSA, cleared her throat. "It's not, at least not in the traditional sense. I believe those in attendance with a medical background will concur." Although she said this to the president, her eyes were on Martha.

Martha nodded. "We've found nothing to indicate this can be transmitted from person to person like a virus—it's not airborne, there is no abnormality in blood or bodily fluid, nothing like that."

"Yet, they are infected." The president mulled over this for a moment, then said softly, "This can't be a goddamn sound. Especially something generating from below the surface. This must be some new Chinese weapon, or Russian. We're missing something."

At the curse, several eyes fell on the cardinal.

Martha wasn't accustomed to the president speaking so frankly, different from television. Apparently, the others weren't, either.

Harbin looked over at the general. "Can you play the beginning of the first video again? When the minivan begins to back out of the parking space?"

The general raised the remote and brought up the file, then hit Play.

As the woman loaded her children into the vehicle, Harbin said, "Watch the top right of the screen as the people start to run across the frame. Maybe slow the image down a little bit, if you can. This happens quickly."

When the first of the runners darted by the back of the minivan, the general slowed the video to half-speed.

"Keep your eye on that man in the dark leather jacket leaving the mall."

Martha didn't see him at first. He was far off in the distance, nearly hidden behind other cars and a light pole. As more runners entered the frame below, the man dropped the bag he was carrying and doubled over, pressing his hands to his ears. A moment later, he rose again and started running back toward the mall.

"Is he going for cover?" Brazzell asked, puzzled.

Harbin shook his head. "He's joining the others. He's running." He looked back to the general. "Rewind it again. This time, watch the cars around him."

The video sped backward, then restarted. As the man doubled over, the windows in the car next to him blew out, spraying the ground in glass.

"Okay, pause," Harbin instructed.

The image froze.

He stood and walked over to the monitor and drew an imaginary circle. "We noticed in Barton the sound increased in volume until glass shattered, including the security camera lenses. I was curious why this particular video didn't cut out as that one did. You can see it here. I think it's because the camera that shot this footage is too far away. If you look really close, you'll see all the vehicles around this man blew out and the damage extends in a radius of about four or five cars deep around him, then it stops—other cars in the lot remain untouched."

"Are you saying he was targeted?" The president frowned.

Harbin shrugged. "Either that, or he was caught up in some smaller random event than the one that affected the horde."

"Like an aftershock with an earthquake?"

Harbin nodded.

"A weapon from Russia or China still makes the most sense to me."

Samantha Troy said, "Sir, we've got every available satellite listening in on that part of the world, and there's been zero chatter regarding any type of weapons test. Our assets are squeezing their contacts. All due respect, if a capable weapon existed, we would have heard about it. The development process alone would have spanned years, there would have been some type of testing phase, something would have slipped out. This is unlike anything in development here or abroad."

"Well, here we are," the president said flatly. "Somebody created it."

The cardinal leaned forward and looked down at his hands.

The president blew out a breath and turned to him. "Do you have something you'd like to add?"

"You know what I think." The cardinal's voice was soft, yet gruff. He spoke in deep, measured tones.

The president shook his head, more annoyed than in any type of agreement. "I'm not willing to go there. I may be a man of faith, but I'm not ready to point an accusatory finger up at God."

"This is not the work of our Lord," the cardinal replied. "But I do believe we are experiencing the start of some sort of cleansing. A new flood to wash the planet clean of our filth."

"Forgive me if I'm not ready to climb aboard an ark."

The cardinal gestured at the walls of Air Force One. "I believe you already have."

The president closed his eyes and rubbed his temples. "If they're not eating, not drinking, how long can they keep this up? Won't they burn out?"

"Even if the weaker ones start to drop off, it won't matter if they keep adding to their numbers. The horde is growing far faster than it's dying," the general replied. "They're moving at a good clip, too. An average of ten miles per hour. That puts them in Gresham in a little over six hours, Portland after that." He paused for a second, choosing his words carefully. "Sir, without a complete understanding of how this infection is spreading, we can't risk them reaching a large, populated area. Best case, they leave sizable destruction in their wake. Certainly more deaths. Worst case, they infect others, further increase in size, and continue on."

"What's the population of Gresham?"

"111,053 souls in Gresham at last census. 647,805 in Portland."

"What's the size of the horde now?"

The general hesitated before answering. "We're estimating their size to be approaching one hundred thousand. There's no way to get an exact figure."

"Jesus. A hundred thousand?"

"Yes, sir."

"You understand what you're implying, right?"

This time, the general didn't hesitate. "Yes, sir. I'm telling you we need to consider options to either reroute or eliminate this group before it's given the opportunity to expand. I see no other solution."

"A cure," the president shot back. "That's our other

option. We cure those who are infected and inoculate those who are not."

"In six hours?"

He was right, Martha thought. Even if this were a virus and she had the cure on hand, six hours wasn't enough time to produce the quantities they would need to inoculate that many people.

The room fell silent for a long moment.

"Sir, if we're going to mobilize in time, you need to issue the order within the next hour," the general pushed.

The president brushed this off, stood, and went to one of the windows. "I need a minute."

Several others got up and stretched, talked in small groups.

The cardinal rose and came over to Harbin and Martha. His voice low, he said, "Anahshim is mentioned in the Old Testament as well, but you already knew that, didn't you?"

Harbin gave a grave nod.

Harbin had told Martha earlier, but he hadn't been serious. At least, she didn't think he was. He had told her in the Old Testament, Anahshim was a demon.

CHAPTER FIFTY-EIGHT

TENNANT

TENNANT SAT IN A cold metal chair in the far corner of the room and watched the strange man hovering over her sister. He wore thick, rimless glasses, and his beady dark eyes seemed a little too close together for the size of his face. His hair was gray, and it must have been awhile since he cut it. She'd been told his name was Dr. Fitch, which didn't seem right—it was too close to *finch,* the small bird, and he reminded her more of an opossum than a bird.

Sophie was still unconscious, wearing a straitjacket, and bound to the gurney the soldiers had used to transport her from home.

Dr. Fitch hovered over her for a moment, then took out a small recorder, pressed a button, and spoke into it. "Subject is female and appears to be six to eight years old— "

"She's eight," Tennant informed him.

He gave her an irritated glance, then turned back to Sophie. "Eight years old, restrained and unconscious due to a mixture of..." He reached for the clear plastic bag hanging from a pole over Sophie and read off some long words Tennant didn't recognize. "Per Lieutenant Colonel Fraser, she's been unconscious for approximately three hours. Blood pressure is extremely elevated at 183 over 122, heart rate is highly erratic. I've checked three times now and the lowest reading was 133 beats per minute, the highest was 174—far above expected for a child of this age, particularly in a near comatose state."

He reached to the table behind him, picked something up, and ran it over Sophie's forehead. "She currently has a temperature of 102. Again, this presentation is uncharacteristic considering the medications being administered. That said, the medications appear to be slowing the progress of this affliction, potentially preventing it from running its course. It's too early to know if her condition has in any way reversed."

Dr. Fitch set the recorder down on the table, examined the end of the IV tube, the needle the other doctor had inserted in Sophie's neck. He began peeling back the tape holding it in place. "I'm removing the cannula now." He glanced up at the clock. "Discontinuing all medications at 1642." He yanked out the tube and let it fall to the floor. Several drops of liquid came out and shimmered on the white tile.

Tennant jumped up in her chair. "What are you doing? She needs that to get better!"

The doctor reached behind him and clicked off the recorder. "Your sister is lost, young lady. Dr. Chan made a valiant effort to save her, but it's not working. All she's doing is holding back the inevitable, prolonging your sister's suffering. At this point, the best use of your sister will be in allowing her condition to run its course, document the progression, and utilize the resulting information to prevent this infection from spreading to others."

"Best *use* of my sister..." Tennant repeated the words, let them fall off her tongue as she contemplated their meaning.

"Yes. Best use." Dr. Fitch repeated.

He clicked the recorder back on and began speaking again, but Tennant didn't hear what he said. She couldn't hear much of anything behind the blood rushing in her ears.

Tennant lunged at him.

She was across the room and on his back in less than a second, a feral thing. She went for his neck, as Poppa had taught her when defending herself, but before she could strike, she felt strong arms snake around her waist and pull her back.

Tennant had no idea how the two soldiers got in

there so fast, but they had. They yanked her away from the doctor and slammed her down to the ground. Both her arms were pinned, and she couldn't move. All of this seemed to happen in less than a few seconds.

Dr. Fitch brushed off his sleeves and looked down at her. "We're also concerned about the lasting effects of the exposure you endured." He looked up at a camera mounted in the opposite corner of the room. "Note, our second subject is demonstrating increased hostility. However, she doesn't appear to have the increased strength documented in our first subject. This may present later as the infection spreads through her."

"I'm not infected!" Tennant spat out, jerking her head away from the soldier's hand.

"Put her back in that seat, please."

They lifted her off the ground, carried her back to the chair, and set her down. Both continued to hold her at the arms and shoulders so she couldn't get back up.

"If necessary, I'll have you restrained as well, at least while I'm in the room, but I'd prefer not to do that," Dr. Fitch told her.

Tennant jerked sideways, tried to break free, but they were too strong.

"Hold her still so I can draw some blood."

Their grip tightened as he jabbed a needle into her arm and filled four small vials. When Dr. Chan had done this, she wiped her arm with alcohol first. Dr. Fitch didn't. When he pulled the needle out, he wiped away a lingering drop of blood and quickly covered the spot with a Band-Aid.

He knelt down in front of Tennant, his face close to hers. "Do you still have a headache?"

Tennant did, she still had an awful headache, but she wasn't about to give him the satisfaction of an answer. Her broken nose still hurt, too, though it had stopped throbbing.

"I believe you received a slightly diminished exposure from your sister, but you were exposed. I'm curious to see if the illness progresses." He got to his feet. "I suppose we'll know soon enough."

With one last glance back at Sophie, he gathered his recorder and the blood samples and left the room.

The soldiers went out the door behind him.

She heard a heavy lock twist into place as she got up and ran to her sister's side.

CHAPTER FIFTY-NINE

TENNANT

IT STARTED ABOUT TEN minutes ago, the murmuring. Sophie was still unconscious, but her body had begun to twitch and shudder on the gurney. Her fingers jumped up and extended as if a jolt of electricity found her. Then they slowly settled back down. Her tiny toes curled tight, then relaxed again a moment or two later.

The straitjacket was on the floor in a heap, as were the leather straps. Sophie's favorite flowered dress, the one with purple lilacs on it, was soaked in sweat, torn in some spots, and shredded in others. Tennant slipped it off and dropped it on the floor with the rest. From the sink in the room, she wet several paper towels and went to work gently wiping away the horrors of the past days. Her poor little sister's skin was scratched in so many places, it was a wonder none of the wounds had grown infected. Most likely, *their* medicines had something to do with that, but those were gone now. Dr. Fitch had someone clear them away moments after he left. If Momma were here, she'd use garlic, honey, ginger, echinacea, goldenseal, clove, or maybe oregano to help with infection, but Tennant had none of those now. She had water and the box of crackers one of the soldiers had given her, nothing else.

In one of the cabinets under the sink, she found T-shirts and sweatpants, all new, still wrapped in plastic packaging. Tennant had never owned new clothes; neither had Sophie. Everything they wore came from others in the village. The community clothing yurt had been a round tent on the far end of their settlement. Tennant and Sophie had loved picking together through the boxes and crates of outgrown or discarded clothing. They'd never do that again. The yurt was gone now, along with everything else.

The sweatpants were far too large for Sophie, meant for an adult. The T-shirt would reach her knees, nearly as long as her dress, and it would have to do on its own. She redressed Sophie, then looked at the items on the floor. She couldn't bring herself to put the straitjacket back on but she replaced the leather straps, although a little looser than they had been. She didn't want to, but she had no idea what her sister would be like when she woke, and she couldn't risk her hurting her or herself again.

Aside from the clothing, the cabinets around the sink were bare.

There was a small air-conditioning vent near the ceiling, not large enough for either of them to fit. The door was made of steel. Four cameras looked down at them, one in each corner. Each camera had a harsh red eye that blinked every other second. She tried not to look up at those.

Sophie's skin felt warm but not hot like earlier, and Tennant told herself that was good. She was still sweating, though. Not as bad, but still...hopefully that was her body forcing out the poison, fighting this nasty, evil thing growing within her.

"Help me, Tennnnant. I die. I to die. You watchin' me to die."

The words drifted up from Sophie's lips so quietly, at first Tennant thought she imagined them. Then Sophie's eyes opened. Narrow slits, as if unable to look out upon the harsh lights from above.

"Sophie?" She brushed the hair from her sister's forehead with her fingertips and touched her again. Without a thermometer, it was difficult to be sure, but she felt even cooler. With a damp paper towel, she wiped the sweat away and dried her skin. The telltale glisten of perspiration didn't return. "Can you hear me?"

Sophie's eyes opened a little more. Her dilated pupils shrunk, focused, found Tennant. "Where we?"

"They took us to an Army base somewhere in Washington, I think. How do you feel?"

Sophie's head slowly turned from one side to the other, taking in the small room. She pressed her eyes shut again, as if in pain. "Annnna Shimm calling. Calling sooo loud, Tennnnnant."

Tennant gently slapped her cheek. "Stay with me, Sophie."

When her sister's eyes opened again, they didn't seem so red. The yellow was gone, too. "You look much better."

"I dying. I need to go, Tennnant. I don't go...I die."

Tennant shook her head. "No. You need to fight this."

"Her voice beautiful, like music. Like Ma's records. Beautiful music. She need me, my Annna Shimm."

"You need to stay here with me," Tennant insisted.

Sophie's eyes grew wide. "Noooo. You go with me. You run with me. You run with Annnna Shiiim. All run with Anna Shim." She turned her head again and faced the sink. "Sooo thirsty."

Tennant tugged a paper cup from the dispenser on the wall, filled it, and brought it back to Sophie. She helped hold her head up so she could drink.

The cracks in her sister's lips had healed some. They weren't bleeding anymore.

Sophie tugged at the leather straps on her arms.

"Take these off. I nooo hurt you. Not no more. Okay now."

She did seem much better, but Tennant wasn't sure she could trust her. There was no place for her to go, though. They were locked in. No doubt soldiers right outside the door. More beyond that.

Tennant unfastened Sophie's right wrist, let the strap fall to the side of the gurney. When her sister made no move to hurt her, she undid the left one, too. Sophie rubbed both her wrists as Tennant undid the straps on her ankles.

Sophie rolled to the edge of the gurney and sat up. She flexed her feet and rolled her head on her stiff neck. Her gaze settled on one of the cameras. She slowly turned and found the others, then smiled at Tennant. "We poke out their eyes now."

CHAPTER SIXTY

TENNANT

SOPHIE SLID OFF THE edge of the gurney and dropped to the floor. She padded across the tile on her bare feet and looked up at the underside of one of the cameras. The fingers of her tiny hands flexed and curled into fists. She slowly shifted her weight from her left foot to her right and back again, her body swaying. Tennant could hear her breathing, this thick, raspy sound as phlegm and mucus caught in her throat.

All went suddenly silent.

In a blur, Sophie's knees bent and she leaped. How she was able to jump so high was lost on Tennant, but somehow her sister shot nearly straight up, curled her fingers around the wiring between the camera and the wall, and tore it out as her weight brought her back down to the floor. The second camera, the third, the fourth, they all came apart with equal haste and by the time Tennant's eyes found Sophie again, she was standing at the sink, shuffling again—right to left, left to right—agitated, growing faster.

Sophie leaned in, gripped the water pipe under the sink, and yanked it free. A metal ring and chunks of plastic blew out across the floor as water sprayed out with a loud hiss from the damaged pipe—soaking her and her new clothes, spilling out over the tile.

All of this played out in a matter of seconds, and Tennant found herself standing in a growing puddle of water. She watched as it sprayed out across the room, reached the walls and door.

Would it fill the room?

Would they drown?

Sophie crossed back over to the gurney and stood behind it, her fingers wrapped around the cold steel, her eyes on the door.

She screamed this horrible, gut-wrenching shrill cry with no end—no pause for breath, no break at all, only a horrible shriek that caused the hair on Tennant's arms to stand on end.

The door handle jiggled, the door swung open—one soldier quickly surveyed the room while a second had his eyes down on the ground, watching the water lick at his shoes a moment longer than he probably should have.

Sophie's grip tightened on the end of the gurney. She pushed the heavy metal table forward on wobbly wheels and barreled into the first guard, catching him in the gut. He slipped and tumbled back into the second guard, who tried to grab the wall for support but missed. They both fell to the floor in a clatter of guns and limbs, the gurney rolling over the top of both.

Sophie vaulted up onto the gurney and rolled off the opposite side into the hallway. With a quick glance in both directions, she was gone.

"Wait!" Tennant cried out after her. She was halfway out the door when one of the guards grabbed her by the ankle. She kicked him with her free foot, connecting with his jaw, then stomped on his forearm.

He yelped, released her, and she ran off after her sister, moving as fast as she could but not fast enough. She almost missed Sophie turning right at the end of the hallway and disappearing from sight.

She yelled again as she ran, but that did little good. Her sister moved with impossible speed, a wild animal free of the noose with hunters at its back.

Tennant rounded the corner an instant after Sophie burst through a metal fire door at the opposite end. Two more soldiers were on the floor in the hallway—one on his back, the other on her side leaning against the wall—both stunned and wide-eyed at whatever they'd just seen. Tennant managed to get around them and to the door before either recovered. As she pushed through the outer door, the cool evening air lapped at her. Although the sun wouldn't set for several more hours, thick rain clouds choked the sky and blotted out the light, casting everything in a gray haze.

Tennant looked wildly about and spotted Sophie nearly sixty yards away, running alongside a low concrete building. Her long, wet shirt slapped against her skin. Rather than sway at her sides, her arms were perfectly straight, held down and back. Her fingers were splayed out as if reaching for the ground.

A loud siren came to life somewhere nearby, then another farther off.

Footsteps clattered on the tile behind her. A soldier shouted, "Don't move!"

Tennant *did* move. She darted off after her sister, ahead of several people running behind her. Growing up on the mountain, spending most of her time outdoors, she knew she was physically in good shape, probably better than any of the soldiers, but she also knew if she looked back she might trip, or falter. Her sister was at least eighty yards ahead now, the distance growing. Tennant sucked in air, willed her body to work harder. The muscles in her legs burned, her chest hurt. She ignored it all and pressed forward.

Additional soldiers appeared all around, joining the chase. Tennant caught a glimpse of a Jeep racing toward them between buildings on her right.

A hundred yards ahead now, Sophie was nearing

a chain-link fence, nothing but forest on the other side. Tall redwoods and thick brambles. The fence had to be at least ten or twelve feet tall, maybe more. It was topped with spools of razor wire, and even from this distance, the large red-and-white signs warning of electrocution were visible, posted every twenty feet or so.

Sophie hadn't slowed at the sight of the fence but somehow managed to speed up, and all Tennant could think about was how she had jumped up so effortlessly and destroyed the security cameras. She'd either die trying to get over the fence, or even worse, she'd make it and disappear into those woods. She'd lose her sister forever.

The Jeep blew by Tennant on her right, at least five people inside, maybe six. When the driver caught sight of Sophie up ahead, he gunned the gas and the engine roared. They overtook Sophie, skidded to a stop at the fence line, and the soldiers scrambled out. They formed a line and knelt down. Their guns went up, each pointed at her sister.

Tennant tried to scream, but she was so out of breath nothing came out but a stuttered gasp.

A second Jeep raced by.

Sophie neared the fence—sixty yards.

Forty yards.

The second Jeep came to a stop next to the first.

Twenty yards.

Sophie sped up. Somehow she managed to find more speed, and Tennant knew she was going to try and jump over.

Ten yards.

The first shot was the loudest.

Although the bullet didn't strike her, Tennant felt the blast in her chest as if it had. Three more guns went off a moment later in quick succession.

Tennant watched in horror as Sophie's legs came out from under her, and she tumbled forward. She hit the blacktop hard and rolled, her tiny body twisting awkwardly as her head cracked against the ground with a sickening thump.

This time, Tennant did manage to scream. She yelled so loud her vocal cords felt as if someone sliced them with a razor blade. She closed the distance and fell to the ground next to her sister.

Sophie wasn't moving.

Dr. Fitch climbed out of the second Jeep, holding a stopwatch. "Thirty-six minutes. That's all it took for this little girl to not only recover from the sedatives in her body, but to escape a high-security facility and reach a potential exit. That's remarkable." He turned to a woman next to him. She was holding something that looked like a ray gun from a science-fiction comic. "How fast?"

The woman studied a display on the back. "Thirty-seven miles per hour at the end there and she was still picking up speed!" She looked up at the doctor, her mouth hanging open. "The fastest person on record is Usain Bolt—twenty-eight miles per hour in the hunded-meter. This is extraordinary!"

Tennant stopped listening. She scooped Sophie up into her arms and pulled her close to her chest. They hadn't shot her with bullets. Instead, her body was riddled with darts.

CHAPTER SIXTY-ONE

MARTHA

MARTHA AND HARBIN WATCHED the new video for the umpteenth time and tried to wrap their heads around what they'd seen. They were in a small conference room two buildings over from the hangar where they'd met with the president. Fraser was still aboard Air Force One with the others. They'd been told neither of them had a clearance level high enough to remain for the conversation currently taking place.

This new video had come in about ten minutes before that over a secure satellite feed, and it had everyone spooked, including her.

They'd tracked the horde from the shopping mall in Herdon, Oregon, to another town about ten miles away. The footage was shaky, taken from a helicopter. Fraser had told them the name of the town, but Martha didn't remember. It didn't matter. It might as well have been Anytown, USA.

The horde came in from the east. First a single runner, then several more, then this flood of bodies. Men, women, children, pressed so tightly together they looked like a single organism bursting out of the woods into the street. They didn't slow for cars, signs, poles, buildings, nothing. When they encountered an obstacle, they either ran through it, over it, or trampled whatever it was. If someone tripped, if someone got caught up underfoot, they were dead, crushed. The more Martha watched the video, the more she was convinced dying was better than the alternative—joining those who ran. When she froze the picture, she could see the utter exhaustion in their blank faces—the drawn, tight skin of severe dehydration. The yellow jaundice of failing livers. Some ran with broken limbs. One man ran on a bloody stump, his foot gone. Yet, somehow, they were unable to stop. Unable to slow down. And they moved with incredible speed. These people would run until their bodies failed them. While this was terrifying, it wasn't the worst part. She had rewound the video and played it side by side with the one from the shopping mall several times before she realized the worst part.

Harbin leaned in closer. "My God, you're right," he said softly. "It makes no sense. How can this be happening?"

Martha had no answer, only watched the video play out again.

As the horde encountered people from the town, those people joined the runners. Unlike the previous video, there was no hesitation, no panic, they simply dropped whatever they were doing and began to run. Within seconds the giant mass swallowed them whole and grew that much larger.

"They're just joining the others—no sound as a trigger," Harbin said more to himself than to her. His finger traced the screen, hovered over glass storefronts and car windows—unlike the previous video, most were intact here. Anything broken appeared to have been caught up in the path of the horde, not shattered by the sound as a precursor.

"We don't know what they're hearing on the ground," Martha pointed out. "All you can hear is the damn helicopter in this footage."

"Remember what Fraser told us about the private jet over Mount Hood, though. They were in the path of the sound and went down. How is this helicopter able to fly over? The only thing that makes sense is the problem is evolving. The horde itself is now infecting people, not just the sound anymore."

"Maybe the horde is generating the sound?" But even as she said this, Martha saw a flaw in her logic—they had a chicken and egg scenario—the sound came before the horde, right?

There was a loud knock at the doorway.

Martha and Harbin turned to find Fraser standing

in the opening, the lights above casting him in shadows. He stepped into the room, his face long and tired. He looked at them both and slid a tablet across the table. "It's out. The media has footage. I'm not sure where they got it. They don't know what to make of it, but images are popping up everywhere."

Martha gave Harbin a sidelong glance, then pulled the tablet closer. On one of the news sites, the headline read CROWD STORMS MCDONALD'S and there was a short video clip taken from a camera at the drive-thru. This wasn't the Volkswagen they'd found in the drive-thru in Barton, but somewhere else. When Martha clicked Play, a rush of people came into frame. They ran around the side of the cars, up and over. The employee working the window had her arm extended when they appeared, holding out a bag—her arm got caught in the rush and snapped backward, cracked against the window frame. She fell back into the restaurant and out of sight.

From the speakers of the tablet, the noise shrilled out, quickly growing louder. Martha's fingers fumbled over the mute button and switched off the sound. A moment later, the image went dark, most likely due to camera damage. The video stopped, and she hit the Back button on the browser. The screen filled with search results—hundreds of stories. Many of the headlines claimed it was a hoax, like some kind of flash mob gone wrong. A few others used words like *unprecedented* and *disturbing*. Others simply said, *What happened?*

"A local network out of Eugene got it first. CNN after that. It's everywhere now. They're not sure what to make of it, not yet," Fraser explained. "Aside from the clip you just watched, there are three others. All taken from security cameras. That seems to be slowing things down a little bit—there's no cell phone footage. Nothing from camcorders or other devices, only fixed security cameras."

"Why is that?" Then Martha understood. The answer was in the video she had just watched with Harbin—anyone close enough to film the horde joined the horde.

"The sound was captured in the video... that noise," Harbin said. "It's muted, distilled, but still painful to listen to, even as a distant recording—at least for me. I can still hear it, like a ringing in my ears. And this pressure similar to the beginnings of a migraine."

"Same here," Martha said.

Fraser nodded. "Dr. Fitch ran some earlier tests based on the recording we brought back from Barton. The noise brings on severe physical discomfort in everyone who hears it. He documented physiological changes in blood pressure, heart rate, and brain activity. He asked for additional neuroimaging equipment. It arrived about ten minutes ago. He believes the sound induces a reaction similar to one we might feel the moment before a car accident or similar traumatic event, but rather than this being a limited reaction—a microsecond or two—it's prolonged. The body continues in this heightened state the entire time it's exposed to the noise."

Martha considered this, but it didn't make sense. "The body couldn't keep that up. It would be fatal. Like running a car on nitrous for too long, the engine burns out."

Harbin pulled the tablet closer and scrolled through all the stories. "This isn't just the news networks. People are sharing the videos on all the social media sites, probably peer-to-peer with text messages and email, too. If recordings have this detrimental impact, what will happen when people are exposed to it repeatedly from all these different sources?"

Fraser sighed and tapped his fingers nervously on the edge of the table. "We're not sure yet. Dr. Fitch is hoping he'll learn more after extended exposure with the two survivors from Mount Hood."

Martha's face flushed with heat. "He's *experimenting* on the girls? He's supposed to be treating them!"

Lieutenant Colonel Alexander Fraser was a large man. He towered over Martha, but when she stood up and started toward him, he took a step back. He held both his hands up. "Dr. Chan, this is an epidemic. We need to fully understand exactly what—"

She glared up at him. "Take me to them now!"

CHAPTER SIXTY-TWO

TENNANT

"SOPHIE!"

Tennant screamed out her sister's name for the dozenth time, unsure if she could even hear her. They pulled Sophie from her arms back near the fence and took her away in one Jeep while soldiers held Tennant back and drove her off in another one. Instead of returning to the room that looked like a doctor's office, they'd brought Tennant to someplace that looked like a jail cell. There was a small cot in the corner bolted to the floor and wall, a stainless-steel sink, and a toilet with no lid. Dim light streamed in from a small window up in the corner—a window that was far too narrow for her to slip through. Not that she could even if she did fit—a steel mesh was embedded in the glass, and there were bars on the outside. The walls were cinder block, painted white, and the door was heavy steel.

There was a camera, but unlike the other room, this one was built into a box in the wall and covered in thick plastic or glass. Tennant glared up at it. "Where is my sister? What did you do to her?!"

She knew someone was watching, probably that doctor, but she hadn't seen him since they took Sophie away. They had implanted something in her neck, too. Under the skin. About the size of a grain of rice. The surrounding skin felt hot to her touch, inflamed, angry.

"Tennant, can you hear me?"

This was the doctor's voice. It came from a speaker in the wall near the camera.

"Where is Sophie?"

"Your sister is fine. She's doing wonderful. You'll be permitted to see her soon, but first there are a few things we need to check. If you cooperate, this will go much easier, much faster, and I think we'd all prefer that. Of course, if you feel the need to fight us, you may. I suppose I understand why you would want to, but that will really just make things worse…for the both of you."

"I want to see my sister!"

"Here we go," he said.

Then the noise came.

Although it came from the same speaker up in the wall, for Tennant, the noise only seemed to start there. Like water from a faucet, the noise poured out of the metal grille, splashed off the walls, ceiling, and floor, and quickly surrounded her. Tennant found herself backing up, but there was no place to go. When she reached the wall, she turned around and pressed her forehead against the cinder block, pressed her palms tight against her ears. The noise only grew louder, seeped around her fingers, inched down into her ears and scratched at her brain.

Through the increasing volume, she heard the doctor's voice. "Can you describe what you're feeling?"

"Sophie!"

"If you cooperate, and tell me what you're feeling, I'll let you see your sister. I promise."

His voice was so calm and quiet. She wanted to hit him. She wanted to beat him to a bloody pulp.

The sound grew louder.

The doctor said, "Your pulse rate is elevated, but not beyond what I would expect under the circumstances. With your sister, we noticed substantial changes in neural oscillations. Are you familiar with brainwaves? There are four different kinds—high amplitude, low-frequency delta, low amplitude, and high-frequency beta. With your sister, we found increases in all four, similar to receiving an electric shock. Is that what this feels like to you? Like getting an electric shock? Are you able to concentrate? Can you focus on the sound of my voice and respond, or is exposure making that an impossibility?"

When she didn't answer, he said calmly, "I'm going to increase the volume again. Stand by."

Tennant sucked in a breath.

The pressure around her head increased, like someone had a leather strap around her skull and was slowly tightening the band. She dropped to the ground and pressed her body into the corner on her knees. Her eyes were squeezed tightly shut. Tennant was afraid if she opened them they'd pop. "Please stop!"

"Soon. You're doing wonderfully."

"I can't..."

"Can't what? Are you able to respond to my voice?"

"Yeees...please stop."

"That's excellent. Thank you."

The noise stopped.

When Tennant finally opened her eyes, she found herself lying on the ground, on her side. She didn't remember how she got there. Her nose was bleeding. Her ears, too. The blood wasn't fresh, though. It was tacky, partially dry.

"You passed out. Twelve minutes ago," the doctor said.

The lights of the room seemed horribly bright.

Tennant forced herself to sit up. All her muscles ached as if she'd spent the last day working in the gardens or hauling water.

The doctor said, "If I were to open your door, let you out, what would you like to do first?"

Tennant glared up at the camera, at the speaker. "Please let me see my sister. You promised..."

The red dot blinked.

"Soon."

CHAPTER SIXTY-THREE

MARTHA

DR. FITCH LOOKED UP as Martha stormed into the room with Fraser close behind. "Ah, Dr. Chan. I think you'll find this very—"

She tried to lunge at him, but Fraser held her back. He'd been expecting it and grabbed her around the waist.

"You said you'd remain calm," Fraser said from behind, twisting around and pressing her tight against a wall.

Her feet were barely touching the ground. "This *is* me being calm!"

Martha quickly took everything in—Dr. Fitch was standing at a long desk with two other people, both dressed in scrubs. Nearly a dozen large monitors glowed around them displaying vital signs, the words SUBJECT 1 and SUBJECT 2 in bold white letters at the top. Two other monitors had a video feed—

Tennant in one room, Sophie in another. Tennant was huddled down on the ground.

"What the hell are you doing?" Martha growled.

Dr. Fitch's eyes went nervously from her to Fraser, then back again. "Dr. Chan, you must understand our current circumstances are extraordinarily unique and call for unprecedented measures. We have less than four hours to determine a means of stopping the advance of this infection, and these two subjects may be our only chance at insight or clarity into how the infection spreads." He paused for a second, considering his words. "I know this isn't an infection in the traditional sense, but that's the simplest way for me to describe what's happening to those I report to, so I've taken to calling it that. As a medical doctor, I'm sure you—"

Martha spit at him.

She'd never in her life spit on anyone and could think of no one more deserving than this squirmy little man.

Unfortunately, she missed.

Dr. Fitch took a step back anyway. "I could use another pair of skilled hands, but if you're going to let emotions blind you, you're useless to me. We don't have time for it."

From behind her, Fraser whispered, "He's got the president's ear, and I'm under orders to follow his instructions. If you want to help the girls, you need to control yourself."

Martha fought the urge to kick Fraser, break away, and take another rush at Fitch, but she knew he was right. They'd haul her out of here, and she'd never see these two girls again. Finally, she relented and nodded softly. "Okay. I promise."

Fraser released her slowly. Martha stepped away from him and slowly circled the room, studying the monitors. On one, Tennant huddled on the floor in the corner of a room, nothing more than a cell, her face buried in her hands. On the other, Sophie was standing at the center of a similar room, slowly rocking back and forth, shifting her weight from one foot to the other and back again. Other monitors displayed their vitals. Although elevated, Tennant's appeared normal. Sophie's hadn't changed much since she'd last checked—blood pressure well beyond normal and a body temperature of 100.2. She was breathing in long, thick gasps, but they didn't seem as erratic as earlier, as urgent. "What are her current medications?"

Dr. Fitch remained at a distance, eyeing her warily. "Nothing. I felt it was important to observe her without any external interference."

"You mean you felt it was more important to let this... infection... run its course rather than attempt to save this girl's life," Martha stated.

"While the medications you administered may have appeared to hold the infection at bay, I think they may have been doing more harm than good. With each dose, I noticed a marked increase in her body's reaction, as if the infection stepped up to combat the medications. Her liver, kidneys, all vital organs were being taxed beyond their capabilities, to near failure. When I discontinued, she leveled off...somewhat. Although the infection itself is also very damaging."

"She's still running a fever, and BP is high."

"Leveled off somewhat," he repeated. "She's still far from normal, but I don't believe her life is in danger anymore. At least, not at the moment."

On the monitor, Sophie continued to rock back and forth.

"How are you tracking their vitals?"

"Implants." He pointed at the back of his neck. "Right here. Painless, I assure you."

A phone on the wall rang. One of the men in scrubs answered, listened for a moment, then handed the receiver to Fraser. He spoke softly, then hung up. To Martha, he said, "I need to get back to the president. Can I trust you here?"

She nodded.

His eyes lingered reluctantly on her for a moment longer. Then he left the room, pulling the heavy door shut behind him.

When he was gone, Dr. Fitch continued, "I asked for an fMRI machine less than an hour ago. It's a Corean Level 4—last I heard, those were still in the testing phase and the only working model was in Israel, yet, they found one and it's already on base."

She'd only read about functional MRI, or fMRI, a machine that measures brain activity by detecting changes associated with blood flow and metabolic function. It would allow them to monitor the effects of the noise on brain chemistry itself, even beyond the three-dimensional picture they would see with traditional MRI or a CAT scan.

He crossed the room and tapped several keys on one of the keyboards. "You need to watch this."

Martha stepped over to the monitor. An image of Tennant filled the screen. The time stamp read about fifteen minutes earlier.

Fitch asked, "Are you familiar with antiphase technology?"

Martha shook her head.

"It's the core principle behind noise-canceling headphones. You take a sound, any sound, and invert the phase, basically create an opposite or a negative version of the sound, then play it back at the same amplitude as the original. The two cancel each other out so neither can be heard. What you're about to see is a recording of us playing the noise you recovered in Barton. We've implemented antiphase technology, so the subject can hear it, but we can't. This allows us to hear what's happening in the room without the negative impact of the anomaly's noise present."

"Her name is Tennant, not the subject."

"Tennant, right."

He pressed Play, and the video ticked forward. About ten seconds in, a message flashed across the bottom of the screen—ANOMALY RECORDING INITIATED.

Martha watched in horror as the girl screamed for her sister, tried to shield herself from the sound, and collapsed in the corner of the room, blood trickling out from her eyes, nose, and ears. The poor girl must have been in horrible pain. Martha wanted to tell him to turn it off, to stop, but that would do no good—what she was watching had already taken place.

Fitch said, "Exposure to the noise ultimately rendered her unconscious for twelve minutes. I'm going to fast-forward."

The time stamp sped up, and when Tennant stirred, Fitch pressed Play again and returned to normal speed. Martha heard Dr. Fitch ask her what she would do if he opened the door; Tennant only pleaded to see her sister.

"How is that helpful?" Martha asked. "You're torturing her. You realize that, right?"

Fitch didn't respond. Instead, he loaded up a second video, this one of Tennant's sister. "Watch how this sub . . . Sophie . . . reacts to the same exposure."

As she had been in the live feed, Sophie stood in the center of the room, slowly rocking. She didn't appear to be looking at anything in particular. Although her eyes shifted back and forth, Martha got the impression the girl's thoughts weren't focused on the room itself but elsewhere. As if caught up in a daydream or unaware of her surroundings. Her mind in some far-off place. Sophie's lips were moving, but Martha couldn't make out what she was saying. "Can you turn it up?"

Fitch reached for the volume and increased it to the maximum.

Martha still couldn't make out her mumblings.

The anomaly recording message flashed.

"The noise playback starts here," Fitch said.

Sophie's head jerked up, twisted from side to side. Then she smiled, this sly, peculiar grin.

Martha shivered as a coldness crept up her spine.

"Annna Shiiimmmm," Sophie said softly, her head nodding. "My Annnnnaaaa Shimmm."

Her feet and legs began to move faster. She ran to one corner of the room, then to the other, back again. She started to circle the room with ungodly speed. Her vitals were superimposed over the corner of the screen, and Martha watched the girl's heart rate increase to dangerous levels; BP, too. The girl somehow ran faster. She ran directly into one of the walls, then without hesitation, she turned and ran back in the opposite direction, crashed into the other wall.

Martha's hands covered her mouth. "Oh, my god."

Fitch paused the video. "There's no need to watch

more. She stopped the moment the anomaly recording did." He rewound the video to the beginning and pressed Play again.

Sophie mumbling.

"Best we can tell, she's rattling off names in quick succession," he explained. He stopped the video and returned to the live feed. "Still is. We think they're names of the infected, but we have no idea how she would know them—at least five match residents of Barton." He removed his glasses and wiped the lenses with his tie, then put them back on. "It's too early to be sure, but I believe the older one may be building up some kind of tolerance with each exposure. Similar to receiving a flu shot—her body is adapting, learning to fight back. While the sound itself is still highly unsettling and painful to her, her physiological responses appear to be lessening. Her sister has obviously adapted as well, but in a very different manner. Frankly, I find her reactions... disturbing." He added, "I think all of this may be related to their initial exposure. Something about their initial exposure was different from all those who simply joined the horde."

Martha couldn't watch the videos again. All she could think about was her own children back home, the growing horde. Finally, she said, "I need to see them."

CHAPTER SIXTY-FOUR

MARTHA

MARTHA TOLD DR. FITCH to wait in the other room. She didn't want either girl to see him right now.

When the door swung open, Tennant shrunk deeper into the corner, away from the opening, her eyes frantically glancing around. Martha got the unsettling feeling she was looking for some kind of weapon.

Martha held her hands up and slowly stepped inside. "I'm so sorry, Tennant. I had no idea he would do that to you. I never would have left you and your sister alone with him if I had."

Tennant's eyes narrowed, and she glared at her as she scurried deeper into the corner. "They shot Sophie! You said we'd be safe!"

"From what I was told, Sophie attempted to escape, and they sedated her," Martha said softly. "Had she reached that outer fence and somehow got through it, or over it, she'd be gone right now. Maybe forever.

I'm sure it was difficult for you to witness that, but they saved your sister. She's not well. You don't want to lose her, do you?"

"I want to go home," Tennant fired back. "I want to take Sophie and go back home to Momma and Poppa, to the mountain. They won't know how to find us. They don't know where we are. We were safe at the mountain!"

"Your sister was dying, Tennant. I know it may not seem like it, but those soldiers saved your lives. The treatment your sister received, that saved her life. Whatever happened back at the mountain to your village, it happened again, multiple times. If you were still there, you would have gotten caught up in it. You'd be gone now, both of you. You're safe here, with us. With me."

"How do you know it won't find us here?"

Martha didn't know and she didn't want to lie to this girl. "I don't."

"Then let us go home."

Martha eased down onto the floor and sat beside her. "Can I show you something?"

Tennant nodded.

One of the orderlies handed Martha a laptop. She lifted the screen and angled it toward Tennant. "I'm not supposed to show you this, but I'm going to anyway. I don't care what they do to me. I want you to understand what we're dealing with. I think you're old enough to understand. What's happening right now is bigger than just you and your sister, bigger than all of us. You may find it difficult to watch, so if you need me to turn it off, just tell me, okay?"

Tennant nodded.

Martha spent the next ten minutes showing her all the video footage they had accumulated, including the one from Barton. With that one, she left the sound on and made careful note of Tennant's reaction. Fitch had been right; the noise didn't seem to bother Tennant as much as it affected both her and the orderly standing in the room.

When the final video ended, she let the silence hang in the room for a moment before speaking again. "We don't fully understand why, but you and your sister weren't affected by the anomaly the same as all these other people. Both of you seem to be building up a tolerance, although in very different ways, and understanding that tolerance could provide someone like me with the information I need in order to help all the other people who have been affected."

When Tennant finally spoke, she sounded much younger than her sixteen years. "Do you think Momma and Poppa are part of that group?"

Martha thought of the crevasse. All the bodies they'd pulled out of that hole were now baking in a tent back at Zigzag. She looked down at her hands, because she couldn't say this part to the girl's face—what needed to be said. "They very well might be. Others from your village, too. If you help me, I may still be able to help them." This was probably a lie, but Martha had no choice. She needed this girl to cooperate.

"What happens if they reach Gresham?"

The Army will never let them reach Gresham.

Martha turned to her. "We don't have much time."

Tennant seemed to consider all of this. While her concern fell primarily with her sister and her family, Martha could tell she understood the bigger ramifications of what was happening. "Okay."

Martha felt a flood of relief wash over her, because there was one other thing she hadn't told Tennant. If Tennant and her sister didn't help voluntarily, the president and those in charge would most likely instruct Fitch to continue anyway.

Martha got to her feet and reached a hand out to Tennant. "Let's go see your sister."

Sophie was two doors down.

Three soldiers were positioned outside her door, and they grew noticeably tense when Martha asked them to step aside so they could go in. She knew Fitch had been watching her speak to Tennant on the monitor, and she was certain he had also talked to these soldiers. Luckily, he was smart enough to stay out of sight. Martha had no idea how Tennant or Sophie would react if either girl saw him, and she really didn't want to find out. There was no time for that.

Sophie was still standing in the middle of the room, still mumbling names. She looked up at them as they entered, her hands balled into tight fists. "Tennnnnant."

Tennant went to her and threw her arms around her sister's neck. Sophie let her, but didn't reciprocate. She kept her arms at her sides, her eyes filled with suspicion and locked on Martha. Tennant leaned closer and whispered in her sister's ear. Martha couldn't make out the words, and she found herself looking up at the camera, wondering if the same person who had been reading Sophie's lips was also deciphering what Tennant had just said.

When Tennant stepped away from Sophie, the younger girl blinked several times. She unclenched her fists, flexed her fingers.

In the hallway, Martha had swapped out the laptop for a tablet. The screen detailed vitals for both girls, fed by the implants in the back of their necks.

Tennant had told her the headache she'd felt immediately after exposure to the noise had faded away. According to her vitals, aside from a slightly elevated blood pressure, she was normal. Sophie's temperature had stabilized around 102.

Martha reached for Sophie's hand. She let her take it. Didn't pull away.

"I'm going to help you," Martha said.

CHAPTER SIXTY-FIVE

FRASER

THE FEELING ABOARD AIR Force One was thick, palpable. Although the plane was spacious, Fraser couldn't help but feel claustrophobic, trapped inside the cylinder. He'd been here, stationary, for the better part of a day.

He kept looking at his watch and thinking about the two-hour time limit Holt had imposed on the scientific teams. During his initial briefing, he'd been instructed to limit excursions near 45-121 to two hours as well. Nobody had told him why. As a soldier, he hadn't asked, only followed his orders. To no one in particular, he asked, "What time did Air Force One arrive here on base?"

The president looked up at him, exhausted. His eyes had sunk deep into their dark sockets, his hair ruffled and unkempt. General Westin didn't look much better. Neither did Samantha Troy, the acting director of the NSA. She was on a phone in the corner of the room. The president's deputy press secretary had excused herself to one of the bedrooms to fight off a migraine. Shortly after, the president had ordered nearly everyone else out of the room, too. Along with Lieutenant Colonel Fraser, only the three of them remained. The rest had moved to other portions of the plane and regrouped, most in the guest and press areas near the rear of the aircraft. The president offered his private office to Cardinal Kitzmiller. He was in there now with that scientist from NOAA, Dr. Harbin.

The president said, "We arrived at 1300. Why? Concerned about the window?"

"Should I be?"

General Westin exchanged a look with the president, then waved a dismissive hand. "You're on board the most secure aircraft in existence, housed within one of our country's best-defended bases. There is nothing to worry about."

Fraser said nothing.

General Westin continued. "The fact that we've been here for more than four hours is testament to that."

"I only bring it up because I was told to adhere to a two-hour window when first deployed. If you're not concerned, then I won't be, either."

"I've been assured this aircraft is a hundred percent

soundproof. Even if the anomaly were somehow able to strike here on base, it wouldn't get past the exterior of the plane," the president said. "Aside from that, we know where the horde is and where they're going."

Fraser nodded.

Several satellites had been repositioned and were transmitting images of the horde in near real time to one of the monitors on the wall. At their current speed, they would reach Gresham in a little less than four hours. The military had been deployed and had attempted to evacuate some of the smaller towns and cities along the way, but that had done little good. The moment the horde encountered them, the soldiers broke from ranks, joined the horde, and began to run. They were lost. Further deployments were kept at a ten-mile distance from the horde, but that proved ineffective as well—as civilians were evacuated and relocated, the horde shifted direction, adjusted just enough to target the new location. The horde somehow sensed large groups of people and was drawn to them like a moth to flame. Forcing people to relocate to evacuation centers only created more viable, condensed targets. Grew the horde faster. Airlifts were the only way to get people out of harm's way, and there was no way to transport all those in their path. Even if they could, it wouldn't keep the horde from reaching Gresham or another large city. At best, they'd only slow them down. In just the past two hours, the size of the horde had increased to at least a hundred and twenty thousand. The towns left in its wake had been decimated.

"Sir, I know this isn't what you want to hear, but I don't see any alternative but some type of clinical strike," General Westin said.

"You mean kill them, General," the president fired back. "Let's not sugarcoat. Don't call them actors, don't call this a theater. I want you to be perfectly clear—you want to kill American citizens."

"I see no other alternative." He stood and went to the monitor. "Eagle Creek, Dover, Springwater—each of these towns will add another three to four thousand to their total number. There are dozens more little towns just like these between the horde's current location and Gresham. We continue to feed it, the monster just grows stronger. Soon the size will become completely unmanageable, and a strike will be off the table, too. We need to act while we still have a window—thin their numbers, weaken this beast."

"Hypothetically, you do that," the president replied. "Let's say you wipe out every last one of them. How does that prevent the anomaly, that sound, from striking again? We could have a new horde in a matter of hours. You commit mass genocide, and we're right back here again looking at the same scenario. Looking at killing more Americans."

"We buy time, Mr. President. We secure several more hours and possibly come up with another solution in those hours. Right now, this is all we've got, and we need to act."

In the corner of the room, Samantha Troy hung up the phone and looked back at them grimly. "Attempts at discrediting the reports in the media and online aren't working. We're picking up chatter from intelligence agencies—they're beginning to see this as a threat."

Everyone in the room understood what this meant, but the general spelled it out anyway in an attempt to drive his point home. "If we wait much longer, someone other than you may decide a strike is necessary to protect their own population."

"You think China or Russia would start a war over this?"

Samantha Troy said, "They've both repositioned satellites to get a better look. Israel, too. Several European countries as well. It's too early to fully understand how they'll react, but I think the general may be right—if these other countries are having similar discussions to ours—realizing the horde could reach unmanageable proportions after absorbing the population of a major city—and they feel we haven't acted adequately to resolve the problem, they may decide we're unable or unwilling to solve the situation. That's when they're most likely to act, do whatever they feel is in their own best interest."

"Sir," General Westin interrupted. "If one of them acts, I can guarantee they won't do so with the precision we're capable of. Loss of life would most likely be far larger. We'd see collateral damage well beyond those who are infected."

The president rose and went to one of the windows, looked out into the hangar. "Dr. Fitch wants to catch one."

"And, what, waste more time studying it?" General Westin scoffed. "He's got both those girls in a cage and hasn't learned anything."

Without turning, the president replied, "He feels those girls weren't infected at the same level as the others. He thinks that may lead us to a possible inoculation. He also thinks the entire group is acting with some sort of hive mind and the only way we can fully understand that mind is to capture a member of the horde. He wants to approach this from two directions—an inoculation from the girls, and stop the horde from within; take out the hive."

"We have less than four hours," the general reiterated. "There is no time."

The president didn't reply, only stared out the window.

CHAPTER SIXTY-SIX

MARTHA

MARTHA STOOD ON THE tarmac with Harbin and several others and watched Air Force One climb into the sky and disappear from view. Something about that moment made her feel desperately alone. The president, the people on that plane—they should have inspired confidence, strength. Instead, all she could think about were the worried looks on their faces as the door closed. It felt as if they were fleeing.

How do you outrun a sound?

Fraser came up behind them, and when Martha turned, she noticed he wasn't watching the plane but was staring down at the ground, his face filled with concern.

"What is it?" she asked him, keeping her voice low. "Where's Fitch?"

"In the lab, studying some of the tissue samples from Mount Hood."

Fraser looked defeated. "There's no easy way to say this, so I'm going to just come right out with it. We lost contact with Zigzag several hours ago. I sent in a recon team... we've got six dead, everyone else is gone, missing. The walls we built around the camp have been breached in several places. They didn't find any expended rounds, no evidence of a firefight. Whatever happened, happened fast."

Harbin's mouth fell open.

Martha felt her heart sink.

Joy Reiber.

Russel Fravel.

Brenna Hauff.

Brian Tomes.

Their only other survivor, Raina Caddy.

When she spoke, her voice cracked. "How is that possible? The horde is miles away, heading in the opposite direction—they're nowhere near Zigzag anymore. Could it be something else?"

Fraser was slowly shaking his head. "Most likely they experienced a recurrence of the original anomaly, one of those 'aftershocks' Dr. Harbin mentioned. An echo." He went quiet for a moment, forming his words carefully. "The breaks in the walls... they were breached from the inside out. They weren't attacked or overrun like those videos we watched. We think the noise infected our people and they fled the camp on foot, same as that initial village. Their tracks tell us as much. We're attempting to locate them with heat signatures, but the tree cover on the mountain is so thick we haven't been able to pinpoint anyone. We suspect they're heading west, following a similar path as the original group, but there's no way to be sure." He looked up at both their faces in turn. "We're on our own here now."

Harbin asked, "Are we safe here? On this base?"

Fraser didn't answer. He didn't have to.

Martha thought of Air Force One disappearing into the sky. When she looked back up, the plane was gone. The wind had picked up the contrails, smudging their tracks. In a moment, those would be gone, too.

Harbin said, "Cardinal Kitzmiller told me tensions with foreign governments have grown substantially in the past several hours and the president isn't returning phone calls. He's been off-grid now for the better part of a day. That's making a lot of people nervous."

Martha tried to rationalize. "It makes sense for him to remain mobile. I wouldn't sit in the White House, either."

"The cardinal also said procedures dictate the president should be in the air prior to launching an air strike or if the imminent threat of a strike from a foreign body exists."

"Launch an air strike?" Martha frowned at Fraser. "He wouldn't attack those people, would he?"

Fraser didn't answer her. Instead, he looked at Harbin. "What else did the cardinal tell you? Your meeting lasted nearly as long as mine with the president."

Harbin shuffled his feet. "He's convinced this is the act of some higher power. Some kind of reckoning or global cleansing. He believes military options will prove ineffective and it will only be a matter of time before the president realizes regardless of what he does, the outcome of this situation is beyond his control."

"And what do you think?"

Harbin shrugged. "I may be a man of science, but I try to keep an open mind. I'm willing to accept there is far more in this universe we don't understand than that which we do."

"Even demons?" Martha said.

With this, Harbin let out an uncomfortable chuckle. "The Old Testament is an odd thing. Much like the New Testament, I find it to be an interesting read, but whether it is fact or fiction is not for me to decide. There are some interesting distinctions, though. In the Old Testament, although the God we recognize today is depicted as the one who created the world, the 'true God,' the God of the Old Testament is not consistently presented as the *only* God who exists. That is something that changed or evolved between both Testaments. The Old Testament abounds with others, Anahshim . . . the god of Tahor being another."

"Tahor?" Fraser repeated.

"Loosely translated, it means *pure*."

"The God of Pure."

Harbin nodded. "Or the God of *Cleansing*, as the cardinal alluded to. What I find fascinating is that all religions have a similar deity. All walks of life. The Hindus have Shiva, also known as the Destroyer. Cherokee Indians have Uyaga. Even Islamic texts, which in current form preach a single God, much like the New Testament, have ninety-nine different names for God, or Allah. Over the years, those names have evolved to become attributions rather than individuals, as if many deities became one. In those earlier writings, they have al-Mumit, the Bringer of Death. Whether you believe religion to be gospel or a complete fabrication, all seem to share similar origins. As if each of these ancient texts or ideologies came from a singular, much older, source. From a time before our current records."

He paused for a second and studied the ground. "Even if you put religion aside and focus purely on science, modern humans have only existed on this planet for two hundred thousand years or so. The planet itself is 4.543 *billion* years old. The universe is 13.8 billion years old. It's naive to think this planet is ours. We're merely the latest short-term residents. To ignore the possibility that something far older than us or our understanding has possibly returned to reclaim Earth would be equally naive. That is what the cardinal believes as well. That is what he is communicating to the president." He sighed. "None of this provides answers, only more questions. And it's answers the president needs right now, if we have any hope of avoiding a military solution."

Behind them, about halfway down the tarmac, two large helicopters with twin blades came to life. Troop carriers. The blades quickly gained speed with a loud and steady *whoop, whoop, whoop*.

"The president authorized me to try and capture one of the horde," Fraser said flatly. "Fitch convinced him we need a live sample. Someone fully infected, not half-baked like that little girl."

"Sophie."

"Sophie, right." He repeated her name, but his mind was elsewhere. No doubt thinking about what he was about to attempt. "In four hours, that horde will reach Gresham and potentially double in size. This may be our last chance to try and control this."

Martha stood in silence, not sure what else to say. She wasn't sure they ever had this under control.

As Fraser turned and started toward the helicopter, Harbin shouted over the growing noise. "Are you sure about Zigzag? They're all . . . gone?"

Fraser stopped midstep, turned half toward him, and nodded softly.

CHAPTER SIXTY-SEVEN

FRASER

WITH A TOP SPEED of 196 miles per hour, the two Boeing CH-47 Chinook helicopters made quick work of the distance between McChord Air Force Base and the horde, now just a little more than two hours outside the city of Gresham, Oregon.

Strapped into his seat in the lead chopper, Fraser's hand drifted down to the item in the pocket of his fatigues. His recon team had recovered the small hard drive back at Zigzag. If not for the crushed remains of a laptop above it in the dirt, it might have been lost completely. Air Force One had been gone by the time his team had returned and given it to him. He told himself that's why he didn't turn it over directly to the president and his superiors on board, but that didn't justify why he hadn't told the president or his commanding officer that they had recovered it.

He hadn't told anyone.

Not yet.

He would.

As soon as he determined *who* he could tell.

He'd only had time to review a few of the videos from Frederick Hoover, but that had been enough for him to realize the significance of this find. It also raised a serious concern—there was no way the president wasn't aware of DARPA's findings, not if Holt had had this. Surely Samantha Troy, as acting director of the NSA, knew. Why hadn't any of it been discussed aboard Air Force One? Was the president keeping this information from his senior staff? Or worse—was his senior staff keeping it from the president?

He'd have to figure all that out when he returned to McChord. For now, he had a job to do. "Distance to the horde?" he said into his microphone.

"Twelve-point-six miles, sir. A little over three minutes," the pilot replied.

"Maintain a ten-mile radius and circle around to the front of them. We don't want to risk getting caught up in their audio backwash."

"Copy that."

"Sir, I'm already picking up the noise."

This came from a soldier across from Fraser on the opposite bench, his face buried in a laptop. He looked to be no more than twenty-three or -four. Brown eyes and shaved head. He wasn't a Ranger, but Fraser recognized him—he had worked with the communications officer once before in Afghanistan. His name was Mertz. He was frowning.

"What is it?"

Mertz continued to stare at the screen. "The sound emanating from the horde is measuring at 190 decibels."

Prior to leaving McChord, Fraser had been told satellite readings confirmed the horde was somehow generating a noise comparable to the ones recorded in Barton. They had also recorded a similar sound with listening devices placed throughout Zigzag. They hadn't determined *how* the horde was generating the noise, only that they were. Somehow that sound grew with their numbers as if emanating from the members themselves like human speakers.

"That's damn loud," Fraser said.

Mertz hesitated, then said, "Theoretically, no sound on earth can exceed 194 decibels due to a natural limit. Air pressure can't drop below a vacuum, so the loudest possible sound would be a pressure wave oscillating between vacuum and plus two atmospheres. To the best of my knowledge, that's never occurred naturally, only in a lab. For this group of people to somehow create a sound so close to physical limits is...well...unheard of." He picked up the modified headphones sitting beside him on the bench and studied the speaker inside one of the cans. “I’m not sure these will be a hundred percent effective.”

“I’ve been assured they will be.”

“They’re using antiphase. That means they have to produce a sound of equal and opposite levels in order to cancel it out completely. At best, these max out at 120 decibels. That won’t be enough. We’ll still hear... something.”

“But it *will* limit our exposure, correct? Take the noise down to a safe level?”

“A typical conversation, the volume you’re hearing me at right now, is about sixty decibels. A chainsaw is around 120. What we’ll hear will fall somewhere in between. I’m not sure what would be considered a *safe* level. Will this be loud enough to damage our hearing? No. Will it be loud enough to infect us? That I can’t answer.”

There were nine Army Rangers on each helicopter. Six teams of three. Each in heavily armored body gear. Hard men who had seen their share of combat. While none said anything, they’d all heard this entire conversation, and several looked uneasy. It was one thing to face a known enemy on a battlefield, look them in the eye, a tangible target. These soldiers were being asked to capture American citizens while combating a sound. An intangible, invisible thing.

Fraser looked down the length of the helicopter’s interior. He studied each of their faces. “All of you were briefed before we left McChord. You know exactly what is at stake, and you know what we've been asked to do. The technology is what it is. This is the best we've got. It's *all* we've got. That said, if any of you are having second thoughts and don't want to participate, I understand. We can set down right here and let you out. In a moment, we'll be entering what is effectively a combat zone, and there will be no turning back. I'm going in, and I expect those on my right and left to be as fully committed as I am. You're Army Rangers, the best of the best, and your countrymen need you right now. Does anyone want to get off the bus?"

Nobody said a word.

"Good." He picked up his headphones from his lap. "Now, as Mertz said, these will limit our exposure. I've been told we'll be within safe levels. I've personally heard several recordings of the sound at levels near what our exposure down there will be, and I walked away without any lasting effects. That said, we need to move fast. I don't want any of us to risk exposure longer than necessary to complete our mission, and our mission is simple—we are to safely capture and return to McChord three infected members of the horde. More, if we can get them, but no less than three." He held up his headphones. "Once these go on, they stay on. No exceptions. Not even for a second. They're linked to our communication system, and since we're using bone-induction microphones, we should have no problem hearing each other without worry of retransmitting the noise. If for some reason audio communication is compromised, go to hand signals or flares."

Fraser allowed that to settle in, then set down the headphones and picked up his weapon. "Each of you has been provided with a Pneu-Dart G2 X-Caliber assault rifle. This is the most powerful and accurate gas-based RDD projector ever built. While it may feel lighter than the weapons you're accustomed to carrying, make no mistake—it is effective, accurate, and versatile. They've been modified to hold five darts. Each dart is loaded with ten ccs of midazolam. That is three times the recommended dosage to take down a two-hundred-pound human. From shot to drop should be no more than ten seconds. Do not use more than one dart on a single target." He set down the gun and unclipped a large black cylinder from his belt—it looked like a heavy flashlight—and held it up. "Your secondary weapon is Lanthum Net Gun. This device will deploy a ten-by-ten net a distance of fifteen yards. Possibly farther, but at the cost of accuracy. You've got four shots total. Use them sparingly." He returned the net gun to his belt. "Work in teams of three—dart, zip-tie, prepare for transport. Fast, efficient. In and out. When you've got one, launch a green flare and the chopper will come to you. If for some reason you need emergency evac and communications aren't working, launch a red flare."

When Fraser looked up, he realized none of them were watching him anymore. All eyes were on the port-side windows. He stood and looked out.

Even from a distance of more than ten miles, the horde was clearly visible, a wide stampede sending thick plumes of dust up into the air. It was enormous.

They'd picked a location that was fairly flat and open, flanked on one side by the Sandy River on the north, a heavy tree line to the south, creating a choke point.

Over the open comm, Fraser said, "Chopper Two, hold back. Follow our lead. Maintain your cargo until I give the order to go to ground. We're going to take a run at this first."

"Understood."

To the pilot of his chopper, he said, "Circle around the front, keep your distance at no less than two miles. Each team will rappel out on the north shore of the river—I want to keep the water between our men and the horde. Three groups. One quarter of a mile between each. I don't want you in the thick of things until absolutely necessary."

The pilot nodded, then swapped out his headset for the same noise-canceling model the soldiers had.

CHAPTER SIXTY-EIGHT

FRASER

THE CHINOOK CIRCLED AROUND to the front of the seemingly endless horde and dropped each team of three two miles ahead of the mass of people. Fraser watched the last soldier go out the door. Then he moved to the edge, snapped into the line, and jumped. The moment he was on the ground and free of the line, the helicopter pulled up and right and banked away, increasing its distance. The second Chinook shot by and followed at a height about a thousand feet above the first.

Fraser's body armor was heavy but surprisingly flexible. It didn't limit movement as much as he'd expected. He checked his rifle, then unsnapped the decibel meter from his belt and activated it. The device was linked to the others:

TEAM 1—43dB
TEAM 2—31dB
TEAM 3—28dB

The ambient noise level was 36 decibels where he currently stood with the two Chinooks still trailing off in the distance. He heard none of it through his headphones. "All teams, stand by."

"This is Team One, we have visual."

Fraser said, "Keep the water between you and them. Take your shots carefully. Just tag 'em and bag 'em. Don't attempt to secure or remove your target until it's clear to do so. Wait for the rest of the horde to run by, if necessary."

"They're close. Less than a quarter mile. We're at 61 decibels now."

Fraser glanced down at his meter and watched their level tick up to 72, then 81. It continued to climb. The other teams as well. He was at 41.

"This is Team Two, we see them."

"Team Three here. Us, too."

Fraser could see the dark cloud of dust now, as if a thousand vehicles were driving across the dry dirt.

"I . . . I can't hear them, but I feel the ground vibrating. We're reading 120 decibels."

When Fraser looked back at his meter, Team 1 had ticked up to 141. All readers were over one hundred now, including his own, at 106.

"Do you guys hear it? It's like... someone screaming over a deep hum."

"Stay focused," Fraser said.

"My nose is bleeding."

Fraser wasn't sure who said that.

"Mine, too," someone else said.

"Stay focused!" Fraser repeated forcefully. "Team One, what's their distance?"

There was no response.

"Team One?"

He looked down at the meter. There was no longer a reading for Team 1. Team 2 was at 168 decibels, Team 3 was at 134. "Team One, do you copy?"

"This is Team Two, they're crossing the water."

Fraser quickly said, "How's that possible? It's too deep. Do you have visual on Team One?"

"No line of sight on Team One. They're just running into the water, trying to get to this side—trying to get to us. Holy hell, this is loud. Hurts. They're... if someone falls, slips, the others are just running over them. The bodies are just building up, creating a bridge. We need evac—this isn't going to—"

A red flare went up. Fraser wasn't sure if it came from the first team or the second.

The pilot broke in over the communication channel. *"Lieutenant Colonel, are we go for evac?"*

Fraser pulled the binoculars from his belt and scanned the horizon but couldn't see anything—he'd been dropped behind a slight bend in the river, and the trees blocked his view. The sky had grown dark, though, thick dust swirling above the tree line.

"Sir, they're crossing the water! They're— "

The voice cut out.

To the helicopter pilot, Fraser yelled, "Chopper One—Evac! Pick me up last—get our men out of there! We need to try something else!"

"Affirmative. Stand by. On approach."

Without hearing even a hint of the heavy aircraft, Fraser felt the large Chinook shoot up from behind him and fly over. It flew in low and fast, no more than fifty feet off the ground. The displaced air swirled and nearly knocked him off his feet as it zipped by. He held steady and watched the chopper disappear behind the bend.

Another red flare went up, arched over the trees, and faded away.

"All teams, sound off."

"Team Three here!" a voice shouted.

Nothing else.

Fraser said, "One and Two, respond."

Nothing.

The ground at Fraser's feet began to vibrate. When he was a kid, he used to stand on the train tracks, feeling the freight trains a mile or two away. He was reminded of that. He also remembered the pennies they would leave on those tracks—the paper-thin flattened pieces of copper they would find later. "Teams One or Two, respond."

Fraser heard a low hum. He'd forgotten the decibel meter in his hand. The display no longer reported a signal from the three teams. His own reading was at 151 decibels. "Chopper One, report."

A moment ticked by.

"No visual on One or Two . . . two members . . . of Three on board. Third . . . clipping in . . . now." The pilot sounded like he was in pain, his voice low and choppy. Forced.

About a quarter mile away, Fraser spotted the Chinook. It climbed above the tree line for a moment, then dipped back down. A second later, it was climbing again. Someone was dangling from the paracord at the open door. The chopper rocked unsteadily, climbed higher.

The hum grew, took on this high-pitched whine.

Fraser's decibel meter read 162 decibels.

He felt something wet on his upper lip, and when he touched it, he realized his nose was bleeding. He shuffled backward several steps, nearly tripped. "Pilot, get them out of there!"

The pilot didn't respond.

The hum, the noise, this horrible sound, grew louder.

The Chinook hovered for a moment, seemed to steady as the man beneath climbed the cord and reached the netting hanging from the door. An arm reached out and grabbed him, started to haul him in, then the Chinook tipped awkwardly—the front end shot up, the back dropped. The helicopter rocketed forward and up, nearly vertical, crested about five hundred feet above the trees, then rolled in the air—the nose came down, the back end wobbled above it. For one brief instant, it froze there, and Fraser thought they might be okay.

The helicopter came down hard, like a rocket set on embedding itself a thousand feet into the dirt. Fraser heard none of it over the growing noise, but the impact knocked him to the ground. A giant fireball burst up, igniting the dust-filled air.

He scrambled backward on his hands and feet, shuffled like a spider before spinning, getting up, and bursting into a full-out run in the opposite direction of the approaching horde, the butt of his rifle slapping against his chest. "Chopper Two—evac now! Evac now!"

No response.

"Chopper Two!"

The second Chinook came in fast, dangerously low. Someone threw a paracord out the door. The end smacked the ground and dragged, kicking up dirt and weeds. They slowed only a little as Fraser jumped for the line, got his left wrist around one end, gripped the cord, and fashioned a loop with his right hand above that, and pulled his bulk off the ground. He got his leg wrapped around the cord and secured himself as best he could while simultaneously shouting, "Go! Go!"

The Chinook whipped in a hard circle, the back end rolling past the front like a car in a slide on a drifting track. Fraser nearly lost his grip as he was jerked around beneath the aircraft, tossed nearly thirty feet from one side to the other.

As Fraser hauled himself up toward the open door and outstretched hands, he caught a glimpse below as the horde came around the trees and crested the small hill, some on the north side of the river, others on the south, some in the water. A thick mass moving forward, unhampered by anything in their path. Twisted pain-filled faces staring blankly forward. He felt the heat of them, all those bodies. As the sound burned at his ears, he fought the insatiable urge to let go, fall, and join them.

CHAPTER SIXTY-NINE

FRASER

SEVERAL HANDS GRABBED HIM, pulled him over the lip of the Chinook's doorway, and dragged him to the center of the aircraft, where Fraser collapsed in an exhausted heap. His hands went to the headphones, started to pull them off, and two of the soldiers batted his fingers away. When he looked up into their faces, they were pale, eyes wide with fright. Blood trickled down from their noses, their ears. One of them had blood in his eye.

The helicopter banked hard, and he rolled across the floor. Then they shot forward and up, increasing the distance between them and the horde as quickly as possible.

Fraser didn't remember passing out, but he did. Only for about a minute, maybe less. The noise told him so—the loud, grating scream that threatened his very sanity vanished with a shudder of his eyes.

All-encompassing one moment, gone the next, nothing left behind but a cold, empty void not unlike the day after a migraine. When his eyes opened again, he found nine new faces staring down at him from the benches of the second Chinook, and his stomach twisted into a knot as he realized what happened to the nine men who had been with him in the other helicopter.

He forced himself to sit up, got to his feet, and made his way to the front of the aircraft on wobbly legs, holding on to the netting fixed to the ceiling for support.

When he reached the pilot, the man didn't look up at him. His gaze remained fixed on the horizon. Blood had dripped out from the bottom of his headphones to the shoulder of his fatigues—three little red drops.

"Report," Fraser managed to say, his throat horribly dry.

"What do you remember, sir?"

Fraser remembered more than he wanted to. "We lost contact with all three ground teams in rapid succession. Chopper One went in for evac. I saw them go down."

"Permission to speak freely, sir?"

Fraser waved an impatient hand at him.

"Best I can tell, they just got too close. I've known Cory, their pilot, since training at Rucker. Prior to going in, we agreed to switch to B-channel and run the letters. Do you know what that is?"

Fraser shook his head.

"When the first helicopter pilot flew over Chernobyl, his superiors hadn't told him how dangerous it would be. He was actually assured it *wouldn't* be dangerous. All the pilots had their suspicions, though. They'd seen what happened to the first responders, heard the stories. There was little choice—they needed to drop sand on the reactor, slow the meltdown. They understood the mission was far more important than their own lives. In order to succeed, they needed to fully understand where they could fly and where they couldn't. They weren't given any type of radiation meter. Radiation is invisible. They had nothing to go on, so they worked out a simple system. Each pilot agreed to repeat the alphabet over an open channel as he flew over the hot zone. On the ground, other pilots charted their progress. If their superiors were telling them the truth, nobody would be the wiser. If something happened, the other pilots hoped to use the data when determining future routes. They all knew they'd be flying into that fallout zone sometime soon. Most likely, repeatedly. The very first pilot, he drifted a little too close to the blown reactor, his voice started to falter, he started skipping letters, then went down. It all played out in a few seconds. He managed to get to the letter *R*.

Cory, when he flew over the horde to try and evac those teams, he only got to *G*. He struggled through those last couple letters. I could hear the pain in his voice. He tried, sir. He did his best."

"I'm sure he did."

The pilot continued, "When I went in for you, I got a few letters past that, but I gotta be honest, sir. Another twenty seconds and I might have ended up on the ground, too. I've got no memory of turning us around. I snapped back a little before you probably woke up. Muscle memory flew us out of there, not me."

"Your skill got us out of there."

The pilot reached over and flicked several switches on a panel to the right of his seat. "The men in back, me, the ones we just lost—we all understand the importance of this mission. We knew going in not everyone would make it back. I'm only telling you all this so you understand our limitations, *my* limitations in particular. If I fly us back into that thing, and I have no doubt I'll need to do that, I may not be able to get us back out if we're there beyond the letter *J*. And for this mission to succeed, I *need* to get us out of there. I need to get us back to base, future cargo intact."

He eased the stick slightly to the right, maneuvered a pedal, and the Chinook turned slowly as it hovered in the air. Two miles off in the distance, the horde came back into view, swinging in from left to right across the windshield as they turned. The sheer size of the mass was jaw-dropping. The fast-moving group stretched for nearly half a mile, a black stain on the earth. Dark dust loomed above and behind, this giant rooster tail so thick, visibility was probably nonexistent behind them.

"Can this chopper fly in that?"

"The dust?"

Fraser nodded.

"A Chinook can fly in damn near anything, sir."

He had an idea.

CHAPTER SEVENTY

FRASER

FRASER TOLD THE PILOT to circle to the far end and come in on the tail side of the horde. He did so with an incredibly wide arc. The decibel meters were useless inside the loud Chinook, but that didn't really matter. They could all *feel* the horde, the now familiar pressure on the inner ear that grew to inscrutable pain as they drew near. The pilot maneuvered the chopper in such a way to test those external limits: slowly drifting closer until both he and Fraser felt the slightest tickle in their ears, then moving in closer still, in short hops, plotting out distances and their corresponding pain levels. Because of the fast-moving nature of the horde, this has proven impossible while on the ground—nobody had gotten close enough and escaped the pull of the group—but the helicopter provided a unique vantage. They learned even with their modified headphones, the call of the horde began to affect them at about a half mile out. At a quarter mile, they could still tolerate the pain, probably a seven on a scale from one to ten, equatable to a severe migraine, but any closer than that and things got dicey. That was a problem, because they obviously needed to get much closer.

"What about autopilot?" Fraser asked. "Can you program in a route that takes us down and over the horde, holds above there for maybe thirty seconds or a minute, then pulls back out to a safe distance?"

"I thought about that, but we need to get too close to the ground. May need to execute precise maneuvers when we're there. We've got trees everywhere, and the horde itself is moving. There are too many factors, too many variables. What if we still have men on the ground when the autopilot is programmed to pull back out? If we needed to execute a maneuver at altitude, maybe autopilot would work, but I wouldn't trust it with such a low ceiling." The pilot's eyes were fixed on the horde. "I need to do this. Get us in, hover long enough for you to capture your cargo, then get us back out. I don't see any other way."

Fraser had his binoculars out. "The tail end is our best bet. The crowd is thinner in the back. Those people are slower, weak, injured. I'd be willing to bet the noise is weaker there, too. We come in from the back and the horde will be running away from us, too. They'll clear out even if we can't."

"Or they turn tail and run toward us like they did with the first three teams. They were willing to cross the water to get to them. They may come after us, too. When they sense us close."

Fraser knew he was right. They'd tripped over each other, some *died* trying to get to his teams. They were like sharks to blood.

"I could program in an auto evac on a trip-switch," the pilot thought aloud.

"Explain."

"Never mind." He was shaking his head. "It wouldn't work. Somebody would need to be conscious enough to hit the switch."

"Tell me anyway."

The pilot pointed to a bank of switches to the left of the throttle. "I program the autopilot with an altitude and coordinates away from the horde. We use one of these buttons to engage it. Push the button, the chopper goes up and high, then maneuvers to that waypoint and hovers. We treat it like an ejector seat in a jet, a last resort. But like I said, someone would need to be conscious enough to punch it, and you saw what happens when we get too close."

What Fraser *saw* was that they didn't have a choice.

Together, they hashed out a plan, and Fraser hoped to God it would work.

CHAPTER SEVENTY-ONE

FRASER

BOTH SIDE DOORS ON the Chinook were open. Of the nine soldiers, four crouched at the edge of each opening. The men on the port side had their G2 X-Caliber pneumatic dart guns at the ready, the men aft were holding all eight net guns, one in each hand. Each net was secured by a cord to one of the rafters in the ceiling of the chopper. Although thin, these lines were designed to hold nearly a thousand pounds each. They'd spaced them out as best they could, wary of getting caught up in them.

Several of the soldiers had wrapped their heads and headphones with thick strips cut from cargo blankets and secured everything with duct tape, the pilot included. Whether the added protection would help was yet to be seen. It certainly couldn't hurt. The ninth soldier was in the copilot's seat, not because he knew how to fly the chopper, but for the sole purpose of keeping a finger on the evac switch programmed by the pilot. If one of the two men saw the other pass out or become incapacitated, the other was to immediately hit that switch.

Fraser stood in the center of the cargo area between both sets of men, his dart gun in one hand and his fingers twisted into the netting on the ceiling for balance. "On my mark."

"Copy," the pilot replied. He had the Chinook at a right angle to the back of the horde a half mile away, visible through the open port-side door.

The dust and debris kicked up by the large crowd was so thick, the people themselves weren't visible. On some level, Fraser was thankful for that. "Go!"

Without hesitation, the Chinook shot toward the horde, moving sideways on its double blades as swiftly as if it were flying dead-on. Fraser felt the pressure from the noise almost immediately.

The pilot began rattling off the alphabet. "A... B...C..."

The dust hit them first. Fraser pulled a pair of goggles down over his eyes and covered his mouth with the neck of his shirt.

The lack of sound created by the headphones was very disorienting. He knew exactly how loud the Chinook was. He'd been in his share, and he imagined the engines were screaming right now, but he couldn't hear the helicopter at all. Nor could he hear his own breathing. There were only the subtle noises picked up by the soldiers' bone-induction microphones, the pilot speaking, and the quickly escalating sound of the horde's noise. That sound was somehow loud enough to cut through the thickest silence.

"D!"

Although the sun wouldn't complete its descent for at least another thirty minutes, the dust and grime in the air turned twilight into the deepest witching hour. Directional floodlights flicked on, beating back against the dark from the outer shell of the chopper, but they did little good, like using your high beams in a heavy fog.

"E!"

Fraser pinched his eyes shut for a moment, tried to will the noise away, but it only grew louder. The now familiar low hum was joined by this high-pitched wail, a keening, thousands of people crying out in horrible pain. He pinched his eyes shut tighter, tried to bury those voices beneath the black, but one by one their faces came to him, materializing from the shadows, racing forward toward him, bulging eyes wide and mouths agape—faces he knew—the people he left behind at Zigzag. The soldiers he just lost in the other helicopter. Soldiers he lost in past missions. In his mind's eye, his father ran toward him, arms stiff at his side, legs pumping like pistons, his screams joining the others.

"F!"

Fraser's eyes snapped open, and he realized he was screaming, too. Not just him, but some of the others, their voices picked up by their bone-induction microphones and mixed with those of the horde. He forced himself to stop even though the rest of his body welcomed it, craved the relief it brought. He wanted to move. Wanted to run. Every muscle in his bulky frame needed to flex as if he'd been sitting still for hours and finally had the opportunity to stand and stretch. He looked out the open door of the Chinook, surprised by just how close to the horde they now were, and fought back at the urge to jump. Oh, how wonderful it would be to leave the confines of this metal death trap for the open fields below, to run with all the others, to run for—

Anna Shim.

The name came to him, a whisper among all the screaming voices, and for a moment he wasn't sure if he actually heard the name or simply recalled it from the debriefs with that little girl they'd picked up on the mountain. That was when he heard it again and the voice that spoke that name sounded so calm, so serene, so . . . welcoming. A warm blanket on the coldest of nights. A beautiful woman smiling from across the room. A siren's song—and when that particular thought popped into Fraser's head, he also saw the image of an old ship. He thought it might be a schooner, turning toward a rocky shore, cracking against the stone and taking on water, all while the men looked on in stunned silence at a woman perched upon those rocks smiling back at them, beckoning them, come to Anna Shim.

"G!"

They were directly over the back end of the horde now, barely visible through the haze. The floodlights trying to cut through but only offering glimpses. Fraser watched as one of the soldiers jumped from the open door and fell from view. This quick moment played out like a scene from a movie, and for that brief instant, Fraser wasn't sure he actually saw it happen. Then his mind snapped into the present, and he realized there were only three men holding dart guns and four others behind him with the net weapons. He wanted nothing more than to go out the door behind that man, and that's when he realized all the soldiers were probably having similar thoughts, that was why they were easing toward the openings. He began to hit them. He didn't know what else to do. He worked his way through them as fast as he could, slapping some, punching others in their backs below their Kevlar, where they'd feel it. He jolted each of them out of their reveries, and in his headphones he heard their screams drop away from the noise, he heard each of them come back, regain control.

"Fire! All of you, fire!" Fraser shouted. "Fire now!"

They did.

He watched as white gas expelled from the dart guns, the adrenaline pumping through his body with such intensity all time seemed to slow. He saw the darts leave the guns soundlessly, saw them sail down toward the runners. As he went to the door, he watched several of those runners stumble and slow, try to regain their footing as other runners pushed past them, ran over them.

"H!" This came from the pilot in one long, drawn-out gasp, *aaaaytch,* and Fraser knew they didn't have much time.

The Chinook drifted forward over the horde, and the men with the net guns opened fire, too. He hoped they were aiming for the stragglers, those embedded with darts, but there was no way for him to be sure. He wasn't certain they could even see well enough to make that determination.

"I!"

As the nets deployed, several of the attached cords went taut. A cord near the back of the helicopter snapped tight against the shoulder of one of the men firing darts—the impact threw the man out the open door to the ground below. They weren't more than twenty feet up, but Fraser knew he was lost. If the fall didn't kill him, the stampeding feet around him surely would, and that end would be about as merciful as any.

Through the pain, confusion, and screaming in his head, Fraser shouted for everyone to reload and fire again—darts, nets, all of it. Several of the cords, tight like razor wire, dragged against the open doors, weighted down by whatever the nets had managed to grab. He caught a glimpse of at least two people wrapped up in the netting below, their arms and legs flailing wildly as they tried to escape.

He waited for the pilot to shout out the letter *J*, but that never came. He fell to the floor and rolled hard against one of the benches as the Chinook shot straight up into the air, then banked hard to the right.

Someone had pressed the emergency evac button.

CHAPTER SEVENTY-TWO

MARTHA

MARTHA SHIFTED HER WEIGHT on the metal bench and watched as Tennant ate her third helping of macaroni and cheese, second hot dog, and took another bite from a brownie before pausing only long enough to wash everything down with a swig from another can of Coke. The girl inhaled the food as if she hadn't eaten in a week. For all Martha knew, that might not be too far off from the truth.

Harbin lowered himself onto the bench beside her and handed the girl an apple from his tray. "When we find your parents, I at least want to be able to tell them we attempted to feed you well while you were in our care."

Tennant picked up the apple, rubbed it on her shirt, then took a large bite before setting it down and returning to the mac and cheese. "We're not gonna find my parents. You don't have to lie to me."

"I prefer to believe we will," Harbin replied, spooning out a bit of tomato soup.

Martha had the iPad sitting between them on the table. A live video feed of Sophie's room filled the screen. A moment ago, she'd been pacing the outer walls, circling the space again and again at a fast clip. Now she was standing still in the center of the room, her eyes on the ground and her head cocked slightly to the side.

"Your sister looks much better," Martha said.

Tennant glanced up at her but said nothing.

"She's still running a temperature and her blood pressure is high for her age, but otherwise her vitals are normal. I think she might be out of the woods."

Tennant's hand hovered over her tray for a moment, then swept down and scooped up a dinner roll. "She's got the devil in her. Ain't no amount of medicine gonna drive *him* out." She pushed the entire roll into her mouth with the tip of her finger, chewed twice, and swallowed.

Harbin took the roll off his tray and gave it to her. "What makes you say that?"

Tennant snorted like this was the stupidest question she'd ever heard. "What else could it be?"

Martha was about ready to agree with her.

She'd tested for everything else, why not the devil?

She and Fitch had spent the last two and a half hours running every test imaginable on both girls, everything came back negative. Nothing in their blood. Nothing visible on full-body CT scans or MRIs. Even the fMRI, the system Fitch had been certain would provide an answer, didn't pick up anything abnormal.

Her temporal lobe—the part responsible for understanding language, behavior, memory, and hearing—appeared slightly more active than baseline said it should be, but that would hardly account for her behavior. It certainly wouldn't explain her increased speed or strength. Sophie's cognitive functions seemed to be improving, but because she hadn't known either of these girls before, understanding what their *normal* might be was total guesswork. Although Tennant's language sometimes appeared clumsy, it was obvious to both Martha and Harbin she was intelligent. Tennant had told them different members of their village "schooled them" in different subjects, pulling from their own education and experiences before leaving what Tennant called *the rushed world* for a simpler life in the mountains. She had a solid handle on advanced mathematics, physics, even medicine.

When Fitch had been going over the results of Sophie's blood work, Tennant had pointed to Sophie's white blood cell count and sighed. "Not an infection. This would be elevated, right?" He and Martha must have looked shocked, because Tennant added, "Dr.

Baggins was with us for almost ten years. He said I had the makings of a doctor, so he'd been teaching me. He moved from Los Angeles after twenty years of practice in oncology. People think just 'cause we live in the mountains we're dumb. Ask me and I think anyone payin' thousands of dollars each month for rent, payin' for a car they gotta pay to park, payin' taxes, payin' for electric when God gives us solar for nothing, living off bottled water, they're the stupid ones. Our village might be the most beautiful place on earth, and living there is free but for some hard work and a little sacrifice."

Was, Martha had thought, but she didn't say anything.

Harbin hadn't touched much of his food. She caught him staring up at the clock on the back wall.

In less than an hour, the horde would reach Gresham, and they had no idea how to stop it. She felt like they should still be in the lab, but she wasn't sure what else she could do. She needed a quick break to regroup her thoughts. She needed sleep, too, but that certainly wasn't going to happen anytime soon.

"We should take some food back for Sophie," Tennant suggested. "Other than whatever she got through those IVs, she hasn't eaten at all. Even the devil's got to eat."

On the screen of the iPad, Sophie's head jerked up.

Her eyes darted anxiously about. Her nose wrinkled as she appeared to smell something.

Dr. Fitch appeared at the open doorway. He was slightly out of breath, as if he'd run there. He looked at both Harbin and Martha. "Lieutenant Colonel Fraser is back. You need to come with me."

CHAPTER SEVENTY-THREE

MARTHA

THE THREE OF THEM followed Fitch out the cafeteria to the Jeep he'd left running just outside the building. Harbin climbed in front, Martha and Tennant in back. Tennant had brought her extra roll and the remains of the brownie. She held them both out to Martha, who shook her head.

The girl made quick work of them before frowning down at the iPad on Martha's lap. "No signal."

She was right. The screen had gone blank. "Maybe it will pick back up once we get inside."

Harbin instinctively reached for a seat belt, realized there weren't any.

Martha asked, "Where are they?"

"Hangar off Tarmac 12. Hold on." Fitch dropped the Jeep into drive and they shot forward, loose chunks of blacktop crunching under their wheels.

Night had settled over the base, and with it came an

icy air. Part of her was thankful to be outside, away from the sterile stillness of the lab. The other part listened to the various noises all about, wondering when one of them might turn against her.

The base was larger than she had first thought. It took them nearly five minutes to get to the tarmac. As they rounded a corner and the open runways came into view, she spotted one of the helicopters about a quarter mile away, surrounded by bright lights and about two dozen people bustling about. At least half had weapons drawn. The other half appeared to be dragging something out of the cargo area and down a ramp at the back.

My God, they got one.

The Jeep skidded to a stop. Fitch left it running. "Come on."

Martha told Tennant to stay put and climbed out the back.

They found Fraser barking orders up at the soldiers on the helicopter ramp. There were three of them, each holding the end of a nylon cord and pulling it tight. At the center was a man in ragged clothes and one shoe, a torn net twisted around his frame. A broken zip-tie hung from his left wrist. His head swiveled as he glared at each of them with bulging eyes. Dark blood stained the sides of his face, and spit flew from his lips. Aside from deep, ragged breaths, he was oddly silent.

"Slow! Keep the ropes tight! Guide him down!" Fraser shouted. To Fitch, he said, "We put six darts in this one on the way back. That's on top of the three it took to bag him."

"That's—"

"Ninety ccs of midazolam over the past hour," Fraser finished for him. "Barely slowed him down. Pissed him off more than anything." They reached the bottom of the ramp, and Fraser pointed to the hangar behind him. "Put him next to the other two."

"You captured three?"

Fraser shook his head. "We got four. Come here." He quickly went up the ramp and disappeared inside the helicopter.

They followed after him. In the back corner was another net. Half the white nylon was stained red. Someone had tossed a green tarp over it but only covered about half. Beneath it all was a woman, probably in her fifties. The left side of her head was caved in, one eye ruptured, her wrists and ankles zip-tied. Martha knelt and checked for a pulse she didn't expect to find. The woman was obviously dead. Her skin was still hot to the touch, though. If she was anything like the ones they had back at Zigzag, her temperature would continue to rise. "What did you do to her?"

"We didn't do anything to her. Right after we got her secured, she started banging her head against the floor. We hit her with a few more darts, but like that other guy, that just aggravated her and she beat her head harder. There was nothing we could do." He dropped the tarp back over the woman.

Fitch let out a sigh. "We may still learn something from her."

Fraser turned on him, his face filled with frustration. "I sure as shit hope so, Doctor, because this little exercise of yours cost me the lives of thirteen men, and I can guarantee you, the ones who came back won't be the same. Not ever." He smacked the side of his head. "I can still hear them—we all can—that damn noise, their screaming, whatever the hell it is. It's stuck in here. It's not as loud as it was when we were near them, but it's still there. I can't get it out. And hearing it like that, all faint somewhere in the back of your head? That may be worse than hearing it at full volume. It's like someone following you into an alley, the way your skin crawls, or being trapped in a dark room with a mosquito. That feeling you get. You know they're close, you know they'll attack, you just don't know when. I want it out of my head."

"We're doing what we can."

Fraser pulled his sleeve up and looked for a watch that wasn't there. "What time is it?"

Martha didn't have to look, she could feel the seconds ticking away. "Ten after nine. We've got about fifty minutes before they reach Gresham."

He looked over her shoulder at Tennant, still back at the Jeep. "What have you learned?"

She didn't have to answer. He could tell from the look on her face.

"Fuck." Fraser stomped out of the helicopter and down the ramp. He ordered two of the soldiers to follow and went into the hangar with Fitch chasing after him.

Martha waited for all of them to disappear inside. When she spoke to Harbin, she kept her voice low. "Did you see that?"

"He's clearly upset."

"That's not what I meant. His eyes are bloodshot, and he was sweating even though it's what, maybe sixty degrees out here?"

"You think he's infected?"

"He said he still hears the sound. Said his men do, too."

Harbin considered this. "We have no way to test, do we?"

Martha shook her head. "Temperature seems to be the only real indicator."

From inside the hangar, Fraser shouted, "Both of you, in here, now!"

Martha helped Tennant out of the Jeep. "Stay close to us, okay?"

Tennant nodded.

CHAPTER SEVENTY-FOUR

MARTHA

IT WAS WARMER INSIDE the hangar than out, the heat from the day still trapped and hovering in the still air. As the three of them stepped inside, the iPad in Martha's hand beeped and the screen filled with an image of Sophie. She tilted it toward Tennant. "We're back on the wi-fi."

Tennant only half heard her. Like Martha and Harbin, she was staring at the six chain-link cages standing at the center of the hangar, three of which were occupied. Each cage was freestanding, about eight feet square with about three feet of open space between them. The tops were covered by metal beams in a tight crisscross pattern. The bottoms of the cages were bolted down into the concrete floor of the hangar. Several soldiers patrolled around and between them, walking at a slow pace, weapons ready. Others had been assigned to stand farther away, creating a secondary line of defense should someone get beyond the first.

All the lights in the hangar were on. In addition to those, large halogen lights on steel racks had been positioned around the cages, the harsh beams pointing inward.

The three captured runners, two women and a man, each stood on the left side of their cages, all three facing the same direction, their arms motionless at their sides, slowly swaying on their legs. If they noticed them enter the room, they didn't acknowledge them.

"Sophie did that, too," Tennant said. "That back and forth."

"They're facing south, toward Gresham," Harbin pointed out.

Martha glanced at the iPad. "So is Sophie."

Both of them looked over at Fraser, about twenty feet to their left, but he wasn't facing south at all. He was leaning forward with both his hands on his knees, his head hung low.

Fitch was circling around the center cage with a long pole. He stuck the end through the chain link, brought the tip up behind the man inside, and jabbed it against his neck. There was an audible *pop,* and he yanked the pole away. He didn't seem to notice at all.

"Implant?" Harbin asked.

Fitch reloaded the end of the pole and went to the third cage. "Same as the one we have in Sophie—they transmit vitals and location."

Tennant stepped closer. "I know that one."

Martha looked down at the girl. "Which one?"

Tennant pointed at the woman in the cage on the far left. "Rosalin Agar. She's from my village. Used to work in the pharmacy at Walmart before she came to us. About three years ago."

Before Martha could stop her, she started toward the cage.

"Hey!" Fraser shouted, his hands still on his knees. "Control her, or get her out of here!"

The sound of his voice froze Tennant midstep, about ten feet from the cage.

Fraser's eyes were bloodshot, skin pale. He had yet to clean away the dried blood from his face. When he shouted, a bit of spittle rolled down his chin. He wiped it away with the filthy sleeve of his fatigues. Several of the soldiers looked no better, most likely the ones who had just returned with him.

Ignoring Fraser, Harbin took several steps closer to the cages, then stopped. "Can...can you hear that? Is it something mechanical in the hangar somewhere, or—"

"It's coming from them," Fraser interrupted. "I don't know how."

Martha heard it then, too, a low hum, nearly

imperceptible. As she stepped up beside Tennant and Harbin, the sound grew louder.

Fitch finished implanting the third tracker and set the pole aside. "Can vocal cords produce a sound that low?"

Martha didn't know the answer to that, but it didn't seem likely. This sound was a deep, deep base. A much lower tone than anything she had ever heard produced by a human, or an animal, for that matter. As she drew closer, she felt it nearly as much as she heard it. This steady hum. Too steady. "To produce sound, vocal cords vibrate, they modulate the flow of air being expelled from the lungs during phonation. There's only so much air in the lungs, though. At some point, you run out, have to inhale. Even the best singers have to carefully monitor their breathing in order to produce a sustained note. This sound isn't fluctuating. There's no break as they inhale. If you look at the way they're breathing, those quick inhalations and exhalations, the timing is completely off to produce a sound like this even if it were feasible."

Harbin considered this, then looked down at the iPad in her hand. "Can I see that?"

Martha nodded and handed the tablet to him.

Harbin went to the device settings, made several adjustments, then brought up the camera. He held the screen up and pointed the iPad at the woman Tennant had identified as Rosalin Agar. He held it there for a moment, then turned slightly and pointed the tablet's camera at one of the halogen lights.

Martha didn't understand. "What are you doing?"

Still pointing the camera at the light, he said, "When plugged into alternating current, AC, halogen bulbs flicker. Albeit, very quickly. Somewhere in the neighborhood of a hundred and twenty frames per second. I adjusted the iPad camera to the lowest setting of twenty-nine frames per second, and if you look at the screen, the flicker is visible. The human eye detects nearly one thousand frames per second, which absolves that flicker, renders it undetectable to us by blending so many images together, but when you limit the images, things change."

Martha looked at the screen and saw what he was talking about. On-screen, the bulb flickered like a fast strobe, but if she looked directly at it, she couldn't see that. The light seemed steady. When he turned the camera back on the woman, Martha understood what he was getting at, although she had no idea how such a thing was possible. "They're vibrating?"

Harbin nodded and slowly panned over the other two.

On-screen, the motion was barely visible but it *was* visible, their bodies moving so quickly they had a soft shimmer around the edges. They appeared slightly out of focus.

Martha only stared. "I thought the camera on

Sophie was older, or maybe dirty. I never considered..." she looked back up at the three people captured from the horde. "Their bodies are producing the sound through this constant vibration. We couldn't really hear it with Sophie alone, but three make it audible."

Fitch was nodding. "Imagine hundreds of thousands. Body mass, size, age, all of those things would be factors in the pitch. Each person would create a unique vibration and add to the whole."

"We have less than an hour," Fraser said from the far side of the cages, his voice a mix of pain and rage. "Unless you can tell me how we'll use this information to stop them, it's meaningless. A waste."

Harbin and Martha exchanged a glance. Then Harbin turned the iPad toward Fraser, lined him up square in the center of the display.

CHAPTER SEVENTY-FIVE

MARTHA

FRASER WASN'T VIBRATING, BUT he understood what they were doing. "Satisfied?"

Martha looked up from the screen. "This could be a breakthrough. A way to identify the infected."

"I'm not *infected.* This feels more like some kind of hangover from the exposure. It's pretty clear who the infected are. We don't need a test, we need a cure." He crossed over to a cart of medical supplies someone had brought in, checked several labels, and took a handful of ibuprofen. He tossed the bottle to one of the other soldiers who didn't look much better than he did before turning his bloodshot eyes back on Martha and Harbin. "Whatever the noise did to me will pass. I'll worry about me and my team. You need to focus on them. Find a way to stop *them.*" He gestured toward the three captured runners, all three still facing south. The movement of their legs reminded Martha of a jogger stuck at a traffic light. If she opened one of the doors, would they bolt out? She was certain they would.

The one closest to her mumbled something, but she couldn't make it out. The others started, too. All three turned slightly, faced the open hangar door.

Fitch stepped closer to the center cage with the man inside and tried to make out what he was saying. "Pollen? Tabran? Itabran? Pollen Itabran? Maybe pull, not pollen. Sounds like they're all saying the same thing."

All three grew more agitated. Their voices grew louder, angrier. Their movement increased—from a gentle sway to a more desperate shuffle. The man banged his head against one of the steel support posts. His forehead started to bleed from a cut above his right eye.

Martha retrieved her iPad from Harbin and switched back to the video feed of Sophie. Her fists were clenched and she was also shuffling in place, inches from the wall. Unnerved. Like the others, she no longer faced south. Her lips were moving, and when Martha turned up the volume, Sophie's voice blended with the other three—all of them repeating the same phrase in unison.

The man banged his head again.

The soldiers had grown tense, their fingers nervously playing over the triggers of their weapons. Several stepped closer to the cages, and the ones near the outer doors closed ranks.

"Doctor..." Fraser said softly, stepping closer to Fitch. "If you think we need to hit them with sedation darts, give the word. We can't risk them hurting themselves. We don't have the time to get more. I don't know if I can put my men through that again."

"Not yet," Fitch replied. He retrieved an iPad from the cart with the medical supplies, clicked through several screens, and studied the display. "This is incredible. Body temp on the older female has risen from 102 to 105 in under a minute. Her blood pressure is through the roof. She shouldn't be conscious, let alone active, even in such a diminished cognitive state."

The woman Tennant had called Rosalin Agar ran toward the side of her cage, cracked against the metal, and bounced back. The other two started doing it, too. The moment they regained their footing, they ran again. On his third attempt, the man in the cage beside her got his hand caught between his torso and the chain link of the cage. When he impacted, three of his fingers bent back, and Martha was certain she heard them snap. He didn't seem to notice, just ran again.

Two soldiers came through the hangar door, pushing a gurney with the body of the dead captured woman on it. The sight of her set them all into a frenzy. They began screaming. The hum emanating from their bodies grew louder; Martha felt the vibration creeping over her skin, like ants crawling on her back and neck or a low electrical current. All of them screaming—*"Pull! Itabran! Pull! Itabran! Pull! Itabran!"*

"Get that body out of here!" Martha shouted at the soldiers.

The two men quickly turned and wheeled the gurney back out the door, but not before one of them tossed a wallet to Fraser.

All three captured runners began to calm. Onscreen, Sophie did, too, her frantic movements returning to more of an aggravated sway.

Fraser had the wallet open and was holding up the woman's driver's license. "Her name is Paulita Brannan. That's what they're all repeating. Paulita Brannan."

They didn't react to his mention of the name aloud. Martha wasn't sure they even heard him—they were listening to something else entirely. All three shifted position again, their gazes returning to the south. Their voices dropped low, became a soft mumble.

Harbin rounded Rosalin Agar's cage and snapped his fingers several times less than an inch from her face. She didn't react at all. Her eyes stared blankly forward, fixed on something none of them could see. "They're clearly operating with some kind of hive mind. Not necessarily present here with us, but mentally somewhere else. Trancelike."

"We should bring Sophie here," Fitch said. "Maybe she can talk to them."

Martha looked back down at the iPad. Sophie was staring up at the camera. She'd stopped moving. But that was impossible. She couldn't have heard that.

But the others did, her mind whispered back. *And when one hears, they all hear.*

She wasn't sure she believed that, either. She looked down at her watch. The horde was thirty-eight minutes outside of Gresham. What she believed didn't really matter at this point. They were grasping at straws.

Tennant leaned in close to Martha. "I don't trust these people with my sister."

Martha brushed a strand of loose hair from the girl's face. "I'll get her, okay? You can come with me."

CHAPTER SEVENTY-SIX

MARTHA

SOPHIE DIDN'T RESIST, BUT that didn't stop Fraser from putting her in full restraints. Before he agreed to allow her out of her room, a thick leather belt was secured around her waist. Handcuffs on her wrists and ankles were fastened to the belt with chains through metal rings. The unnerving contraption forced the small girl to lean forward and walk at a slow shuffle. Martha had seen similar restraints used in prisons. She didn't want to know where Fraser managed to find one sized for an eight-year-old so readily.

Seeing the little girl like this tore at Martha's heart and made her think of Emily and Michael back home, hopefully sound asleep right now, unaware of all this.

Tennant had held her sister's hand while they put the restraints on, and Martha was surprised to see

Sophie react positively to her sister's touch. She hadn't said anything, but she watched all of them closely, and that lucid behavior was encouraging.

They moved as quickly as possible, but that wasn't fast enough.

The moment they got her out of the Jeep back at the hangar, Fitch cornered them outside and was quick to point out the location of the horde. "They managed to get somewhat close with a drone before the sound took out the camera. The microphone didn't stand a chance—that was gone a half mile out. They're picking up speed the closer they get to Gresham, like sharks heading to a feeding frenzy. We've got maybe ten minutes before they reach the edge of the city. They've picked up so many people along the way, we've lost track of their total numbers."

"Why aren't they warning anyone?" Tennant asked, still holding her sister's hand.

Martha knew they wouldn't. Even if they did, what would they say? Any kind of warning would do nothing but start a panic. "Let's just get Sophie inside."

The little girl grew visibly tense at the sight of Fitch. At first, Martha thought she was frightened by the man, but that wasn't it at all. There was a disdain there. Sophie said nothing, but her eyes followed him as he turned and quickly made his way back into the hangar.

Harbin was standing off to the side of the hangar

door, holding a black plastic crate. She wasn't sure what was inside.

Martha and Tennant helped her walk.

Fraser remained several paces behind them, and while he tried not to be obvious about it, Martha noticed his hand never ventured too far from his sidearm, even when he caught her looking.

When the cages came into view, Sophie froze. "Let 'em go. You're gonna kill 'em."

That might have been the clearest Sophie had spoken since they pulled her out of that shelter, and Martha found herself exchanging a look with the others.

The three runners turned toward Sophie in unison. All three rocked back and forth, their pace quickening at the sight of her. Martha heard the sound emanating from their bodies intensify like the buzz of bees. She rubbed at her arms and realized the hair was standing up, her skin covered in gooseflesh.

"Let 'em go," Sophie said again, more defiantly this time.

Martha stroked the girl's hair, tried to soothe her. "We can't do that."

The sound grew louder, and Martha realized it was coming from Sophie, too. Not as loud as with the others, but it was there.

Sophie balled her fists and stepped closer to the nearest cage, this one holding not the woman from their village, but the older woman. Her gray hair was matted to her skull with greasy sweat, and the lines of her face were filled with grime. The woman eyed Sophie, incoherent ramblings dripping from her lips. Sophie tried to reach out to the woman, but the chains on her wrists kept her from doing so. This seemed to aggravate her even more. "Anna Shim wants her children back. You're all her children now."

Again, her voice was clear, nothing like it had been before, that didn't make her words any less disturbing.

Fitch was studying the iPad with her vitals. "Her temperature is only 101. That's the lowest we have on record. BP is only slightly elevated."

Harbin set down the crate, reached inside, and came up with a pair of headphones. "Sophie, would you allow me to place these on you? They've been designed by the military to block the sound. I know it's all around us, coming from them, from you. I know you can hear it. I'd like to see what happens if you're severed from it. Do you know what that means, severed?"

If Sophie heard him, she didn't acknowledge it. Her gaze remained locked with the older woman in the cage, the two of them staring into each other's eyes. The man in the center cage, as well as Rosalin Agar, were both facing them, slowly shifting back and forth.

Harbin handed out headphones to the rest of them,

including the soldiers standing guard, then placed a pair on his head. "We'll be able to communicate with you through the built-in radio, but you won't hear anything else." He waited for Martha and others to get their headphones in place, then knelt down next to Sophie. "Okay, here we go."

Like the three in the cages, Sophie was also rocking from side to side. Harbin timed his movement with her and brought the headphones down on her head as gently as he could, pulling them down until the padded cans covered her ears. It was obvious he had adjusted them to the smallest possible size, but even still, they were large on her, meant for an adult, not a child. Certainly nobody as young as her.

Sophie's eyes remained locked with the woman, both of them rocking together.

Harbin produced a small remote from his pocket. "I'm switching them on."

When he pressed a button on the remote, Martha noticed a little red light come to life on his headphones, Sophie's, all of them. Her world went completely silent. Gone were the gasping breaths of the runners, the drone of vehicles outside the hangar, all the ambient noise of the world relegated to the background of life. Everything vanished into a noiseless void.

Sophie stopped rocking. She went completely still, rigid. Her eyes grew wide, and her mouth fell open as she quickly looked around. She gave the impression of a sleepwalker waking midstride in an unfamiliar room. Her face filled with a mix of shock and fear.

"Sophie? Can you hear me?"

This came from Harbin. Martha heard his voice only in her headphones, and she found this slightly disorienting.

Tennant, standing beside her sister, reached for her hand and gently squeezed her fingers.

Sophie looked up at her and blinked several times but said nothing.

Martha touched the girl's arm. She still felt warm, but not as bad as even minutes earlier. "Sophie, do you know where you are?"

"Her vitals appear to be improving," Fitch said, tapping at the iPad. "I can see her temperature dropping, nearly a half-degree already, BP, respiratory, everything."

Harbin, still kneeling, grew excited. "Sophie, I believe by blocking the sound, we've broken whatever hold it had over you, do you understand? I don't know how long this will last. There's a good chance the moment I switch off those headphones, the noise will grasp you again, pull you back in."

"Anna Shim," Sophie said softly.

Harbin nodded. "Yes, Anna Shim will try to take you back. But know that if this works, we can break the link again. If you slip back, we can bring you back to us. We can keep you safe. We'll find some way to make this permanent. For now, though, we don't have much time. I need you to answer a few questions for me. Do you think you can do that?"

She hesitated for a moment, then nodded.

"When you heard the noise, when it...controlled you...were you able to communicate with the others? Could you *hear* these people?"

He gestured toward the three in the cages. Like Sophie, they had stopped rocking. They were completely still, their eyes locked on her.

Sophie looked up at them, seemed to think about this for a moment, then turned to Harbin. "They're very sad. They hurt. They want to stop."

"That's good. That's *very* good. We're here to make it stop," he told her. "I want you to think about this part very carefully, because this is very important. You could hear them. Could they hear *you*?"

Again, she nodded.

"And what about the others? The large group approaching that town, could you hear them? Could they hear you, too?"

"Yes."

"Do you think you could tell them to stop? Could you tell them that a lot of people will die if they don't, and they have to stop?"

Sophie's face grew pale. "She'll be angry with me. She would be *so* mad..."

"But you could, couldn't you?"

Sophie's eyes fell to the floor as the seconds ticked. She looked at the three caged people, then back to the floor.

"Sophie? Could you tell them to stop?"

Martha hadn't noticed it at first, there was so little. The thin trickle of blood slipped out from under Sophie's headphones, down the side of her neck, and found her shirt. Barely visible. Only a few drops. But there nonetheless, and Martha knew something was wrong.

Sophie looked back up at Harbin, leaned in close to him. "She wants you to understand how mad she would be. She says you need to understand."

She screamed.

Amplified by the headphones, Sophie's horrible, shrill cry stabbed at Martha's ears like the sharp edges of broken bottles twisted and forced into her flesh.

She heard herself scream, she heard everyone screaming.

CHAPTER SEVENTY-SEVEN

MARTHA

FITCH WAS FIRST TO tear off his headphones and throw them to the ground, and Martha was about to do the same when Harbin grabbed her hands and pulled them away. He fumbled with his remote and managed to press a button that somehow muted Sophie's cries. Not completely, but enough. Martha sucked in a deep breath and fought the urge to pass out.

Fitch was on the ground, his body convulsing, and Harbin ran to him, tried to get his headphones back on, but the man batted him away, struck out and caught his jaw with an errant fist, then twisted and rolled to his side.

Martha was about to help when she realized two of the soldiers had ripped away their headphones, too—both were on the ground—one was rolling back and forth, his hands pressed to his ears; the other had managed to sit up and was trying to raise the stubby barrel of his weapon toward Sophie. He held the rifle at an odd, twisted angle, his fingers fumbling for the trigger. Both his eyes were pinched shut, blood trickling out from the corners as his mouth moved in a scream Martha could no longer hear.

"Don't shoot!"

Wasted words. She knew it the moment she shouted, because her microphone had been muted with Sophie's. That didn't keep her from screaming again as she dove toward him.

His muzzle flashed and what must have been loud reports were only dull thuds to her as he pulled the trigger. He held the gun cradled loosely in his right arm, and the moment he pulled the trigger the kickback sent the weapon flailing in a wide arc as the bullets were expelled in a wild hail.

Martha wasn't first to reach him; one of the other soldiers was faster. The bulky man dove from Martha's left and dropped over the soldier on the ground without hesitation. His knee came down hard on the man's firing arm, pinning the weapon between them, but not before two of his shots hit the second soldier in the chest. Martha watched as one of those shots burst out the bulky soldier's back and disappeared somewhere in the ceiling. Both men stopped moving.

The soldier who had been rolling had gone still. His mouth was open impossibly wide, as if his jawbone had snapped. He'd bit his tongue clean off, and a lumpy chunk rested on the side of his face. What was left of his eyes was nothing more than dark congealed jelly oozing from the sockets.

The bullets.

The wild shots.

Off to her side, Harbin still struggled with Fitch. The doctor's arms flailed, his head jerking from side to side.

Martha's head swiveled around and she found Sophie unharmed, standing perfectly still. Tennant was behind her and had her arms around her sister in a tight hug, her face buried in the little girl's back.

Sophie was still screaming, pausing only long enough to suck in more air.

Martha had lost track of Fraser, and when she found him she realized he had circled around the cages and managed to get right behind both girls. His eyes met Martha's, and in that instant, she understood exactly what he planned to do. She also realized she was too far away to stop him.

She cried out again in another plea rendered silent by the headphones and ran toward him anyway, ran toward the three of them, and had she been just a little bit faster, if her legs were only a little longer, she might have made it.

She didn't, though.

Fraser came up behind both of them, reached out,

and yanked the headphones off Sophie's head. They skittered across the floor and cracked against the far wall in a mess of black plastic and electronics.

Sophie's body jerked with such force Tennant was tossed away, landing hard off to her side.

His balance gone, Fraser fell awkwardly on his shoulder. The impact wrenched his headphones off, and they shattered on the concrete.

Sophie collapsed, unconscious.

Martha scrambled over to her, cradled the little girl's head in her lap.

An instant later, Tennant was there, her headphones gone as well, her face twisted in pain. She was screaming, crying out, her fingers clawing at Martha's headphones, trying to take them off, and at first Martha fought her—she thought it was the sound, that godawful noise—using Tennant as it used Sophie, but then Martha realized she was only crying out in anguish at the sight of her sister; she was screaming at Martha, trying to talk to her. Tennant ripped at Martha's headphones and she let her, and the moment they pulled away from her ears, her world filled with sound.

"—elp her! You gotta help her!"

Martha waited for her ears to bleed, for her eyes to rupture, waited for a pain that didn't come but that did little to slow her gasping breaths or her heart, beating so hard it was a wonder it hadn't burst.

"Please, Doctor!"

She only half-heard her. About ten feet to her left, Harbin rolled off Fitch onto his back, yanked his headphones off, threw them aside, and just lay there, exhausted. His nose was bleeding, but judging by the redness on his cheek, this was most likely from being struck, not the sound.

Fitch was clearly dead. Like the soldier, his eyes were gone. Blood had pooled under his ears on both sides of his head. One of his arms was pinned beneath him.

In the cages, having smashed against the bars and walls, the man and the older woman were both dead, their bodies twisted in piles on the ground. Only Rosalin Agar was still alive. She stared down at Martha and Tennant, at Sophie, frantically moving from her left foot to her right and back again as if standing on hot coals. Yellow mucus dripped from her nose to the corner of her lip, and she mumbled incoherently. There was a large gash on her forehead, just below her hairline, most likely from hitting the bars like the others.

She wants you to understand how mad she would be. She says you need to understand.

Fraser groaned.

In her arms, Sophie stirred.

On the wall, the clock read three minutes after ten.

CHAPTER SEVENTY-EIGHT

PRESIDENT

THE PRESIDENT SAT AT the head of the conference table aboard Air Force One. Under his hands, the table was damp with sweat. He'd given up wiping it away with his shirtsleeve. Normally he didn't hear the drone of the engines, monstrous things built by General Electric, but he heard them now. On his first flight aboard the plane, he'd been told each of the four had a thrust rating of 56,700 pounds. He'd nodded, smiling, pretending he understood what that meant. Everything about the plane had seemed impressive, why not the engines? Turned out, these were the same engines found on any other Boeing 747. Airbus used them, too. Nothing special at all. When his staff assured him Air Force One was the safest place he could be during a conflict, that he was untouchable here, he thought about those commonplace engines.

Reminded himself that safety was a carefully crafted illusion.

The people of Gresham, Oregon, had returned home from work, from school, eaten dinner with their families and friends, sat in front of the television or played games or read, and many were probably retiring to bed right about now. They'd tucked their children away and lain their own heads down on their pillows believing they were safe because the people in power, the people they trusted, told them they were. That carefully crafted illusion.

General Westin was on the president's left, acting director of the NSA Samantha Troy on his right. He didn't want anyone else in the room, not now. The three of them had their eyes fixed on the large monitor on the wall, the satellite image of the horde.

He didn't need to hear from Dr. Fitch or Lieutenant Colonel Fraser to know the team left behind at Lewis–McChord had failed.

For the most part, the horde had followed the Columbia River west. And had they remained on that course, their impact, while still devastating, would have been far less. They hadn't remained on that course but instead veered slightly south just before a small town called Corbett where the mass picked up another two thousand people. From there, they went on to Springdale, a town of nearly four thousand. Mount Hood Community College came after that, with a student body of nearly thirty thousand more. His advisors hadn't mentioned these places as possibilities until after the horde made the southern adjustment on their way toward Gresham. At that point, it had been too late to do anything. Not that they had a solution. Their solution had been Fitch, and he failed.

When his crack team of advisors had briefed him only hours earlier, he had been told the size of the horde would be around a hundred thousand when it reached Gresham, but they had anticipated a more or less straight line, following the river. They hadn't considered the horde might adjust and target additional population centers along the way. *They should have,* but they didn't, and that little oversight proved to be damning. Turns out there was a fair number of small pockets of people along the way.

Based upon the sheer footprint of the horde as seen from satellites—which was their only means of calculating numbers—General Westin had just informed him they had amassed somewhere in the range of a quarter-million people. He hadn't mentioned the total number dead in their wake—he didn't need to. The president had seen enough predictions, stats, and assumptions to know that number was roughly 10 percent. One died for every nine others who joined. The occasional person escaped, but that number was so small it hadn't made any of the reports. The survivors had become an afterthought.

On the monitor attached to the far wall, the president watched as the horde breached the outer edge of Gresham where it would no doubt add another hundred thousand. Simple math—total population of 111,053—99,947 new runners, 11,000 dead, a handful of survivors who would most likely prefer to be part of one of the other two groups when they raised their heads and looked out upon what was left.

"That's North East Division Street," Westin pointed out as the runners bolted out across lawns and from the trees onto the pavement. First just a few, then many. Then even more. No different than the smaller towns along the way. "This here is Interstate 26. If we take out a swath of the road, we can slow them down, maybe divert them."

Bombs.

He meant bombs.

The president licked his lips. They were so damn dry. His head was pounding with a headache that refused to go away. "We've seen them run through forests, water, across some horribly rugged terrain. What makes you think they won't go around whatever hole you put in front of them? Or worse, let it fill up with the bodies from their numbers until the pile is high enough to get across?"

They'd given up on the use of troops. They tried to make a stand about half a mile outside the community college with rubber bullets and gas. Crowd control bullshit. The horde made quick work of that, too—the soldiers dropped their weapons and joined the runners. The equipment vanished under their feet. They didn't even slow down.

Westin said, "There's only one real solution to this problem. You're not willing to consider it."

The president said nothing, his eyes still fixed on the screen, grateful they had no sound.

"There's another half-million people between Gresham and Portland. That puts their numbers at three-quarters of a million *before* absorbing the six hundred thousand in Portland. They're a million and a half strong by the time they leave Portland. From there, they're either heading south down the seaboard or north toward Seattle—Olympia, Tacoma—they'll pick up another million and probably target Vancouver next if they continue to focus on large populations. That happens, do you really think the Canadian government will sit by and watch? They won't let this group cross the border. If we don't stop them, they will."

"Canada will not lob a bomb across the border into US territory."

"How certain of that are you? What would you do if this thing were heading south from Canada toward us? Would you let them run right across the border onto US soil? Attack Americans?"

The president didn't reply. On the monitor, the dark mass of the horde flooded into the streets and yards of Gresham. Because the view was from above, he could only see the rooftops of homes and businesses. He wondered if those who had gone to sleep had time to switch on a light before the sound found them, before thoughts of such mundane things were pushed aside.

Westin was still rambling. "On the off chance they turn south, we've got Salem, Eugene, Medford, Redding—they pick up another half-million just in those four cities, who knows how many more in between. Sir, they could easily have numbers in excess of two million by the time they reach California, and if you think we had a problem before, what do you think will happen next? They're currently in a relatively unpopulated area of the country. That changes if they're allowed to get to California." He pulled out his map again, that damn map, and started pointing. "Sacramento, 501,901 people. San Francisco, 884,363. San Jose, 1.3 million. Los Angeles, *four million*. There are forty million people just in the state of California. At their current size, we still have the means to stop them. That will change, sir."

"You don't think I fucking know that?" the president shouted, slamming his hands down on the table.

Startled, Samantha Troy jumped.

Westin went quiet.

Two secret service agents were in the room, weapons at the ready, before his voice got swallowed up by the engine drone. The president waved them off, took a deep breath, and rubbed his temples. "Somebody get Dr. Fitch on the line. I want to speak to him alone."

CHAPTER SEVENTY-NINE

FRASER

"DR. FITCH IS DEAD, SIR."

Lieutenant Colonel Alex Fraser sat at a conference table in the Lewis–McChord dead room—an acoustically clean room with no true right angles or reflective surfaces. The walls, floor, and ceiling were covered in sound-absorbing foam. The outer walls themselves were more than a foot thick: two layers of concrete surrounding a Faraday cage, a metal structure designed to block all electronic signals. Nothing got in or out of this room unless routed through secure McChord communication channels. The dampening effect of the various soft and curved surfaces was disorienting. The still air seemed to eat sound.

A video monitor sat on the conference table, the president's drawn face filling most of the screen. "What happened?"

Fraser told him.

With the briefest, most concise statements he could muster, he detailed everything that had taken place in the past hours, from the loss of his men as they attempted to capture several of the runners to their failed attempt to speak to the horde through the little girl.

Through all this, the president listened. He was in his office aboard Air Force One and had made it a point to tell Fraser he was alone and could speak freely. That statement had made Fraser think of Holt's recovered hard drive, still in his pocket. Several times he considered mentioning it, then decided not to. Not until he fully understood which side of this the president fell on.

The president asked him the one question he'd been dreading, because the answer meant several different things well beyond the handful of words making up that question. He knew his response could trigger something he didn't want on his shoulders—a decision that wasn't his to make.

"Are these people conscious of what they're doing?"

"With all due respect, sir, that's a loaded question."

"You understand the position I'm in. Dr. Fitch was tasked with deriving a medical solution. In the absence of that, his sole purpose was to get me an answer to that single question."

"Dr. Fitch is dead, sir."

"Which is why I'm asking you."

"So you can formulate a response."

"Yes."

"May I speak freely?"

"I already told you that you could."

Fraser measured his words. "Whether they are aware of their actions or aren't, does that really change the plan on the table?"

"I think your reluctance to answer gives me my answer."

"They're operating with some kind of hive mind. We've learned that much. All of them linked together somehow, somehow following instructions from—"

"Anna Shim," the president interrupted with the wave of his hand. "A demon."

Fraser shook his head. "Dr. Chan believes the little girl's mind just came to that conclusion to rationalize what's happening in terms she could understand. She took some story she heard at some point, some campfire tale, and put a name to it, a face. There's no demon, no entity, no alien race . . . none of that. She could have just as easily named Santa Claus or the Tooth Fairy as the voice in her head."

"Then what?"

Fraser again thought of the hard drive in his pocket. He thought of the noise. He'd be damned if he couldn't hear it right now—an impossibility within this room, but there it was anyway. Barely a hum, but there. "Dr. Chan and Dr. Harbin both believe we need to break the link. They think the individual conscious mind is still intact and if separated from the collective, they'll be capable of independent thought again."

"Isn't that what you just tried?"

Fraser nodded. "Dr. Harbin attempted to sever the link by blocking the noise itself. That obviously didn't work, but the theory was sound so Dr. Chan is attempting to find a medical means of doing the same. She's trying to isolate the portions of the brain impacted by the noise, then block it chemically. There may be a way to build up a tolerance, too. She's studying that as well."

"With the older girl."

"And me. Some of my men. Anyone who has survived multiple exposures."

There was a knock on the door. The president's gaze remained fixed on Fraser. "Yes?"

Fraser heard a door open, then a hand reached across the president's desk and gave him a folded note.

The door closed. The president opened the single page and read the contents. It was obvious by the look on his face it wasn't good news. He looked back at Fraser. "I've got statisticians running probabilities, attempting to determine where the horde will go next. Everyone agrees on Portland. They seem to be drawn by large population pockets. From there, things get sketchy."

"North or south..."

"Exactly. The next large city to the north is Seattle, but there is a lot of rough terrain in between, even more if they continue up into Canada." The president set the paper down on his desk. "Everyone seems to be in agreement now. After watching satellite imagery of the horde near the river when you attempted your capture, it's believed as a group they're operating with some intelligence. They're not running for population centers blindly; they're purposely attempting to increase their numbers. At Portland, the Columbia River is a half mile wide with a depth of fifty feet. Until now, they've crossed bodies of water on the backs of their dead—they keep running in until enough bodies accumulate to create a bridge. That won't work with the Columbia near Portland. They'd all die trying. Every last one of them." He tapped the paper. "Their path to the north is effectively cut off by that body of water. My people are now telling me with near hundred percent certainty the horde won't even attempt to cross on the northern face. They'll head south toward California after Portland." The president looked up again, his eyes filled with defeat. "We've got to make some kind of stand at Portland. This needs to end there. That's our last shot at containment."

"Have you considered evacuation?"

"There's no time. They're two hours out. The situation is no different from Gresham and the others. A warning would just create a panic, traffic bottlenecks... It wouldn't matter, anyway. I've been told the horde would just redirect to the evacuation zones, they'd follow the people. Nothing would change. It's a zero-gain solution."

Zero-gain solution.

That was a military term. If the president was using terms like that, it meant General Westin had his ear. Fraser knew Westin well enough to understand the solutions he'd recommend.

Fraser said, "How long has General Westin given you to decide on a military solution?"

The president looked as if he might deny it, then must have realized there was no point. "He wanted a green light on that hours ago. We're too late for any meaningful troop mobilization. You've seen what happens with that, anyway. We'd just lose the personnel to the horde. He's preparing an air strike and autonomous vehicles. That's all we have left."

There was another knock at the door, and the president muted his microphone and looked up. He nodded several times, then returned to Fraser. "I want reports from you and your doctors every thirty minutes."

"Yes, sir."

There was no good-bye. The screen went blank and switched to the presidential seal. Fraser was up and out the door in an instant. He hoped to God Chan and Harbin had something.

CHAPTER EIGHTY

MARTHA

MARTHA AND HARBIN BOTH stared at the body on the examining table, neither sure how what they were seeing was possible.

"One sixty-three," Harbin said. "Still climbing. Climbing fast."

Harbin had a nasty bruise under his left eye from his struggle with Fitch. Martha had suggested he ice it, but he insisted they didn't have time for that sort of thing, and he was probably right. Fitch was dead, several soldiers, two of their test subjects. Fraser would be back any moment looking for answers, and they had none, only more questions.

"One sixty-eight."

He was pointing one of the infrared thermometers at the dead woman on the table, the one who had bashed her head in on the helicopter with Fraser's team. What was left of her remaining eye looked out at the two of them, milky with cataracts and beginning to liquefy from the increasing heat. Brownish-yellow pus dripped from the corner, down the side of her face, to the aluminum table. There was a little pool of it.

The smell was horrendous.

"One seventy."

They'd seen something similar with the bodies back at Zigzag. They had increased in temperature post-mortem, too, but not like this. Not this fast. She'd only been dead for about two hours.

After what happened, Fraser insisted they lock Sophie in one of the cages. The two dead captured runners had been removed and brought to this room—an exam space off to the side of the hangar. Martha wasn't sure where they put Dr. Fitch and the soldiers who lost their lives, but she imagined they were close.

She'd ordered all her medical equipment to be brought here in order to stay near the test subjects. From the hangar, both Rosalin Agar and Sophie were whining in unison, their voices rising and falling together in this horrible chorus that seemed to combine with the low buzz of the noise coming from their bodies. Tennant refused to leave her sister's side. She tried to go in the cage with her but finally agreed to remain on the other side when Martha told her they'd take off Sophie's restraints.

"One ninety-two."

Steam began to rise off the woman's body, this humid mist that crept around the edges of Martha's surgical mask. She'd rubbed petroleum jelly under her nose, but it did little to block the scent. Rot, sulfur, and turned earth, that's what it smelled like.

"Should we cool her? Maybe with ice or water?"

Harbin shook his head. "If she's representative of the dead members of the horde, we need to let this play out. They're losing people as they go, and those bodies are out there. My God, 207 and still climbing."

"I'm taking another sample." Martha uncapped a syringe and plunged it into the woman's arm, drawing blood. Even through her latex gloves, when her fingers brushed her skin, the heat singed her. She jerked away, embarrassed, as if she'd gotten an electrical shock. She shook it off. "Hand me that scalpel. I want epidermis and dermis, too."

Harbin found one, placed the scalpel in Martha's outstretched hand.

As she cut open the woman's thigh, they both heard it.

Sizzling.

The hum was there, too, faint but growing louder.

"Two thirty-six," Harbin said. "We need to hurry. It's accelerating."

A soldier appeared in the doorway. "Ma'am? We have the fMRI machine."

"Two forty-nine," Harbin said.

Martha pointed back to the hangar. "Set it up near the cages. I need you to restrain the remaining test subject and get her inside. I'll be there shortly."

She saw the hesitation in his eyes, but he nodded anyway and disappeared around the corner. With a pair of forceps, she took the sample of the woman's flesh and carefully set it on a glass slide and positioned it under a Micron compound microscope. When she peered down into the eyepiece, she felt her breath leave her. "This is incredible. I've never seen anything like it. We've got active bombardment at the cellular level. I don't know what could possibly be fueling it—there's no blood flow, no continuation of oxygen saturation, but yet..." Speaking aloud, it came to her. She looked up at Harbin. "Skin is an organ. I remember reading the dermis layer of the average adult is capable of absorbing as much as a liter of water during a one-hour bath. It sucks in oxygen as well. I've got no explanation for why this is continuing postmortem, but that's clearly what's going on. The active bombardment is causing vibration and friction. That friction is creating the hum we're hearing. But the dermis alone can't possibly..."

"It's her entire body," Harbin finished the thought for her. "Every organ, every bone, every ounce of her being. I believe it's perpetual—the energy created by the friction exceeds the energy necessary to create the friction. Running must burn this excess away, but now that her body is stationary, the excess has no escape, which is resulting in residual heat. A rising buildup. This reaction is similar to a nuclear meltdown, just on a much smaller scale. I can't think of any other way to explain it." His eyes were fixed on the thermometer display. "Three eighty-four. That's more than a hundred-degree increase in the past minute. This isn't slowing down—just the opposite, we're heading toward possible combustion. We need to get her outside."

The room had filled with haze, and Martha realized he was right. She looked around, spotted a door marked EMERGENCY EXIT in the far corner. "There."

The body was on a gurney. They quickly kicked off the brakes and wheeled her toward the door. The metal was heating up, too, and Martha had to keep moving her fingers around to avoid getting burned. An alarm sounded as they pushed through the door and out onto the tarmac.

A soldier appeared from around the corner, and Martha shouted at her. "Get a fire extinguisher!"

They wheeled the gurney out into the open, about thirty feet from the side of the building, and had to let go. The metal had gotten too hot.

Harbin checked the temperature again. His eyes narrowed as he stared at the tiny display. He pulled the trigger again. Then a third time.

"What is it?"

He kept pulling the trigger, taking new readings. "Six twenty-two. Six forty-one. Seven oh-three..." he started to back up. "This is impossible..."

The body began to smolder.

When a soldier came back with a fire extinguisher, Martha snatched it from her. The hum was loud now, mixed with sizzles and pops. The body was visibly vibrating, the gurney, too, even with the brakes on.

Harbin shouted to be heard. "Nine twenty-six! Nine forty-three! One thousand and six!"

A flame burst from the woman's chest, a spire of orange and red. Smaller flames shot from her eyes, mouth, ears.

"One thousand four hundred and twelve!"

The flames went from orange to white as the temperature continued to rise. A blanket of blue light cascaded over the length of her, so bright Martha found it hard to even look.

"The fire extinguisher!" Harbin screamed. "Put it out! Put it out!"

Martha yanked out the safety pin, pointed the nozzle, and squeezed the trigger. Unlike a typical home fire extinguisher, this was a Class B, designed to fight flammable liquids—oil, gas, fuel. The expelled foam contained a mix of monoammonium phosphate and sodium bicarbonate. When mixed together, the two created a chemical reaction that effectively ate all available oxygen and starved the flame. Martha only knew this from her time in a lab back in college. There was very little a Class B extinguisher couldn't quench. As the foam came in contact with the burning body, she had no explanation for what occurred. The foam caught fire, and that flame trailed back over the arch of her spray, toward the nozzle, toward her—

Harbin slammed into her waist with enough force to jar the extinguisher loose. The two of them crashed against the blacktop and rolled off to the side as the body erupted into a geyser of white flame, a sudden burst reaching into the heavens. Even with her eyes pinched shut, her head turned away—the light was incredibly bright, this flash followed by the force and pressure of an explosion.

A moment later, it was over. The roar, the hum, all of it replaced by silence.

When Harbin sat up and Martha was able to turn her head, they both realized there was nothing left of the body. Half the gurney was gone, twisted metal and melted wheels, smoldering on the blacktop. And both of them had the same thought at once—the bodies of the two dead runners were still in the building behind them with Sophie, Tennant, and the others.

CHAPTER EIGHTY-ONE

MARTHA

TEN MINUTES LATER, AS Fraser's Jeep skidded to a stop, Martha barely had the energy to look up at him. The remains of three gurneys stood on the tarmac, half a dozen soldiers around them along with one of the emergency fire vehicles. Hoses snaked all around, and the asphalt was covered in blackened foam.

The door to their makeshift exam room was open, the remnants of thick, steamy mist curling from the opening toward the heavens. Someone had managed to disable the alarm. At least there was that.

"What the hell happened?"

She told him as best she could. Everything happened so fast.

"Why haven't we seen evidence of this before?"

One of Harbin's latex gloves had partially melted. He picked pieces from his skin as he spoke. "If the cellular friction is causing the noise, it's present in all of them, both dead and alive. Something just accelerated the process here. I believe this will happen to all of them."

"Could it be some kind of defensive reaction? Because we captured them?"

Harbin shrugged. "At this point, your guess is as good as mine. We don't know how long these people have been infected. That could also be a factor."

Fraser stared out at what was left of the gurneys. "I'm supposed to brief the president on progress again in less than fifteen minutes, and now I have to tell him every one of these people is a potential weapon. You know what his next question to me will be, right?"

Harbin fell silent for a moment, his eyes tired and heavy. "If he's considering a military option, you need to tell him that may not be viable. Killing these people—"

"He *can't* kill these people. That would be like killing someone who caught measles or chicken pox," Martha interjected. "They're sick. They're not responsible."

Harbin gave her a sidelong glance. "*Killing these people,* particularly on a large scale, could result in a far more devastating destructive reaction, almost retaliatory. What we just saw...I can't imagine if that were multiplied by the thousands...hundreds of thousands. God forbid, a million. Aside from the initial damage, we have zero understanding of the residual left behind." He gestured toward the smoldering ruins. "What will that do to the atmosphere? Both immediate and long term?"

Fraser walked in a slow circle. "We've got another problem."

"What?"

"People are gathering outside the gates of the base, demanding to get inside. They think it's safe here. Not just here at this base, but dozens of others around the country. Roads are starting to get congested, people fleeing major cities."

"Where do they think they can go?"

Fraser shrugged. "Speculation is growing on the internet. Theories, too. They know population centers are a problem, so they're seeking out isolation. Some people are trying to get to the caves in the Blue Ridge Mountains, go underground. Others are boarding boats and ships and heading out to sea. People are everywhere, though. They're just tripping over one another."

"We found those girls isolated up in the mountains. Their whole village was isolated. You can't hide from this. They're better off staying in their own homes," Harbin pointed out.

"I saw photos of a man in Dover. He handcuffed himself to a water pipe in his basement. Two pairs of cuffs, behind his back." Fraser held his arms behind himself, mimicked the position. "Must have done it right before the horde passed through. One of my teams found him. Looked like he tried to chew his arm off to get out. There were marks on the floor from him running in place. He bled out right there. There's no place to hide from this thing."

A soldier had appeared from inside the hangar and was standing off to the side looking nervously at Martha, apparently waiting for a moment to break in. She let out a frustrated breath. "Yes?"

"You asked us to secure the last one. We've got her ready for that machine."

Fraser asked, "The machine?"

In all the craziness, Martha had nearly forgotten. "The fMRI. Fitch had theorized if we can isolate the parts of the brain impacted by the noise, we may find some way to block the specific receptors."

"If there's a chance at obtaining even a remnant of positive news I can communicate to the president, we need to get on it."

Martha didn't respond to him, didn't know what to say. When she tested Sophie with the fMRI, she found nothing out of the ordinary. They were grasping at straws now. She pushed by both men and went back inside, doing her best to ignore the stench lingering in the air.

CHAPTER EIGHTY-TWO

MARTHA

MARTHA FELT SOPHIE'S EYES on her as she stepped back into the hangar. The girl stood at the side of her cage, her hair ruffled and partially covering her face. Tennant had set up a folding chair on the opposite side of the chain link but was standing now. She looked up at all of them nervously.

Martha's eyes jumped from Sophie to Tennant. "Did she say something?"

Sophie hadn't spoken since they pulled off her headphones.

Tennant shook her head, but there was a hesitation there. She took a step back from the cage. The girl was lying.

Fraser saw it, too. "Now is not the time for— "

He started toward her, but Martha grabbed his shoulder and held him back. She told him softly to let her handle it, then went to Tennant.

Tennant stiffened as she approached, her eyes bouncing nervously over all of them.

"It's okay, you can tell me," Martha said.

Tennant glanced over at her sister, who was facing south again, as if none of them were in the room. When she turned back to Martha, her voice dropped low so nobody else could hear. "For a second there, it was like she was back. She even smiled at me. She asked if I wanted to see Momma and Poppa again, and I told her I did. She said she could hear them and they were *so* happy, happier than they'd ever been, and we'd all be together again soon. She said all of this would be over soon."

Her eyes fell away, and Martha knew there was something else. Something the girl didn't want to tell her.

"What is it?"

"Nothing."

"Tennant..."

Again, she looked at her sister nervously. This time when she turned away, she faced the ground, unable to look Martha in the eyes. "She said she can't wait to play with Emily and Michael. She said even though she's never met them, they will still have *sooo* much fun."

Martha felt a pang in her chest at the mention of her children's names.

Emily and Michael will run with Anna Shim. You all will. We *all will.*

Sophie had said this back at Zigzag, and she still had no idea where the girl had picked up their names. She told herself she must have overheard her talking about them with one of the others. She was so quiet and still, it was easy to forget she was there when speaking, but after that first incident, Martha had wracked her brain trying to recall where she'd let the names slip and couldn't remember a single incident.

Fraser had come up behind them.

"She's just messing with you, Doctor. We don't have time for this."

Without facing them, Sophie said softly, "Ben and Eldridge have been running a long time, too."

Martha didn't recognize the names, but Fraser clearly did. His face went white.

"Who are Ben and Eldridge?"

Fraser quickly recovered and went to the gurney holding Rosalin Agar. "Doesn't matter. She's just trying to distract us. We need to focus."

Sophie said in a low, scratchy voice, "Mark would rather screw that bitch Allison than watch those little brats. He *can't wait* for Emily and Michael to run."

"Enough of this." Harbin joined Fraser on the opposite side of the gurney, and together they started wheeling her toward the fMRI.

Unlike the other gurneys, this one was made of plastic, designed to slide inside the large donut-shaped machine. Rosalin twisted and faced them, drool spilling out from her partially open mouth. The woman had wet herself. There was a dark stain on her torn jeans, and she reeked of urine. At some point, she tore her sweatshirt, and pasty skin was visible beneath, lined with blue and purple veins. Her eyes had the same yellow, jaundiced look like the others. Martha went to the LCD monitor and computer attached to the machine and began turning it on, prepping it for use.

Fraser was looking at his watch. "How long will this take?"

Martha didn't answer, still flustered by what Sophie said.

"Doctor? Did you hear me?"

"I heard you. I can either take time to answer you, or I can focus on getting this done. Your call." She didn't stop moving. A neck brace was attached to the side of the machine with Velcro. She snatched it and tossed it to him. "Get this on her."

Fraser flipped the plastic brace around in his hand, then nodded at two of the soldiers standing by. "Give me a hand."

The soldiers gripped the woman's head and held her still as Fraser got the brace under her, fastened the straps, and secured it to the gurney so she could no longer move her head.

With a triple chime of tones, the computer completed its boot-up cycle. The LCD display came to life, and Martha flipped through several screens, calibrating a baseline. When finished, she double-checked her entries, then turned to both men. "Okay, slide her in."

Fraser and Harbin gripped the gurney and wheeled her inside. Her body jerked as the large device closed around her, but the various straps and braces held her still.

"What's the difference between this and a regular MRI?" Fraser asked.

Martha cycled to another screen. "A regular MRI only provides static pictures. With this, we'll be able to monitor her metabolic functions in real time."

She pressed a button and the device whirred to life. "Here we go."

A loud clicking filled the room, enhanced by the concrete on the ground and the metal of the hangar.

Sophie continued to face south but began rocking from her left foot to her right again, picking up speed in time with the steady clicking of the fMRI's large magnet.

Inside the machine, Rosalin Agar began grunting, those grunts turning into short, gasping screams as the device got louder.

She handed Harbin an iPad. "We're capturing all her vitals with the implant. Keep an eye on her temperature. We don't want whatever happened outside to happen in here. You see anything out of the ordinary, let me know. We'll abort if necessary."

He nodded.

On the screen, Martha brought up an image of the woman's brain and began speaking, pointing out sections to Fraser. "These are live shots of her neural pathways. You can see the various synapses as they fire. The colors indicate the intensity of the activity. Red is moderate, yellow is higher. Blue and white are the strongest."

Even as she told him this, her mind flashed back to the colors of the burning bodies outside, and she tried to force the thought out of her head. "I don't see anything irregular here. Her pain receptors appear to be elevated, but not much. That could easily be the stress of being in the machine."

Fraser produced an iPod. "We need to wire this in."

Martha knew exactly what *this* was and that made her think of Finch's experiments on the girls, forcing them to listen to the noise. She also knew they didn't have a choice anymore. What was happening went well beyond this one woman.

The fMRI came equipped with speakers meant to play music for the person inside as a distraction from the loud clicking. Many people got claustrophobic, and it helped with that as well. She took the iPod from him and plugged it into the audio jack under the LCD monitor with an existing cable. Then she looked over at Harbin. "How is she?"

"No different than the others. Highly elevated temperature and blood pressure but otherwise normal. No significant changes."

She let out a breath and slipped her thumb over the Play button. "Okay, I'm switching on the sound."

The woman's legs stiffened. Her arms tugged at the plastic zip-ties, but the bindings held. The hum emanating from her body grew loud enough to hear over the fMRI's clicking magnet.

"Harbin?"

"She was at 103 when we started. She's at 106 right now."

Martha looked up at the LCD screen, and her mouth fell open.

"What is it?" Fraser asked.

"This part here, lighting up in blue and white, is the nucleus accumbens, the brain's reward center. She's experiencing an incredible sense of pleasure, a high. Her body must be pumping out record levels of dopamine and serotonin. But then when you look over here, we've got an equal reaction."

"What's that part of the brain?"

"Pain. Inconceivable levels."

Harbin said, "Her temperature is still rising. One-oh-nine now. I'm more concerned with her heart rate. She's at 168 beats per minute and climbing.

This woman appears to be in her sixties—activity that high could trigger a cardiac episode."

The hum emanating from the woman grew louder, mixed with the noise from the speakers. Martha felt the hair on the back of her neck stand on end. She felt as if ants were crawling all over her skin.

"Turn it up," Fraser said over the noise. "Unless you've learned something conclusive here, turn it up. Otherwise, this is pointless."

Tennant tugged on Martha's sleeve. She hadn't noticed the girl come up beside her. When Martha looked at her, she pointed at a phone on the wall. She couldn't hear it ringing over all the noise, but a red light was flashing on the handset.

"Sophie says that's for him—" Tennant shouted out, pointing at Fraser.

CHAPTER EIGHTY-THREE

FRASER

FRASER EYED THE GIRL for a moment before snatching up the receiver, turning his back on the loud machine and covering his other ear. "This is Lieutenant Colonel Fraser!"

He had to shout—didn't have much of a choice over all the noise.

There was nothing at first, only static. Then a distant voice. Barely audible.

"Speak up! I can't hear you!"

"You . . . need to stop . . . this."

He pressed his hand tighter over his ear. "Who is this?"

"Stop it . . . or I will."

The voice was clearer now, louder. Fraser thought he recognized it, but it couldn't be.

". . . Dad?"

He said the word so soft, barely audible, but it felt like the loudest thing he'd ever spoken.

"This is not...your fight...son."

"What the hell is this?"

"You're interfering...in the natural order...of things."

The static was back, threatening to drown him out. The voice slipped away to near-nothingness.

"Let it...happen."

Fraser turned back around and faced the little girl.

Sophie had stopped moving and was glaring at him, her face blank, her lips slightly parted.

"This is you!" he shouted at her. "Some kind of trick!"

His father's voice faded back in, fighting the static. "...over soon."

The noise erupted from the phone receiver. This screeching, terrible sound. Far worse than the recording, worse even than what he experienced in the helicopter over the horde. It felt as if a knife blade shot from the speaker in the phone and plunged into his ear. Fraser tried to pull the receiver away and found that he couldn't. Instead, his hand pushed it tighter against his head, squeezing his ear between with enough force to crush the cartilage. He heard himself screaming and couldn't stop that, either. He twisted hard to the right, slammed his back against the wall, then against his arm holding the phone, but his grip only tightened.

He caught glimpses of the doctors in the room, the

two girls, and Fraser had no memory of pulling his sidearm from the holster, but he caught a glimpse of that, too, the 9mm coming up. Felt his finger tighten on the trigger—once, twice, six times—the first shot targeting a soldier, then Harbin, finding him before turning on the others. The shots no doubt loud but unheard over all else.

"So proud, son," he heard his father say.

CHAPTER EIGHTY-FOUR

PRESIDENT

WHEN THE VIDEO CONFERENCE connected in the main cabin of Air Force One, the president stared up at the screen. Fraser looked out at the room with dead eyes. There was no other way to explain it. Distant, unfocused. The man looked like he was sleepwalking.

On the president's left, General Westin leaned forward, narrowed his eyes at the screen. "Soldier, are you okay?"

The question seemed to take a moment to process. Then Fraser nodded. "Yes."

"You don't look okay."

Fraser shifted nervously in his chair. "It's been a trying day, sir."

The president let out a breath. "That it has."

"I'm afraid I don't have good news for you, sir." He paused for a second, adding, "On several fronts."

"Explain."

Fraser did. He told them what happened with the bodies postmortem.

"Like some kind of spontaneous combustion? How is that possible?"

He went on to explain about the vibrations causing the noise. The friction on a cellular level somehow creating unprecedented levels of heat in the dead, that heat igniting when it had no place else to go.

His words came slow, forced.

Probably just tired. They all were.

Westin was the first to respond. "So we can't just kill them. We need to incinerate them before that combustion takes place, is that what you're telling us?"

Fraser didn't answer. He only stared at them blankly.

"Soldier?"

His eyes blinked. "Sorry. I... I don't know if that would work."

"You have test subjects there. Test it!" Westin fumed. "Incinerate one of those bastards!"

The president placed a hand on the man's arm. "General, that's enough."

Westin's face grew redder. "We're about to lose the western seaboard. The time for any morality—perceived, real, or otherwise—is long gone!"

The president was ready to object when Fraser spoke again.

"The test subjects are all dead, sir. The last one died a few minutes ago during an fMRI scan."

"Christ."

"What did you do to the body?" Westin asked.

"We managed to get it outside before it combusted, but it was close. Faster than the others. Dr. Harbin theorized it was because she was one of the original runners from Mount Hood. He thinks the longer they've been infected, the faster the reaction after death."

The president said, "This explains all the fires cropping up behind them. We thought they were secondary, caused by damage to the infrastructure after the horde passes through, but that didn't explain the ones back in the mountains—there's nothing left of Zigzag." He paused as another thought entered his head. "What happens if they stop running?"

"Harbin believes that may be a trigger, too," Fraser replied. "Their bodies are producing excessive amounts of energy, they're burning much of it by running, by keeping in motion. This buildup seems to occur when they're still . . . dead or alive."

The president looked down at the table. "Then our plan won't work."

Westin turned to him. "It *will* still work if we add a final component—we blow the bridges, trap the horde, *and* incinerate them."

Fraser cocked his head. "Plan, sir?"

“Remember what I told you about the Columbia River?”

“They can’t cross. The river is too wide.”

The president nodded. “The Willamette River runs along the eastern edge of Portland and poses a similar challenge for them. To reach the city, they need to cross the water, but it’s deep in most parts. General Westin has suggested blowing all the bridges between the horde and the city as they near it.”

“Before they have a chance to react and alter course,” Westin jumped in. “We blow the bridges, trap them on one side of the water.” He looked back at the president. “Sir, that’s our window, our *only* offensive option. While they’re backed up at the river’s edge, stumbling over one another trying to get around that water, we take them out.”

“By killing them,” the president said flatly.

Westin was no longer holding back. “Every last one, yes, sir.”

“How do we know a bomb won’t trigger this spontaneous combustion and create a secondary explosion, something we don’t have control over?”

“We use a thermobaric weapon,” Westin told him. “A fuel-air explosive. Thermobarics use all the surrounding oxygen in their blast wave. Without oxygen to fuel it, there is no secondary explosion.”

“You don’t know that. Not for sure,” Fraser countered.

Westin glared at the screen. “Do you still have the girls?”

Fraser nodded.

“Then test the theory. Put one of them in the hyperbaric chamber at McChord, suck the air out, and see what happens.”

Fraser didn’t reply. He seemed to be waiting for the president to object.

The president didn’t.

Fraser finally said, “It wouldn’t be a valid test. Neither girl appears to be a hundred percent infected. The older one is no longer showing symptoms, and the younger one is somewhere in between.”

Westin turned back to the president. “Sir, we need a decision on this. If we’re going to mobilize, we need to do it now.”

The president said, “Have your doctors come up with another option? Some other way to stop them?”

“I’m afraid not, sir.”

The president fell silent for a moment. He felt additional eyes on him but didn’t turn to see who had entered the room. It really didn’t matter anymore. Westin was right. They were out of time. He needed to act. “Then we no longer have a choice. Our closest assets are at McChord, Lieutenant Colonel. I’ll need you to coordinate this from the ground under General Westin’s command.”

“Yes, sir.”

Westin said, "Report to the airfield and stand by, soldier. I'll be in touch shortly."

The president reached forward and pressed a button on the conference table's embedded panel, disconnecting the call.

"You're doing the right thing, sir," Westin told him.

How could killing nearly one million Americans be the right thing?

The president didn't answer. Instead, he rose and started back toward his office.

Westin stopped him at the door. "Sir. Thermobaric weapons should be effective. There's also no radiological effect. They're the perfect first choice."

"But..."

Westin fell silent for a moment, choosing his words carefully. "We've also got the capability to launch a nuclear strike from orbit. Surgical, defined." He hesitated. "I'd like permission to align those assets as a backup plan should the thermobaric fail."

The president couldn't look at him.

"I need a moment."

He pushed by and entered his office, closing the door in the general's face.

CHAPTER EIGHTY-FIVE

MARTHA

AS THE PRESIDENT'S FACE vanished from the monitor in the Lewis–McChord dead room, Fraser cocked his head over his shoulder. "You can untie me. I'm okay now."

Martha stood in the shadows off to the side, Harbin opposite her, both purposely concealed from the video conference camera. With his good arm, Harbin was holding a 9mm against his thigh, his index finger hovering over the trigger guard. Martha had told him she didn't want a weapon.

"It wore off, whatever she did to me with that phone call. Untie me."

Stepping behind Fraser's back, Harbin looked over at her, a light sheen of sweat on his pale face. She'd bandaged his arm as best she could with such limited time. The bullet had managed to avoid the humerus and gone straight through, but the bleeding hadn't stopped, only slowed. He'd need stitches.

Fraser's neck was red and angry where she'd hit him with the heavy battery, the only thing that had been within reach when he started shooting.

When he had pulled his gun, things seemed to move in slow motion.

Martha saw the sweeping motion of his arm, watched as he took aim, first at one of the soldiers, then at Harbin. The soldier had been facing away and went down instantly. Harbin managed to rock to the side, more of a flinch at the harsh sound of the first shot than an attempt at evasion, and that probably saved his life. Even as Fraser fired, it was clear he tried to fight whatever commanded him—he threw the phone receiver aside, his arm shaking. After the shot that hit Harbin, he swung the weapon to his left and down, putting four bullets into Rosalin Agar, killing her while she lay bound and immobile in the fMRI machine. His gun was rising and aligning with Sophie when Martha picked up the battery and brought it down on the back of his head, at the base of his neck. The awkward angle with which she struck sent her to the ground right behind him, and her head hit the concrete a few inches from the phone receiver. For one brief instant, she heard a voice on the other side of that call, an impossible voice: her little girl, Emily.

Come home, Momma. Come run with me.

When she scooped up the receiver, there was no one there, only dead air.

Martha shook off the memory and peered at Fraser in the dimly lit dead room.

Although clearly agitated, his voice remained calm. "I don't know how she did it, but now that we know she can, we can prevent it. We know it's not real."

"What did you hear?" Harbin asked him.

Fraser's eyes fell to the top of the conference table, but he didn't hold back. "My father."

"Your *dead* father."

He nodded. "Ben. Ben Fraser. The other name that girl mentioned, Eldridge, is my grandfather. I don't understand how she'd know either of those names."

Martha had brought the iPad. She pointed the camera down at Fraser. She studied the screen for a moment, then turned it toward Harbin so he could see, too.

Harbin said, "You're not vibrating. You're not infected. At least, not now."

"Untie me."

Martha only glared at him. "The president ordered you to kill the girls."

"And now he knows I won't do that. Do you think I'm the last person he'll ask? There's too much at stake, especially if they consider her to be a source of the infection. They might be on the line with someone else right now. Untie me."

"So you can what? Get out to the airfield and run point for Westin?"

"Yes. Do you think you'll somehow stop our response by keeping me here? The military option is already in motion. You had your chance; it's too late. If the horde absorbs Portland, this is over. It will overrun the country, the continent, possibly beyond that if some other government doesn't shut it down first."

"Your orders are to corral all these people so that general can exterminate them. I can't be part of that," Martha countered.

Harbin had fallen oddly quiet. He was slowly pacing the floor. When he stopped, there was a resigned look on his face. He reached over and gently squeezed Martha's shoulder. "We need to let him go. He's right. He has a job to do. We failed."

Martha turned on him. "One million people! They're going to kill one million people!"

"The president has no other option. We were meant to provide one and we failed. It's time to step aside."

"Look, Doctor," Fraser said, "I know this is difficult to hear, but if the president doesn't act, if he doesn't stop this, some other government will. Maybe not today, maybe not tomorrow, but they will. There's already chatter coming out of the European Union, Russia, Korea, China... You've seen how fast this spreads. If it's allowed to continue for a week, how many will die then? How many in two weeks? How long before it can't be stopped at all?"

Martha shook him off and took a step back. She couldn't believe what she was hearing. "We're close. We're missing something. We can't just give up."

"We're out of options. Out of time."

She looked back down at Fraser. "The man you found in Dover, the one handcuffed in his basement. You said he was alone, right?"

Fraser nodded.

"That's what I don't understand. If he was alone, how was he infected?"

"The noise," Harbin replied. "That sound somehow reached him."

"We've all been exposed to the noise at some level and we're not infected, at least not completely. Those two girls most of all. Tennant has recovered and Sophie is... she's something, but not full-blown infected, not like the others." She looked up at them, her eyes growing wide. "We know the people in the horde are generating the noise but what if that's only part of it? What if the noise isn't the source of the infection at all but some kind of by-product? What if something else is infecting everyone and the noise is the result of that infection rather than the other way around?"

"Could it be two things?" Harbin suggested. "The noise, when combined with something else, leads to full-blown infection? C4 is benign until you run a current through it. Bleach is fairly harmless until you mix it with something acidic, then you get chlorine gas. Maybe that's why we're having so much trouble identifying the source—there are two sources. Two halves to a whole." To illustrate this he held out both his arms and brought them together, clasping his fingers. "That still gives us a chicken and egg scenario—what came first, the noise or the infection? Where did it come from?"

Martha looked over at Fraser. "You said USGS believed the noise was generating from underground."

"I was told that's initially what they believed."

"But not anymore?"

Fraser didn't answer.

"We need to speak with Frederick Hoover."

"It's too late, Hoover's a waste of time."

There was something in the way he said that last bit, both Martha and Harbin heard it.

The 9mm twitched in Harbin's good hand. He knelt beside Fraser's chair. "You know something. You're holding back."

Fraser's gaze went from Harbin to Martha and back again. Finally, he said, "Hoover's a dead end."

"How can you be so sure?"

Again, Fraser went quiet.

"We're close, I know we are," Martha said, attempting to control the emotion in her voice. "We can't stand around and wait for the bombs to drop. Let us try."

A long moment passed, Fraser studying both of them. Finally, he said, "My right pants pocket."

Martha looked up at Harbin who nodded; she reached into Fraser's pocket. She found a small hard drive and held it up to the light. "What's on it?"

Fraser ignored her question. "I need a radio. I've got to speak to one of my men."

"No way."

He looked her dead in the eye. "You either trust me or you don't."

"Do you hear the noise anymore?"

Fraser shook his head.

"What about Sophie?"

"Nothing. I don't hear a damn thing. I'm fine. You can trust me."

Harbin leaned closer to Martha and said softly, "What choice do we have? Without his help, we'll be locked in a room watching this play out."

She didn't trust that man, not one bit, but Harbin was right. They had maybe an hour before the horde reached Portland. The president's plan was in motion, already decided. Even if Fraser somehow betrayed them, they'd be no worse off for it. She reached for the radio transmitter on the conference table and held the microphone out to him.

Fraser said, "Put it on channel one thirty-eight."

Harbin studied the controls, twisted a knob, and nodded at Martha. She pressed the transmit button.

Fraser cleared his throat, "McMichael? This is Fraser. Copy?"

"Copy, sir."

"I need you to prep a chopper on runway beta. Radio ahead and tell LaValley to ready for flight. Dr. Harbin will accompany you."

"Destination?"

Martha snatched the microphone from him. "Why not me and the girls? Why just Harbin?"

Fraser looked up at her, his face hard. "This only works if someone gets out unnoticed. There are too many eyes on the girls and I need you to stay with them, keep the young one... stable."

"He's right," Harbin agreed. "We'd never get Sophie out of that hangar."

"Destination, sir?" McMichael asked again.

Martha reluctantly agreed and held the microphone out again, pressing the button.

Fraser said, "Renton Forty-Nine."

The soldier didn't reply.

"McMichael?"

"Renton Forty-Nine. Confirm, sir?"

"Confirmed. Renton Forty-Nine."

"Understood."

Fraser licked the blood on his lip again, then said, "McMichael, this mission is your ears only. Tell LaValley he's flying dark. No radio contact. We've got hostiles at the gates of the base and it's believed several have made their way on base. Watch your six on the way out. We're transporting the doctor under cloak, understand?"

"Sir, yes, sir."

Fraser looked back up at Martha and Harbin. "I spent time with both of these men in Afghanistan. I trust them explicitly. You can, too. Runway beta is near the hangar you've been using, you'll see it. Take my Jeep. Move fast, don't hesitate. Don't give anyone a reason to stop or question you."

Martha asked, "What's Renton Forty-Nine?"

"It's a DARPA black site outside of Seattle." He hesitated for a moment, then added, "It's Frederick Hoover's last known location."

Martha felt the weight of the hard drive in her hand.

Fraser said, "One other thing."

"What?"

"Untie me."

This time, Martha did.

CHAPTER EIGHTY-SIX

MARTHA

MARTHA AND HARBIN PUSHED through the double doors of the building housing the base's dead room and found themselves at the center of organized chaos. Vehicles and personnel raced purposely through a chilled night air thick with the looming anxiety of what was to come. The roar of engines thundered above with a mix of transports both coming and going. An armored Humvee rolled by on her left, and a confused moment passed as Martha realized the vehicle had no driver but was somehow operating autonomously.

Fraser's Jeep was right where they had left it after rushing him inside at gunpoint, and even though all that felt like a lifetime ago, Martha realized it had been less than an hour.

She drove, ignoring the speed limit signs, as Harbin plugged the hard drive into a laptop he'd taken from the dead room. Several minutes passed before he slumped back in his seat and looked over at her grimly.

Martha frowned. "What is it?"

"You'd better pull over for a second."

She pulled the Jeep into a narrow alley between two concrete buildings, turned off the headlights, and shifted into Park.

Harbin turned the screen so Martha could see, then clicked on a file. The familiar image of Frederick Hoover of DARPA filled the screen, and his voice found them through their headphones:

"I apologize for the short notice, the ways and means necessary to bring each of you to your current location. As you may have already surmised, the nature of the anomaly requires the utmost secrecy, and your cooperation is greatly appreciated. I would be remiss if I failed to point out the NDAs you've signed clearly state a violation of the Secrets Protection Act of 2008 carries a minimum of five years in military prison and a maximum penalty of death under the Treason Act as defined in Article III, Section three of the United States Constitution. Should you speak to any unauthorized personnel, those individuals will be subject to the same. At this point, all your communication devices should have been turned in to an appropriate handler. If you've retained any form of communication device, you are hereby ordered to relinquish it immediately. Failure to do so will result

in immediate charges, imprisonment, and replacement on this team. I ask that your handler pause the video at this point in order to give you the opportunity to turn in any remaining forms of communication."

Hoover went still for a moment, but without Holt to press Pause, he continued several seconds later.

"I imagine you to be curious as to why you are here. Understandably so. And while I would like to offer an explanation, I'm hesitant to do so. I fear sharing of our current theories and/or analysis of the anomaly may prejudice your own opinions and theories, and we'd prefer you approach this situation without such handicaps, at least for your initial exposure. We will reevaluate upon debrief. In a moment, you will be transported to the anomaly. We ask that you do not consult one another until after your individual debrief and return to base. Each of you possesses a particular skill set, and as with sharing current theories, we'd prefer to hear your individual thoughts before you compare notes."

The video stopped.

Martha said, "That's the video Holt showed us at Zigzag when we all first arrived. I don't understand. Why would Fraser think it was important? He doesn't say anything useful."

"The content of the video isn't the real problem."

"The *real* problem?"

Harbin held the laptop closer to her and pointed at the file name. "Look at the date it was recorded."

Martha had to squint, the text was so small. She found herself frowning. "That can't be right."

"It is, though."

"...but that's more than six months ago. It's only been a few days since—"

"—we were *shown* the video a few days ago, but that's not when he recorded it," Harbin interrupted. "There's more. There's a lot more."

Harbin scrolled through the folder, and Martha realized there were several hundred videos there, dating back nearly nine months. "This didn't just start. It's been going on. Zigzag, the girls' village on Mount Hood, that wasn't the first, only the most recent. Some of these videos are other teams just like ours, brought in to review the aftermath. Other videos capture the effects of the noise as it's played for animals and other people—"

"They purposefully exposed *people* to the noise?"

Harbin nodded. "Prisoners, mostly. To better understand what it does. If this got out, the implications would be devastating."

"How did they keep it quiet? You saw what happened. How fast it spread."

Harbin's face went grim. "I think they killed them before it got a chance to get out of hand. This last one, at Mount Hood, it got away from them."

Martha's chest tightened. "We need to tell someone—get this out in the open."

Harbin worked through several screens on the laptop, then let out a frustrated grunt. "This thing is on the military network, but there's no access to the outside world. No internet or email."

"I haven't been able to reach anyone since we got to Zigzag. Not my ex-husband or my children. Even when I had access to the internet at the base, it was running through some kind of proxy. All the social media sites were blocked."

Harbin leaned back in his seat and closed his eyes, a look of defeat washing over him. "Why didn't I see it..."

"See what?"

"They've been blocking us. Keeping us from reaching the outside world. They have been since we arrived. I thought it was for security reasons, but that's not it at all." His shoulders tightened, and a quake entered his voice. "They put our team together to solve problems for which they already possessed the answers. This was never about *stopping* the anomaly." He gestured at the hard drive. "All these experiments...this was someone trying to determine how long it would take a group like ours to figure out what was really happening."

Martha understood then. "*Groups,* not *group*. We're somebody's sample. Part of the experiment. An average on a spreadsheet. They're trying to weaponize this, and they needed to understand how long it would take for us to help organize a response so they could better deploy."

Harbin nodded.

Martha felt her stomach sink.

She turned the headlights on and pulled back out onto the road.

Neither of them spoke.

If the base was organized chaos, the adjoining airfields were a dance of precision. Numerous aircraft lined the runways preparing for takeoff while others came in for a landing, rolled down the tarmac at great speed, slowed with a rush of air, and moved aside to load or unload moments before the next plane approached.

Runway beta was deserted, and judging by the potholes and weeds growing up through the blacktop, it had been some time since it had been used by a plane. The various hangars and low-lying structures were in serious disrepair, abandoned some time ago. Martha was beginning to think Fraser had led them into some kind of trap when they came around the side of the remains of an old warehouse and the helicopter came into view—an EC135, Martha now recognized. The rotors were spinning, picking up speed.

She skidded to a stop about twenty feet away and left the motor running.

Two Humvees rounded the corner of the warehouse

from the direction they just came and seemed to pick up speed when the helicopter came into view.

A soldier came running up and identified himself as McMichael. He had to shout to be heard over all the noise. "Fraser wanted me to go with you, but I can't!" He gestured toward the two approaching Humvees. "I need to run interference, or you'll never get out of here! You gotta go!"

Harbin climbed out the Jeep, favoring his injured arm, the laptop under his other, and turned back to Martha. "Stay safe! Keep the girls safe! I'll find some way to get back in touch with you!"

"Sir, now!" McMichael yelled, taking Harbin by the shoulder and quickly leading him to the helicopter. The moment he was on board, McMichael slammed the door, knocked twice on the glass, and the chopper lurched up and vanished.

The first Humvee pulled right up to McMichael out on the tarmac. The second skidded to a stop next to Martha. Through the open window, a soldier shouted, "Dr. Chan? Ma'am, you need to get back to the hangar!"

CHAPTER EIGHTY-SEVEN

MARTHA

MARTHA FOLLOWED THE HUMVEE back to the hangar and was still rolling to a stop when Tennant rushed out.

"Doctor, it's Sophie! Come on!"

Tennant grabbed Martha from the Jeep and pulled her arm so hard it felt like the girl might yank it out of the socket.

She led her inside where Sophie stood in the middle cage, still facing south, her eyes closed, her fists balled up. The other cages were empty now. After the incident with the phone, Fraser had insisted they put her back in restraints. Martha wasn't sure what good that would do, but she had complied anyway. He had also wanted her to put a gag on the girl. She had *not* done that. None of this mattered because all of her restraints were now lying in a heap near the door.

Martha turned to Tennant. "Did you take those off?"

"How could I? Her door's locked."

When Martha looked back, she realized the girl was right. The heavy padlock was right where she'd left it. Her hand rummaged through her front pocket and came out with the key.

"Forget the restraints," Tennant said. "Listen."

The hum was there, louder in this room than it was next door.

The air held the same stillness as an open field moments before lightning reached down from the heavens and scorched the earth. A slight tinge of electric ozone.

Sophie's lips were moving. Barely perceptible, Martha realized she was whispering. As she stepped closer, she could make out the words.

"Jayne Bergh, Aja Holmberg, Naomi Pilger, Jaunita Haakenson, Hershel Simonton, Elna Blanco, Darcie Chidester, Lanette Quinn, Forest Balch, Bethel Deakins, Shauna Blizzard, Suzette Marcinek, Fernande Bittner, Yu Jessop, Kimberly Dansereau, Greg Marasco, Paul Wasilewski, Ellie Pizarro, Cedric Lesko, Michaela Vandever, Elia Magrath . . ."

"She started about five minutes ago. I recognized a couple of the names, but not most. Do you think they're all infected?"

"How could she know that?"

Tennant shook her head and went over to the bank of computer and video monitors Fraser's people had been using earlier and began switching everything on.

"What are you doing?"

"While you were gone, it started. They're scrambling fighters and bombers out there. I overheard two of the soldiers talking about what they'd seen on video footage coming back from some of Fraser's advance teams. I want to see if—"

One of the video screens came to life with a shaky image of the horde—grainy and tinged in the green glow of infrared. Thousands of people running. A readout in the bottom corner said they were moving at an incredible pace of twenty-one miles per hour. To Martha, it seemed physically impossible they could sustain such momentum, but there they were. Several of the runners jerked and dropped to the ground and because there was no sound, it took Martha a moment to realize what was happening.

Tennant saw it, too. "They're shooting at them!"

As bullets struck, people dropped and fell beneath the feet of others, trampled in moments.

What could they possibly expect to accomplish by shooting them?

The footage must have been coming from a vehicle, something racing alongside the horde. Probably a Humvee or an ATV. There was no way to be sure. It was too low and jarring to be from a helicopter.

Tennant said softly, "I heard a soldier say they modified the noise-canceling equipment and they can get closer now. They're operating some of the equipment remotely, too."

One of the other monitors had a detailed map showing the current location of the horde, all military vehicles and major cities. Martha studied it for a moment. "At this speed, they'll reach Portland in less than an hour. Closer to forty minutes."

Behind them, Sophie continued to whisper, "Elisa Sine, Berry Redding, Cassaundra Pasha, Shakia Kiel, Melinda Visitacion, Millie Rowse, Murray Raymond, Lucila Arms, Hugo Majeed, Gabriel Rollo, Leora Hickel, Estelle Bodin, Alice Mccutcheon, Gwyneth Haverly, Takisha Millender, Donita Kalis, Loria Higgs, Amanda Truluck..."

Tennant let out a gasp. Her finger rose and pointed at the screen.

"What is it?"

"Poppa and Momma..."

Martha hit several buttons on the attached laptop and froze the image. "Where?"

Tennant stepped closer and touched the screen. Her index finger left a streak on the plastic. She traced a man and a woman on the outer fringe of the runners. The man was wearing a single boot, his other foot glistened in the hazy green light with what could only be blood. As Martha looked closer, she realized his pants leg was shredded and damp.

How far were they from Mount Hood? Had he really run all the way like that? At that speed?

She thought of Rosalin Agar. She had run the same distance. Why not this girl's parents?

"We need to help them!"

Martha's voice fell soft. "Tennant, there's nothing we can do."

"Tell the soldiers to stop!"

"They won't listen to me."

"They have to!"

Tears welled up in Martha's eyes, and she wiped them away. She tried to offer Tennant a hug, but the girl shook her off.

"All over soon, Tennnnant."

The two of them looked over and realized Sophie had moved to the side of her cage closest to them. Although she faced them, her eyes open now, she didn't appear to be looking at them. It was as if she saw through them to some distant place or object.

"Over how, Sophie?" Martha asked.

Her voice dropped low and mimicked Harbin's accent. "We're all going to die, Doctor. Is that what you want to hear?" Then, in her own voice, she added, "We're all going to run."

She started on the names again after that, this endless list.

"Carla Santani, Isaura Corella, Aurelio Sines, Normand Escareno, Marx Welle, Mallory Cargo, Era Vida, Yelena Brin, Kathy Tryon, Danna Germann, Eddy Fleagle…"

CHAPTER EIGHTY-EIGHT

HARBIN

RENTON 49 WAS A square structure about six stories tall sandwiched between half a dozen similar buildings on a street that could have been anywhere. There were no lights on the roof, nothing to indicate a helicopter could set down. Nothing to indicate the building was even occupied.

At some point, their pilot had switched off their running lights. They came in fast and dark, and for a moment, Harbin thought they were going to crash.

At the last moment, the pilot pulled up and set them down with a blast of dust and a soft thud. "You need to hurry. The door is on the east end of the roof, past those air conditioners." He motioned in that general direction with his left hand. "I pulled my GPS beacon when we left the base, and they've been on the radio trying to locate me. I need to get to the Portland staging area before someone figures out where I really went."

Harbin yanked up on the door latch and winced before climbing out with the laptop under his arm and gun back under his belt at the small of his back. He had redressed his bullet wound while en route—the bleeding had finally stopped, but without painkillers his entire arm throbbed.

Harbin leaned back inside and shouted at the pilot, "Good luck, son."

The pilot gave him a half wave, and the moment he closed the door, the helicopter lifted off into the night sky and was gone.

Harbin quickly stared off in the direction the pilot had indicated, rounded the three large air handlers from the building's HVAC system, and found the door inside a brick portico with a steel-slat roof.

Metal.

Painted a dull gray.

Locked.

Harbin found no keyhole or latch.

He beat on it with the back of his hand.

No keypad, intercom, or visible camera.

He hit the door again, harder this time, and felt the pain reverberate up the length of his bad arm.

Nothing.

No response.

He could try to get to the ground level and find

the front door, but something told him that would be locked, too.

"Who are you?"

The voice was female, and Harbin had no idea where it came from. Electronic, though, some kind of speaker.

"I'm looking for Frederick Hoover. Lieutenant Colonel Alexander Fraser sent me."

"Who are you?" the voice repeated.

Harbin looked around for a microphone, and when he didn't find one, he just spoke up. "Hoover knows me. Tell him it's Doctor Sanford Harbin with NOAA. We worked on a project together for the Navy about six years ago. I imagine he recommended me for this team. Tell him I'm here."

Nothing for a moment, then—

"Where is Holt?"

"He's dead," Harbin said. "Died up near Zigzag."

"Doctor Fitch?"

"Dead, too. Everyone's dead."

"Why aren't you?"

That question took Harbin by surprise, and at first he didn't say anything. He wasn't sure what to say. He held up the laptop. "We've got the only survivors from Mount Hood at Lewis–McChord. We've studied them. I'm sure I can access all the data from here. Maybe if we compare it to whatever you have—"

A loud click came from the metal door, and it popped open, swinging slowly out toward them.

"Get inside."

Harbin grabbed the edge of the door and tried to open it faster but realized he couldn't. It was far heavier than it appeared, and the hinges were motorized. The moment it had opened wide enough, he slipped through and the motion of the door reversed. It closed behind him with the weight of a bank vault. There was no handle or lock, no manual means to open it again from this side.

The hallway was stark white, lit by bare bulbs strung along the ceiling with no signage or markings of any kind.

"Follow the hallway to the stairs. Take the stairs down to the lowest level."

Like outside, there were no visible speakers or cameras in the walls, yet he knew he was being watched. The voice seemed to come from all around him.

"Hurry."

Harbin moved as fast as he dared, favoring his good arm.

CHAPTER EIGHTY-NINE

FRASER

FRASER HADN'T LIED WHEN he said he no longer heard the noise or Sophie. His mind had been quiet as he sat in the dead room, as he talked to Chan and Harbin. The moment he stepped out, though, as he made his way to the airfield to report for duty, to prepare for his mission, he heard it again.

Not the little girl, he was sure of that, but something else. He was reluctant to call that *something* a *someone* because whatever she was, to compare her to humans would be no different than comparing a gnat to a supercomputer. She was *something* else, something...far more. He wasn't even sure why his mind considered this thing to be female, he had no evidence of that. The idea of male and female seemed far beneath her, a trivial description left to those things that crawled out from the mud, yet that understanding was present, too. That *knowing.* This was a she, whatever *this* was.

He stood on the western end of the Burnside Bridge, the near-midnight air swirling around him.

While he couldn't hear the cries of the horde from here, their hum was in the air, much like the vibrations of an approaching freight train, a heavy, unstoppable force felt long before it's heard.

The child in him wanted to put a penny down on the tracks. Something he could find in the aftermath.

The fencing had gone up fast. Cement barriers beneath twelve-foot chain link topped with razor wire. He knew this barrier stood no chance of stopping the horde. He'd seen that with Zigzag, but it would keep the people of Portland off the bridge as they prepared to blow it. Similar blockades had gone up at Hawthorne Bridge, Tilikum Crossing, Sellwood, Fremont, even the various railroad crossings. His team hadn't informed the media, the local government, or anyone, for that matter. There was no time and General Westin felt there was nothing that could be said that would quench the fear of those caught behind the opposite side of those fences. How do you tell someone they're safer in a cage when their only instinct is to escape and flee?

Above him, dozens of Boeing CH-47 Chinook helicopters filled the night sky. Some carried additional materials for blockades; others carried tanks and armored vehicles not only from Lewis–McChord, but every nearby base in the western continental United States. While each vehicle would be manned by soldiers outfitted with noise-canceling headphones, they could also be operated remotely if those soldiers were compromised. Because their cameras were housed behind thick ballistics glass, the hope was they could survive the vibrations created by the noise long enough to aid in stopping the horde. Fraser was under no such illusion. He'd seen the destructive power of that sound up close, but he was under orders and would follow those orders.

His skin prickled.

The air was electric.

The hum.

The noise.

So close.

The crowd on the other side of the fence had grown within moments of the barrier going up. First with the occupants of cars and trucks stopped dead, then with people on foot. As word spread of these fences surrounding Portland, more people came, their shouts and cries desperate and pleading. The ones in front pressed so tight against the chain link by the momentum of those behind, he was certain several were dead already, crushed. He wanted to tell them the Army had only blockaded the eastern side of the city, they could still get out from the west, but there was no point.

"Sir?"

Fraser was so lost in his own thoughts, at first he didn't hear the soldier come up beside him. Didn't see her holding the satellite phone.

"I've got General Westin for you, sir," she said.

He took the phone from her and pressed it to his ear.

Was that buzz on the line, in his head, or really just growing in the air?

"General," he said. Surprised by the distant sound of his own voice.

"I'm getting reports back from our advance teams, and it's not good. We've lost two scout planes and at least six Humvees. They get within a quarter mile of those people and our personnel succumb. Some abandon the vehicles altogether and join the horde on foot. It's the ones left behind who become problematic. We've had several instances of soldiers turning and fighting us when we switch the vehicle to remote. You need to instruct your people to destroy the overrides before you deploy."

"Understood."

"Are your laser beacons in place?"

Fraser turned to his right. He could see the one on Burnside Bridge. A small box laser, no more than four inches square, on a tripod at the center of the bridge. This was the last one to go up. "Yes, sir."

"I'll have one of our pilots confirm visual." The general cleared his throat. "One of our gunners managed to get close enough to fire some rounds before we lost them. With the kill shots, we still saw the spontaneous combustion you mentioned. Some faster than others, but each person we took out eventually lit up. The slow ones, the weak ones, near the back, they seem to go up fastest. I've got a secondary wave coming in. We're going to focus efforts on those stragglers with distance shooters. We don't want to risk someone moving slow and avoiding the blast radius. Best to take them out."

Fraser didn't reply.

"Operation Achilles will commence in twenty-four minutes. Four F-15s and three B-52s will be airborne momentarily, coming in from multiple directions. They're all crewed but capable of going completely autonomous if compromised. I'm not leaving anything to chance. A full payload of laser-guided Maverick missiles in the F-15s, sixty thermobaric bombs between the three bombers. Each with a blast radius of thirty-three square meters. Enough to erase this mess three times over. There won't be so much as a roach crawling around in the dirt after these things go off."

Fraser turned from the people behind the fence to all the armored vehicles in movement on the opposite end of the bridge, on land. Hundreds of soldiers, people under his command. Both his squads moving into position. How would he get them out in time? Then, he realized, maybe he was never meant to.

Westin was still talking. "...the moment the full horde is in range, we're a go. The F-15s will strike first. They'll launch from five miles out and follow your lasers in, then they'll make two visual passes and fire at will if any portion of those bridges are still standing. Two flyovers—watch for them—then deploy your first squad. Sweep in from the north and south and the back end of the horde. I need you to bottleneck them, box them, and hold them in the pen, give our B-52s time to get into position and deploy. When I give the order to drop, you and your soldiers will have one minute to evacuate the hot zone."

That's not enough time.

"Understood."

"Post detonation, your second squad needs to move in. Ensure none of these things were missed. *Not one.* Execute with extreme prejudice. Come in from all sides and meet in the middle. Squeeze any remaining life from this monstrosity."

How am I supposed to get any of my people out of here?

"Understood, sir."

The hair on Fraser's arm was standing up. He felt it on the back of his neck, too.

The hum had grown louder. He saw a number of

people looking off into the distance. You could feel it coming, feel *them*.

"...those two girls."

Fraser covered his other ear. "I'm sorry, sir. I missed that last part. Repeat?"

"Have you made arrangements to deal with those two girls?" Westin said.

"I don't follow."

Westin's voice dropped off again, but this time, it wasn't because of the connection or all the noise in the air. He was choosing his words carefully. "The president's orders are explicit. All carriers are to be eradicated. This infection dies today. Understood?"

Even this second time, Fraser barely heard him over that growing hum.

My God, is it getting loud. Strange, how it doesn't hurt so much anymore.

"Soldier, do you copy?"

"Yes, sir. Understood."

CHAPTER NINETY

HARBIN

THE HALLWAY ENDED WITH an emergency door at a stairwell—Harbin pushed through and followed the stairs down eighteen flights.

His arm throbbed with each step, and he did the math in his head to try and distract himself from the pain—the building appeared to be six stories tall from the outside; eighteen flights would put him at least three stories underground. The odd thing was he hadn't passed a single door or window. Not in that initial hallway on the top floor or as he reached each landing on the lower floors, nothing but concrete walls, as if the entire building were solid.

At the base of the final flight of stairs, he came upon another steel door, identical to the one above. There was another loud click, and it began to swing open before he reached it. It was open about halfway when a woman appeared—fortyish with black hair pulled back in a ponytail, dark-rimmed glasses, gray slacks, and a navy blouse.

The woman glared at him. "Get in here—hurry."

Harbin stepped past the woman and back in time.

There was no other way to describe the space.

The walls were concrete. Once painted a pale yellow, they were now streaked with old water stains and cracks. A crooked framed photograph of former president Lyndon B. Johnson hung on the wall, the glass tinged and colors faded, a tattered American flag on a pole beside it. In the far corner of the room stood an old cabinet stereo with a stack of records on the floor, similar to the one Harbin remembered at his grandparents' house. Near a doorway leading into a hall lit by bare fluorescent bulbs was a cigarette machine advertising Lucky Strikes for forty cents a pack. A Coca-Cola machine with bottles for fifteen cents. An old rust-orange crushed velvet couch was off to his left. It stunk of mildew. A bank of ancient reel-to-reel computer cabinets lined another wall. One of them actually appeared to be working.

"What is this place?" Harbin asked as he turned slowly, taking in the room.

"Gimme that!" The woman snatched the laptop out from under his arm and tossed it back out the door. It hit the concrete with a crack and skidded to a stop in the far corner near the base of the stairs. "Do you have any other electronics? Anything?

Phone, computer, tablet, hearing aid, pacemaker, smartwatch, anything? Anything that plugs in or charges?"

"No, nothing," he replied in a stunned voice. "They took all that from us at Zigzag."

"What about weapons? Do you have any weapons?"

"One gun."

"You wanna stay, you gotta hand it over. Nobody gets a gun."

Harbin appeared to consider this, realized there wasn't a choice, then reached behind his back, retrieved the gun, and handed it to her.

She held it in her palm for a moment, as if testing the weight, then slipped it into her waistband. "Nobody gets a gun here," she said again, more to herself this time.

The woman's mouth was open slightly, her eyes wide. She looked nervously out toward the stairs, at the shattered laptop, then hit several buttons on a keypad next to the door. The buttons were bulky and made a loud click with each push like an old television remote. The heavy door reversed direction and started to close.

"I have an implant."

The woman turned on him. "What?"

Harbin's fingers went to the back of his neck. "They put it right here. To monitor my vitals after I was exposed to the—"

"Goddamn, Fitch..." With a heavy frown, the woman slammed her palm down on a large red button under the keypad. A loud buzz erupted from a box speaker in the corner of the ceiling, and the door stopped moving. "It was Fitch, right?"

Harbin nodded.

"Stupid, stupid, stupid..." The woman went to a long table, shuffled through a wooden box, and found an old pack of razor blades. She pointed at another table under a bank of black-and-white tube televisions. "There's a lighter over there somewhere. Get it."

"You can't be serious?"

"The implant comes out right now, or you leave."

Again, he had no choice. He went to the table, found the lighter, and tossed it to the woman.

Her eyes shot nervously back to the door. "We need to get that fucking thing closed."

She peeled open the ancient pack of razor blades and took one out, flicked the lighter, and held the blade over the flame. When hot enough, she said, "You know this will hurt, right?"

Harbin nodded.

The woman lifted her ponytail and pointed at a rough scar on the base of her neck. "Easier than getting my own, though."

She made the incision with a practiced hand. Fast. No hesitation. Then, with her thumbnail, she forced the implant out. No bigger than a grain of rice.

Harbin watched it clatter across the concrete floor when she flicked it through the open doorway.

She dropped the bloody razor blade on the floor and glanced down at her watch—an old wind-up with Minnie Mouse on the face. "I should have never opened the damn door. There are bandages in the end table next to the couch," she told him hurriedly. "Antiseptic ointment, too."

Harbin watched as she returned to the door and entered the code again.

The heavy door began moving, lazily swinging shut with a thud. When closed, she leaned her back against the steel, closed her eyes, and let out a long sigh.

"Are you Anna Shim?" Harbin asked her.

With the door closed, the windowless concrete room took on the feeling of a tomb, and his words echoed slightly, resonated, his voice sounding deeper.

She looked back at him, her mouth open slightly again, then let out a nervous cackle, one she quickly stifled. "You don't know shit, do you?"

CHAPTER NINETY-ONE

FRASER

THE NEW HEADPHONES WERE bulkier than the ones his team had worn when they captured those runners—*Was that really only a handful of hours ago?*—and Fraser felt the weight of them on the top of his head under his helmet as his Apache helicopter lifted off from the east end of Burnside Bridge and flew toward the horde. With all the bridges barricaded and laser guides in place, he'd instructed all his teams to pull back and move in to intercept positions.

"This is strange, sir."

Apaches were configured similar to fighter jets—rather than sitting side by side, Fraser was in the seat up front, in the copilot/gunner position, and the pilot sat behind him.

Fraser turned his head slightly but he couldn't see him. "Strange, how?"

"I don't hear the chopper at all. Not even a whisper."

"Will that compromise your ability to fly?"

"It will just take a little getting used to, sir. Engine noise is useful when judging strain on the aircraft. Back in the desert, we had to listen for sand. It got in everything and had a distinct sound. Sound was the first tip-off of a potential problem. The alarms would eventually kick in, but we always heard the sand first, gumming up the equipment."

"No sand here."

"No, sir, I suppose not."

His voice dropped off for a moment as they banked around over the water of the Willamette River, then back east. They were flying low, only about a thousand feet off the ground.

"You've flown in this before, haven't you, sir? I was told you had."

"Yes."

"Can...you tell me what to expect?"

The pilot had been prepping for takeoff when Fraser climbed in; he'd only caught a glimpse of him. Probably mid-thirties. Black guy. Shaved head. He had a slight southern accent, probably one of the Carolinas. "What's your name?"

"Dorset, sir."

Well, Dorset. Imagine the sound someone might make if they were filleted without anesthetic, cut maybe a thousand times, then dropped in a vat of hot salt water. It sounds a little something like that. Oh, and that pain they'd feel? It's gonna feel like that's between your ears. Then it gets worse as you get closer.

"I'm sure we'll be okay with these new headphones."

"Yes, sir."

Fraser spotted the horde a moment later and felt his chest tighten.

How had it grown so much in only a few hours?

This black stain on the earth the size of a lake or a river, that's what it looked like from the air now, the bodies packed so tight they moved as one, a wall of dust above them. Autonomous military vehicles bounced alongside, floodlights reaching across the void, but even they seemed to peter out and vanish, as if the light turned back, unwilling to brush against the infected.

"Sir, do you hear that?"

Fraser did.

The hum.

The noise.

"How are we able to hear it but not the helicopter?" Dorset asked. "No way it's louder, right?"

Fraser didn't answer that question—it wouldn't do any good. "Just keep your headphones on. What's our current distance?"

The pilot didn't respond.

"Dorset?"

"Sorry, sir. We're a quarter mile out."

A quarter mile? That was good. The new headphones

were good. It had been much worse earlier at this distance.

The hairs on his arms were standing again. His skin felt electric.

"Sir, my left ear is bleeding."

"Did you remove your headphones?"

"No, sir. I just felt something wet on my neck."

Fraser touched his own neck, and his hand came away dry. Nothing under his nose or his eyes, either. Dr. Chan said he'd built up a tolerance. "Are you compromised?"

"Compromised, sir?"

"Your ability to fly. Are you able to keep flying?"

"I'm . . . I'm fine, sir."

"Take us in a little closer. Up near the front."

At first, the helicopter remained steady, and Fraser thought he'd have to tell him again, but then they swooped down and over and narrowed their distance by about half.

The hum grew louder, but still felt tolerable. At least to Fraser.

"Dorset? You okay back there?"

" . . . I'm . . . okay."

The helicopter jerked slightly, then steadied.

Fraser peered out the window again.

Dorset had brought them down, only a few hundred feet off the ground, even with the lead runners, an endless wall of people behind them.

He watched as a woman out front tripped and vanished under a thousand pairs of feet. There one second, gone the next. An old man was running next to a teenage girl, somehow keeping up as her legs pistoned, both of them staring forward toward some invisible brass ring, their arms dangling at their sides like dead weight.

All of these people were going to die. Every last one. His finger pulling the trigger.

Fraser felt pressure between his ears. As if someone placed their hands on either side of his head and pushed.

Bad.

Not as bad as earlier.

He could take it. He'd power through.

His right leg started to twitch, like a spasm. Involuntary.

He tried to shift his position but the belts held him tight.

The space felt so small, even surrounded by the Apache's windows. He felt like he was in a box, the walls inching closer, pressing against him. Pressure, like his head, all around.

"Dorset, what's our current distance from the bridges?"

When had Dorset started screaming?

"Dorset, what's our current distance from the bridges?!" Fraser repeated, shouting, more firm this time.

Christ, this cockpit felt small. Warm, too.

He reached up and loosened the safety harness.

Both his legs were twitching. The muscles in his left leg tightened up, the start of a charley horse. There was no room to stretch. He'd kill to stand, stretch out, move around.

"Dorset, damnit! Answer my question!"

The man stopped screaming.

Thank God for that.

"Two . . . tenths of a mile . . . sir . . . ETA one minute."

Fraser hadn't heard the F-15s fly over them, but when he looked up, he saw their jet wash—these dark streaks on a darker sky. He saw the missiles deploy. Watched dozens of them cut through the air on bright blue flames, arch down, and ride the lasers to their targets.

He toggled the channel on his microphone. "Command, this is team leader. Bridges down."

He wasn't sure if they heard him—Dorset was screaming again.

Fraser looked down at his hands. His headphones were sitting in them, balanced on his lap.

He didn't remember taking them off.

Funny—the noise didn't sound so unpleasant anymore.

His legs were jumping now. He really needed to move.

"Take us down, Dorset."

The ground came at them far too fast.

CHAPTER NINETY-TWO

MARTHA

THE NAMES WERE STILL coming, faster now:

"Colton Matsuo, Leola Carpio, Valorie Wideman, Madaline Eaves, Manual Aldridge, Rigoberto Kogan, Danial Havens, Lajuana Bertolini, Hildegard Edman, Maire Fullwood, Marty Barb, Felicidad Zabriskie, Fabian Overman, Milagro Toole, Jona Dowler, Nicolas Theodore, Jude Manhart, Meredith Carroll, Arlene Lindstrom, Tia Gau..."

Sophie bounced from left foot to right foot and back again with each name, this rhythmic dance. There was no break in the words, not even to draw in a breath, as if speaking alone was enough to fuel her. Her face was this odd mix—the excitement of an eight-year-old girl discovering something for the first time, and something else, something far older, something that made Martha want to turn away.

The monitor with the frozen video image of the

horde was attached to a metal stand on wheels. Tennant grabbed it and angrily shoved it at her sister. She pushed it so hard, it crashed against the metal cage.

"That's our Momma and Poppa! Are you really going to let them die?!"

"Audria Kinne, die! Leland Pepe, die! Nevada Burchell, die!" the little girl chanted back at her, her legs moving so fast.

"No, Sophie! Nobody dies! Nobody!"

"They all run! They all run! *We* all run!"

The hum coming from Sophie's body was loud enough now to rattle the cage. Martha watched a pen on a table jump several times and drop off the side. The hangar, the metal roof and walls, the large lights above, everything rattled and bounced. Martha felt it in her bones, in her teeth. The sound growing louder with it.

Her feet still moving, running in place, Sophie's tiny hands reached out and grabbed the door, her fingers wrapped around the metal so tight they went white. "Tennnnant."

Tennant hesitated a moment, then took a step closer.

One of the soldiers started to go to her, to hold her back, but Martha grabbed him by the arm and shook her head.

Let her, she mouthed.

"Luuuv you, Tennnnant."

Tennant's eyes filled with tears. Her fingers curled around her sister's, squeezed her hand. "You need to stop this."

"Caaan't."

"You can hear them, that means they can hear you. You need to tell them all to stop. They're all going to die if you don't. The soldiers are going to kill everybody. Tell Anna Shim, tell all of them. It's not too late. You can save Momma and Poppa, all of them, you need to try…"

"…must run. All…"

Tennant looked over her shoulder at Martha. "She's *so* hot."

Martha reached for the iPad—Sophie's temperature was 126 and climbing.

"Don't let her burn up like the others!" Tennant pleaded. "I can't lose her, too!"

Martha knew there was nothing she could do, but she ordered one of the soldiers to get some ice anyway.

Tennant turned back to her sister. "I've got nobody without you. Everybody's gone."

"Not gooooone, running."

"They're gone, Sophie. Unless you stop this. Do you understand? They're dead. The soldiers are going to drop bombs and kill everyone. They'll be gone forever. They're like the rabbits in my traps. That noise they're making, that's like that horrible sound the rabbits make when we snare them. These people, they're all running into a trap."

Martha considered telling her to stop, prevent Tennant from detailing the plan, but realized it didn't matter at this point. The bridges were gone. They'd heard the report over one of the radios. All those people had no place to go, nowhere else to run. Surely, whatever force was behind this knew exactly what was happening.

"You stop them, Sophie, you make them better, and we'll all go back to the mountain. We'll rebuild our village, you and me and Momma and Poppa...all of us. We can rebuild. Remember the storm two years ago? You were so small then, but that was the reason Poppa built the shelters, in case another storm came. Half the village vanished overnight, but we rebuilt. We put it all back, better than before. We'll do it again."

Sophie's blue eyes scrunched, filled with frustration, and at first Martha thought what Tennant said had angered her, but then she realized this wasn't anger, this was frustration.

Was Tennant getting through to her?

"Not enough," Sophie forced out.

"What's not enough?" Tennant asked.

Sophie's legs started to move even faster. They were nearly a blur.

According to the iPad, her temperature was 134.

She shouldn't be conscious. She shouldn't be alive. Her face and hair were greasy with sweat, and the hum, the noise, grew impossibly louder.

"What's not enough?!" Tennant shouted.

"Us... Them."

"I don't understand!"

Sophie pulled out from under Tennant's hand, took several steps back, then ran forward with incredible speed. She crashed into the metal door, backed up, and ran again.

"Sophie, stop!"

"Must run!"

"You're going to hurt yourself!"

"Run!"

"Run to what?! What are you running toward?!"

"Not tooooward, run away. Must run away."

CHAPTER NINETY-THREE

HARBIN

HARBIN FOUND THE OINTMENT—a metal tube of some brand he'd never heard of. The expiration date stamped in the base of the tube read January 1972.

The woman told him, "It's still good. Most expiration dates are bogus. That's something manufacturers came up with to build in obsolescence. Gotta throw stuff out, buy more. Throw stuff out, buy more . . . " She kept repeating this as she went back over to the long table below the television monitors. She began flicking each one on, moving from right to left. Five in total.

"Who are you?" Harbin asked her.

"My name is Dr. Amanda Cushman. Until very recently, I worked for DARPA. I haven't officially tendered my resignation, but unofficially, I am no longer under their employ. We've had several differences of opinion lately, and I've decided it's best we part ways."

As she moved, Harbin noticed a dark stain on the crotch of her pants, partially dry. It had been there awhile. He tried not to stare.

Dr. Cushman tapped on one of the televisions, then put her ear to the small speaker in the front. "I believe you came to see Dr. Hoover." She waved a hand toward a metal door with a narrow window on her left. "He's in there."

Harbin stepped up and peered inside. He had to cup his hands to see through the haze, and he realized the glass was smeared with blood and the room filled with a damp steam. There was blood on the filthy concrete walls, the floor, everywhere. When a gasp fell from his lips, it wasn't brought on by all the blood but by the man inside.

Frederick Hoover was in a straitjacket, suspended from the ceiling, his legs pumping as he ran in place, moving so fast they were nothing but a blur. His skin was yellow, deeply jaundiced, his unblinking eyes red and glaring at some unseen point, spittle dripping from his mouth as he jerked in the air with the movement.

Still looking up at the television monitors, Dr. Cushman said, "I couldn't take him running around in circles anymore, smacking the walls and the door, so I sedated him and got him in the air. I frankly didn't think he'd last this long, but he's holding in there. Last I checked, his temperature was around

120. He'll blaze up soon enough. Those walls are a foot thick, solid concrete. We'll be okay out here when he goes. Just keep that door shut."

Harbin stood there for a long moment before he asked, "How did it happen?"

"Have you ever told a child not to do something? Don't do this, don't touch that... as soon as you tell them, that's all they want to do, they become obsessed. That was Freddy when I told him not to listen. We took to sleeping in shifts a while back, and I'd wake up to find him listening to it... just little bits here and there, but he was convinced that if he listened in short spurts, he could build a tolerance. We'd seen it already in others. Immunity was a pipe dream *but a tolerance*? That brass ring wasn't hanging too high, and he wanted to grab it. I told him to stop. That only made him want it more. He did it for months, and it seemed like it was working, until the day it didn't. I'm not sure how long he listened that last time, but I woke when I heard the clatter of him running. Took half a day to get him into that room."

"When was that?"

Her face scrunched up as she thought about it. "What's today's date?"

Harbin told her.

She seemed slightly taken aback. "I've... we've been down here a long time. You lose track. I guess he's been running for about six days now. Like I said, he'll blaze up soon. None of them seem to last much longer than that."

Six days.

"What exactly is this place?"

She didn't answer, only stared at the blank televisions. He was about to repeat the question when she said, "Blast from the past, isn't it? The building you're standing in, known affectionately as Renton Forty-Nine, is an old government bomb shelter left over from the Cold War. If you head down that hall in the back you'll find food, water, showers, bunks . . . all the comforts of a third-world prison. This one was meant to house Seattle's mayor, a couple senators, and anyone else stupid enough to seal themselves away in an oversize tin can for ten thousand years. How they expected to arrive in the ten minutes they'd probably have to get here is beyond me, but here it is. Our tax dollars built thousands of these, all over the country. DARPA picked this one up because of its unique structure—the building is a solid block of concrete with metal mesh layered inside. They did that for support, but the unintended consequence was they created a double-layered Faraday cage. No electronic signals in or out, unless they're hardwired."

"Like the dead room back at the base," Harbin said.

"Yeah, like a dead room."

Having finally warmed up, the five televisions began

to glow—four with nothing but static, a shaky gray image on the middle one.

"How's that signal coming in?" Harbin asked.

"Best I can tell, back in nineteen-whatever when they built this place, someone had hardlines put in from here to the local television stations up the road. I guess they figured they didn't want to spend eternity without *I Love Lucy* on standby. I've only gotten a picture on this middle one, though." Dr. Cushman stood and snapped a switch on a timer screwed into the wall. Plastic numbers began to whir, counting down from two hours. "We can watch for a little while, but make sure this is off before it hits zero. It's possible to recover from exposure under two hours, not more than that. It creeps up on you but doesn't seem to be cumulative. Don't forget."

She hit the screen with the back of her fist.

The horde came into view, this giant black mass writhing like some unholy living thing.

The picture flickered, and she hit the screen again. "That's the Willamette River there holding them back," she said, tracing the side of the screen. "Portland on the other side. Looks like the military blew the bridge. Probably all of them."

The image flicked out and went to static like the others.

"Goddamnit." She hit the television again, but the picture didn't come back.

She hit it again, harder this time; still nothing but static. "We had communications with Washington up until a few days ago, but there's something wrong with our radio." She gestured toward a rusted-out metal box to the left of the couch.

The glass display was shattered. The cord attached to the receiver had been cut into at least half a dozen pieces, and it looked like someone took a sledge-hammer to the rest, pulverizing the body and inner electronics.

There's something wrong with our radio.

Dr. Cushman let out a sigh. "You came here looking for the illustrious Dr. Frederick Hoover, but I'm guessing you really want to talk about this."

She flicked a switch, and the noise screamed out from every speaker in the bunker.

CHAPTER NINETY-FOUR

FRASER

FRASER TUMBLED OUT THE shattered windows of the Apache cockpit and collapsed in the grass. Half a dozen feet away, one of four rotor blades protruded from the earth. He couldn't tell by looking at it if it had just snapped off or if the other half was buried in the ground. The chopper was on its side, ass-end up in the air, one of the missile pylons under the wing propping it up. Black smoke poured out the back.

Fraser managed to turn his head and caught a glimpse of Dorset about a hundred feet away. His right arm was gone, nothing but a ragged stump at his shoulder, yet the man was running. Trying to. He was awkwardly shuffling toward the horde, blood pouring from the wound, down his side, his leg, his body slowing with each step. For a second there, Fraser thought he might make it, and if he did, maybe the momentum of all the others would carry him along like discarded trash in a rushing river.

But Dorset collapsed about fifty steps short. He went down face-first, dragging himself forward with his remaining arm, but only managed a few more feet.

Fraser forced his body to work through sheer will more than anything, because he was pretty sure it no longer wanted to move. Nothing seemed to be broken (a miracle, considering the drop they just took) but he was cut up, and every one of his muscles felt as if someone had stretched them out like taffy. He got to his feet, wobbled for a moment, and waited for the world to stop rocking.

His eyes locked on the horde.

Christ, there were so many, and they were so loud. Even above the noise he could hear the thunder of their feet. He was reminded of cattle in an old western, a stampede across an open prairie. The cowboys on horseback had been replaced by autonomous military vehicles running alongside. Cameras rolling, remote gun turrets shooting. He imagined a dozen soldiers in a building half a world away lined up in front of computer monitors, high-fiving each other with each kill in this real-life video game. He wondered if they even knew what they were really shooting at. He watched several of them roll by, picking off random runners as they went, and realized just how fruitless that effort was. They were swatting at single bees in a hive a million strong. This was nothing more than a useless effort ordered by someone who felt the need to do something and could think of nothing better.

The F-15s raced overhead, back in the direction of Portland, and he watched as they deployed their missiles for a second time.

Fraser could see one of the bridges from here. Hawthorne, maybe? He wasn't sure, but the first wave of missiles had done a number on it, and as the second wave cracked into the remaining metal and concrete, several of the large support struts crumbled and two large spans of steel and blacktop collapsed down into the water. He imagined the other bridges had fared the same. Nobody would be crossing this one anytime soon, and off in the distance, he could see the F-15s circling back for their final pass.

No doubt, the first of the runners had reached the water's edge and were either tumbling in or stopped there. He couldn't see the front of the group from here, but he could see enough of them to know they were backing up at those bridges, at the water, unable to move forward.

Something wet dripped down the side of his head, and when Fraser touched it, expecting blood, he realized it was only sweat. He had no idea what happened to his headphones—maybe still in the Apache or maybe a thousand feet away in the dirt, he only knew they weren't on his head.

The noise screamed so loud on the night air he could taste it. Every molecule was alive and riding the wave of that sound, vibrating with it. He wondered if the sound was coming from him. What would Dr. Chan see if she held up her iPad again?

Unlike the others, he felt no need to run.

He was curious. He wanted to go after them to see what was happening, but that undeterred urge to run? He didn't feel that at all. Not anymore. Part of him wanted to feel it, and that frightened him a little. *Not* feeling it, and standing out here in the middle of the noise without any protection, no longer feeling the pain, no longer wanting to run, that frightened him a lot. Because it meant he was something different. No longer normal—not one of them, either, but different. He wondered if this is what that little girl felt.

Yes.

He didn't know where the single word came from. This wasn't a conscious thought on his part, certainly wasn't something he heard, but there it was. An answer to his question, and he'd be damned if it hadn't popped into his head with that little girl's voice.

Beside him, a Humvee rolled up and skidded to a stop.

Fraser walked over to it and peered inside.

In the driver's seat, a soldier's lifeless body lay slumped over the steering wheel, his fingers coiled around a 9mm. There was a black burn mark under his chin where the bullet had entered and a much larger hole in the top of his head where it had come back out. The ceiling above him glistened with the man's last thought.

There was nobody in the passenger seat. Nobody in the back.

Like the other vehicles, this one had cameras mounted all around under thick ballistic glass and several automated machine guns on turrets attached to the roof. One on Fraser's left was still clicking, out of ammunition but still firing in the direction of the horde.

Also like the other vehicles, this one had been modified to operate remotely. There was a bulky contraption attached to the steering wheel and another one at the pedals. The dead soldier's limbs were still entwined in these things, but that didn't seem to keep them from working.

In the center of the dashboard was a small LED screen. Two words blinked on the screen:

GET IN.

CHAPTER NINETY-FIVE

MARTHA

"RUN AWAY FROM WHAT, SOPHIE?"

Tennant nearly screamed the words in order to be heard.

Martha didn't need a camera to tell her Sophie was vibrating; she could see it with her naked eye. What should have been sharp lines—the girl's nose, her arms, her legs, the creases of her clothing—were all blurry, as if Martha were watching her through a veil of water. Sophie's cage was rattling, too. The discarded restraints on the floor inched along with the vibration, moving toward the opposite wall. The hangar shook. The tables. The computer monitors and LCD screens flickered. One cracked—a tiny break in the topmost left corner crept and grew across the screen in a web, distorting the image of the horde more than a hundred miles away. Before it flicked out completely, Martha caught a glimpse of an enormous black mass building at the edge of the Willamette River, Portland on the opposite side, and what seemed to be a giant fireball between where the bridges had stood earlier. Then the cracked screen went black and shimmied across the concrete.

Martha's legs shook beneath her, and she reached for a steel support beam to steady herself. That did little good. The beam was vibrating, too.

"Sophie! Run away from what?!" Tennant shouted again.

Sophie didn't answer but instead shuffled to the back wall of her cage and ran again for the door, slamming into it with enough force to stress the steel hinges and lock, but not enough to break it.

She took several steps back, pinched her eyes shut, and clenched her fists. "Run from all, but no place to go! It's everywhere!"

The words came out muddled, nearly incomprehensible.

"She's at 136!" Tennant called out.

Martha glanced frantically from the little girl to him. "We need to get her out of that cage! Maybe if we let her run, she'll burn off some of the energy, keep from..."

She didn't finish the thought—she didn't have to. They all knew what would happen.

Behind them both, two soldiers near the hangar door raised their weapons. They didn't point the guns at Sophie, but they made it clear they could get them there if they needed to. The one closest to Martha yelled out, "We're under orders—she doesn't leave the cage, and she doesn't leave this hangar! Don't make us shoot a child, ma'am!"

"She'll die if we leave her in there!"

"She *can't* leave this hangar!" the soldier repeated.

With that, his eyes shifted over to Tennant for a second, and Martha read something there. Something worse. He wasn't talking about only Sophie. They'd all been exposed. The military action taking place wasn't just to wipe out the horde but to wipe out the infection. *All traces of the infection.* That included the two sisters, Harbin, herself...hell, General Westin might not stop there. Martha inadvertently looked up at the ceiling of the hangar, the heavy lights swaying back and forth above her, and imagined what might be flying above them right now.

Her fingers tightened on the support beam. "If you kill these girls, if you kill all of us, that won't stop this thing. Everyone on this base has been exposed on some level. How far do you think the general will go? How do you know one of those B-52s isn't circling around right now? Or maybe one from another airstrip? They could target us from space or a ship or detonate something already here on base, make it look like an accident if they want to." She pointed at the cameras all around them, several lying on their sides. "They're watching us. They see this girl implode, they'll use that as an excuse to take out everyone here, including you, and they'll find some way to cover their tracks!"

The soldiers shuffled nervously but said nothing.

"One forty-eight!" someone called out.

Sophie was running in place. Her fists clenching and releasing. Her head bobbing as she sucked in air and let it back out in labored gasps.

"We have orders, ma'am! I'm sorry! Don't open that door!"

Tennant was back at the cage door, but without the key, she couldn't open it. "Sophie! Listen to me. You need to fight this! Focus on my voice! Ignore everything else. Tune everything else out like we do with the rabbits. Don't listen to any of it! Whatever they're telling you to do, they're lying!"

Sophie stumbled forward, her eyes still closed, and gripped the metal door near the lock—one hand above, the other below, her legs pumping.

The noise grew louder.

Under her touch, the cage joined the blur that was Sophie. This violent vibration cracked the metal frame against the brackets and bolts that held it to the ground. The welded corners and seams shook with an incredible force coming not only from the girl but from the air around her.

The noise became deafening, raining down from

the heavens, growing up from the ground, riding the air as if every living thing had joined this devil's chorus.

Martha tried to cover her ears, but it did no good. She was vibrating now, too. Her, the others, everyone. The noise was screaming at them. It continued to cry out as the lock snapped and fell away, as the cage came apart. As Sophie stood there, finally free.

CHAPTER NINETY-SIX

FRASER

WHEN FRASER CLIMBED INTO the passenger seat of the remote-controlled Humvee, he made several assumptions. He assumed the powers that be, watching from their far-off place, had seen him scramble out of the fallen Apache and away from the wreckage on one of the many cameras, or maybe a satellite, and had ordered some freckle-faced kid, also in a far-off place, to redirect the remote vehicle to Fraser's location. He had also assumed, when he fell into the seat and tugged the door closed behind him, that the vehicle would quickly turn and rush him away from the current theater of operation and the soon-to-be bomb zone. Instead, the Humvee shot forward, not away from Portland but toward it—toward the blown bridges and the growing horde at the river's shore.

Fraser grabbed the keyboard dangling under the

small monitor and quickly typed: GET ME OUT OF HERE! YOU'RE GOING THE WRONG WAY!

The response came impossibly fast, within a millisecond of him hitting Send.

NO.

Then, CONNECTED. YOU MUST SEE. STAND BY...

These words lingered on the screen.

See what? He keyed that in too, but there was no reply. The Humvee only picked up speed, sliding on some muddy grass, then finding traction.

Should he jump out?

Even as the thought entered his head, the Humvee veered to the right, toward the horde. The desperate faces didn't turn to look at vehicles, not even a glance, but somehow, the runners opened up a gap, and the Humvee eased into it. Then the horde closed in around him, swallowed him, *absorbed* him.

The faces surrounding him were both blank and horror-struck, forced into movement against their will, without the ability to stop. A teenager tripped directly in front of the Humvee and vanished under the hood. Fraser felt the vehicle bounce with a sickening thump.

Overhead, the F-15s made their final pass. The last of their missiles swooped down out of the sky and crashed into the earth ahead. The ground shook as the bombs tore through the last remnants of the bridges. Others pummeled the earth along the shore, and others still slipped beneath the surface of the Willamette River and erupted in geysers spouting at the heavens.

Fraser knew the sounds of war intimately. He waited for those sounds to come, but they never did, not over the sound of the horde. There was nothing louder than the scream of the horde.

Not hundreds of thousands of individual voices anymore, but one singular voice containing the pain of all—the pain of life and death, disease and infection, pollution, suffocation, and suffering in a chorus of only crescendo. If this were a wave, it would be a tsunami a thousand feet tall.

Fraser knew it was wrong to listen to it. He reached over and plucked the headphones from around the dead soldier's neck. He tried not to think about the sticky mess on the band as he pulled them on his head, down over his ears.

The outside world went silent, and for one brief second he heard the military's radio chatter—*"F-15s clear. Bridges gone. Bombers inbound. And—"*

The pain started right behind his eyes, quickly wrapped around to the sides of his head to his neck, his chest, his arms and legs. It was worst at his ears, though, as if someone had set the headphones on fire. He smacked at them, knocked them off his head, and watched them fall into the footwell through blurry vision.

On the monitor: DISCONNECTED. RECONNECTING. STAND BY...

The runners were packed so tight around him, there was nothing but a wall of bodies. Torn flesh and open wounds covered in dust pressed against the windows, smeared the glass. The air was hot with the stink of them, seeping into the Humvee.

He couldn't see a damn thing.

With the keyboard, Fraser quickly typed: STOP THIS VEHICLE!

No response.

The Humvee lurched and picked up speed instead. Two more runners fell beneath the wheels and vanished.

Fraser reached up, pushed open the top hatch, and stood.

He nearly fell back down into his seat.

The sky was crimson and thick with smoke, and so hot. Where one of the bridges had once stood—he had no idea which—the waters of the Willamette were burning. Directly ahead of him, less than a hundred yards away, many of the horde followed the torn blacktop and tumbled over the edge, but more still had stopped. Those coming from behind ran directly into those already there, and a wall of bodies had begun to form, this human traffic jam—tripping, falling, and pushing over and around each other trying to get by with no place to go as the noise caused the air to shimmer.

Fraser's Humvee raced directly toward them, toward that water, with no means to stop, knowing the bombers were not far behind.

CHAPTER NINETY-SEVEN

HARBIN

THE NOISE STOPPED ALMOST as quickly as it began, but even that brief exposure felt like an icepick in Harbin's ear and he found himself doubled over, both hands pressed to the sides of his head, when it ended.

Dr. Cushman threw up her hands. "Sorry, sorry, sorry. My bad. I meant to play this one."

Before he could react, she flipped another switch and the noise again poured out of the speakers, only this time it brought no pain. There was none of the discomfort Harbin had come to expect, only the ugly sound.

"This recording has gone through a series of filters. It's harmless. I'm going to slow it down for you. I want you to tell me what you hear."

She reached for a dial and began slowly twisting it counterclockwise. The pitch of the noise shifted, dropped lower, became less of a constant tone and more of a series of sounds.

When Harbin recognized it, he almost didn't say anything, because he couldn't possibly be right. But it could be nothing else. He finally said, "That sounds like an old fax machine. The sound they would make when they connected. Or an old modem. Dial-up."

Dr. Cushman was nodding. "Acoustic exchange protocol. The sound was used to establish speed and exchange identification. Binary tones represented as varying pitches." She turned back to him. What was it you called me?"

"Anna Shim. Sophie said the sound was Anna Shim."

This seemed to amuse her. "We never used that phrase outside of the group, but if she's connected I imagine she had no trouble finding it. Children appear to be the most adaptive."

Tugging open a metal drawer, she pulled out a thick sheaf of papers bound together with a clip and dropped it on the table between them:

DARPA INITIATIVE 769021473

ANALOG SYMBIOTIC HUMAN INTERFACE MECHANISM

She underlined the first three letters of *analog* and the first letter of each additional word:

ANALOG SYMBIOTIC HUMAN INTERFACE MECHANISM

ANA SHIM

Anna Shim.

"I don't think anyone expected it to work, until it did," Cushman said, running the dirty nail of her index finger over the pages. "We were tasked with finding an efficient way to connect people and computers without the need for an implant or intrusive surgery of any kind. That seemed like a tall order, until we broke down the problem." She tapped the side of her head. "Our brains are organic computers, and our five senses—touch, smell, sight, sound, and taste—are forms of input. We spent years working with light, following the same principles as fiber-optic lines but using the visual cortex of the brain to decipher the signal. In many ways it worked, but it wasn't very forgiving. The test subject had to look dead-on, and something as simple as blinking disrupted the message. Sound, though—sound was a different animal. When we switched to sound, everything changed. Low volume, high volume, close, far…none of that mattered. There was nearly zero signal loss. We had it. The possibilities were endless—imagine learning to play the piano in a millisecond or learning a foreign language. Learning *every* language. Reading a book instantly with perfect retention. Controlling artificial limbs. Controlling vehicles or other hardware. We were so close. We were right there."

Dr. Cushman slumped back in her chair and wiped her nose with the back of her hand. "That wasn't enough. They wanted the internet. They wanted soldiers to be able to communicate directly with satellites, they wanted a connection without any special headphones or speakers. To do that, we needed two things—a carrier signal and a viable transmitter/receiver. The signal was easy. The internet is everywhere—cellular data networks, Bluetooth, wi-fi—everything is connected now, transmitting and receiving. You step out that door, and you're bombarded with it. You may not see it, but it's there. That left the human aspect. How do we teach the brain to talk to that signal? If a telephone rings next to you, and you don't know what a telephone is, you just let it ring. But if someone shows you how to pick it up, how to answer and use it..." She tapped the side of her head again. "Once you know, it's there forever. It practically becomes an involuntary action."

Her eyes drifted back down to the stack of pages, and she fell silent for a moment as the memories came back. "It was Hoover who came up with the idea of treating it like malware. Just like our experiments with language, he wrote a snippet of code that taught the brain how to connect, how to interpret the signal, how to transmit, how to receive...He converted it to analog audio, and using what we learned, he played it for our Patient Zero, this homeless man from Oregon. The damn thing worked. He connected, but he ran hot. No matter what we tried, we couldn't control the speed of the data exchange—the human brain is hungry, starving for knowledge, but the man's body couldn't keep up. You've seen what happens—perpetual energy created and burned until *poof,* they blaze."

Dr. Cushman watched a daddy long-legs spider ease down off the wall, skitter across the desk, and vanish down below. When she spoke again, her voice was somber. "We thought we could control it, but we were wrong. Someone at a much higher pay grade than me thought they could weaponize it. They were wrong about that, too. Turns out, we were wrong about a lot. At some point, like any good malware, this one learned to spread. At first it just seemed to spread person to person—their bodies gave off that hum, the noise, and infected others, but then we realized it had also spread to the internet, to all those connected devices. And anything electronic that could generate sound became a host, too. All of it infecting, infecting, infecting."

She shuffled through several items on the table, found a pen, and scribbled something in the corner of the Anna Shim document.

Harbin tried to process all this. He had so many questions, but only one that mattered. "So how do we stop it?"

This made her laugh, the sharp cackle of someone unwell. She leaned back in her chair and called out over her shoulder, "Hey, Freddy, he wants to know how to stop it! How 'bout you take that one?"

Dr. Cushman waited a moment, as if expecting Hoover to answer. Then she tilted her head and told Harbin, "It's not gonna get me. Let me show you how to stop it."

Reaching forward, she snatched up Harbin's gun from the table, flicked off the safety, and put the barrel in her mouth.

She pulled the trigger without hesitation, and Harbin's body jerked with the loud report. Her head cracked back, the bullet exiting and embedding in the concrete wall behind her.

Harbin stood there for a long time, unable to move, the echo fading and dying around him, the room filling with utter silence—this complete silence, the only silence he'd heard in days. When his arms, legs, and body would finally obey him again, he managed to turn the thick sheaf of documents and read her words among the speckles of blood—

GIVE GENERAL WESTIN MY BEST.

CHAPTER NINETY-EIGHT

FRASER

FRASER DROPPED INTO HIS seat and jammed his leg down into the driver's-side footwell onto the brake pedal, mashed it down along with the dead driver's foot. There was no response. He recalled from some long-ago briefing that manual controls disconnected when these vehicles switched into autonomous mode but had hoped he'd remembered wrong. He had no idea how to disconnect the remote system. He'd be pulling wires blind.

Fraser grabbed at the steering wheel, but it spun under his grip, small servos turning it hard right, then back to the left. The Humvee smacked into runners on both sides, as if attempting to force them back, clear a path, but it did little good—the moment they straightened back out, the horde closed back in around them, bodies pressed right up against both sides, chasing from behind.

The runners in front of him hit the wall of standing runners without even a hint of slowing down, and the Humvee crashed into their backs. Even over the roar of the engine, the screaming noise of the horde, his own cries, he heard the crack of bone as legs and spines and arms splintered and snapped. He was thrown forward, his shoulder smashed into the dash with an unsettling sound and knew something broke even before the rush of pain confirmed it. The broken bodies of several runners flew, others went under, and the Humvee lurched to a stop amid a tangle of death.

The engine switched off, and the text on the LCD monitor updated: GET OUT.

Even if he wanted to, there was no way he could.

Runners crushed into the Humvee from behind, at both sides. Several ran right over the top and kept going over the writhing bodies at the water's edge and vanished.

The text updated again: ALL WILL CHANGE SOON.

Fraser pulled the microphone from around the dead soldier's neck. "This is Lieutenant Colonel Alex Fraser! I'm in Humvee"—he located the identification plate on the dash—"Six oh one nine three! I need immediate evacuation!"

Without the headphones, he didn't know if anyone could hear him, but he repeated all of this several times before tossing the microphone down to the floorboard.

The horde pressed tight all around him, filling every inch of available space outside the Humvee. He reached up and yanked the overhead door shut when a leg dropped down through the opening, kicked at the open air, then pulled back out. He managed to get the door closed as footfalls rained down, as the horde choked the vehicle from above. As the metal groaned under the growing weight, he tried not to think about all the crushed cars he'd seen in the past several days.

BOMBERS INCOMING. ETA ONE MINUTE.

He stared at the five words. He was going to die here.

A hand slapped against the window beside him. A man's hand, an Army Ranger ring on the third finger identical to the one his father had worn.

Fraser twisted and tried to get a look at the man, but he was gone a moment later as others pressed against the side of the Humvee and pushed him out of the way. The roof over the backseat buckled inward and the portion above Fraser followed. He slid deeper down.

Thick ballistic or not, he knew the glass would go soon under the weight. Christ, it was hot.

He remembered what those doctors had told him happened to the other bodies when they stopped moving, the captured runners back at the hangar. He thought of the makeshift morgue back at Zigzag.

He understood where the heat was coming from.

A woman's face was up against the glass on his right, distorted by the pressure of so many others behind her. At first, her eyes held that same blank gaze as all the others. Then something changed. She seemed to see him. She seemed to realize where she was.

He'd never seen anyone look so scared.

Sweaty steam lofted from her skin and smeared the window. Her cheek split open, the blood singed the glass, then went white with a light so bright Fraser had to turn away. He felt the heat of it and realized the metal of the Humvee was glowing, too, burning hot and red. When the woman ignited in a flash, a boy beside her did as well. The ones around them both followed. All of them, one after the other, as if someone took a flame to a book of matches.

Fraser sucked in one last hot breath as three final words appeared on the LCD screen:

UPLOADING. STAND BY . . .

CHAPTER NINETY-NINE

PRESIDENT

THE PRESIDENT AND A dozen others clustered around the video monitors aboard Air Force One.

He kept telling himself he was doing the right thing.

The people around him *assured him* he was doing the right thing.

None of that calmed the churning in his stomach or settled the migraine gaining traction behind his eyes despite the three Imitrex he'd swallowed in the past hour. He'd taken his tie off hours ago. The top two buttons on his shirt were undone, yet he still felt like he was being choked. He had a glass of water on the table but refused to pick it up, worried someone might see just how bad he was shaking if he did.

General Westin looked up at him, a phone pressed to his ear. "The bombers are in range, sir. Deploying in ten seconds, on my mark. I need confirmation from you—are we a go?"

The president looked back at the monitor on his far left. The feed came from a McCoy 828 satellite. The image was remarkably clear—the lights of Portland, the brighter lights of the fires along the Willamette River—and to the east of Portland, at the river's edge, the enormous black stain of the horde. He told himself the horde were no longer people, but a deluge of death and destruction. An organism, a monstrous cancer. The contrast between those two things—the bright lights of Portland and the deep black of the horde—helped him to think of what was happening there not as a *them* but as an *it,* and that separation got him over the last hump, brought him to what he must do.

The president nodded at Westin.

"I need verbal confirmation, sir. For the record."

The president swallowed. "You're authorized to deploy."

He hadn't realized how quiet the room had gotten until Westin spoke back into the phone. "Achilles is a go. Weapons drop authorized at your ready."

The president forced himself to breathe and stepped closer to the monitors. He found his eyes locked on that ugly black mass. It was so damn big. "How long?"

He could only manage the two words, but this was enough for Westin. He understood what he was asking.

"Deployed at a height of fifty thousand feet, the bombs will reach the surface in approximately three minutes."

The president stepped closer to the monitor, narrowed his eyes, and tapped the screen. "If the bombs haven't reached the ground, what is that?"

Westin followed his finger.

A pinprick of incredibly bright light had started at the easternmost edge of the horde, growing thicker and somehow brighter.

The president understood then, and the words dropped from his lips. "They're combusting. We forced them to stand still, and it's like the doctors said—without running to burn off the energy, it's building, igniting."

Westin was back on the phone. His face grew red as he barked at someone, then listened. "We're reading temperatures on the ground in excess of a thousand degrees and climbing. This is some kind of chain reaction—they're lighting off one another!"

The president couldn't take his eyes off the screen. "What does this mean for the bombs?"

Westin didn't answer. His mouth was hanging open as he listened to whoever was on the other end of the phone.

"General?"

Westin held up a finger. Into the phone, he said, "Repeat?"

On the screen, the image was so bright, it obscured everything else.

Westin looked up at him. "We lost one of the bombers. Whatever this is, it's reaching up through the entire atmosphere. Deep into the stratosphere—twenty miles straight up, maybe higher. Extremely high temperatures..."

"Will the bombs stop it?"

Again, Westin ignored him.

"General?"

"There are no more bombs—that's what I'm trying to tell you. They were incinerated along with that plane! The air above them is superheating, and..." His voice fell away as he listened again.

The satellite image turned pure white, then the screen went blank. Samantha Troy mumbled, "I think we lost the satellite." She went to a laptop, made several entries, and another image came up, much farther out. "This is HornetEye 413, one of our high-altitude recon units. It orbits about ten miles higher than the McCoys." She clicked through several screens. "This is... this is really odd..."

"What?"

"...aside from taking images, HornetEye records atmospheric disturbances. That thing is burning everything above it. It's pulling every ounce of energy and heat around to keep going. It's punched a hole directly through our atmosphere and—"

On the screen, the burning horde somehow managed to grow brighter still, then vanished with an implosion that left anyone watching it seeing spots.

Anyone unfortunate enough to witness this from the ground, the president thought, must surely be blind now.

CHAPTER ONE HUNDRED

MARTHA

SOPHIE DIDN'T RUN.

Instead, Martha watched as the little girl, this blur of vibration, stepped forward on legs that seemed to operate independently of the rest of her body.

When her eyes opened, they seemed to shine with blue light. Her head swiveled and took in her surroundings as if looking out on the hangar, on them, for the first time.

Tennant dropped to her knees beside her sister, stifling a gasp. "My God, Sophie. What have they done to you?"

Sophie's eyes closed. When they opened again, she drew in a sharp breath—then, despite the rattling metal of the cage, the lights, the hangar itself, Martha clearly heard the little girl speak in the softest of voices. Martha realized she heard this not only from the girl across the room, but in her head, in her thoughts, this voice's slightest whisper perfectly clear and eerily calm.

"I can see Momma and Poppa and Grammy and...everyone. Tennant, I see everyone. I *feel* everyone. I hear everything."

Martha glanced down at the iPad in her hands. The screen was covered in flashing warning messages—temperature, blood pressure, blood oxygenation—all beyond logic. This girl shouldn't be alive, let alone speaking.

Tennant tried to take Sophie's hand but jerked away when she came in contact with her sister's skin. She cradled her fingers like she'd touched a hot oven.

"It's okay...I'll be okay...I know that now."

Sophie drew in another harsh gasp and pinched her eyes shut. When she opened them again, the bright blue had returned, and the fear was washed from her face. She looked out at them with the gaze of someone far older than her eight years. The voice that spoke was still hers but also not, as if mixed with many others.

"Transcendence...is coming. A new world. A wonderful world. All will run. All will run with those who have been and all will run with those to come. Our body is one. Our mind...is one."

Sophie sucked in another breath and her back stiffened for a moment. There was a quick glimmer of the girl who was, then she was gone again.

Martha had to tell herself this was another's voice, not Sophie, someone, *something* else. A great being. As impossible as that might be to accept, she knew it was true. She got as close as she dared. She could feel the heat radiating out, rising from Sophie's pores. "Who are you?"

The girl who was once Sophie looked at her, the voice that was not hers said, "I am we. I am all there is. I am what is to be."

Her body vibrated with such speed, such force, she was a shimmer against the harsh lines of the cage behind her. Martha realized just how loud the noise around them had become. There was no blocking it, no hiding, no way to avoid the sound that crept over every inch of her body, worked down through her pores, and shook her bones. Two of the soldiers were down on their knees, hands pressed to their ears against the noise.

Tennant looked like she was in shock. Blood trickled down the sides of her face, but like Martha, she made no attempt to block the sound. She only stood there and glared at what was once her sister and was now something else. When she shouted, her voice cracked against her tears. "You can't take my sister—she's all I have left!"

Sophie lowered her gaze to the ground and shook her head. "Those who run, they run from all you have done and the hate and the anger and the fear.

They run to what is next. They run to the cleansing. Rebirth from ashes."

Her eyes closed then.

Martha could do nothing as steam rose from the child's flesh, as she glowed with a heat so intense the air itself threatened to ignite, far exceeding what she and Harbin had witnessed with the runners.

Sophie ignited in the brightest white. This flame that poured from her flesh leaped straight up, burned through the roof of the hangar, and continued skyward until it vanished somewhere in the heavens with a deafening roar.

Martha, Tennant, the soldiers—they all recoiled from the light.

Then Sophie was gone.

And silence engulfed them all.

CHAPTER ONE HUNDRED ONE

PRESIDENT

THREE HOURS LATER, FROM the far corner of the room, the president looked out at the podium of the James S. Brady press briefing room at the White House, a location familiar to all Americans, second only to the Oval Office.

They had considered a ball cap and windbreaker and maybe an outdoor speech, but decided that might give the impression that things were unresolved, that the worst was yet to come. He needed to stem a panic, not fuel one.

An Oval Office speech might come later, if need be. To provide additional closure. Maybe a fireside chat.

He wiped the sweat from his palms onto his trousers as one of his interns straightened his tie.

A woman with a rolling cart carrying enough makeup to cover the cast of an entire television production for a season dabbed more powder on his forehead.

He waved the hastily drafted speech at his press secretary. "Are you sure about this?"

"It's a valid explanation. It leaves room if we need to adjust the narrative later. We'll track the response in the press and on social media and make adjustments as necessary. This is the right thing to do."

The right thing.

As opposed to the truth.

The president frowned. "Where's General Westin? Maybe he should stand up there with me."

"He's on with the Joint Chiefs, sir. If necessary, we'll have him do a follow-up speech later today. We'll see how this one goes. Best to hold him in your pocket for now."

Drawing in a deep breath, he crossed over to the podium and set the pages on top. An identical copy of the speech had been loaded into the teleprompters, but he'd been told the use of paper would help with the image they were trying to portray. Urgent, yet organized.

The president looked out over the rows of chairs and fought the urge to squint. The lights were always so damn bright. He cleared his throat. "At approximately eleven fifty-one last night, the largest solar flare on record reached across the cosmos and touched down just outside of Portland, Oregon. This flare, traveling at 1,250 miles per second, provided no warning and left immense devastation in its wake. It's still very early, but I've been told the death toll will amount near one million American souls. Our thoughts and prayers are with the families and loved ones of all those involved." The words PAUSE HERE flashed on the teleprompters, so he did, lowering his gaze for a moment, before swallowing and going on. "The damage to property and infrastructure is also substantial but inconsequential in relation to the loss of life. We can and will rebuild. We will honor our dead. I've declared a national emergency. Resources and aid are en route, joining the military already on the ground in this trying time. Our scientists, along with teams from around the world, are currently analyzing not only the immediate effects of the flare, but the long-term implications."

He looked up. "I'm still getting reports, but I'll do my best to answer any questions you may have." The first hand went up in the back, and he pointed.

"What about the reports of mass hysteria? There are recordings and images all over the internet of people running toward the place where the flare hit. Like they were drawn to it."

The president's palms felt like they were dripping with sweat, but there was no way he'd wipe them on national television. He placed them calmly on the top of the podium. "I've been told prior to this flare, there were a large number of smaller microbursts. They reverberated through virtually any electronic device relying on radio or wireless signals within reach. This was nothing more than radio interference, solar static."

The president raised his hand and pointed to his right. "Yes?"

"Can this happen again? You mentioned microbursts leading up to the large flare. Is this like a volcanic eruption or an earthquake? Should we expect more?"

He swallowed again. They'd rehearsed this, several times. The delivery was key. He lowered his voice and looked just a little to the right of the central camera. "This has happened before. At four fifty-one p.m. EDT on Monday, April 2, 2001, the largest flare previously on record left the sun and just missed our planet. On March 6, 1989, another did reach us, and knocked out half the power grid in Canada. There are hundreds of smaller ones on record. This is not a rare occurrence. That in mind, we are a difficult target to hit. Like asteroids and meteorites, most pass us harmlessly by or jettison out into space with little or no impact on our planet. Can it happen again? Absolutely. Is it likely? No, it is not. I've been told the events on the sun leading up to this flare are currently waning. It may be millions of years before something like this happens again."

"Any idea when the power grid will be restored? We have reports of outages nationwide. More than a hundred million homes. Well beyond the Pacific Northwest—most of the country appears to be in the dark."

He nodded bleakly. "I've been told there was a cascading effect and residents should check with their local municipality for restoration estimates."

"How do you expect them to make those phone calls without power?"

He caught someone from the corner of his eye giving him the signal to wrap things up. Turning, he placed both hands back on the podium. "We have many questions at this point, and I'd love to address all of you, but as you can imagine, I've got a lot of people vying for my attention this morning. We will continue to release information as it comes in. We Americans are strong. We're resourceful. And we are never deterred. An obstacle is something to be tackled, overcome, and conquered. While this event is devastating, I have no doubt we will not only persevere, but we will thrive in the wake of this disaster. We will prosper *because* we are Americans, and that's what we do. We owe that to the people we lost." He forced a smile out over the seats. "Thank you for attending at this early hour."

The president stood there for a moment, gripping the podium.

Off to the side, someone said, "And... we're out."

The bright lights switched off, and the president looked out over the empty chairs. Other than a handful of his staff tasked with shouting out prepared questions, there was nobody in attendance.

The briefing room set was quickly dismantled—the backdrop, the podium and stage, the walls—all of it would be back aboard Air Force One within ten minutes.

Samantha Troy took him by the arm. "We need to get you back on board, sir. We'll be airborne again as quickly as possible. We need to keep moving."

They had landed at Fort Wainwright in Alaska.

"How long can we keep the nation's power grid off?" he asked her. "There must be a better way to block the internet."

She directed him toward the stairs leading back up into the plane. "We'll discuss options once we're back in the air, sir. We need to move."

"Where are we going?"

"We plan to remain airborne for the foreseeable future. Refuels will be in the air. Until we understand the implications of what's happening and how best to avoid it, we'll stay out of harm's way."

"You didn't answer my question."

"No, sir. I did not," she replied.

1 WEEK LATER

CHAPTER ONE HUNDRED TWO

MARTHA

"THE PRESIDENT'S SPEECH WAS bullshit. You all know that, right?"

Senator Michael Raffalo rolled his eyes, scratched his thinning hair, and took a quick drink of water before responding. "Dr. Chan, you've been told twice now, we're on the record here, there's no need for that kind of language."

She glared up at him at the center of the large oak monstrosity of a desk, flanked by Senators Greg Hastings and Amber Roush on his left and George Lummin on his right along with an empty chair and a nameplate for Rosario Cortez, who had yet to arrive. Aside from a few whispered comments to Raffalo, the other three had remained relatively silent for the several hours they'd already spent in this room deep in the Capitol building. Martha was beginning to wonder what any of them were doing there. "Come on, solar flares?"

"He was…is, trying to avoid a panic."

"It's a little late for that, don't you think?"

"Can we please just stay on task? Your outbursts are only prolonging our time together."

"My outbursts—"

Harbin reached over and squeezed her wrist. He shook his head softly.

The two of them were seated alone at a long conference table facing the members of the Senate Intelligence Committee, their backs turned on a galley designed to hold at least a hundred people but today stood completely empty due to security concerns and the varying degrees of secrecy all these people insisted on continuing.

"'Give General Westin my best.'" Raffalo cleared his throat. "Dr. Harbin, those were Dr. Cushman's final words to you?"

Harbin turned from Martha and looked back up at the senator. "Her final spoken words to me were, 'Let me show you how to stop it,' she then shot herself. She wrote the message about Westin on the document I surrendered to the soldiers I found graciously waiting for me outside of that DARPA black site."

Raffalo glanced at the notepad on the desk in front of him. "Renton Forty-Nine."

"Yes."

"The location Lieutenant Colonel Alexander Fraser transported you to?"

"Yes."

"A location that does not exist."

Two days ago, Harbin had taken Martha to Renton 49. They'd found the remains of the building in the middle of a dead-end street in Seattle, surrounded by a ten-foot chain-link fence. A homeless woman had told them the property was an abandoned textile factory, vacant for nearly a dozen years. Construction crews had imploded the structure a week ago, within twenty-four hours of Harbin's visit. The homeless woman said she'd watched the building come down, listened to the workers complain about the excessive amounts of concrete and how much time it would take to haul it all away. A sign on the chain-link fence advertised the future location of six luxury lofts, expected completion in two years. It had been hanging sideways, one of the bolts meant to hold it in place missing.

Raffalo continued reading from his notepad again, "You're referencing the document you said was titled 'DARPA INITIATIVE 769021473, *ANA*log *S*ymbiotic *H*uman *I*nterface *M*echanism. Ana Shim.'"

"Yes."

"The document nobody on this committee has seen or heard of even though the people you see before you control all of DARPA's funding."

"Maybe you should ask General Westin about the program."

"In due time, Doctor. Today we're here to talk to you and your colleague and, like uncontrolled outbursts, chiming in with unsolicited commentary will also extend your stay. So, let's focus, shall we?"

When Harbin didn't reply, Raffalo scribbled something down on his notepad and continued, "Dr. Cushman told you this program was a means to connect the human brain to the internet through the use of sound, correct?"

"Yes."

"And she said they succeeded in this endeavor?"

"Yes."

"And it's your belief, the belief of your team, that success led to the destruction and loss of life you followed in the Pacific Northwest?"

"Yes."

He turned back to Martha. "Dr. Chan. As the only remaining medical doctor from your team, can you explain to the committee, in your own words, how exactly this worked?"

"No, sir. I cannot."

"Why not?"

"Because medically, it shouldn't work."

"But it did, didn't it? So give us your best interpretation."

She looked to Harbin again, who only gave her a

soft nod. Martha placed both her palms on the table and explained as best she could. "As we currently understand it, the noise itself is an acoustic virus and can be generated in one of two ways—electronically, as a reproduced recording meeting very specific standards, or by a human host infected with the virus—vibrations on a cellular level that generate an audible signature. In both instances, the virus is capable of spreading, infecting others with a near one hundred percent success rate. This…sound…contains information. That information teaches the human brain how to connect to the internet using any available carrier signal—cellular, wi-fi, Bluetooth, possibly others unknown to us. Once…connected, the brain—which tends to starve for information—suddenly had an unlimited source of data, and it only wanted more. This caused transmission speeds to increase, and like any computer taxed heavily, this created heat, and that excess heat became energy the body was compelled to burn. *Had* to burn."

"By running?"

"Yes. By running," Martha replied. "As we saw with several test subjects, when they stopped running, the heat—the energy—became unstable, perpetual. They created more than they used, which eventually led to combustion."

"Even after death?"

"*Especially* in death," Harbin interjected. "This

connection didn't just occur in the brain but in every cell, every molecule of the infected individual. And it didn't stop with what we consider *clinical* death. The sudden stoppage of motion brought on by clinical death left no place for the energy to go. I guess, to put this in the simplest terms, this would be like disabling the radiator in a car while the accelerator is held to the floorboard—the engine would burn."

"Like a nuclear reactor in meltdown?"

"Exactly."

Senator Roush leaned over and said something to Raffalo behind a cupped hand. He nodded and said, "If this infection had a near one hundred percent success rate, and you, Dr. Harbin there, and those girls from Mount Hood were all exposed, why weren't all of you infected?"

Harbin leaned forward. "When initially exposed, Tennant Riggin had wax in her ears. She was...checking rabbit traps...and put it in purely by happenstance in order to block out their cries. Her sister, Sophie, did not, but both girls were rushed into an underground shelter by their father before the noise hit them in full force. Some combination of these circumstances limited their exposure on varying levels, Tennant more so than her younger sister. Dr. Hoover believed exposure in small doses could possibly build a tolerance in some people, maybe even an immunity."

At this, Raffalo raised his index finger and silenced Harbin as he conferred with two of the other senators for nearly a minute, wrote something else down, then looked back at him. "Have you been able to replicate this . . . immunity?"

Harbin shook his head. "Not with any kind of regularity. In studying people around the Portland area, we have learned that younger individuals seem to be more adaptive. When exposed in limited doses—doses low enough to avoid infection—they recovered faster. This could be due to their ability to hear a wider range of audio frequencies—we lose that as we get older. I don't really have an answer there. Both Dr. Chan and I were exposed numerous times and don't seem to suffer from any lasting ill effects, same with Tennant Riggin. With Lieutenant Colonel Fraser, well, we've all seen the recordings."

"So you don't believe he removed his headphones because they were ineffective?"

Harbin considered this, choosing his words carefully. "I honestly don't think he needed them anymore. In the video captured by the Humvees, he leaves the downed helicopter and gets into another vehicle without showing any signs of discomfort from the noise even though it was at its strongest all around him. I think he became one of the connected while also remaining in control of most, if not all, of his own faculties."

"He didn't feel the urge to run," Raffalo stated flatly. "I think he managed to make the connection Dr. Hoover and the people at DARPA had hoped to create in everyone without the adverse effects, yes."

"Is that what you saw in the child? Sophie Riggin?"

Martha reached for the pitcher of water on the table, refilled her glass, and took a drink. The water was warm; dust floated across the top. "Sophie was different." She set her glass back down on the table. "We now know she did connect—that was how she knew the names of my children, the names of many of the infected, knew a number of things she shouldn't have—*the hive mind,* the collective consciousness of all the connected, used her as a conduit in those final moments as a means to try and communicate. But it was all too much, her body couldn't handle it."

"She burned."

"Yes, she burned."

Senator Lummin raised his hand. "If you would have allowed her to run rather than lock her in a cage, would she have survived?"

Martha felt her face flush. "It wasn't my decision to—"

Lummin waved his hand dismissively. "If *anyone* would have allowed her to run, would she have survived?"

Martha leaned forward, glared at him. "I don't know."

"But it's likely she might have managed this perpetual heat you mentioned and found a way to survive?"

Harbin cleared his throat. "I don't think any of us can be one hundred percent certain she is dead."

He'd brought a metal case with him and he reached for it now, setting it on the table before him. He gave Martha a glance before pressing the buttons on either side, releasing the latches.

He lifted the lid and turned the case toward the panel.

Senator Roush jumped up out of her chair.

The others remained still, their faces going ashen.

Raffalo was the first to speak, his voice cracking. "Why the hell would you bring that in here?"

Inside, set in black foam to hold it still, was the old tape recorder Tennant had used to record a message to her parents in the shelter back on Mount Hood.

CHAPTER ONE HUNDRED THREE

MARTHA

"I'M NOT COMFORTABLE WITH this at all," Senator Roush said. "How did you even get that past security?"

Harbin carefully lifted the tape recorder from the case and set it on the table. From his pocket, he took out four batteries and began inserting them into the recorder.

"Okay, now you're going too far," Raffalo said. "Somebody take that from him and escort him out!"

One of the Capitol security guards watched from the doorway but made no attempt to approach him. Instead, he took several steps back.

Harbin said, "It's fine."

Senator Lummin clearly didn't think so. He shoved his notes into his briefcase, got up, and started for the door. "I'll be in my office. Have someone get me when this is over." He was gone a moment later.

Hastings was the only one who didn't appear nervous. "You've done this before?"

Harbin nodded, inserting the last battery and slipping the plastic cover back in place. "Several times. I assure you, it's safe."

"Give us a moment," Hastings said, turning to his two remaining colleagues. They began to speak in hushed whispers.

Martha looked over at Harbin and although he was attempting to remain collected, his temples glistened with sweat.

Raffalo made another note and said, "Proceed with caution, Doctor. You're on very thin ice."

Harbin nodded.

The volume control on the tape recorder was a small wheel on the side. Martha watched as he turned it from four to ten, the highest setting. Then he pressed the bulky Play button.

Static poured out from the speaker, followed by Sophie's voice, sounding distant—

"Tell Tennant to go to big rock."

This repeated two more times.

"Tell Tennant to go to big rock."

"Tell Tennant to go to big rock."

Harbin pressed the Stop button.

"I don't understand," Raffalo said. "What is *big rock*?"

"We didn't know, either," Martha replied, "so we

asked Tennant. She said big rock was an outcropping a short walk from their village on Mount Hood. Someplace the girls would go to play or to hide from the adults."

"I still don't understand."

Harbin said, "We provided the coordinates to the Army and they dispatched a team to investigate. They found the Riggins' dog hiding there—dehydrated, malnourished, impossibly thin. Another day or two and he may have passed away. Sophie saved him."

The three representatives fell silent for a moment. It was Amber Roush who first realized the significance. "When exactly did she record that?"

Harbin eyed the three of them. "The message first appeared two days after she combusted, *after* she was gone."

Hastings said, "You're saying she somehow recorded this after she died."

Harbin shook his head. "She didn't *record* anything." He turned the machine around and hit the button that would have ejected the cassette had there been one inside. "There's no tape. There hasn't been one in this machine since Fraser first found it and turned it in after returning to base."

This seemed to confuse them even more.

"How is it playing, then?" Raffalo asked.

"I'm not sure *playing* is the correct word for what's happening." Harbin settled back in his chair and pulled the device closer. He studied their faces for another moment, then turned to Martha, who gave him a reassuring nod. He leaned closer to the recorder, pressed the Play button again, and spoke in a soft voice, "Sophie, can you hear me?"

At first, there was nothing, only static coming from the single speaker, then they all heard it, quiet at first, barely a whisper. Sophie's voice.

"Yes, doctor. I can hear you."

Hastings let out an audible gasp.

Amber Roush's eyes grew wide and she seemed to sink down into her seat.

Raffalo didn't move at all. His face had gone horribly pale. When he spoke, he sounded like a frightened child. "How is that possible?"

Harbin spoke into the recorder. "Sophie, can you tell us where you are?"

"I... I'm not sure."

"Is it a place?"

"It feels like I'm... everyplace... all at once. It's cold. I'm cold."

"Can you see me? Can you see Dr. Chan and the others?"

"Yes. I can see... everything. Everyone."

Hastings frowned. "Is that tape recorder connected somehow?"

"Not with wi-fi or any other conventional connection method known to us... but somehow it is,"

Harbin said. "Sophie, how are you able to speak to us through this device?"

She ignored the question. *"Can I talk to Tennant?"*

"Maybe later."

"I'd like that."

Harbin glanced up at the senators, their eyes fixed on the recorder. "Who else is there with you?"

"Everyone is here."

"Your mother and father? The people from your village?"

"Everyone. We all run now. We all run together."

Harbin pressed the Stop button and the recorder clicked off. "For some reason, this only works when we hit Play. It's the only time she hears us. I haven't figured out why. Although Sophie is the only one who speaks to us through this particular device, we think all those who were infected, all those who *connected,* are there."

"Where?" Raffalo said, clearly much louder than he had hoped.

Martha said, "We believe their consciousness uploaded to the internet. To the cloud."

"You do understand how far-fetched this all sounds?"

"Yet, here we are."

At the corner of their table, one of the candles flickered and went out, the other four were still burning as were the half dozen or so up on the desk with the senators. Others placed around the chamber fought back the dark but were losing. The Capitol building had very few windows, and without power, the darkness inside was thick.

After Portland, when groups of runners were spotted in Little Rock, Denver, and outside of Atlanta, Homeland Security had taken the extraordinary step of shutting down all internet service providers, *severing* the country's internet backbone.

That hadn't been enough.

The ANA Shim virus spread.

Less than a day later, large groups of runners appeared near Los Angeles and downtown Dallas.

Other places, too.

The ANA Shim virus spread.

The nation's power grid was taken offline less than twenty-four hours later.

The ANA Shim virus still spread.

Amid all of this, when Martha had first heard Sophie's voice, a single thought had come to her, one that frightened her more than all others—

Death didn't mean the same thing anymore.

Martha found herself eyeing every shadow, second-guessing every cold pocket of air. She tried not to think about the ghosts huddled within the corners of this particular building, one of the oldest in the country—the wars, the disease, the death—this building had seen throughout history. John Quincy

Adams had died in this very room. Two hundred years of specters watched them now. Listened. She wouldn't turn to the dark galley at her back for fear of what she might see. She hoped to God none of those here found a voice; hearing Sophie was enough.

Hastings cleared his throat. "You expect us to believe the dead are speaking to you?"

Raffalo had one eye pinched shut and the tip of his finger in his ear, scratching at something deep.

From his briefcase, Harbin took out a thick manila envelope and set it on the table next to the tape recorder. He tapped it with his index finger. "At first, we didn't believe it, either, but the more we talked to Sophie, the more we realized it was true. It's amazing, actually. Her consciousness seems to have not only joined with the internet but all the others who have passed on, what we referred to as the hive mind. Their thoughts have become collective, a *single mind.* Together they've been able to seamlessly and almost instantly pick through data on any electronic device—not just those connected in a traditional sense but things like this tape recorder, anything and everything that uses electricity. They created their own means to transmit data. I imagine it would have taken a government team months, maybe years to figure out who was actually responsible for mutating the virus, who took Dr. Cushman and Frederick Hoover's work and attempted to weaponize it and began this... infestation.

With the two of them dead, we may never have figured it out. But Hoover is part of that collective mind now, too, up there in the cloud somewhere, and he didn't want that knowledge to die with him."

A door opened on the side of the room and General Westin stepped in with Tennant, one hand on her shoulder. The door closed behind them. Tennant looked nervous. Martha had suspected Westin had been listening somewhere nearby but she hadn't been certain. Without releasing Tennant, he silently stared over at the two of them.

Hastings and Roush glanced at the general but said nothing.

Senator Raffalo gave up on his ear and made several more notes. The corner of his mouth twitched. When he looked back at Harbin and Martha there was no hiding the anger brewing behind his flushed face. He made no attempt to conceal it.

Harbin wasn't about to get flustered. He continued. "Through our connection with Sophie, through this tape recorder, Hoover provided not only the names of those responsible but every detail from their first contact with him to everything they've done since. Every action they've taken to attempt to cover their tracks. This new mind, this *hive* mind, doesn't forget. They don't seem to miss anything." He patted the thick envelope again. "The amount of information here is staggering."

Martha turned to General Westin. "When Dr. Cushman said to give you her best, I think we all misunderstood. It wasn't some kind of slight. She wanted you to have the DARPA document."

Senators Hastings and Roush had been whispering to each other but had fallen silent.

Westin's eyes fixed on Senator Raffalo, who had his finger in his ear again, his free hand attempting to write something. "She must have known I'd get the information back to the president," Westin said. "I wouldn't allow it to . . . vanish, as some might. She was right. We reviewed not only the ANA Shim information but a copy of the data Sophie Riggin provided. Had any of that information ended up here . . . with this committee first, with you in particular, Senator Raffalo . . . I hate to think where it might have gone."

Martha expected Raffalo to deny the accusation, to maybe stand and storm out of the room, but he did neither of those things. Instead he pressed his finger deeper into his ear and turned to Senator Roush. "Do you hear something?"

Either because she was still processing what Westin had said or because she didn't know how to respond to that question, she said nothing.

"Well, I hear something."

At this, she shrunk back, eased her chair away from Raffalo, nearly rolled into Hastings beside her. "Don't you wear a hearing aid?"

Raffalo scribbled something else down on his notepad and shook his head, his finger buried in his ear. "I've got a cochlear implant. You don't hear that? Like a hum."

This was enough for both Hastings and Roush to stand. They crossed around to the other side of the large desk.

Westin looked over at Harbin and Martha. "Can the sound generate here? From an implant?"

Martha stood, got a better look. "You're not wearing the external component, are you?"

His finger twitching in his ear, Raffalo shook his head. "It's in my desk. I haven't worn it since this business started." His free hand scribbled something else down on the notepad.

Martha said, "Cochlear implants use conductive transmission. Without the external component within range, there's no microphone, no power, it's nonfunctioning."

"Well, I hear something, damnit, and it's getting loud," Raffalo shot back. His finger looked like it was buried down to his knuckle.

On the tape recorder, Harbin pressed Play again. "Sophie, is the sound about to generate here? In this room?"

"The bad man needs to run."

"Sophie, Martha and I are in here. Tennant, too. You don't want to hurt us, do you?"

"The bad man deserves to run."

Raffalo tried to stand, got halfway to his feet, then fell back in his chair. "Ah, Christ, stop it! Get it out!"

"I want you to come and run with me, Mr. Raffalo. Will you come and run with me? With all of us?"

"I don't hear anything, do you?" Martha asked.

Harbin shook his head.

"His nose is bleeding," Senator Hastings said, stepping farther away.

Raffalo slammed the side of his head down on the desk. Not once, but twice.

He dropped back into his chair, his eyes bulging. His breathing went to sharp gasps, every muscle in his body tensed and he twisted to the right and back again, his bloody finger digging impossibly deep in his ear.

"We're all waiting for him."

Raffalo's eyes fell on the pencil in his other hand and without any hesitation, he grabbed it with bloody fingers, shoved it into his ear, and slammed his head back down onto the desk. There was an audible *crunch,* a sound Martha knew she'd never forget, and he fell forward, still.

A hush fell over all of them.

The room dropped into silence.

Harbin said, "Sophie, did you do that?"

Her answer was immediate. *"No. Not me. But the bad man deserves to run."*

Tennant was the first to move. She stepped away from General Westin and crossed the room, went to the large desk at the front, and eyed the dead man for a moment before reaching into her pocket.

The Bluetooth speaker wasn't large, smaller than her palm, JBL printed on the side. Below that, was a flashing white light. Wrapped twice around, a rubber band held the external half of Raffalo's hearing aid against the black plastic. Tennant switched the speaker off and softly said, "For Momma, Poppa, Sophie . . . everyone," before setting it next to the dead senator's head.

Martha went over to her, wrapped her arms around the girl, and tried to pull her close, but Tennant wouldn't move. She was reading the notes scrawled by Raffalo in a hand impossible to ignore. The same phrase written hundreds of times across every inch of the notepad page:

Lieutenant Colonel Alexander Fraser says hello.

Lieutenant Colonel Alexander Fraser says hello.

Lieutenant Colonel Alexander Fraser says hello.

According to current calculations, 4,390,000,000 souls around the world are connected to the internet.

That number might be larger than we think.

ABOUT THE AUTHORS

James Patterson is the world's bestselling author and most trusted storyteller. He has created many enduring fictional characters and series, including Alex Cross, the Women's Murder Club, Michael Bennett, Maximum Ride, Middle School, and I Funny. Among his notable literary collaborations are *The President Is Missing*, with President Bill Clinton, and the Max Einstein series, produced in partnership with the Albert Einstein Estate. Patterson's writing career is characterized by a single mission: to prove that there is no such thing as a person who "doesn't like to read," only people who haven't found the right book. He's given more than three million books to schoolkids and the military, donated more than seventy million dollars to support education, and endowed more than five thousand college scholarships for teachers. For his prodigious imagination and championship of literacy in America, Patterson was awarded the 2019 National Humanities Medal. The National Book Foundation presented him with the Literarian Award for Outstanding Service to the American Literary Community, and he is also the recipient of an Edgar Award and nine Emmy Awards. He lives in Florida with his family.

J. D. Barker is the international bestselling author of numerous books, including *Dracul* and *The Fourth Monkey*. His novels have been translated into two dozen languages and optioned for both film and television. Barker resides in coastal New Hampshire with his wife, Dayna, and their daughter, Ember.

For a complete list of books by

JAMES PATTERSON

VISIT
JamesPatterson.com

Follow James Patterson on Facebook
@JamesPatterson

Follow James Patterson on Twitter
@JP_Books

Follow James Patterson on Instagram
@jamespattersonbooks